To Stephanie,
 The only 1
We put on our

e

MW01268429

The Holedigger

a novel about living and dying

Arthur Nelson Thornhill

" May your life be long
 and may your love be strong."
 —"old Irish Toast"—

RED LEAD PRESS
PITTSBURGH, PENNSYLVANIA 15222

The contents of this work including, but not limited to, the accuracy of events, people, and places depicted; opinions expressed; permission to use previously published materials included; and any advice given or actions advocated are solely the responsibility of the author, who assumes all liability for said work and indemnifies the publisher against any claims stemming from publication of the work.

ISBN: 978-0-8059-8571-9
Library of Congress Control Number: 2007936233
Printed in the United States of America

First Printing

For more information or to order additional books, please contact:
Red Lead Press
701 Smithfield Street
Third Floor
Pittsburgh, Pennsylvania 15222
U.S.A.
1-800-834-1803
www.redleadbooks.com

Chapter 1:
White Lightning

A Texaco sign marks the front of a weathered old country filling station and general store. The store is just a front for Charlie "Nub" Hooper's " likker bin-ezz." They call him "Nub" because his left arm was cut off just below the shoulder, leaving nothing but a stub. Nub Hooper and his family have made and sold moonshine whiskey here in Georgia for years, with their "load runners" occasionally crossing into a few other bordering states.

The road in front of Nub's store starts way up yonder in the far north. It snakes down out of the Tennessee mountains then wiggles south across Georgia all the way down over the Florida line and eventually curls up in the sun somewhere near Miami beach. The store squats, looking out at the road in a long rectangular building, with a shingled, protruding roof that extends from the middle to overlap two gas pumps, one for regular and the other for ethyl. The shade of that overhang is a gathering place for boys living within a few miles of it.

Underneath the cover of that open transom is a well-worn, dry dirt floor with three grease-stained, wooden straight chairs. Two of them are usually placed so that, by leaning back, you can prop against one of the posts on either side of the pumps. The third person usually straddles the last chair to look at the occupants of first two and also to see cars go by, or pull in off the road. For more than three people, there is a long bench with its back against the side of the store. Nub often keeps the store open all night to sell moonshine, and he seems to enjoy having 'the boys' around. When his sales are going strong, he will often give all of them "Co-Colas."

Nub also has a pinball machine and a jukebox inside the store, that he

1

lets the boys play for free. He pretends he doesn't know that they have found a way to play them without money, since none of them usually have any. The jukebox is a beautiful Rock-ola with a solid wooden frame. Backing up to it, and kicking it with the flat of a foot, jars the coin slot and clicks up six plays, the same as when a quarter is put in it.

All 'the boys' need, to get the pinball machine started, is a single nickle, because all of them can win games easily, now that they know the tilt function does not work very well. Also, when they win a game, the machine makes a buzzing sound, clicks up the free game, then buzzes again. They also know that by cutting the machine off, with a toggle switch underneath, after it clicks up a game, then quickly cutting it back on, it will buzz and click up another game. The cycle is just repeated until the maximum of 99 games credit is clicked up.

Nub has a great voice that sounds just like his favorite singer, George Jones, and he loves to sing. He also enjoys hearing them playing the pinball, almost as much as he loves the music they play on the jukebox. The importance of that jukebox just can't be overstated. A world-wide musical revolution is taking place, and every major event in our lives will forever be etched in our brains by the songs we hear. We are all listening to the words and rhythms of songs that are as vital to our lives as the beat of our hearts. In these explosive times, it's like Nub's craving, we have to have it. Drunk or sober, Nub understands how much that music means to everyone.

Anytime Nub's name is mentioned, within earshot of the boys, somebody will say, "Yeah, Old Nub's alright." Out of sincere respect for him, before the kicking and the clicking starts, they always wait until Nub goes outside to the pumps or to the well.

A good deep well is outside, and out of sight, behind the far corner of the building to your left if you're propped up against a pump post. Nub keeps his pint bottles of white lightening in the cold well water, until he either wants to sell it, or drink it.

The two-thirds of the building, to your left, was meant to be a small house for the family who built the store. Nub's store takes up about a third of the building, from the left start of the overhang to the right end of the building. To the right of the overhang, you have to take one short step up to enter the store, through an opening made by double doors. They are always open to the inside, unless they're pulled together with a big padlock in the center, indicating that the store is either closed, or Nub is too drunk to fool with anybody, and has, most likely, gone around back to enter the house.

Nub is an alcoholic and you probably would be too, if somebody chopped off your left arm with a pick ax. The boys don't know it for a fact, but some of the Hooper family say that Nub first started drinking the day he lost his arm. If you ever taste white lightning, you can easily believe that if you chug-a-lugged enough of that clear liquid, it would help get your mind off your chopped-off arm. As the Roger Miller song says:

"Chug-a-lug, Chug-a-lug, Makes you wanta holler, HI DEE HO!
Burns your tummy, don't 'ya know. Chug-a-lug, Chug-a-lug"

The boys do suspect that it took a long time for Nub to get over the pain of it all, and a lot of drinking to drown out the endless frustration, from trying to do things that get pretty darn hard with only one arm. As you will soon see, he did get over all of that, and in some ways, the drinking seems to help. Some people would argue that it did more harm than good.

Anyway, one thing for sure, he did become a full-fledged alcoholic. One time he had been drinking so much that his family was afraid he was going to kill himself, so they hid all his liquor. The next day the boys found him passed out inside the store. He must have had the "craving" bad. There were many small bottles all over the floor, where he had drunk a full case of Vanilla extract, because it has about fifteen percent alcohol in each bottle. One of the boys they call "Bocephus", was just a child when it happened, but he can still remember how good that store smelled. "Bocephus" still talks about how much he likes the smell and taste of vanilla.

By now you could be thinking that there is nothing so special about Nub. But you would be dead wrong. He isn't just a typical old, one-armed drunk. He is remarkable, because he finally got sick of feeling sorry for himself, and began to figure out ways he could get back to doing what he wants to do, using just one arm.

For example, here's a story "Bocephus" told the boys about Nub and his love for rabbit hunting. One night, after "Bocephus" becomes good friends with Nub, he takes Bocephus "rabbit-shining". By sweeping the beam of a flashlight into the dark woods ahead, the rabbit is spotted by the red glare of his, or her, eyes, when she, or he, freezes momentarily, looking back at the light, and the hunter has the chance for a kill by getting off a quick shot at the glare. Since rabbit and dumplings are a favorite food hereabouts, "Bocephus" already knows about rabbit shining, but he just can't see how a man with one arm can do it.

Here's what Nub does. He ties a flashlight on his head so that it will shine where he is looking, and leave his one arm free, to wield a 12-gauge, double-barreled, sawed-off shotgun. He takes a long strip of cloth that he rips off a sheet, and ties a loop on one end with his only hand. Then he runs the other end of the long strip through the loop, making it a lasso that he places over his head, and cinches tight under his chin. Next, he places a flashlight on top of his head, wraps it with the rest of the sheet, and tucks that end under the first noose and ties it snug. When he is ready to start the hunt, all he has to do is hold his shotgun between his knees, put shells in it, and reach up to turn on the flashlight. Now, when he looks ahead of him, the beam will follow the movement of his head. If you don't think this is amazing, just try doing it with one hand behind your back. Nub also has a lot of strength in his one good arm. When the glare of a rabbit's eyes pops up in the light, he throws the gun straight out, with his one arm rigid, and cuts loose with both barrels. "Bocephus" says he never saw him miss. "Bocephus"'s job is to pick up the dead rabbits and put them in a croaker sack. Back at the store, "Bocephus" will skin and clean them, put all but one of them in the freezer, then leave the store whistling into the dark. As he walks home, thinking about eating rabbit and dumplings, he sings a happy song.

> *"The first time I saw Bo Weevil, he was sittin' on the square.*
> *Next time I see Bo Weevil, he's got his whole damn family there."*

There is a long gravel entry to the store that runs in an elongated crescent shape in front of the pumps and back onto the asphalt highway.

> *"Just looking for a home*
> *he wuz looking for a home."*

On the right side of this drive, a deeply rutted red clay path runs alongside an embankment, parallel to the main road, up a hill that leads to an assortment of trees and shrubs, surrounding the house that Nathan Fulton built.

Chapter 2:
Looking for a Home

The house that Nathan Fulton built stands high on a hill, with ancient oaks shading the lawns. A rich forest stretches out behind it for miles, until the branches of mature hardwoods overlap the muddy Chattahoochee river. Lightening rods stick straight up from the roof, like spears with fancy globes gripping their centers, as if ready to hurl them against an unseen enemy above. The lightning seems to mock them as it streaks laughingly across the dark night sky.

A single gable with a large lighted window protrudes from the slanted housetop, forming a cozy alcove to the only room upstairs. The solid silhouette of a woman casts a big ugly shadow, that seems to slide down the roof, onto the top of the porch, as Thera Fulton approaches the window to watch the symphony of shadows being orchestrated by the storm outside.

"Bomb...bomb, bomb, bomb...BOMB!" She throws her finger triumphantly high at the final note in perfect harmony with a loud crack of thunder.

Thera remembers the bombs over London; the phosphorescent clouds they made burning her nostrils, with a smell as acrid as that of the matches beside the kerosene lamp on her desk. The lightning outside her window is different from the bombs. The afterglow is missing. It is more like flint sparking in the dark. It throws stark shadows that quickly close ranks, leaving it darker still until the eyes adjust. Yes, the sparking adds lively illusion to the ghostly stirring of the cold, dead scene. Ghoulish winds moan around the house and meet screaming on the front porch, then race down the steps, mercilessly whipping everything before them.

On both sides of the long rectangular flowerbeds, evenly spaced yews sag like weary pallbearers lugging giant coffins, heavily laden with the ossiferous remains of what had once been a glorious array of colorful flowers.

Through this window, Thera has watched their full concert: they have sung hymns to the sunshine, waltzed in the gentle rain, done a teeth-chattering tango to autumn's bittersweet music, then their lovely locks shriveled and fell, as frost's final curtain covered them in its white shroud, turning them as colorless as the strand of grey she plucks from her charcoal hair.

Now, all that is left of her beautiful flowers are their cadaverous bodies, stiff and bald, being lashed by the cruel wind,

'Dance you stilted skeletons! Step lively!'

Aged azalea limbs bow to pining petunia twigs, as chrysanthemum corpses lock stalks with zombie zinnias. Each time they pause, a flash of lightning exposes them, trembling and naked, as the fierce wind beats them with added fury,

The path runs through the middle of a row of trees, that seem to dance in place, across the lawn, with their limbs waving wildly. The yard vanishes abruptly just beyond the trees. The front half of the hill was chopped off, years ago, to make way for the chain gang to lay a ribbon of asphalt, for the main road that is used by most people heading across, or into, or out of the state.

Twenty-one years ago, Thera's mother followed that road south out of Georgia and never came back home. With her went the few playful days, and peaceful nights, of Thera's childhood.

Ida Maye Fulton sent presents from Florida. The gift for her eight-year-old daughter, Thera, was a glass paperweight, filled with water and tiny bits of seashell, that looked like snow, when it was inverted then turned upright. The snow fell on a miniature nativity scene. Nathan had called it blasphemous, taken it away from her, and smashed it. Days later, he had tried to make it up to her by giving her a small white Bible, with her name pressed in gold on the cover.

Thera sat in this room crying, as she tore every single page out of the bible into little bits. She went to the top of the open staircase, and made one big snowstorm over the room below, where Nathan sat in a rocker sharpening his cheap gift - a pocket knife with a pink flamingo on the handle. Nobody knew it yet, but the grim reaper was also sharpening his scythe, deep in the thick woods behind the Fulton house.

Nathan made a good living from the timber on his land, but nothing could hide the fact that he spent his life among pulp wood workers and sawmill hands. Nathan's warped sense of values became a constant source of embarrassment, as Thera grew older. The way he spent money, simply confirmed his lack of education and poor taste.

Thera is drawn from her reverie by tonight's stiff wind, causing a loose lightning rod to quiver and screech on the tin roof, above her window. It is loose because, at one sad moment, she had climbed out the window to pull it down, but she had found the housetop too steep, and the rods firmly fastened. All she did was loosen its bracket, before slipping, and scraping the side of a muscular calf.

Thera still views the rods as a monument to Nathan's extravagant ignorance. At her desk, she picks up a framed news photo of Nathan, in a Derby-like hat, flashing even teeth, under a white walrus moustache. The caption reads:

NATHAN FULTON ATE FOUR LIVE BEES on the steps of the courthouse yesterday, "Just to prove to his friends that he could do it." -Woosterville, Georgia , October 11, 1943-

Nathan had died shortly after this photo was taken. Thera learned, from the autopsy report, that a Black Widow spider had bitten Nathan, when he stuck his hand into a bee hive. He died thinking he had only been stung by a bee. So much has changed since Thera learned that the Black Widow often builds her web in bee hives. Everything seems to be changing in her world.

'Death is the most fearful, tearful change.' muses Thera. In war-torn London, she felt it most looking in the eyes of people whose loved ones had been killed. And she still feels it when people who used to be around her, are not here any more. The year before Nathan died, his oldest son, Victor, was shot down over North Africa on April 10, 1942. The year before that, Nathan's youngest son, Ned, died at Bataan on December 8, 1941, the day after the Japanese attacked Pearl Harbor. 'Places with missing faces just aren't the same anymore.'

Thera Fulton studies her reflection in the large oval mirror on the wall above her desk. She looks older than her twenty-eight years.

"Thera is just gonna be plain...all her life." she had overheard Nathan say to her mother, just before Ida Maye left for Florida.

"As if anybody looking at my face couldn't see that." Thera says to her image. "Plain broad forehead, plain heavy chin, plain bulbous nose... with a plain ugly pock mark on my cheek that I can't ever cover with makeup." She draws her mouth down at the sides to make a clown face, then rolls her lips inward. "Niiceeee eeveen teeeth...." She hisses. "And the eyes are definitely not plain."

"Her eyes're purty... but nobody ever notices 'em" Nathan had added in response to the tears in Ida Maye's eyes, just before she left Georgia.

Thera places Nathan's picture behind two larger frames. One is her degree from William and Mary College, where she won a scholarship, to get away from the people she had known all her life. The other is from a school far away from home. The most treasured moments of her life are the times she spent studying at Oxford, in war-torn England.

7

Thera picks up the last of the four frames from the center of her desk. It is a snapshot of a man making a mock bow, toward the closed door of a royal carriage, that just happened by as she took a picture of him, in front of Buckingham palace. His eyes were blurred behind thick glasses. The blur had gone out of his eyes, and into hers, when he kissed her right on the pock mark, and whispered that she had the prettiest grey eyes he ever had seen.

Just eight months after she came home to Nathan, following the news that her brother Ned had been killed, Thera received a short note, that is tucked behind the snapshot, and imprinted forever on her brain:

Dear Lady Greyeyes,
The world is mad. I'm trying to get to you. - Rabun D. McTanis

A second letter came two months later, from an Oxford professor they both knew, notifying Thera that a British cargo ship, sunk by a German U boat, had taken an American stowaway with it to the bottom of the sea. The American was known to be the distinguished scholar, Rabun Daniel McTanis, PHD. Reportedly, none of the unfortunate souls aboard the ill-fated ship had survived.

Chapter 3:
Born To Lose

Although it had been weeks after Nathan's funeral, when she sat at this desk and read that letter, it was the first time in Thera's life that she had felt completely alone.

After her brother Victor was killed, Thera thought it only fitting that Victor's widow, Becky, and their son Daniel, the last male Fulton heir, should share the big house with her and Nathan. Becky had other ideas. Shortly after attending Victor's funeral, Becky remarried and moved to a mill village in town, near the foundry where Billy Ray Shirey, her new husband, works. After it became clear that the man Becky married had little interest in her young son, Daniel, she allowed Thera to keep Daniel with her in the big house. Eventually, Thera's goal was to convince Becky to let Daniel simply move in, and stay with her full time. Now, he stays with her a lot on week days, and with his mom and sisters on most weekends.

Thera's younger sister, Carol, is married to a fine young man from Alabama - Alton Newman - and everybody seems to like him a lot. The Newmans are struggling financially. Carol had to give up her job, when she became pregnant, several months ago. Thera prepared the rooms on the right side of the house for the Newmans, and easily persuaded them, that it just made good sense for them to use some of this big old house. Earlier tonight, the three of them decided that it was time for Alton to get Carol checked into the Woosterville hospital, on the other side of town.

The loud bang of the wind slamming an opened screen door on the veranda, at the back of the house, echoes through the big empty hallway, beneath her room, and Thera realizes that Alton and Carol are leaving for the hospital, as planned. With the matter settled, Thera had said goodnight and come up to her room. She isn't frightened being alone, but this old house sure sounds lonesome on nights like this. Hard rain begins drumming the tin housetop and making her sleepy, as it drowns out the sound of Alton's truck warming up outside.

***

The old pickup slips down a muddy, rutted path, with its worn tires spinning, as it hits a gravel drive sending rocks flying, until the tires grip the asphalt paved road. Sharp pain jabs the pregnant Carol, as she rests her sore back against her husband. She shuts her eyes tight as the pulsating grows stronger. The truck speeds around treacherous curves, and she feels Alton's thigh tense, as he pushes the gas pedal, until they are going so fast that she can hear the swish of passing pines. Carol Fulton Newman is scared. She opens her eyes just a little, as if she is afraid to look. Through her wet lashes, she sees knife-edge rays flickering, from rain and asphalt. Beyond the truck's lights is total darkness. Carol rubs Alton's leg nervously, as pain rips through her abdomen like a dull saw. She feels a sudden flood of release, and digs her nails into his leg.

"Oh my God! My water broke!"

He snaps his head toward her as her eyes widen in terror. Bright lights blind him as he hears, then feels, a violent jolt that drives twisted metal and broken glass through his body.

Alton is dead when removed from the mangled cab. Carol is an unconscious mass of torn, tender, flesh. Their newborn son lies in a pool of blood, still attached to his mother by a taut umbilical cord.

The car they met head-on that night was driven by Elroy Leondus Knox. He was badly shaken, but, he has only minor injuries, and a serious hangover from drinking too much of his precious cargo. He was on a "short run," to deliver ten gallons of moonshine whiskey to Charlie "Nub" Hooper, at a country store next door to the Fulton house, where the light from the gable window proclaims that Thera Fulton is still wide awake upstairs.

***

Thera is pleased by the sheer joy Carol is discovering with Alton. 'Love is so good for them. Carol is such a beauty. Do men only feel that way about such women? Had Rabun McTanis felt that way about her? She must truthfully answer no.' His love for her had been different. He had seen beyond her physical appearance. Most men never look that deep. She is proud that her young sister can see others for all that they are as whole people. Carol's love for Thera is not all that different from the love she had with Rabun McTanis. But the love Alton feels for Carol is much more and it seems so grand. 'Do plain women ever know such love?'

She thinks not.

'How is sex tied to such love?' Would she have viewed sex more favorably without Rayford's terrible introduction of it? She can't imagine a more loveless demonstration. After Rabun McTanis's death she had often wished she had tried it with him. He was a tender, gentle person. She has masturbated while thinking of his smooth, gentle hands stroking her body. How could any man think it possible for a woman to find pleasure in the ugly crude way Rayford had taken her? Is the beauty of the woman related to the way a man treats her body?

'Are women no different from flowers; pretty ones admired and handled carefully; ugly ones ignored and trampled among the weeds?'

Thera feels that she has missed something of value in her life because she has never been loved by a man as Alton loves her beautiful sister. Her disappointment goes well beyond that. She also feels a sense of loss because she has never been on the receiving end of the attentions and compliments men give women they find attractive. She despises the embarrassment in men's eyes when they look at her after complimenting an especially attractive woman.

She also despises the feelings inside herself that yearn for release. These feelings actually make her uncomfortable around the virile young body of, TJ, her own son! She delivered him into this world and scrubbed his tiny penis and butt until he was old enough to do it himself. She is sure that he would not be embarrassed standing nude before her. But, now that he is fast becoming a man at age fourteen, she is so conscious of his maleness that she is certain that he senses it.

Is TJ's budding sexual awareness stirring dormant sexuality in her? She does seem more conscious of all males around her. She can not deny it. Try as she might, she can not help but wonder about the hidden parts of their bodies. What would Jack Fisher look like undressed?

'Shame on you!' She scolds herself.

Thera can admit that she has missed a lot because she is not pretty. All the advantages of being a woman seem reserved for pretty women. She has had all the disadvantages without such compensation.

And the disadvantages are many. Doors have been closed to her throughout her life. She has forced some of them open, but she has never had an important one opened for her by a man. She fought to take high school courses needed to prepare her for college. Women were encouraged to take home making, typing, and on and on. The jokes in biology. The trouble getting a lab partner in chemistry. And on and on. At best she is treated like one of the boys. But, she's not one of the boys. She's a woman.

'Why can't I apply for this scholarship?'

'"Why, Thera, because you're a woman."' With the implication that any fool should know that.

College was not much better. On a sandlot near her dorm, she discovered that she had a knack for throwing a baseball. The school's baseball team was all male.

Then on to liberated Europe. Her thesis professor, Doctor Jenkins, won the admiration and gratitude of countless male students for holding forty hour final re-write sessions in his quaint little village cottage. After Thera received her Doctor of Philosophy degree, she asked him why she had not been invited to attend these sessions in his home. "My Gowd, Miss Fulton; I wouldn't think of having a woman enter my bungalow alone." He tugged at his perfectly trimmed beard. "The villagers would talk forever. I could even lose my membership in the bowls club."

'Sexism? A lovely word for tyranny. Perhaps she hasn't missed so much after all. Isn't the adoration of a pretty woman just another means of gaining the upper hand? Isn't sex just another such trick? Is there really any difference in the way Rayford took her and the way many men take their wives, who often submit only because they are in no position to refuse?'

'Yet, I can't be cynical about love. All that is needed to support the beauty of love is one look into young eyes on a day when they have found it and the most cynical heart will surely melt.

'Jack Fisher wants me to run for a seat on the state legislature. Perhaps I will have a chance; provided I win the support of the right men!' Thera laughs at the thought of getting rid of them all by just snapping her fingers.

'Women can not allow themselves to be treated like flowers;" She concludes. "pretty ones admired and handled carefully; plain ones ignored and trampled among the weeds?'

Thera turns out the light, undresses and climbs into bed. She lies watching her toe-tepees as flashes of light spark the alcove beyond the foot of her bed. Carol has dainty feet. Her pretty little sister once told Thera that she had a firm foundation. She must visit Carol and Alton at the hospital tomorrow. Their baby could come any day now. She pulls the sheet over her head.

***

Carol Fulton Newman hangs on for a dozen horrid, nightmare ridden, days, driven by sheer determination that her child will live. She sees her older sister, Thera Fulton, during flashes of consciousness, amid long fits of screaming agony. In her tortured mind is an image of a younger Thera, bending with her hands between her legs, and weeping :

"It hurts so bad, Carol... That mean man just wouldn't stop hurting sister Thera."

Rabun Duel Newman's birth comes at a time when change is rocking the earth. He enters this world with these dramatic events shaping the songs of his childhood.

Chapter 4:
I Will Fear No Evil

"Doodlebug, doodlebug, please come out. Your house is on fire." Frustrated by the chant not working, Daniel throws a handful of fine sand into the hole. A little puff of dust rises to remind Thera of the two devastating atom bombs that had, just weeks earlier, severely tested the thinking of humanity.

People felt as helpless against such power as the tiny insect in his hole, but most of them went back to work, with the same determination as the doodlebug, and an undying belief, that each time they moved a grain of sand, they changed their world forever.

Some changes are like the stars on a stormy night; you know they are out there although you can't always see them, and even when you do, they're still a mystery. Other changes are like catfish in muddy water; you want them so bad you can taste them, but you're never sure if they're down there, or if it's the right time for them to bite, or even if you're using the right bait, and you know you might as well be patient, because they're gonna come in their own sweet time.

Thera finds, in her case, the changes that have come into her dull life to make it better have been more than worth the long wait. For her, it is a miracle that at this late time in her life, God has given her charge of these beautiful children. She sits in the shade of an elm tree, watching young three-year-old Daniel play, under the corner of the high front porch. The baby she named Rabun Duel Newman frowns as he tests the grass beyond the blanket she spread for him, beside her chair. From the day she brought him home, Daniel's mother, Becky, started calling him "baby RD".

Southerners are very partial to nicknames. For no reason at all, Daniel started referring to him as "Bocephus" Thera was thankful that one didn't stick. Soon everyone settled on RD, except Daniel, who still calls him "Bocephus" on occasion. Daniel got that stubborn streak from Victor.

Daniel is the "spitting image" of his father. But there will be no more Victor Fultons. No more heroes. Before the big bomb, people could praise the Victor Fultons of the world while they secretly dreamed that deep inside them was the same well of courage ready to spring forth in the face of death. But no more. With people now forced to live every day knowing that a big bang can take it all away at any moment, they can't kid themselves anymore. People are scared! And they know it! With everybody cowered in the face of such awesome destructive power, who would appreciate those who risk their lives? Yes, she concludes, the Atom bomb definitely changed everything in a flash.

Some changes do come swift, like lightning splitting a tall pine tree lengthwise to the ground, while others are slow and lazy, like heavy raindrops pelting a slick bank of Georgia clay, until rivulets are running red as blood.

"RED! Oh my God! Oh..baby! Get outta there!" Thera knocks over the armchair rushing to snatch the baby from under the porch. "Daniel! That's a Black Widow spider!"

Daniel calmly grinds the spider into the dirt with the same rock she was under when he found her. When he steps out into the yard, Thera takes his hand and with baby RD on her hip she leads him up to sit on the porch swing.

***

Years later, in that same swing with Daniel, now eight, and RD age five, Thera tells them how to recognize the Black Widow spider, by the red hourglass shape on it. She explains why it must be avoided, by telling them that a Black Widow spider had bitten Nathan Fulton, when he stuck his hand into a bee hive. He died thinking that a bee stung him. Daniel asks why the spider was in a bee hive, and Thera explains that the Black Widow often builds its nest in bee hives.

Then she asks him how he feels about Billy Ray and Becky coming to live with them.

"I think I'd rather be a bee with a Black Widow in my hive," Daniel grins. "than a Fulton with Billy Ray Shirey in my house."

"Oh, Daniel, they're having such a hard time making ends meet. Your mom does so need to be with us, too."

Seeing the troubled look on Thera's face, he adds. "As long as he don't mess with me and "Bocephus, I'll just have to put up with him."

Thera hugs him and RD close to her. "Daniel, if he ever decides to mess with you or RD, I promise you, I will knock him down with my big iron skillet, and tell him to find another place to live." Daniel has never heard that kind of talk from his Aunt Thera, but he knows she means it and he also knows she can do it.

"You can only do what you must do, Aunt Thera. Me and Bocephus will just have to get over it! Just get on with your life, Bocephus. That's all you can do." So says Daniel.

The next weekend Becky and Billy Ray move into the right side of the house where Carol and Alton had been. Daniel and RD share the left front bedroom and Thera sleeps upstairs. Theirs is a peaceful co-existence for a few short years, mostly because Daniel is seldom at home, and Aunt Thera proves to be a strong and capable mother protecting and taking good care of the two boys.

Also, being fair, Billy Ray does work very hard, and long, hours at his job in the iron foundry. He is a very strong, muscular man. He has been lifting and pouring molten iron into molds for many years. He has flaming red hair, and freckles all over his body, and a quick, winning smile, that he flashes freely. He loves hard work. He loves life.

And, most of all, he loves Becky, more than anything in the world.

He also loves homebrew and hunting. Years ago, he went drinking homebrew and hunting with CC Paylo, who, in the thick of the chase, fired a shotgun too close to him, and left several small buckshot balls imbedded in the lobe and back of his left ear. His friends started calling him "Shotgun" Shirey and the nickname has stuck ever since.

Shotgun is not really a mean man, but he does have a temper. Most people know to stay out of his way when he is mad, which isn't really too often.

Eventually, it has to happen, and it does, when Daniel is about eleven years old and RD is
almost eight. Fortunately, the trouble comes at a rare time, when Thera is away from home. She is attending a fourteen-day historical symposium, at the University of North Carolina campus in Chapel hill. She is invited as a guest speaker, to present a study she did with Dr. McTanis on the displaced children of WWII, who were dispersed into the English countryside to escape the devastating bombings in London.

While Thera is away, her two displaced children start their own war at home.

It all begins when Daniel eats the supper that Becky has made for Shotgun, and when he comes home tired and hungry, he gets mad and mean. He starts yelling at Daniel, and chases him upstairs, where he runs straight into RD at the top of the staircase.

Shotgun tries to push by him, but RD will not move. Shotgun hits him hard, with a full blow from the back of his fist, that sends him tumbling all the way down the steps. It seems that Shotgun is himself surprised at the force and result of his swing, He immediately bounds back down the steps and, with tears in his eyes, lifts RD and tells him over and over that he is so sorry. But, it is too late.

RD says nothing, but he will not forgive, and he will not forget. He goes deep into the woods to think about what he must do. He makes a decision at age seven that will begin to shape his young character. He vows to himself that he refuses to live in fear. He would rather die than live his life afraid of other people. He decides to get mad, get even, and get over it. Then he makes his plan.

RD and Daniel both avoid Shotgun, as much as possible, for almost two weeks. Shotgun is still feeling guilty about hitting RD, and is trying hard to be nice to him. RD acts as if nothing is wrong, and Shotgun begins thinking it is all over. It isn't over. It's just time to get even.

On Sunday morning, RD spies Shotgun sitting on the top step of the front porch, smoking a cigarette. He slips quietly around the house to a barn out back, and finds a two-by-four about five feet long. He then tip-toes through the hall silently, on his bare feet, and ever-so-slowly, eases open the screen to the front porch. Without a sound, he holds his breath until he is in perfect position, then he swings the board with all his might and hits Shotgun so hard, in the back of his skull, that he flips out into the yard, without touching another step.

RD leaves Shotgun unconscious, and calmly walks back to put the cracked board in the barn. Then he goes deep into the woods again and stays there for two days, until Daniel comes to find him, and tells him that Aunt Thera is back home and Shotgun is at work. They agreed to say nothing about what has happened to anybody.

From then on, RD and Shotgun become close friends. Shotgun even earns Daniel's respect, for not telling Aunt Thera about "Bocephus blapping him with a big board," as Daniel phrases it.

After that, each and every time Shotgun introduces the boys, he smiles at RD and says, "Be careful with that one. He never forgets."

***

'Sometimes, you just can't see the changes that are coming your way from the highest limb of a tree overhanging the muddy water, but you can feel them approaching, just as certain as you feel the burning slap of the Chattahoochee river, when you do a belly-whooper.' With his right foot on the grassy slope at the front end of the yard and the other dangling from the steep bank above the highway, RD sits reflecting on his talk with Thera, about how much has changed, in the two years since she made her trip to North Carolina. Thera loves politics. She has been spending a lot of time in Atlanta, and making many other trips the last two years, and she seems so happy now.

'Tomorrow, it will be exactly a year since he felt like he had been slapped hard in the gut when Thera gave him the news that Becky was divorcing Billy Ray Shirey. Shotgun's hot temper had erupted one time too many, and Becky told him she had enough. Shotgun's explosive outbursts killed their marriage, as certain as slaughtering a hog by firing a bullet between the eyes. But, unlike shooting a pig, there was no kicking and squealing. Becky's love for Shotgun seems to have just suddenly gone stone cold dead without warning.

The sticky-hot air has made RD's flesh damp, causing his shirt to stick to his back, as he hugs his knees. He takes a deep breath, scented with the crisp smell from slivers of the grass he has just cut, that are stuck to his moist hands and arms. He removes the shirt and rubs his underarms dry on it, then swings both legs over the bank, and looks across the road to his right. In the fading daylight, he can just make out the pale white image of the unlit pre-fab house that Shotgun built, on the land that Thera gave Becky as a wedding present.

RD turns his head toward his right shoulder, to view the dark form of the Fulton house against an early evening sky. The house seems fast asleep, under a warm sunset blanket, that casts an eerie glow through the glass globe, above Thera's dark window. It is the last rod remaining on the roof. With Thera's enthusiastic approval, before the divorce, Shotgun took the rest of the lightning rods off of her house, and put them on the house he build for Becky. Shotgun discovered that Becky is deathly afraid of thunderstorms, and that she is convinced the rods offer real protection. Shotgun made it clear to everyone, that whatever Becky wants, Becky gets. Sadly, as it turns out, the man Becky wants is not Shotgun.

Becky was strongly attracted to Shotgun's volatility and his strength in the beginning of their marriage. But, the love RD once saw in her eyes, when she looked at Shotgun, slowly began to change, until she began to timidly turn away, to avoid looking at him at all.

Divorcing Shotgun was surprisingly easy for Becky. He truly loves her and he was willing to give her anything she wanted, including her freedom from him.

Chapter 5:
Bye Bye Love

Shotgun still tears up every time he speaks of Becky, but he refuses to say an unkind word about her to anybody. He drinks a lot more homebrew now, and he spends a lot of time in the woods, hunting alone, but he stays away from her, and out of her life, simply because that's what she wants him to do.

Her new husband, Fred Sanders is a significant change for Becky. Becky is attending a church revival meeting with Fred tonight, and they expect to be coming home very late. She seems to be taking an increasing interest in church activities with her new husband. How ironic, since RD believes that her involvement with church functions actually began as a way for her to get away from her second husband.

From Becky's point of view, her marriage to Shotgun was a colossal mistake. Becky had been so lucky with her first husband, Victor, because he was a man who took care of all the problems in her little world, until the big wide world went to war, and took him away from her. Victor's death left her alone and lonely. Her marriage to Shotgun was based on physical attraction, with very little practical thinking. However, Becky did learn a lot from her marriage to Shotgun.

Becky has learned that she doesn't want to live poor. She doesn't want to depend on her family. She doesn't want pity from anybody. She doesn't want to live with a man who makes her feel insecure. Security is, in fact, what Becky needs most from a man. She now wants a husband who is steady, dependable, and most of all, predictable. When he says he will be here at two in the afternoon, he doesn't arrive too early or too late.

Becky explains to RD that this was precisely the case when she first met Fred Sanders. She had looked up at her kitchen wall clock as the doorbell rang exactly at 2pm. She had opened the door, with her best smile, to greet a dapper young man in a white shirt, dress slacks, and hush puppies. He held a clipboard to his chest, and returned her smile, as he offered her his card and introduced himself. "Good afternoon, Ms. Rebecca Fulton. I'm Fred Sanders from Kemp's Carpets. I believe you spoke directly with Mister Kemp about having your home measured for carpet."

She had softly shook his hand, as she took the card from it, and replied. "Yes, Gurald told me to expect you at two. Come right in Mr. Sanders. Your timing is perfect! Please call me Becky."

He called her Becky for hours. She was delighted to learn that he shared her same faith.

Fred took Becky to his church the very next day, and she made Daniel go with them the following week, and every Sunday thereafter. They were married in that church, just three months after he took her measurements.

Daniel took it hard. Daniel bonded with Shotgun, in ways that never would have seemed possible, before RD, so dramatically demonstrated, that he was not afraid to stand up to him. Shotgun's genuine devotion to Daniel's mother, went a long way toward endearing him to her son. It is also a fact that, judging by his actions, Daniel is not afraid of anything on God's good earth. If he is, he never shows it. And Shotgun admires Daniel's spunk. However, his mother's fear of Shotgun definitely destroyed their marriage.

RD decides that people have different fears, and different ways of reacting to them. His friend, Roy Franklin, is afraid of the dark. The Franklin farm is about a quarter of a mile down the road on the right, and Roy won't even walk home from the store by himself at night. RD twists to his left, and looks toward the soft glow that is cast through the thick, cloudlike air, by the light from the Texaco sign.

Chapter 6:
My Boy, My Boy!

Still sitting on the bank in front of the Fulton house, young RD rises. He shakes out his shirt and dusts his pants, then makes his way along the grassy border of the dirt drive down to the graveled area in front of the store. When he reaches the end of the drive, the sharp little rocks hurt his bare feet and he steps lightly, shifting his weight to lessen the sting.

"You should'a seen it....You ain't seen nuthin' that funny."

Bobby Riley's voice booms from under the transom and RD straightens his walk, enduring the painful bite of the gravel. Clyde Addison turns his chuckles into hee-haws as he spots RD, as if to point out that he just missed something hilarious. A skinny little boy springs from the bench and runs to meet him.

"Hey, RD!" His only item of clothing is a new pair of Levis two sizes too big so they will fit after washing. One of his daddy's old belts holds them in folds around his scrawny waist. He tugs nervously at the loose end of the belt.

"Hi, Roy. What are you doing here so late?"

"I been waiting for you, RD. I meant to go on home before dark. ..but....it got dark before I knew it...listening to Bobby and Sammy talk about some of the funny stuff old Coo-Coo does." He eyes the dark beyond the light and tugs his belt again.

Bobby's lean muscular frame is balanced in a chair propped against the corner post to RD's right. He looks like a Charles Atlas disguised as Elvis. He wears slick black pants with pink stitching to match his shirt and socks. The heels of his highly-polished white shoes rest on the bottom rung of the chair, pushing his knees almost as high as his head of ebony hair, swept up on the sides with Wildroot Cream Oil, into a massive roll that spills down onto his forehead. He tries to nurture a rebel look, but when he smiles his even teeth match his pointed shoes. Bobby has an attitude that mimics Elvis singing his favorite song.

"I've never looked for trouble but I've never ran. I don't take no orders, from no kind of man....Well I'm Evil, so don't you mess around with me."

Mister Cool of 1959 lives with his ill and aging mother just up the hill past the church on the right. At age twenty-six, Bobby is the oldest member of the group. He is also the latest person to join them hanging out at the store. But, he has earned everybody's respect, and is good friends with Clyde Addison who lives in the same direction back off the road on the left just past the store.

Clyde, astraddle a chair with his massive arms draped over the back, wears shoes and socks identical to those worn by Bobby. His T-shirt is drenched, as usual, from the hard effort he puts into lifting the weights that the boys put together out of old car parts at CC Paylo's Junk Yard. The bar is an old drive shaft. Flywheels are used for weight discs and are kept on by iron clamps that Shotgun made for the boys at the foundry.

Clyde and Bobby are determined to make themselves as strong as Shotgun. They have a friendly lifting contest that has been going on for more than a year. Eighteen-year-old Clyde looks a lot more muscular than Bobby, but no matter how much weight he manages to lift, Bobby always picks up a few more pounds. RD keeps hoping Clyde will win, but due to his age, he never does.

RD is standing beside the other chair and as he turns to sit in it, he finds Sammy Paylo smiling up at him.

"Where'd you come from?" RD seats himself on the bench beside Roy.

"Crawled out from under a Rockola." Which is Sammy's way of saying that he tired of waiting for Nub to come outside so that he could kick some free tunes on the Jukebox. He is a skinny James Dean ready for a role in a bad gangster movie. He has on a cheap black sports coat over a bright red, high-neck, T-shirt. He is already making a production out of busying himself by cleaning his long fingernails with his switchblade.

"RD, can Sammy really eat a razorblade?" Roy was biting his nails.

"Yeah,,,, I saw him do it one night." RD said lazily.

"How did he do it?"

"He took one of them thin brown Gillette blades...you know the double-edged kind in the red wrapper,,,, and he put it flat on his tongue then he started breaking off little bits with his jaw teeth until he had it all in small pieces. Then he washed it all down with a bottle of RC Cola."

"Sounds dangerous... couldn't it mess up his stomach?"

"Sounds stupid to me..." RD looked directly at Sammy. "I guess the belly-wash soda is supposed to eat up the tiny bits kinda quick."

"So, that's the trick."

"Now you've got it. No big deal."

Sammy gives RD the evil eye just as a car pulls up to the gas pumps and a heavy man gets out mumbling "evening" as he goes inside. Nub comes out shortly to gas the car with the man on his heels, Co-Cola in hand. The stranger has a flat top that looks funny with his big round face and forceful eyes that bulge out like boiled onions. He looks down at Bobby who has his head on his chest and his eyes closed like he's sleeping.

"How much weight you got there?" When Bobby doesn't look up, he turns to Clyde.

"The bar's twenty-five pounds.... each flywheel is about thirty." Bobby answers evenly with his eyes still closed.

Onion-eyes pokes a chubby finger at the weights like he's counting.

"Put 'em all on." Says chubo, and as Bobby ignores him, he kicks the leg of Bobby's chair.

Clyde looks at RD and whispers, "Ohhh...Shit!."

"You want 'em on...you put 'em on." Bobby still has his eyes closed.

Clyde gets up and puts the weights on the bar and clamps them tight.

Onion-head gulps his Co-Cola and puts the bottle in a half-filled rack of Quart cans of oil. He spreads his legs before the weights and opens and closes his hands a few times. He jerks the weights as high as his shoulders and groans as he tries to get them above his head, but his elbows shake and they come back down on his chest. His fat face is as red as RD's bottom was the time he sat down in poison ivy after swimming raw in the river. He bends his knees and jumps the weights up high enough to lock his arms for a moment. Then he just steps out from under them as they drop to the ground with a thud. He licks the onion juice off his thick upper lip and grins until he notices that Bobby still has his eyes closed. He grimaces and draws his lips back so tight that they go white as his cheeks puff out so itchy red that RD unconsciously scratches his buttock. He turns to Bobby and kicks the leg of his chair again.

"You ever seen anybody lift that much weight, Punk?"

"All you did was jump it. He can press it." Clyde says matter-of-fact-ly.

Onion head laughs and Bobby looks up.

"What's so doggone funny?"

"I got a dollar says you can't press that much, Wise ass."

Bobby swings his feet out and the tilted chair rocks upright. He smoothly lifts the weights and presses them five times, then he turns to face the big man and holds out his open palm.

"I bet you ain't even got a dollar." grumbles Onion face.

"Whatdaya mean? I won!"

"Show me your dollar and I'll pay. You can't make a bet without money. No money, no bet. Bet's off, see ya Punk." He turns his back to Bobby, takes out his thick wallet and turns to pay Nub for the gas.

In a flash, Bobby grabs a quart can of oil from the rack, raises it high, and slams it down hard on the big man's head. As his knees collapse, his chubby hand throws money all over the ground around his limp body. Bobby picks up a single dollar bill. Nub begins picking up the rest of the money and puts it back in the wallet he holds between his knees. He has already decided the gas money will cover the dollar the man on the ground lost to Bobby.

"You boys better go. I'll take care of this blob of blubber."

Chapter 7:
Down The Road

The five of them are walking down the road toward the Franklin farm when they hear a siren and see a red flashing light approaching from the direction of the Franklin house. They crouch in the ditch as the ambulance passes on its way to the store. RD feels Roy's arm tremble against his back.

"I gotta get home, RD.....will ya....will ya walk home with me?"

"The baby wants RD to walk him home." Sammy sneered.

"What's the matter, Kid?" Bobby prodded. "You afraid of the dark?"

"Yes, I am." Roy said frankly.

Bobby is amused by Roy's honesty and throws in a sprig of humor

"What if everybody was like that? Everybody would be walking around all night and somebody would never get home." Bobby laughs heartily and Sammy and Clyde snicker.

"I used to walk all over these parts by myself at night when I was your age, Roy." Clyde threw out. "You're too old to be afraid of the dark."

"Why don't we take Roy back into the woods and show him there's nothing to be afraid of at night?" Sammy nodded toward the thick trees on the right.

"I don't mind walking with him. Come on, Roy." RD took Roy's hand.

Bobby stepped in front of them.

"Listen, RD. That kid can't be scared all his life."

RD thinks about the commitment he made to himself at age seven not to be afraid.

"Especially scared of nothing." Clyde enjoins. "It's a nice night for a walk in the woods."

RD respects Clyde's opinion on most matters because he always seems very calm and level-headed and he often has a stabilizing effect on hotheads like Sammy.

"OK, but stop picking on him." RD felt Roy's hand tighten. "They're not going to bother   you, Roy. We'll come back when you're ready."

"I'm ready."

RD throws Roy's hand away from him. "Stop acting like a baby. Just go on home by yourself. You're almost there anyway."

The path that crosses the corner of the woods to the Franklin house is just a short distance past where the bank slopes off and ends.

The others begin climbing up along a dip in the bank toward an old pulpwood trail leading into the dark woods. Roy's eyes glisten with moonlight flickering from them. 'He's got to grow up sometime. And I'm not his keeper.' Thinks RD, as he turns to follow the others.

"Wait for me, RD." RD did not look back. But he stops until he feels Roy's trembling hand in his.

***

Back at the store, Onion head is sitting in Bobby's chair holding a blood-soaked towel on his head.

"I called for an ambulance, You want me to call the law?" Offered Nub.

"Damit, I am the law! I'm deputy sheriff of this whole damn county." He looked as if he wanted to cry. "Who are those boys?"

"Never seen 'em; 'till tonight." Nub pats his head as if he is looking for his flashlight up there. "They're probably with that bunch that's camped out on the Chattahoochee." He handed the deputy his wallet. "If I'd'a known you was a deputy, I'da asked you to run 'em off."

The deputy counts his money. It is all there, including the dollar Nub contributed to replace what Bobby had won.

"Do you know you're breaking the law if you're withholding evidence?"

Before Nub could respond, it rained gravel as the ambulance squeals into the drive and slides to a stop. Elroy Knox is driving and his brother, Irving, is eager attendant on his first actual emergency call.

Irving wraps four rolls of bandages around the deputy's head and insists on strapping him into a stretcher. Once the deputy is firmly anchored in the ambulance, Elroy tells Irving to head for a clinic they know well that is down the road about five miles past the store.

Elroy says he needs to ask Nub a few more questions to fill out his report then he will follow them in the deputy's car.

As they watch the lights of the ambulance disappear, Elroy holds up two fingers and stuffs a five dollar bill in Nub's shirt pocket. "See you in about an hour, partner."

"I'll be here, my friend." Nub watches him get in the sheriff's car as he walks around the corner of the store to the well, a waist high structure of heavy boards with a smooth log crank. Nub slides a square wood cover aside, lowers the bucket into the well letting the log spin freely, and looks around slowly as the bucket drops. Then he hops up on the frame, swings his legs into the opening, hangs by his one arm, and feels with his feet until they hit the ladder he has mounted for climbing down into the well.

At the bottom, Nub kneels on a board just above the water level. He raises a fishing net full of bottles of clear liquid that glisten in the soft rays of moonlight coming down from the opening in the well. He puts four of them in the bucket, climbs out of the well and begins to turn the crank.

Chapter 8:
A Walk In The Woods

The woods seemed a giant black blob sucking them into the dark. They follow the narrow rutted, overgrown trail into the bowels of the forest. The air is rich with the smell of rotting pines - small ones pushed aside to let chainsaws get at the big ones. The smell reminds Sammy of the curly patterns under the bark of dead pines. He remembers that Roy had vomited that time they found a dead possum with maggots wiggling inside its eaten-out guts.

"I wonder how long it takes for maggots to eat up a person when they die?" He said aloud.

"Uck.." Roy rolls his lips down.

"I know it takes awhile for the coffin to rot..."

"I read a story about a little boy that was buried alive." Clyde joins in. "He was stuck in a coffin with his hands tied and a gag in his mouth."

"Can you imagine being in that coffin, Roy? Not seeing a thing with it so dark.. ..hearing them praying and singing....then lowering you down in the grave. Hearing shovelfuls of dirt hitting the casket." Sammy was loving it.

"Hey, knock it off!" snaps RD.

"What scares me is seeing heads chopped off." Bobby visualizes a scene from a drive-in horror movie. "The eyes keep looking for three or four minutes after the head rolls off of the body. One of 'em's mouth kept moving; trying to scream."

"Yeah, I saw that one, too. But, what gives me the creeps are vampires. Sticking their fangs in people's necks. Blood spurtin' everywhere." Sammy makes a teeth-showing face and raises his long-nailed fingers like bat claws as he swoops around Roy.

"Stop it!" RD squeezes Roy's shoulder reassuringly. "He's just trying to scare you, Roy." Sammy holds his bent elbow in front of his face and peeks over it widening his eyes. "After getting a good drink of a little boy's blood, the Vampire turns into a bat and flies into the night. Like <u>that one!</u> " He points into the trees sharply.

"Ka....eeeee......Kaa......eeee." A shrill cry sends shivers down Roy's spine.

"Wha,,,wha,,,what's that, RD?"

"Just a nightbird. Sounds creepy, that's all."

"Ssshhh!" Sammy motions them still. He eyes the clumps of grass between the two deep ruts in the road.

"What is it?" RD whispers.

"I thought I heard a rattlesnake.....lissseeeen..." Sammy hisses.

They all hold their breath and perk up their ears. Roy begins to shake as they do hear rattling.

Clyde takes a quick stride and snatches Sammy's arm from behind his back. He peels Sammy's closed hand open to reveal a small bottle with a few pills in it. Sammy bursts into high-pitched laughter. Clyde tightens his grip on Sammy's wrist until the laughter stops.

"Poisonous snakes are nothing to joke about. These woods are full of 'em and they scare the hell outta me." He threw Sammy's hand away from him in disgust.

"One of 'em almost got me last summer." RD said.

"What kind was it, RD?" Bobby is interested. "Did you get a good look at it?"

"I sure did. I was sleeping in the sun down by the creek and I felt something cold... I looked down and this big snake was crawling right on my belly. I'm not sure what kind it was but it really scared me."

"There are four kinds that I'm afraid of....little ones, big ones, live ones and dead ones." Clyde blurts out. "What did it look like."

"I'm sure it was a viper by the shape of its head....and I found a picture of a copperhead that looked a lot like it. It had brownish-copper scales and a wider body than any other snake that I've seen."

"Holy cow! Whatdidja do?" Sammy asks.

"Nothing. I was too scared. That snake looked right at me with his slick forked tongue slithering under his pearly fangs. Then he just slid off me like he was blind."

"I read somewhere that they are blind when they're shedding." Clyde offers. "That's when they're the most dangerous because they'll strike at anything that moves."

"You're darn lucky you didn't move, RD." added Bobby.

"For sure... Ain't that the truth. I still don't know why he didn't bite me..." RD pats his skinny stomach. "I told Nub about it, and he said that a copperhead is the most dangerous snake on earth because it's the only kind that will strike out of pure meanness. He can have a fresh baby rabbit in his belly, not be needing anything, and he will still chase down and strike a grown man who is being extra careful not to disturb him. Nub says the 'ol copperhead just likes to kill people. He thinks the snake just liked my warm belly."

***

Lester is strapped in so tight that he has to strain to peek over his own belly to see the back of the driver's head.

"Irving, do you know any of the boys that hang out around that store?"

"You say something, Deputy?" Irving cranes his head and shouts back.

"Yeah, damit! CUT OFF THAT DAMN SIREN!" When the wailing winds down, he repeats his question.

"Yeah, I know all them hoodlums. Which one bashed in your head?"

Lester describes the assailant.

"That'd be Bobby Riley. He ain't no good, sheriff. He beat hell out of Elroy for fooling around with Dee Dee Milam. He says she's his girl, but Elroy had the hots for her long before Bobby Riley came along. He lives with his sick old mama in the first house past the church going back toward town." In his side mirror, Irving spotted the lights of Lester's car topping the hill behind them. 'When I tell him Bobby's gonna be tied up tonight, he'll make a b-line to Dee Dee.'

***

The boys are approaching an old graveyard behind a cluster of dilapidated shacks at the far corner of the woods behind the Fulton house. Most of the desolate dwellings are now empty and the few people who still live here come and go on a road from the other side. The graveyard is overgrown with bri-ars and kudsu that cloak decaying, sunken headstones forming ghastly shapes in the pale moonlight. The moon is high and full casting light through scat-tered openings in the limbs above the boys that throws complex patterns of shadows across their path.

RD studies Sammy's sleek form as he steps into a moonlit clearing and turns back to wait for the others to catch up with him. He crouches on the balls of his feet with his arms resting across his thighs. The red shirt under his black coat takes the shape of an hourglass on his stomach. His long fin-gers hang limply between his legs and he seems to spring ever-so-slightly. 'Like a spider waiting for his fly.' thinks RD, as he stops abruptly, Roy bumps him from behind.

"What's the matter?" Roy nearly screamed.

29

"Oh, nothing...I thought I saw a spider."

"Where?! Where's he at, RD?" Roy sounds like he's having trouble breathing. He eyes the ground around his bare feet as his toes appear to curl involuntarily.

"I said I thought I saw a spider...but, I didn't."

"Oh..." Roy sighs with relief, but his toes stay curled.

Clyde is walking back to meet them, then shrugs his shoulders and steps quickly on down the path to where Bobby bends over Sammy whispering in his ear.

"RD, can we please go back?" Roy's eyes are pleading with his strained voice. "I'm really scared....will you please go back?"

"Yeah, I'm ready." RD Cups his hands around his mouth. "HEY... CLYDE! CLYYDDEEE....WE'RE GOING BACK."

"Wait up, RD." Clyde and Bobby walk toward them. "Ya'll com'on. We'll all go back in a little while. We're not going much further."

"Yeah, we ain't gonna be long." adds Bobby.

"Well, I'm tired of walking." RD sits down and crosses his legs. "Roy and me will just wait here until you get back."

Roy puts one hand on RD's shoulder and tugs on his belt.

"Suit yourself. But, we might go back on the old creek road. It's less than a mile the other side of those houses." Bobby points that direction.

RD doesn't get up as Clyde and Bobby walk back toward Sammy.

Suddenly, a large thundercloud passes in front of the moon darkening the woods. Something moves nearby rustling the leaves and causing Roy to twitch. They hear Sammy whistling softly as the older boys walk slowly out of sight, Bobby and Clyde sing along when they quickly pick up the tune.

"Poison...ivv eee eee eee.....Pois..suuun....iiiii....iivveee. Late at night when you're sleepin', poison ivy comes a creepin' uh..rau...rau..rau... round...."

RD pulls himself lazily off the ground, takes a deep breath and fully exhales. "Com'on, Roy."

They catch up with the trio on their second verse.

"Ssshhh...we don't want them to hear us." Bobby feels playful.

"Them? Who's them?" Roy asks.

"Them's the dead people." Sammy smirks. Playing theater usher he leads them down a path that crosses the graveyard, then curls and unrolls his arm to the right pointing out the dark rows of tombstones. "This way, gentlemen. We have a good spot reserved just for yoouuu."

Roy's bony hand grips RD's arm so hard it hurt.

The moon peeks from behind the cloud to reveal a mangy old hound dog lying on one of the graves. When the mongrel sees the boys, she begins to bellow like she fell in a well. As the dog tries to stand, they see that she is bleeding from behind and dried blood is caked on her hind quarters. All her ribs show and her weighted belly hangs like a stuffed brown bag, wet and about to rip. Her wailing now sounds faint and distant. The howling fades into a weak pained moan as the dying dog uses her last breath to empty her pregnant womb.

"Get me outta here, RD...I can't see." Roy's eyes are shut tight.

"That's because you've got your eyes closed." RD notices.

"But...I can't open 'em....RD....honest...I can't."

Sammy slaps Bobby on the back, and laughs. "He's done got his eyes skeered shut."

"It's not funny." RD said firmly. "He's really scared."

Roy is crying now and rubbing his eyes with his tightly drawn fists.

"It's OK, Roy...everybody's afraid of something. We're going home." RD reaches to pull Roy's hands away from his face, as Bobby grabs Roy by the scruff of the neck and shakes him.

"Come on, Kid...Open your eyes." Bobby shakes him harder.

Roy trembles all over but his eyes don't open. Bobby slaps him hard enough to rattle his eyeballs, but they stay shut. Bobby spreads Roy's eyelid open with thumb and forefinger to see the eyeball rolled back so far that only white shows.

"Good grief, Roy!" What's the matter with you?" Bobby pushes the terrified boy's head back so forcefully that Roy stumbles and falls. His fingers are in tight bunches, twisted as if paralyzed. His elbows are pushed into his stomach and he begins to jerk all over.

"You shouldn't 'ave hit him, Bobby." Clyde kneels over the child to hold his legs still.

RD drops to his knees and cradles Roy's head in his lap. Bobby also tries to help steady the legs that are still jerking spasmodically with Clyde's strong hands locked around the ankles.

Roy's head is bumping RD's as he holds him close and tries to console him.

"Everything's alright, Roy. We're going home, Roy. OK, Roy?" The head shakes harder.

The cheeks are hollow, sucked-in, and Roy is making choking sounds. "We're gonna take you home right now. Please stop shaking, Roy.....please, Roy...please..."

It takes a long time for the shaking to stop. Roy's face is washed in RD's tears when the body finally goes slack and the eyes open. The eyeballs are twisted in their sockets and seem to be looking far off in the distance at a scene too terrible to witness. RD notices that Roy has gone quiet and completely still. All life has left his body. His struggle is over. Bobby and Clyde are holding the boy's legs as if they are convinced that the twitching will start again if they remove their hands.

RD lowers Roy's head to the ground and rises, sniffing awkwardly. There is a horrible and unfamiliar smell in his nostrils that he will remember forever

- the scent of death. He staggers to the grave where the she-dog lies lifeless. He thinks he sees her leg move, but on closer look the movement is a new-born pup, apparently the only one alive among the blob of bloody animal flesh. The she-dog's head is thrown back at an odd angle and her long tongue hangs out of the side of her mouth. Her eyes are rolled sideways staring at the moon with a look similar to the eyes of Roy.

With the acrid taste of vomit rising to burn the roof of his mouth, RD remembers Bobby saying the kid was pissing his pants. He remembers the foul odor when Roy's bowels let go. He remembers the stink of fear and the distinct smell of death. And, as he throws up, he remembers a whisper.

"Epilepsy." Without any feeling in Sammy's voice.

Sammy has followed him to the grave and stands poking around in the dead dog flesh with a stick. When he touches the live pup, RD runs at him in a rage, kicking and hitting him until strong arms pull him away. Sammy looks completely baffled, as he squirms away from where he landed right in the middle of the disgusting mess made by the filthy dog..

"What the hell's eatin' you?!" He tries to brush slime and dirt off his coat, and blood from his lip. "It ain't my fault he died."

RD ignores him to lift the live puppy and try to wipe the gook off him with his bare hands. Clyde removes his T-shirt and offers it. RD wraps the blind pup in the sweaty cotton cloth and nestles him against his bare belly.

Clyde carries Roy's body all the way back in his strong arms. He never asks for help and neither Bobby or Sammy offer to carry the burden awhile. As soon as they come to the highway, Sammy turns toward the store without a word.

"I'm going with Paylo." Bobby mumbles timidly. "It's a damn shame that boy dying like that...I guess it couldn't be helped. Rayford's gonna take it hard.. Make sure you tell him it couldn't be helped. Ya hear? You'll do that, won't ya?"

Clyde doesn't answer. He just keeps walking with the same steady pace as when he first picked up Roy at the graveyard to take him home. As Bobby leaves, he speaks to RD in a tired voice.

"You run ahead and let the Franklins know what happened. I'd hate for them to just see him like this without knowing."

"What'll I tell 'em, Clyde?"

"You'll know what to say when you see 'em."

***

Bobby and Sammy find Nub passed out on the bench with three empty bottles on the ground and a half-empty clutched against his chest. It takes a lot of effort to get him awake. When Bobby pries open his lids, Nub's bloodshot eyeballs look like they're floating in pure cane sugar syrup.

"Baa....baaa.....baabaaa....bahbee?,,," Nub slides off the bench with his head just missing a flywheel on the weights bar. They get him seated again and he asks about Clyde. Bobby tells him Clyde is with RD,

***

RD holds the puppy high on his chest and runs hard with his bare feet slapping a steady rhythm on the pavement. When he gets a good lead, he slows to a brisk walk and looks back. Clyde is just at the top of the low hill behind RD. The dead body is beginning to sag in his arms. The dark form of the pair against the moonlit sky reminds RD of a famous statue pictured in an art book.

RD notices the lightening rods Shotgun put up on top of Becky's new house. When she would come home late from church meetings, Shotgun would put his truck on the grass so she could use the lighted driveway. And he always left all of the lights on for Becky. She would be home late tonight, but Shotgun's truck was gone forever and the house was dark as a tomb.

RD takes a small path that crosses the corner of the woods to the back of the Franklin farmhouse. As he approaches their backyard, he pauses to catch his breath and rest his shoulder against the rough bark of a pine tree which serves as corner post for a pigpen. He feels the feeble squirms of the soft, warm puppy and unwraps the T-shirt. A fat sow with her back toward him grunts inside the pen. The faint squeals of piglets are just audible.

PIGLETS!

RD grabs a tree limb, swings over the fence, and feels his feet 'squeesh' into the wallow mud. It's like walking on suction cups as he trudges to the opposite side of the sow. Sure enough, there are five little piglets sucking the sow's teats. RD pushes the pup's nose against a free nipple and his mouth opens to draw it in. The puppy is soon rooting to hold his place among the other babies.

***

"Nub, we saw the meatwagon....did Bobby kill that fat sonovabitch?"

"He's uh..." Nub burps loud and long then wipes saliva from the side of his chin. "He's uh depuhdee..." As if he is just hearing what Sammy said, he laughs and adds, "He's a fat sonovabitch too."

"Well....Zip a dee doo dah. Zip a dee aay!" Sammy throws palms out and bows to Bobby. "You done killed yo' self an officer of the law. You gone big time now, daddyo!"

Bobby's face turns pale. Nub's dull head is slow to notice, but when he does, he is quick to correct Sammy.

"No, no NO! Bobby, you didn't kill him. Didn't even hurt him too bad.

Course that buzzard Elroy and his little turkey-necked brother treated him like he was dying." Nub patted Bobby on the head like he was petting a puppy dog. "Now, what you need to do, Bobby is just cool down and lay low for awhile. The worst that can happen is that you might have to spend a few days in jail."

"That Goddamn Elroy had to be driving that meat wagon!" exclaims Bobby. "Those two are the only buzzards I know that would tell him who I am."

"Shit!" spat Sammy. "Shit, shit, shit."

***

Chicken-droppings mesh with the mud covering his feet as RD swings outside the pen, and walks beside the fence where the messy birds have been roosting, after eating corn from the pig trough. He scraps off the bottom of his bare feet on the fence wire and drags them through the dew-damp grass toward the back porch.

There are no lights on inside the house. RD knows the Franklins are country people who go to bed early and he expects them to be asleep at this late hour. Roy's father, Rayford, is a hard-working hole digger

Rayford Franklin dug most of the wells and many of the graves in and around Woosterville. He is a large rugged man who keeps his hair very short. He always wears overalls on top of a white T-shirt and big red rubber boots with deep-tread soles. He uses a forked stick to find the best spot to hit water without digging any more than necessary. RD is amused that the stick is called a doodlebug. He reasons that the stick got that name because doodle-bugs and well diggers spend a lot of time making holes in the ground.

Rayford Franklin is direct. He likes to get right to the point. RD knows what to tell him. He feels the slick boards under his damp feet as he steps onto the low porch, pulls the screen open, and bangs hard on the heavy door.

"That you, Roy?" Rayford's deep base voice booms. "Door's open."

"Where you been boy?" demands Irene, hurriedly from just inside.

"It's me, mam...RD..."

The door swings open. Irene stands peering down at him, tugging on a robe about ten sizes too big. Her blue-grey hair is pulled high on her head under a brown hairnet.

"Come on in, RD. Where's my boy?" Irene speaks her words faster than anybody RD knows.

As he enters, RD comes face-to-face with Rayford who slips on his glasses with fine gold rims that wrap around the back of his ears. His overalls are hooked on just one side and he is not wearing his T-shirt. The skin it normally covers is pale white in sharp contrast to the ruddy brown of his lower arms and upper neck and face.

"Roy's dead." RD announced. "He had a fit and died."

Rayford sank backward onto the sofa.

"OhGodOhGodOhGod...." Irene rapid-fires, tying and untying her robe.

Rayford is rubbing his face with his hands and moving his head up and down causing his glasses to come loose and fall on the floor.

"Clyde's bringing him home..." When neither of them speaks, RD adds. "They oughta be here in a minute."

Rayford looks up. It is the first time RD sees him without his glasses and he is surprised that Rayford's eyes are the same color grey as Thera's, but they have a blank stare like he can't see.

"Where did it happen?"

"Behind Aunt Thera's house. We were walking in the woods."

Clyde steps onto the porch and all three turn toward the open door. RD pushes the screen and Clyde walks straight to the sofa and places Roy's body where Rayford had been siting. Rayford knocks over a lamp feeling for his glasses. Clyde stands rubbing his aching arms and RD notices his pointed-toed shoe is firmly planted on the glasses. RD kneels and picks up what's left of them.

"Mister Franklin, Clyde stepped on your glasses. They're broken."

Irene chooses this moment to scream as she faints and falls across an overstuffed chair. She looks like a discarded rag doll, with one arm hanging limply over the chair arm and her skinny legs poking out of the robe at odd angles.

"Is there anything we can do to help?" Clyde asks.

"Can you see about getting them glasses fixed?"

As they step down from the low porch, Clyde sounding unusually weary, asks RD what he did with the puppy.

RD's face beamed. "He's eating. Come on, let me show you."

Clyde follows him to the pen, where they find the pup sleeping between two of the piglets with a nipple still in his mouth.

"Well....if that don't beat all." Clyde stoops and gently tugs the puppy loose. The fat sow grunts and her belly shakes. Clyde smiles broadly as he tucks the puppy in the crook of one arm, gabs the low pine limb, and swings over the fence. One of his shoes sticks in the mud. He works his feet free of both of them and lifts them out of the wallow.

They walk in silence to the highway and pass Becky's house where the lights are now off and it still just doesn't look right with Shotgun's truck missing, then RD speaks.

"You're gonna tear those fancy socks on the road."

Clyde takes them off, balancing himself on one foot then the other. "Man, they stink!" He throws them and the shoes into the ditch.

"I forgot to warn you about the chickenshit. I'm sorry you ruined your new shoes."

"I never really liked them anyway, and them pointed toes hurt my feet." Clyde stares thoughtfully into space. "RD, do you want to sell this puppy?"

"Do you want him?"

"Yeah. He feels....so soft...and warm...and...."

"And alive?"

"Yeah."

"He's all yours, Clyde."

"Thanks, RD." Clyde pats RD's shoulder. "I wonder if he'll take a baby bottle nipple?"

"If he won't, we know at least one he will take."

"At least until Rayford runs me outta his pigpen. I guess I need to get his glasses fixed right away." Clyde was thinking hard again. "You know, RD, it might be better if parents didn't raise their own children. They always put too much of themselves into them.

Chapter 9:
All Shook Up

Sammy sits beside the jukebox on the upturned end of a Double Cola case. When Nub goes outside to greet a customer, Sammy stands and kicks the front of the jukebox with the flat of his foot and hears a familiar click. He punches the same Chuck Willis tune six times.

"What am I living for?...dute du du...if not for you?"

Nub hears the music and sings along.

If you ever hear Nub singing from around the corner where you can't see him, you will absolutely swear that George Jones himself is sitting on that bench by the purity of his voice. It is almost impossible to tell any difference in the way they sound. If you listen to Nub do a song that George hasn't done you just know that George would do it the same if he decided to sing it.

"You'll be the only one, my whole life through. Baby, nobody else, .nobody else, will do."

Sammy is patting his knees in time when he feels his hand twitch. He bolts to the door, and almost knocks Nub over in the doorway.

"Where ya goin' in sucha hurry, Sammy?"

"Gotta take a whiz." He flashes a smile, but keeps moving. "Be right back."

***

RD is sitting on the bank watching as Clyde disappears beyond the light of

the Texaco sign. He catches another quick glimpse of him as a car passes from the opposite direction and turns into the store where Nub comes out to greet his customer, pump gas, and collect cash for it.
He hears the hot car spin back onto the highway

RD stands as he sees Sammy rush out of the store. He skirts the bushes and stays hidden, making his way in their shadows toward where Sammy darts around the corner and approaches Nub's well. RD steps out of the shadows just behind him.

"How did you know Roy had epilepsy, Sammy?"

Sammy jumps like a spooked squirrel.

"Goddam it, RD? Whatthahell you mean?...sneakin' up on me like that?" The hand holding his pills is shaking involuntarily.

"Still playing rattlesnake? What're those pills for, Sammy?"

Sammy's right shoulder jerks and the side of his face flinches.

"Holy cow! You've got it too!"

"Yes...Goddam it! Now you know...If you tell anybody...I'll slit your damn throat...you understand?" Sammy tries to open his switchblade in his left hand but it is shaking so bad he drops the knife. He tries to open the pill bottle and also fumbles it.

RD swiftly retrieves the bottle as it falls to the grass.

"How many?" He sees there are only two and throws them into Sammy's open mouth.

Sammy gulps and stumbles to the well, turns the bucket of water on his face and washes down the pills. He hangs on the side of the well with his body twitching for several minutes.

RD stands quietly watching Sammy re-compose himself. He finally stands erect, straightens his coat, and combs his wet hair into a duck tail with the wide-teeth end of his comb then presses the top of it down over his forehead with his palm. He bends to pick up his knife but pops erect and steps back.

"There's a Goddam spider on my knife!"

RD squats and lays his palm flat in front of the spider, letting it crawl into his hand.

"It's just a daddy longlegs. He's harmless." After a long pause, during which Sammy reclaims his knife and flicks it open and closes it nervously, RD adds. "It's the ones with red on 'em that can kill people."

"You just remember what I told you. You tell anybody, you can give your soul to the Lord, 'cause your ass is mine."

RD says nothing, but looks deep into Sammy's eyes, without the slightest hint of fear, and Sammy turns to walk away behind the store where the music continues to play.

"What am I living for?...dute du du...each lonely night?..."

"You need this bottle?" RD tosses it as Sammy turns to snatch it neatly from the air.

Chapter 10:
Show Me The Way To Go Home

RD follows the trail of beat-down grass that leads from the well to the back of Thera's house. He slips quietly across the back porch and feels his way through the dark kitchen. He hears Daniel's heavy snoring in the den and follows the sound to the bed in the far corner beside the solid staircase, which is fully enclosed under the steps and has no rail.

RD loosens his pants and steps out of them as they fall to his ankles. He eases into the bed beside Daniel, feeling very tired but realizing that he will not easily fall asleep. Questions race about in his head like ants pouring out of the ground after his mower spun their mound into a cloud of dust. The Queen question is the riddle of death. He reasons that the dead ants dissolve into the ground and somehow end up feeding the grass. The rabbits Nub shot probably ate the grass, and they in turn made some delicious stew. The grass may also be fed by the bodies of Indians that had long ago been buried under this hill.

So, nothing ever really dies, he decides. Living forms just change into other kinds of living forms when they are dead and buried. It's all just another example of changes in a world that is different every second of every day, always and forever.

Tonight, for the first time, RD is seriously contemplating what happens to people when they die, and thinking about people he knows that are dead. His parents are dead, but he never knew them. Most dead people he knows are faces in photographs. He knows Nathan, Ned and Victor are buried in the Woosterville cemetery, but he didn't see them alive. Roy Franklin is the only real living person that he was looking at the very moment when he died. Until tonight, Roy was always going to be around tomorrow.

Now, where will Roy be tomorrow?

Indians believe their dead go to the happy hunting ground. But, Roy doesn't even like to hunt; and besides, he's not an Indian. Maybe, he'll go to heaven. What will Roy's heaven be like?

What does Roy like? He can't think of anything and this disturbs him. What kind of heaven is there for somebody who doesn't like anything? Then he remembers Roy telling him how much he liked to sit on the bench at the store. And, he likes Baby Ruths!

Roy was probably at this very moment sitting on a bench in heaven eating a whole case of Baby Ruths. Even when RD imagines a very long bench loaded with cases of Baby Ruths, it doesn't seem to be much of a heaven. Of a sudden, RD is struck by a depressing thought. Roy also likes him. When he dies, is he going to spend eternity on a long bench with Roy gorging himself with Baby Ruths in front of a darned old store? Maybe that would be his hell?

No, hell for RD is stretched out on a bed just like this one, dead tired but unable to sleep, all alone, and so weak that he can't move. Then spiders start crawling all over him, wrapping him in a silk cocoon, biting him and draining the blood out of him. He tries to kick free of the cocoon, and spit out the spiders he feels crawling inside his mouth. There is no cocoon, just a sheet that is tightened when Daniel rolls restlessly to the far side of the bed. And there are no spiders, just the tassels on the bedcover he is fond of chewing on when he sleeps.

There is always a chance that Roy is in hell. Hell for Roy is definitely being put in a deep dark hole. How ironic that his daddy is a hole digger. RD lies awake for hours. He tries counting the steps on the staircase. Then he begins making up silly rhymes.

"Along came a spider, and sat down beside her...
And frightened Aunt Thera away...."

The sound of Daniel's heavy breathing comforts him.

"Doodlebugs in the seed bed....Spiders in the hive...
Heroes go to heaven...It's good to be alive."

Heaven for Sammy Paylo is watching somebody put Roy into that hole. He sleeps.

***

Sammy has a long walk - more than a mile back toward town. He walks at a smooth even gait, whistling and singing now and then. As he nears the top of the long hill past the store, he sees Clyde kneeling under the corner of the porch at his house. Sammy eases off the road and stands quietly behind a walnut tree no more than twenty feet from Clyde.

Clyde puts the puppy in a cardboard box filled with soft rags and slides it under the porch behind a washtub used to collect rainwater from the inside corner of the porch. He gives the puppy small drinks of water by repeatedly dipping his finger and putting it close enough for him to lick.. Then he nestles him in the rags, strokes him fondly, and goes inside the house.

Sammy waits for the light inside to go off before approaching. He stoops and lifts the puppy. 'He doesn't even have his eyes open yet, poor little thing.' He grips the tiny puppy by the nape of the neck and holds him above the water. As he drops him into the water, Sammy says aloud.

"Your mother is a bitch and your father is some mongrel bastard. It's best that you never get a look at this rotten world."

"The same can be said for you, Sammy Paylo!" Suddenly, a big strong hand grabs Sammy by his duck tail and forces his head down just above the rain water in the tub. Another hand gently lifts the struggling puppy up out of the water. Clyde firmly pushes Sammy's head under water and holds him there. Clyde heard him singing coming up the road and was aware of him all the time. After going inside the house, he had decided to bring the puppy in to sleep with him. He had cut out the light, and peeked out through the corner of a shade to see Sammy approaching his porch. By using the back door, he was able to come around the house just in time to see Sammy do his dirty deed.

Clyde pulls Sammy up just long enough for a couple of quick breaths then shoves him under water again. He repeats this three more times and then throws the half-drowned scoundrel to the ground.

Weak and still sputtering, Sammy scrambles to his feet and runs back to the highway. When he is sure that Clyde is not after him, he slows his pace and combs the water out of his hair. 'What the hell's got into these people?...first the kid turns on me like that, and now this hayseed goes nuts on me for trying to take that pitiful little turd of a dog outta it's misery.'

Chapter 11:
Thunder Road

Elroy Knox is burning up the road knowing that Bobby is going to jail. He intends to really step on it so that he will be at Henclaws when Dee Dee gets off work. Friday is their biggest night and they're open late. He can just make it. He wheels into the store with his horn blaring anxiously..

Nub appears quickly, hands him two pints, a dollar change, and asks if he wants gas.

"I'm running late, Nub...no time to fill 'er up." He gives back the dollar bill as a tip.

"You got a hot date after work, Elroy?"

"Well... let's just say....When the cat's away... the mice will play. Burma Shave." He shows his ugly teeth.

"How about this one - If you want me the truth to tell.....don't mess with Dee Dee while Bobby's in Jail...or you just might wake up with your ass in Hell! After Shave." Nub liked his rhyme better, but he has always liked old Elroy Knox for a good reason. "You are the best runner I ever used, Elroy.. .and you were smart enough to get out when you did. Now, be smart enough to listen to me when I tell you to leave Bobby's girl alone."

"You know me, Nub. I never pay a bit of attention to anybody trying to tell me what to do. And I'm just too old and set in my ways to start now. Thanks for the hootch, pardner."

"Thanks for the tip. Just don't call me if you get in a tight 'ol buddy."

Knox answers by expertly popping the clutch and flooring the gas pedal, sending a shower of gravel all the way to the highway then hitting second gear, peeling rubber and fish tailing onto the paved road. He skips third and goes directly into high gear so fast that there is not a one second pause in the powerful car's acceleration. He opens a pint and gurgles a good slug of near-ly pure grain alcohol. "Oh, yeah! Life is good, tonight! Just a "short run" for a good "long haul" runner."

***

Sammy moves to the centerline, picks up his whistle, and quickens his step. 'I guess both of them are just upset....RD was the boy's best buddy and all...and Clyde did tote that boy a long way home...so I guess he's just worn out and sick of the whole mess. I guess they have to take it out on somebody.'

Sammy has just gone over the first low hill past the store when he hears the roar of Elroy's engine. He gets out of the middle of the road, just in time, as the Golden Hawk blows by him faster than he ever imagined any car could move. Something hit the road just in front of him and exploded like thunder.

"Holy Shit! What was that?"

***

Elroy had just emptied the first bottle and tossed it out the window. He does-n't even see Sammy, because an announcement on the radio catches his full attention.

"Here's one of the biggest hits from 1956 - The Ballad of..." The DJ paused for dramatic effect..and slowly rolled out the next words in a deep bass tone. "The ballad of... TTHUUUNDER ROOAD!"

> *"Let me tell the story, I can tell it all;*
> *About the mountain boy who ran illegal alcohol.*
> *His daddy made the whisky, the son he drove the load;*
> *And when his engine roared they called the highway "Thunder Road".*"

"Holy Shit!. How about that? They're playing my song!" He turns the radio up all the way and opens the second pint bottle.

> *"Sometimes into Ashville; sometimes Memphis town,*
> *The Revenue-ers chased him but they couldn't run him down.*
> *Each time they thought they had him his engine would explode,*
> *He'd go by like they were standing still on Thunder Road."*

> *"And there was thunder, thunder, over Thunder Road,*
> *Thunder was his engine and white lightening was his load.*
> *And there was moonshine, moonshine, to quench the devil's thirst.*
> *The law they swore they'd get him, but the devil got him first."*

By the end of the chorus, Elroy is high on booze and higher on himself. He is far too intoxicated to be behind the wheel. But telling Elroy not to drive would be like telling CC Paylo to act normal, its just never going to happen, and everybody knows it!

Elroy and his brother Irving have been 'driving since they wuz babies' and driving is about all they know how to do. Elroy was good enough to win some money on the race tracks until he got nailed running moonshine on the back roads between Alabama and Georgia. He did a little time, but got an early release for behaving himself. He managed to get on with his little brother driving emergency vehicles and decided to quit transporting moonshine, but, unfortunately for Dee Dee, he just couldn't stop drinking it.

About a year ago he saw this "Thunder Road" movie at the drive-in. Robert Mitcham had co-written this song for the movie and it got Elroy all worked up. He ran around town telling everybody that they had made a movie about his life story and written a song about him Here are some more of the words to "Ballad of Thunder Road."

"Roaring out of Harlan; revving up his mill.
He shot the gap at Cumberland and streamed by Woosterville.
With G-men on his tail light; road block up ahead,
The mountain boy took roads that even angels fear to tread."

Elroy has moved tons of bootleg hootch for Nub Hooper's family, over every road in the song He always got the load from the stills to "the boys who pay the bills" faster than any runner in Dixie.

"Blazing right through Knoxville, out on Kingston Pike,
Then right outside of Beardon, they made the fatal strike.
He left the road at 90; that's all there is to say.
The devil got the moonshine and the mountain boy that day."

In his dreams Elroy sees himself as the mountain boy in that movie. Well, tonight, he completely destroys the beautiful gold sports car, and comes very close to living his dream by almost killing himself and Dee.

The face of Dee Dee Milam is grotesquely disfigured for life when Elroy's new Studebaker Golden Hawk smashes into a telephone pole at an estimated speed of ninety miles an hour.

Elroy Knox may have seen himself as a legendary race car driver but he did not become famous for his driving that day. Everybody who knew him could add another infamous lament to the lines of his song:

"Evil Elroy drank the moonshine, and drove Dee to hell that day."

Chapter 12:
Just Bumming Around

Irving Knox tows what is left of the hottest car in these parts directly to CC PAYLO AUTO PARTS.

After nearly fifteen minutes of blowing his horn and flashing the spot light on the garage, CC finally comes out with a big flashlight and a single-nut tire tool.

"Elroy said for you to look it over for him." Irving flips a switch and lowers the front end of the crushed Studebaker to the ground, unhooks his rig and runs it back up on the tow truck bed.

"Shine this fer me." CC hands the light to Irving, drops down on his knees and pops off a moon hub cap. He circles the car and removes two more that are undamaged.

The right front fender is pushed almost into the seat on the passenger side and the right wheel and hub are crushed deep into the twisted metal. "Looks like three good 'uns...and one dead 'un."

"Elroy says the insurance will cover it. He said he will talk to you as soon as he can." He climbs up in his truck, starts it, and leans out of the window. "Do you have any questions, CC?"

"Yeah, I do." CC waits until Irving shuts off the engine and gets down from the high cab.

"OK, what's your question?" Irving purses his lips and furrows his brow to show that he is paying close attention. He wonders if he should get his note pad to write it down.

"Do you know why a fart stinks?" a maze of tiny wrinkles crinkles around CC's beady blue eyes as he peers mischievously at his own reflection in one

45

of the moon hubcaps.

"Alright, CC...Why's that?"

"So blind people can appreciate 'em. Huh,huh,huh...huh,huh,huh." his laughter spews a mix of snuff and spit on the hubcap. He rubs it off with his sleeve to get a better look at his merry face. "Huh,huh,huh...."

"Yeah, that's a real good un, ain't it?" Irving turns to climb up in the truck.

He has a big patch on the back of his blue coveralls that reads: BETTER GET BARDHAL.

CC's brown coveralls have a patch on the back that reads:

30 DAYS HATH SEPTEMBER -
APRIL , MAY, AND
THE SPEED OFFENDER.
- BURMA SHAVE

He holds the hubcaps close to his chest and unlocks the cage he built off the back of the garage.

The cage is filled with shiny metal - chrome mirrors, hood ornaments, light rims, door handles,
ornate grills, drag pipes, tailpipe extensions, and hubcaps of every conceivable design. CC rests the new moons on a low bench beside an almost new pair of pointed-toed shoes he found in a ditch.

CC looks up at the wide display of highly polished ones that are positioned so that he can see himself in all of them. He turns on an old console radio with a big dial that he twists until he picks up a station playing a good tune he heard Jimmy Durante sing in a movie.

> *"When ever worries start to bothering me,*
> *I grab my coat, my old slouch hat, and hit the road again you see,*
> *I ain't got a dime, don't care where I'm going.*
> *I'm as free as a breeze, and I'll do as I please...*
> *Just bumming around."*

CC does a little jig, waving the hubcaps in the air like an ancient tribal dancer while enjoying his images. "How's everybody? We got three new 'uns today. They're a little dirty faced but CC's gonna scrub 'em up." He picks up a can of metal polish, a rag, his hubcaps, and his shoes and bursts into a song of his own:

> *"I Got nuthin' to lose...not even my shoes...."*

His chair is an old commode with a shiny stainless steel seat. He rubs the sparkling oval with his polishing rag before he sits down on it. He places a hubcap on his knees and begins polishing it with his head bent down to within inches of the shiny surface. Suddenly he bolts upright, dropping polish, rag and hubcap.

"Lookout! Here comes another good 'un." He slams the seat lid up and quickly sits on the toilet seat and begins to grunt. Satisfied with the explosive outcome, he goes back to polishing his treasures and singing his song:

"I fart and I sneeze..... I do as I please...Just bummin' around."

Coo-Coo is never short on words that rhyme.

Chapter 13:
Goodnight Irene

Sammy's greatest childhood treasure is his memories of Irene's wind- up record player and the few slightly wobbly songs she played on it for him...."Goodnight Irene, goodnight Irene...I'll see you in my dreams." Sammy sings loudly as he walks the highway centerline. A dog runs out barking and gets close enough to see and smell with recognition and barks some more just because dogs like to bark at night. The mutt finally goes back to whatever dogs do at night when they're not barking like crazy.

Sammy tops the final hill and slows his pace. Below him is the maze of twisted metal that stands as a monument to the wrecked and wretched lives of the misfits he lives with in that rundown, overgrown, filthy, smelly excuse for a house behind the scraggly clump of trees, weeds, and briar bushes on his left. Big white letters, on top of the dark barn-like garage, glare out in the moonlight among the rubble of old cars that seem to stretch for a country mile.

C.C. PAYLO - JUNK YARD
USED PARTS CHEAP

Sammy remembers when he was in grade school studying possessive nouns, he asked old CC why he didn't have an apostrophe S by his name on the sign. CC had chuckled hard with his one-of-a-kind disgusting laugh and said:

"HUH, HUH, HUH....HUH, HUH, HUH...The only thing in this world that a man can call his is what he sees his face in.....And he don't have that, unless he's looking at it." He had taken Sammy to a large mirror hanging in back of the garage and shook his finger at their reflection with animated emphasis. "See that?...That's me. That's all I own. See that?.... That's you. That's all you're ever gonna have!"

Oh well, everybody knows CC is a little touched in the head. That's why they call him 'Coo-Coo'. The old fool loves to talk about watching Rayford Franklin raping his daughter Julie, who is also Sammy's mother.

"That hole digger dug Julie's well and out popped Sambo!....HUH, HUH, HUH....HUH. HUH. HUH " It is definitely crazy the way he enjoys repeating the sickening story to Sammy, and how he seems to relish every detail.

"Julie would lay on that quilt in her short-shorts and show her ass off to that well digger 'till he wanted it so bad, he just took it. I seen him do it...with her hollerin' and carryin' on like she hadn't asked for it herself." Then he would laugh like hell.

"HUH, HUH, HUH....HUH, HUH, HUH....." On and on until he had tears streaming down his face.

Sammy hates CC's laugh almost as much as he hates the rotten old shit worm himself. He sits down in the road, just thinking about his mother. Julie is still a pretty woman at thirty-eight, but she has let herself get fat. Sammy has seen pictures of her in those white shorts when she was younger and he can't blame a man for wanting her. But, rape is despicable, and unforgivable! Sammy knows how it feels! CC violated him when he was five and a hard-core cell mate sexually assaulted him when he was thrown in jail as a teenager.

"Shit, man!" Sammy says aloud, as he sees a truck coming his way and moves to the other side of the road. " Even having raping Rayford for a father is not as bad as living with that 'laughing hyena' for a grandpa!"

***

Roy's jeans are soaked with urine and excrement. The dead boy is an awful mess. His mouth is blue and his jawbone is twisted to one side. The sockets of his eyes are dark and the eyeballs are a sickly grey. The smell of him is almost unbearable even to his father's iron stomach.

Rayford pries Roy's mouth open, pulls his tongue out of his throat, and straightens his jawbone. He takes him into the bathroom, puts him into the large tub, and removes the long belt and the Levis. Rayford rinses the nude body with buckets of water he fills from a home-made hand pump that he has rigged himself with plumbing running to the well outside the bathroom window. He gets on his knees and scrubs until the last of the brown-green slime swirls down the tub drain on its way to feed the rich green grass in his yard.

Irene rummages through the boy's room and finds his blue suit, best shoes and a clean white shirt. She takes these items to her bed, sniffs an assortment of perfumes, and chooses a round box of bath powder. Rayford brings in the body and lets it fall across the bed.

"I want him buried on this land." Irene says dryly. "Call TJ. He's a lawyer and he works for the state. He'll know what to do so the fool government don't come out here asking stupid questions."

"Hell, why don't they just leave us alone?" He protests. "I gottta go to the store to call him."

Irene takes a towel from Roy's neck and dries his still damp body a second time. She covers him with the sweet-scented powder from the neck down and gets the clothes on him. She leaves the room and comes back with the long belt in one hand and the only decent pair of socks Rayford owns in the other.

***

Sammy raises his fist in the air pumping it up and down to give the 'blow your whistle' signal to the eighteen-wheeler slowing as it comes toward him. The truck stops beside him and the driver leans from the high cab window.

"Hey, Sonny... You know where I can get some gas around here this time of night?"

"Yeah...about a mile on down the road. Where ya headed?"

"Gotta take this load of tobacco down to Florida and pick up a load of something else and haul it to New Mexico."

"Need somebody to help you drive?"

"Can you handle this rig?"

"I'm a damn good driver......you might have to teach me anything over four gears."

"Hop in, Sonny. You got yourself a job."

"Can you give me a minute to grab some things outta the house?"

"Sure, I was about to stop for a nap anyway."

Sammy packed a small cloth bag with a few clean underclothes and the last bottle of his pills. When he climbed up in the cab, the driver rolled his eyes sluggishly.

"Sonny, I been on the road since I left North Carolina. I gotta get some sleep before I give you a driving lesson. How about we fill this rig up with gas and get a little shuteye before we light out?"

"Sure, I don't want the man in the store to know I'm leaving though."

"You just climb up in that sleeper behind the seat. I'll get the gas, then we can stop a little farther down the road and you can watch the truck while I snooze." He grins and Sammy notices that he has teeth like a squirrel, but his face is more like a Santa Claus without a full beard who needs a shave.

While Nub pumps gas in the truck, Sammy hears Rayford walk up on the gravel and tell him he needs to use the telephone. Sammy is cleaning his long nails and he can't resist thinking how great it would be if he could slip up behind that rotten rapist and slit his throat before he leaves this place.

But, deep inside, he knows that he will never have the strength or the courage to kill a man that powerful. He dismisses his own conscience as it is about to tell him that weak little boys and blind puppies are more his speed.

Within minutes, Santa is back in the cab and they are wheeling out of the drive. Sammy peeks back to see Rayford and Nub walking toward the well.

"That one-armed fella is alright. I reckon he's the one you don't want to know that you're running away....is he?" He smiles a knowing squirrel-ly smile. "Bet, you'll miss this place, too."

"Yeah, I will." But most of all, Sammy starts thinking to himself, he is already missing Irene. He misses her wind-up record player and the old record she says was written about her. She rocked him to sleep countless times to the scratchy sound from that warped and wobbly turntable moaning "Goodnight Irene." Of course, that was long before that bastard Rayford just took her away from him and the old fool.

Aunt Irene is just about the only person in this whole crazy world that really cares about Sammy and the old fool. She is the most loving person he knows. And she loves Roy.

Well, it sure as hell isn't his fault that Roy died! Damit, he has no reason to feel guilty about it! He could've told them to pull his tongue out to stop the choking...but, hell, Roy's better off dead than having a shit worm for a daddy and being raised by raping Rayford.

"Mister, this is a good place to pull off the road for your nap." He points to the shoulder ahead where a path cuts across the woods to the hole digger's house. He leaves the trucker to nap and strolls down the path singing.

"I'm goin'away baby, won't be back no more....Or something like that, I forget the words."

***

Irene stands at the foot of the bed looking down at Roy's body.

The suit is too small. The belt and socks are too big. She decides not to put the tennis shoes on his feet. She ponders the fact that he never wears shoes anyway, and thinks that perhaps she can slip them on her feet when she's feeding the pigs and the chickens. She decides that brushing his hair neatly with a part on the side just looks all wrong.

Irene loosens the two buttons and folds the coat back on his left side. She pulls the extra belt length out and places his lifeless hand around it above his right thigh. She messes up his hair, pulls off the socks, and returns to the foot of the bed.

'Now, that's more natural. That's my boy.' She dabs her eyes with the socks.

"Irene!"

"Whosethat? Whosethat? Whosethat?..." She rapid-fires.

"It's me, Sammy, Irene..."

She runs into the back room and meets him coming through the back door.

"Oh, Sammy! It is you! Comin, comin, comin. Rayford's at the store." She clamps her arms around him with a vice grip hug and begins giving him cold, damp kisses on his cheeks. She feels him become tense and rigid in her embrace, then holds his face firmly between her bony hands and peers deep into his eyes. Embarrassed, he gently pulls her hands down and turns away.

"I'm leaving, Irene... Just wanted to say goodbye." He rubs his cheek with his coat sleeve.

"Oh dear, oh dear, oh dear... I thought you might've come to see your little brother."

"You mean my half brother, Irene." Sammy corrects her. "We don't have the same daddy."

She takes his hand and leads him into the bedroom as he politely gives her his sincere condolences.

"It's a shame, Irene. " Sammy looks without seeing the dead child as he repeats what Bobby said to Clyde. "But, it couldn't be helped."

He leads her back into the sitting room and eases her into a rocker then he takes the overstuffed chair in front of it. Irene immediately crosses to sit on the arm of his seat and puts her hand on his shoulder.

"I don't know if I should tell you, Sammy. But you and Roy do have the same daddy."

"I always thought CC was Roy's daddy." Sammy said uneasily.

"Oh no, oh no, oh NO! CC hasn't had normal sex since he came back to Georgia long before Roy was born." Irene flushes, a tinge of pink in her grey, liver-spotted cheeks. She stands and crooks a finger toward her bottom as she moves back to the rocker. "You don't make babies doing what CC has been doing for years."

Sammy squirmed in his seat. Irene had beat CC off of him with a poker.

"Do you mean Rayford made Julie pregnant with Roy?"

"The same way he made her pregnant with you. He took her by force." Irene was staring at her gnarled fingers. "By force the same way he took me. The same way Carl took me when I was just a little girl." Tears drop on her hands and she takes the socks out of her robe pocket and dabs her eyes.

"Sammy, I don't guess I'll ever see you again after tonight...and I think you ought to know the truth about our family. Me and Carl are the only ones that know and he's plum crazy now. Somebody oughta know." She begins to tell him all she has come to know in her eighty-five years.

"My mother's real name is Mazine. Her father, Claude Hausenzinger, brought his daughter, pregnant with his child, from Switzerland to New

York. He shortened their last name to Zinger. When the baby came, Mazine named him Carl Claude Zinger."

"CC?" Sammy was amazed.

"That's right, my brother, Carl...CC. He was born in 1869."

Mazine's father got her pregnant again before he was shot and killed by hit men while he was driving for a big time gangster." Telling Sammy her awful story seems to steady Irene and she proceeds calmly. "That happened just two months before I was born in May of 1872. We only had one room and one small bed in New York. Mama slept in the middle with me on one side and Carl on the other. She was always turned toward me with Carl curled up to her rear end. She never paid any attention to him. I've often wondered if his preference for backsides was formed in that little bed." Irene stops dabbing at her eyes, props elbows on the rocker arms, and puts her head in her hands. "Mazine was committed to an asylum in 1885. That was the year I got pregnant with Joanie."

"CC?" Sammy was almost afraid to ask.

"Yes. CC..Carl. When they took our Mama away, I was careful not to turn my back to him in our bed. But, he woke me up one night because he had discovered my other side and he raped me. I was barely thirteen when Joanie was born in August of 1885.

I told Carl he was not going to sleep in that little bed with me and the baby. I sewed some stuffed pillow cases together for a mattress and made him up a bed in the bathroom tub at night. I was able to keep him out of my bed for more than a year until we had that hard cold winter in 1886. We were all freezing because we had no money and they cut off the heat. Well, he slid in the bed with his teeth chattering and I was so cold I didn't even try to fight him off of me. He raped me again with me trying to breast feed my crying baby. I had another beautiful baby girl, Ida Maye, in 1886.

"The time I had with my sweet babies was the best few years of my life. But, the welfare people just wouldn't leave us alone. They came and took Ida Maye away from me when she was only three years old and put her up for adoption.

"They let me and Joanie visit Ida Maye at the orphanage until she was adopted by the Addisons just after her fourth birthday. It took us a long time just to find out where they took her.

"Finally, by the time Carl found out the Addisons were living way down here in Georgia and we come to visit Ida Maye, she was twelve years old and they didn't want us to see her.

Somehow, Carl figured out a way to fetch Ida Maye early from school and bring her to visit us. The Addisons didn't know about it. She was a loving and trusting little girl. Carl also found a way to get her pregnant too, but nobody but me knew it was him.

So, we're down here, and we don't have any money. That's another reason we left New York...no jobs...no money.

"What about Joanie? Did you bring her here with you?" Sammy asked.

"No. We got the welfare lady to keep her until we could come back for her.

"So, we had to find work. The only work Carl could find, us being strangers and all, was digging wells, graves, and outhouse pits. After awhile I went into the junk business. Carl quit hole digging and started getting into junk with me. He really liked finding old cars and selling the parts he took off of them. It was him that got the business making money for us.

"Of course all of that took a long time. But, eventually we got a little money together, and Carl went to fetch Joanie. But he didn't come back. He stayed gone over ten years. I hate it, but I believe Carl just wanted to get away from me because he felt so guilty about what he had done to me. I didn't know what had happened to him until Joanie came to live with me in 1900. Turn of the century; that's how I remember.

"When he returned to New York he found Joanie in trouble. Her boyfriend was an illegal alien named Carsio Colon Paylo. This is the name my brother has been using since then.

"Carl got the idea of changing names with Paylo because their first names were a lot alike. They swapped papers and Carl left the country. He bummed all over the world using Paylo's name."

"What did CC...Carl, do all those years he was bumming around?" Sammy asked.

"Said he was a sewage specialist. Said he dug benjo ditches in Japan, unstopped commodes in France, emptied sewage tanks in England, and washed hotel toilet bowls all over Europe."

"What happened to the real Paylo?"

"Oh, they caught him using Carl Zinger's name about six months after he married Joanie and sent him back to Argentina. That's when Joanie came to live with me. We did fine until Carl came back in 1923... the same year Nathan Fulton ran Ida Maye out of Georgia.

"Carl wasn't the same when he came back. He had always been crazy as a loon, but now he was a genuine pervert." Irene crooked a gnarled finger under the seat of the rocker. He started doing to me and Joanie what I caught him doing to you. Said he had the Colon name, so he played the game. Joanie even caught him doing that to me." Irene was crying again and dabbing her eyes with the socks. "It was awful, Sammy. I had to stand guard over Joanie's bed to keep him away from her so she could sleep. I never dreamed he would get after you."

"It's OK now, Irene. I'm getting out of here. You don't have to cry any-more...I'll be OK." He stood behind the rocker and started it moving slow-ly. "Does Rayford bother you?'

"No. He never has. He says my well was dry long before he married me. But, I'll never forgive him for what he did to my girls."

Sammy rocks her gently and sings softly.

"Sometimes I live in the country...sometimes I live in town.
Sometimes I take a blue notion...just to jump in the river and drown."
Irene, Goodnight Irene. Irene goodnight.
Goodnight Irene, goodnight Irene...I'll see you in my dreams."

Sammy leaves her asleep with her hands palms up in her lap.

Chapter 14:
Sick and Tired

Irene is awakened by Rayford's heavy step on the porch.

"TJ says we can bury him here. He'll take care of the paperwork at the courthouse tomorrow. You wanta call somebody?"

"Me...call somebody? Just who in the world do you think I could call?"

"Thought you might want to call your brother."

"CC?! That crazy old loon's the one who got me into this mess." Irene draws her eyebrows down making a deep furrow in her liver-spotted brow. She clenches her teeth and speaks again, enunciating each word. very slowly and deliberately for the first time since Rayford has known her.

"I..DON'T..WANT..ANYBODY!"

"Where do you want the boy's grave?"

"Put him in that well you dug. The water ain't ever tasted right, anyhow. That's a pretty place under the trees. Roy liked that spot." Considering the subject settled, Irene closes her eyes.

Rayford walks from the dark shadow of the house into the bright moonlight. Irene watches from Roy's bedroom as he comes out of the shed with a wheelbarrow and some tools. He knocks down the frame of the well and uses some of the boards to make a small mold. He then mixes concrete in the wheelbarrow and pours it into the mold.

The light from the window casts Irene's still shadow on the ground in the shade of the house. Rayford works most of the night digging a new well near the back corner of the porch and making many trips across the yard, bringing loads of the fresh dirt, until he has a large mound beside the old well. Irene's shadow never moves.

She is still standing at the window when he comes inside to tell her that everything is ready. He folds the bedspread around the boy's body and carries him out to the well. He holds the makeshift shroud over the hole and speaks almost in a whisper as he lets Roy drop from his arms.

"Return to mother earth, my son."

Rayford sees Irene's shadow jump as she hears the body splash. After a moment of silence, he drops on his knees and using a screwdriver he carefully writes on the grave marker still damp in the mold:

HERE LIES ROY
IRENE'S ONLY CHILD

Irene comes to see what he has written and takes the screwdriver from his hand to quickly scratch out her correction:

HERE LIES ROY
~~IRENE'S ONLY CHILD~~
JULIE's BOY

'NOTHING EVER FIT...SO HE DIED OF A FIT' Should be his epitaph, she thought.

A loud truck whistle cuts the still air. Squirrel-face is showing Sammy his new truck horn.

"With good timing, you can even play a tune with it."

"Can you play Goodnight Irene?" Sammy asks as they pull past the Franklin farmhouse.

"__Goooooddd Niiiittte Iiiireeeennn, Goooooddd Nniiiitte Iiirreennn,__"

Rayford begins shoveling the red dirt into the well as the sun breaks the horizon to end another hard night in Woosterville

Chapter 15:
Lonesome

The morning sun is just breaking over the dense pines as Thera wheels into a familiar dirt drive leading to a small trailer that sits halfway up the hill. Cinder blocks are carefully cemented around the underside of it to keep out water, spiders and snakes. Thera sits listening to Hank Williams on her car radio until she sees a light come on inside. A man's heavy shadow peers under a shade, to see her long green Pontiac parked beside his metallic-green, fifty Chevy.

'Good, he's just getting up. I can make breakfast for him. He loves country ham.' She smiles, slides out of her car, and takes a brown grocery bag from the back seat.

He meets her at the door in his jockey shorts. She hugs him and plants kisses on his face. The sounds from the same station she had on in her car radio sound clear and more mournful inside.

"Have you ever heard a robin grieve, when leaves begin to die...
That means he's lost the will to live, I'm so lonesome I could cry."

Thera sits her bag on a small table and starts his breakfast.

As TJ sees what she takes from the bag, he cuts down the radio volume and sings another verse of his own.

"Were you ever starving on a night so long, so hungry you could die?
Then here comes Thera to cook for me, and she sure knows what to buy."

Thera threw a verse back at him.

> *'I never knew a lawyer who could sing, and you're one who shouldn't try.*
> *They can't teach attorney's very much, but you all learn how to lie.'*

They both laugh heartily as he goes in to shave and get dressed, and she reflects with pride on the reasons she loves him so very much.

"What would I do without my Miss Thera?" TJ says aloud as he splashes hot water on his face. He was officially raised by foster parents - Amos and Ellie Prescott who were both mill workers. She began as his babysitter when the Prescotts needed help. As years passed by, Thera spent more and more time with TJ, just because she wanted to be with him. From his perspective, the fact that she took care of him, simply because she "took to him"from the time he was a baby, made her paternal-like love mean even more to him. Without any known obligation or requirement to do so, Miss Thera had always made him feel that he was the most important person in the world. And, in truth, Thera had turned out to be both mother and father to him. TJ bent down to evaluate his lathered image in ths low mirror as he began to scrape off the coarse stubble..

Thomas James "TJ" Franklin - Champion of the poor. His classmates put in the Harvard yearbook. They should add: Destined to die poor himself in Woosterville, Georgia. Every letter from his colleagues questions why the twenty-nine year old honor man stays in this hick town.

"Looking for self, perhaps?" Is his stock answer. His formal education hadn't taught him much about the riddle of self.

It took him twenty years to finally meet his father. Nine years ago, in 1950, Miss Thera helped him get a job with the County Recorder. He discovered two full pages of people with his last name in the county ledger. TJ was sent to investigate a report that an unregistered child was born at the Rayford Franklin household. Roy Franklin died last night at age nine. His short life span was only from 1950 to 1959. He was a baby when TJ came face-to-face with Rayford.

TJ was dumbstruck! He rinses his face and dries it with a towel, studying his own reflection as he remembers rushing to Miss Thera to tell her about seeing Rayford for the first time.

"It's, truly amazing! He's an older version of me!" He nods affirmation in the mirror.

Thera angrily stays his enthusiasm. "Pure coincidence! Nothing more! That hole digger is a mean, vicious man! You are to have nothing more to do with him, TJ. Is that clear?" Then, as if realizing she is not talking to a child anymore, she softens her tone and speech. "Please, TJ, understand that it is very important to me that you avoid that evil man."

He chides her jokingly about her dark secrets then kisses her bulbous nose and tells her one of those blatant lies that all lawyers can spit out as needed. to end a losing debate.

"Well, if it upsets you that much, I'll just let that sleeping dog lie." TJ switches quickly to a more pleasant topic and puts on a drawn-out southern drawl. "My, my, just how on earth am I evah gonna get by way off up thar in that yankee school without Miss Thera?"

She blushes, then smiles, and playfully pulls his hair to accent her instructions.

"I have just three words for you now that you're in a good school. Study, study and study!"

"You can count on it." He suddenly turns sternly serious and looks deep into her beautiful eyes as he gives her a long hug, she knows in her soul that he means what he says.

He comes back to her a good lawyer and she is so very proud of him. But, they both have changed during those years apart. While he was away, she became increasingly involved with her new charge and now her life seems to revolve around young RD. And he has changed.

This morning he thoughtlessly received her in his underclothes. But why did his briefs cause her concern? Concern he sensed, for he quickly donned a robe.

Nonsense! Thera decides to chalk it up to the curse of his profession - a probing mind. She also knows that he was not about to leave that sleeping dirty dog Rayford alone. She knows he has been poking at that hound for the last couple of years. Digging through records and court files he has learned only one fact that he can classify as hard evidence. Rayford Franklin was, in fact, sentenced to ten years in prison the year before TJ was born. 'FOR ASSAULTING AND DEFILING A HELPLESS CHILD." according to the court docket dated 1929.

And now that he has looked that devil in the eye, he constantly throws questions at her that make her uneasy. Thera is not trained to lie and finds it hard to avoid him when he asks her about the details of the case:

"Thera, did Rayford's wife, or lover, desert him because of his crime?"

"Thera, did she simply refuse to wait ten years for him to get out of prison?"

"Thera, could that "HELPLESS CHILD" have been my mother?"

"Thera, ..." She finally stopped him by gently putting her fingers on his lips and shushing him.

"TJ, please stop asking me all these questions. I am not a lawyer and I do not share your interest in the details of that mean man's life." He honors her request, but Thera is fearfully aware that he is still digging up bones.

TJ is not surprised that the victim's name is not in the records. Omitted to protect the innocent? Or the guilty? "THE STATE OF GEORGIA VS

FRANKLIN" protects the family name of the victim. Only in Woosterville could such nonsense determine the content of legal records.

However, now TJ knows that Rayford is his daddy, and by his very nature, and also as a good defense attorney, he throws his full support in favor of the underdog. Whatever Rayford Franklin has actually done, TJ is certain that he has paid his dues in full. TJ has seen enough to know that the poor and uneducated are often railroaded for crimes they don't commit, and more often given unduly harsh sentences for offenses with strong mitigating circumstances that are not even mentioned in their trials. "America has no criminal class except the congress." a great American once said.

Once they had that hole digger in court, the only ,fair was that it was fairly certain he would get a few years in prison for child molestation. He is lucky to still be alive. Other prisoners will often focus their own rage and hate on inmates convicted of this heinous crime. The more he comes to know his father, the more he is convinced that Rayford has both done wrong and been wronged; as is the case with most poor people in this world.

TJ is pleased to have found some of his flesh and blood family. He now considers Roy his brother and his death is a hard blow to take. In recent years, TJ has enjoyed getting out of this cramped trailer to visit the Franklin farm. He had become very fond of Roy.

During that same year Roy was born, 1950, TJ had spoken directly with Rayford and found that it was awfully hard to get any real information out of him. Rayford never talks much, but he always seems pleased to see TJ. He is alone with his father for the first time while Irene and the baby boy are at the store, they sit quietly in front of the cool draft from an empty fireplace with briar pipes making their own smoke until Rayford speaks.

"How did you find out I was your daddy?"

"I didn't exactly find out" TJ thinks about it before he speaks. "I just knew you were the first time I looked at you." He removes his pipe and smiles. "I would 've recognized me anywhere."

"I see." Rayford thinks about it before he speaks. "I'd uh taken care of you if I'd been here." He takes a long puff, removes his pipe, and taps down the ashes in its bowl with his thumb.

"I believe you."

Rayford slowly looks up and smiles. "It looks to me like you done just fine without me."

"I can't complain. I've been cared for very well. I found out you were in prison for ten years."

"I'd uh told you if you'd asked me." He leans over and taps the pipe ashes on the hearth.

"Who was my mother?"

Rayford doesn't look up at him. He carefully stands and turns his back to place the pipe on the mantle. "I can't tell you that. I'm sworn to secrecy."

TJ slams his pipe so hard into an ashtray that fire flies out onto the rug. He quickly jumps up to mash out the hot sparks. "God damn it, Rayford! I have a right to know."

"Well, by God, you won't find out from me."

They are nose to nose as TJ looks deep into that rock hard face and knows that truer words were never spoken.

As he slips on a fresh white shirt and khaki trousers, TJ is snapped out of his reverie and back into the present by the sound of a spoon banging on a pan. In the real world of 1959, he has a lot to do.

"Come and get it!" Thera summons from the kitchen.

This morning Thera seems more free and happy than he has witnessed in a long time. After careful consideration, it is not a good idea to bring up the fact that Rayford Franklin called him last night. Furthermore, it is definitely not the time or place to tell her about the death of the child, his brother Roy. Perhaps it is sometimes wise to hold the cards close to one's own chest.

TJ intends to tell Thera all about the trouble at the store last night. But, to his surprise, throughout their delicious breakfast of country ham, red-eye gravy, grits, eggs, and the best biscuits this side of heaven, she fills him in on most of the details about Bobby knocking out the deputy. She got this information from Nub with this morning's fill-up after driving back early from Atlanta to be here with TJ before her boys knew she was home. She then switches topics and picks his brain about what he expects her to face if she enters state politics. As always, he is reassuring her that a woman with her ability can overcome any challenge thrown her way.

Thomas James Franklin, Attorney At Law, finds little challenge in the legal battles of the Woosterville residents. The young man he talked to last night, Bobby Riley, is a simple example.

He is charged with assault because he gave old "Mo" Lester a taste of his own medicine. TJ would inform the pudgy deputy later today that, on behalf of his client - Mister Riley, he is filing counter charges of THREATENING SPEECH AND GESTURES and FAILURE TO PAY JUST DEBTS OR WAGERS and then use his superior verbal skills to convince old "Mo" that he should just drop his hopeless case before he gets into much more serious trouble.

TJ has not, as yet, secured bail for Bobby, because he feels that a weekend in jail will be good for the young hothead. Or so thinks Woosterville's finest legal mind.

Chapter 16:
Locked Up

Bobby squeezes his fists around the cold bars, shuts his eyes tight, and goes back to a childhood day when his mama had taken him to the Atlanta Zoo. He had gripped similiar bars and pushed his small face between them to peer at an elephant. The caged animal paced to and fro with his wild eyes doing figure eights in their sockets.

Now, he knows the terror trapped in those dumb elephant eyes. He once read a book about how elephants are very smart. Bobby is convinced that the elephant went crazy because he has a brain that thinks, and thinks, and thinks....just like his own brain does!

Anything could happen while he is locked up in this cage. His mama could die, She is awfully sick. The girl he loves, Dee Dee Milam, could find somebody else. That buzzard Elroy Knox has been after her since she was in the ninth grade. They'll all be after her now with him in Jail. There's just no stopping men like Elroy.

Bobby can see him grinning and telling the fat deputy how to find his house. His dark bird -eyes twinkling under his thick bushy eyebrows that come all the way together over his big hawk nose. Nub had it right...Damn if he don't look like an old buzzard!

'I swear, I'll kill that buzzard if he lays a hand on Dee Dee while I'm in here!' Bobby slams his fist into the cell's cinder block wall until his knuckles bleed, then he sits down on the cot and rubs his tender hand.

'What in the hell are they going to do to me?' That fancy lawyer says the usual sentence for aggravated assault is six months on the chain gang. Damn, it's just so unfair. I've just got everything going good....my job at Georgia

Express...able to dress decent...show Dee Dee a good time.....Hell, we would've been married in six months!'

As tears break in his eyes, he cups his aching hand in his lap and sings softly, rocking his upper body in time.

"Hear that lonesome whipporwill, He sounds too blue to fly'
The midnight train is moaning low, I'm so lonesome I could cry.
Did you ever see a night so long, when time goes driftin' by,
The moon just went behind some clouds, to hide its face and cry."

Chapter 17:
Images

"I wonder what time Thera will get home?' Daniel thinks to himself 'Everybody says I'm the spitting image of my father. I've never seen him. Thera says my grandpa Nathan believed my daddy was the greatest man who ever lived. Mama says that grandpa Nathan had cataracts and that he never saw Victor very clearly when his eyes were good. They all agreed that Victor was a very handsome man.'

Daniel knows that he does look just like his daddy from the pictures of a young Victor in Thera's thick photo album. Daniel studies himself in the full length mirror on the door of a wardrobe where Thera stores her coats and pocketbooks. Same broad forehead, pronounced cheekbones, strong squared chin, tightly drawn thin wide lips that part quickly to reveal very straight teeth with a small gap between the two center ones. The later photos of Victor in uniform showed his broad angular shoulders. Daniel spreads his shoulders. 'Well, perhaps one day.'

The last picture of Victor in the book is Daniel's favorite. Victor was sporting a thick moustache. His thin brown hair, already going a shade bald, was flying loose as he stood behind a turning propeller. His wide, long-fingered hand was held high, waving a final goodbye.

The TV across the room is all squiggly again. On the end table where he returns the album is a fancy-framed tinted photo of Becky and her new husband. 'I was just getting used to Shotgun when mom blew us all away with her divorce. Even if she had to get married again, she didn't have to look so pleased about it. The color artist captured her green eyes to a tee; but, her rusty gold hair looked a sickly yellow, just like Fred's. Maybe it was done that way on purpose so Becky wouldn't look too good standing beside that creep.' Daniel snickers, blowing hisses through the slit between his front teeth. He adjusts the rabbit-ears-antenna to stabilize the TV screen on a commentator discussing the morning news. The volume was off so the noise would not wake RD this early on a Saturday morning.

Daniel doesn't realize that the man on TV is talking about Thera. With her help, Jack Fisher has just won passage of a bill to revise voting districts in the state. Thera is playing an active role in state politics and there is talk of her running for election to the Georgia Legislature.

She had called home yesterday to let them know that Jack Fisher and his daughter, Katheleen, would be visiting them Sunday after church.

Daniel thinks he will not be here. Every Sunday he is expected to go with his new family to attend church with Fred Senior and spend the whole afternoon with the finicky Sanders bunch. He hates it!

As it turns out, Fred and Becky decide to leave just after breakfast and spend the entire weekend with Fred's family. Daniel persuades them to let him stay here until Thera gets home. Fred is to pick him up later in the day at the store.

***

On the side of the house facing the store, RD stands at the living room window looking out at the giant oak tree that Thera calls 'Daniel's moping tree.' All he can see of Daniel on the other side of the large truck is a nervously bouncing knee that signals the hard thinking he is doing to memorize the twenty-third Psalms for church tomorrow. A streak of dark brown liquid splits the air in a high arch spotting the bare ground under the tree. Daniel is quiet proficient at sending a sharp stream of tobacco juice through the slit between his front teeth. His skill at spitting is in open defiance of Fred's disapproval of it.

RD places a chair before the wardrobe and steps up to reach the large black book trimmed in gold. He and Daniel know they are not allowed to touch Thera's Bible. 'Why?...' he wonders, as he spreads the heavy book on the sofa and thumbs through giant pages until he comes to an even larger foldout in the center. It's a Family Tree, updated by Nathan until his death, and then continued by Thera. RD studies it with keen interest.

FULTON FAMILY TREE
19 ?? NATHAN DANIEL FULTON(1885-1943)
MARRIED 1903 IDA MAYE ADDISON FULTON(1886-1~~923~~)

RD noticed that Nathan had written in that Ida Maye died in 1923, the year she left Georgia, and that entry had been crossed out by Thera who had told him that her mother had sent her many letters since that time and was thought to be still alive.

CHILDREN
DAUGHTER - THERA (1916 -   )
SON - VICTOR (1920-1942) KILLED IN ACTION WWII
SON - NED (1921 - 1941) KILLED IN ACTION WWII
DAUGHTER - CAROL (1923 - 1944) KILLED IN AN AUTOMOBILE
ACCIDENT

No big secrets in this, thinks RD. 'Wait a minute.....this page has been cut! There was more.... And Daniel's name should be in the FULTON FAMILY TREE. Now where would Thera hide something she cut out of her Bible?'

RD rummages through the wardrobe and spots her Sunday pocketbook. 'Ah hah....I think I'm getting warm.' In a zippered side pocket inside the handbag he finds what he is looking for - a neatly folded square of smooth pale-green paper that precisely matches the Bible foldout.

GRANDCHILDREN
GRANDSON-THOMAS JAMES FRANKLIN(1930 -   )
BORN OUT OF WEDLOCK, GOD HAVE MERCY.
GRANDSON-DANIEL AUSTIN FULTON(1941-   )
BORN TO VICTOR AND REBECCA (1924-   )
GRANDSON-RABUN DUEL NEWMAN(1944-   )
BORN TO CAROL AND ALTON NEWMAN

'Thomas James Franklin? TJ? Roy's half brother? Rayford's oldest boy? But how could he be Grandpa Nathan's grandson? Nineteen thirty...? Ida Maye had been gone for seven years and it's for sure that Nathan would never claim any family tie to her in 1930. Mama was only seven years old....Ned was ten....Victor was thirteen? All of them too young? That only leaves Thera. Thera was only fourteen! Thera had a baby at age fourteen! Thera and Rayford! Holy cow!' At that moment he hears Thera's car outside. He hurriedly replaces the foldout, the pocketbook, the Bible and the chair and runs toward the back door. He mustn't let her see him for awhile.

"RD.....COME HELP ME AND DANIEL WITH THE GRO-CERIES." Thera steps through the front door calling him. As she enters the living room she sees the shiny gold silk ribbon of her Bible swaying gently in front of the mirror. She steps closer and spots the pack of Juicy Fruit gum on the floor that she had put into her Sunday handbag.

Thera drops the groceries.

Chapter 18:
I Didn't Know The Words

Daniel finds RD on Nub's bench. "Thera's really upset. What are you going to tell her?"

"You mean why I wasn't there when she got home?"

"No. I mean why you were messing with her Bible?"

"I don't know."

"Tell her you wanted to learn the Twenty-Third Psalms and I had your Bible."

"That what you told her?" He smiled as Daniel nodded. "Thanks."

"Do you know it?" Daniel smiled as RD shook his head. "Sit back down. I'll teach it to you." Daniel closed his eyes to concentrate.

"Yea though I walk through the shadow of death..."

"Yea though I walk through the shadow of death..."

"I will fear no evil."

"I will fear no evil."

They practice until RD thinks he is fully prepared to walk home and face Thera. He sees her on the porch swing as he climbs the hill. When he steps onto the porch she greets him cautiously.

"Hello, RD. What kind of devilment have you been up to while I was away?"

He knows he must tell her about last night. He also knows that she has MADE IT CLEAR that he is not to play with Roy and that she demands that he stay away from the Franklin house.

"Hi, Aunt Thera. I'm glad you're home." he hugs her and sits close by her in the swing.

"Daniel tells me you have taken a sudden interest in learning scriptures?"

"I know the Twenty-Third Psalms."

"Well, good for you! Let's hear it." Thera pushes her pumps off and toes them away from her swinging feet.

RD struggles through it, She is pleased and hugs him again. "You have something troubling you don't you RD? Do you want to tell me about it?"

"I was just down at the store... Bobby Riley's in trouble. He hit a deputy at the store last night. I was there when he did it."

"I heard about it."

"Who told you?"

"TJ Franklin...He's Bobby's lawyer..I ran into him at the grocery store." She lied.

RD felt uncomfortable. "I went back in the woods with some of the boys after it happened."

"I'm so glad to see you that I'm not even going to fuss about that. Now, you see, all the worrying you're doing is for nothing." She puts her hand on his cheek and kisses his forehead.

He moves his leg and feels a sharp nick on the top of his thigh. Without thinking, he pulls the broken glasses out of his pocket. Suddenly, he stammers. "Roy...Roy Franklin went too."

Thera stops the swing with her stocking feet and draws her elbows against her sides, snapping her furrowed brow at the sight of the glasses.

"Get me a switch, young man!" She pulls him out of the swing by his shoulder and drags him awkwardly to the steps, half pushing him down them.

"AND GET A GOOD ONE! DO YOU HEAR ME?!"

"Yesum.." tears are rolling down his cheeks. He pulls and strips a low limb from a willow tree at the corner of the yard and turns back as she comes off the steps with fire in her eyes.

"You must learn that there are some things you don't understand." She spoke between clinched teeth. "YOU MUST DO WHAT I TELL YOU TO DO UNTIL YOU ARE OLDER!"

She spits out the words as she grabs his wrist with one hand and snatches the switch with the other so hard that it stung his palm. She relentlessly strikes him across his legs and back as he tries to pull away from her viselike grip on his wrist. They pivot in a circle with the strong switch the driving force. He finally drops to his knees, but she continues to pelt his back.

"YOU ARE NEVER TO PLAY WITH THAT FRANKLIN BOY. IS THAT CLEAR?!"

A firm hand stops her arm in mid swing. Thera turns to face the intruder in bewilderment.

"He won't play with the Franklin boy no more. Roy's dead." Rayford's cold steel eyes look blind without his glasses. He heard Thera screaming from below the bank and scaled it to arrive on the scene without warning. "I buried my boy this morning."

He drops her hand and walks straight across her flowerbed to the corner of the yard where he leans down on one arm and swings over the bank.

Thera stands trembling with rage. Her face is pale and colorless except for the the redness in her flooding eyes that are sending jagged streaks of mascara down her cheeks. Her nose is running but her lips are dry and chalky white as if they have dried toothpaste on them. She has big sweat stains under her arms and her stockings are torn and baggy from not stopping to put on her shoes.

***

"So, what happened to your purty white shoes?" Nub was curious.

"Yeah, Clyde... I thought you said you threw away them stinkers?" Daniel eyed the dirty old sneakers Clyde was wearing.

"Them pointy-toes really tore up my feet the first time I took a long walk. So I had to retrieve the old stink-ohs. They sure are comfortable once you get past the smell."

"Speaking of smells, here comes old rotten Rayford in his red go-loshers," Nub waves his hand under his nose and scrunches his lips up like he smells a skunk.

They watch as Rayford stumbles down the bank in front of Thera's house and walks toward the store in the ditch planting each foot like he is setting out fenceposts.

Nub knows what he is after, but he doesn't get up until Rayford stops at the edge of the gravel and bobs his head toward the well. Nub goes through the store and comes out the back with a paper bag twisted around a pint.

Rayford sticks two one dollar bills in Nub's shirt pocket and grabs at the bottle. Nub's powerful right hand does not free it until he has glared straight into Rayford's eyes and harked and spit on the ground. When he lets go, Rayford turns abruptly and stomps off in the direction of the woods behind the store.

***

In front of the Fulton house both RD and Thera are standing mute like a stop frame in a silent movie. Both are stunned by the explosion blowing their emotions into shreds.

This is the only time she has ever physically struck him in anger. But he clearly sees through her ineptitude to the better basic intent. She beat him out of love for him because she takes her responsibility seriously. She knows that her charge is to convince him that evil must be avoided at all costs in a

70

world where unspeakable cruelty lurks everywhere just waiting for the unwary to seek it out or for the innocent to accidently cross its path.

"Forgive me, RD. I had no idea the boy was dead." He has never seen her look so sad. "And, you were trying to tell me..." She lets the switch fall and hangs her head to stare at it.

RD runs to her and hugs her thick waist. "It's OK Thera...I understand....don't cry...please don't.."

She puts her arms around him and her sweaty palms feel the blood on his bare back.

"What have I done, my dear sweet child, what have I done?" She holds his head against her breasts and kisses his hair. She composes herself and eases him away with firm hands. "I am so sorry I lost my temper and that your friend is dead.....There is no excuse for what I have done. I over-reacted to the fact that you disobeyed me in regard to a very important matter. You did disobey me, RD, and that was wrong. But you have never done anything to deserve the way I treated you this day. All I can do is beg you to forgive me, and I will pray that one day I will prove to be worthy of your kindness."

He nods his head. "I am so sorry for what I did, Thera." He never again would call her Aunt Thera,

She takes him inside and cleans his back as he lays across her knees. She rubs his back with Jergen's lotion that has a smell he loves and will associate with Thera for the rest of his life. Today he could see fear in her eyes when Rayford Franklin held her arm, the same fear in her beautiful grey eyes the day she told him, 'Oh, Baby... you scared Thera so bad!"

She tells him she must visit Bobby Riley's mother today. She doesn't tell him that TJ asked her to check on Mrs. Riley, because Bobby is worried about her being sick, and it seems that nobody really knows much about her, except that she never seems to come out of her house. It appears that she is a devout recluse. Bobby says he is all she's got in this world.

Thera leaves RD to make herself a hot bath and freshen her clothes.

He goes back out on the porch and stands on the steps, until she comes out, then he kneels and slips her shoes on her heavy feet. He thinks he should tell her he loves her, but he can see in her eyes that she knows.

Chapter 19:
Your Cheating Heart

Ida Maye Zinger Addison Fulton Jarvis Riley is unloved, seventy- three, sad, lonely, and dying filthy rich. She says she has no religion, but she once told some young Mormons who came to her door that she considers herself to be a devout Recluse, and what she believes is that people like them should leave her the hell alone. When the local undertaker paid her a visit trying to drum up business and sell her a cemetery plot, frilly casket and fancy burial dress; she told him, 'Thanks, but no thanks…that would just make her feel like she was all dressed up with no place to go.' Nobody knows about all the money she has. If they did, they'd be trying to sell her all kinds of junk she doesn't want or need. She knows she's not long for this world and she agrees with that good joke about you never see a trailer being dragged along behind a hearse. And, you never hear about anybody being buried with a big wad of money in their pocket.

Although the temperature is near ninety degrees in her room, "Grace" feels cold. "Grace" Riley, is the name Ida Maye has used since coming back to Georgia with her son, Bobby. Her last husband, Gus Riley used to call her 'his amazing grace' after she had his son, Bobby, in 1933 at age 47. So when he died, she decided to keep the Grace part of it in memory of him. She also thinks it a good idea not to be using her real name around here all these years after she left this state. Especially now that Gus has left her all that money. If word gets out that she is a wealthy Ida Maye, there is just no telling how many greedy relatives will be turning up at her door. She just wants to be left alone…and to be warm.

She tries to light a fire with rolled newspapers under a log in the fire-place, but it fizzles out, leaving her with nothing but smouldering embers on the burned paper. She has a heavy grey blanket over her knees but they still tremble. She tries to keep the rocker moving to circulate the blood in her legs but quickly tires of the effort. There are more liver spots than wisps of thin grey hair on her purple-veined skull. Folds of wrinkled flesh hang from her cheeks and shake when she coughs up phlegm than runs down the side of her sunken, toothless mouth.

"Grace's" sick old eyes can no longer focus, yet in her mind is a clear image of a young man's face. It is still the same as the first time she saw him and fell in love when he was just fifteen.

She is glad to be back in Georgia. Nathan never divorced her, he just ran her off.

'He shoulda just kilt me....' The rocker squeaks and she imagines the wind is howling outside a mountain cabin sending icy drafts into her very soul. Alaska is just too cold for a Southern Girl like her. 'I'd be better off dead...told me to git outta Jawja....jest like that....after twenty years....don't let the sun set on you in this state...git out fore ta'nite!'

"Screetch.....skureeetcheee....screetch.....skureeeetcheeee."from the rocker keeping time with the music on her radio.

"Your cheatin' heart will pine someday
and pray for love you threw away.
The time will come when you'll be blue.
Your cheatin' heart will tell on you."

Her mind ceases for a few slow rocks, then picks up where it stopped.

'I shore got outta Jawja....took nuthin' but tha clothes on my back...hitched uh ride with a trucker....think his name was Jarvis....took me to Florida for awhile....then all the way to Texas...I liked Texas but it was too hot....better than being cold though....went from there to Denver....nice place Denver....met a good man there...my Bobby's daddy...but he died....'

The coughing sets in again, this time bringing out a trace of blood in the mucus running down her chin.

'Then I got hooked up with a damn cranberry picker named Russell....son of a leech took me and my baby all the way off up there in Alaska....I ain't been warm since...he was worse than any of em...I stayed sick the whole time I was with him...at least I never married him....but I aged ten years for evah one I was with him...he gave me a disease they don't even have a name for yet.....finally I just couldn't take it anymore.....I kilt him my own self...nobody evah knew it but I did....'

"When tears come down like falling rain...."

The gnarled hands grip the rocker arms and her head falls back. Her eyes bulge wildly as she screams.

"You'll toss around and call my name....."

The sound comes out a loud gargle, blowing blood-bubbles that pop as they rise out of the gap in her hideous face, but her last conscious thought is...

'RAAAYYFOOORD!'

Chapter 20:
Why, Baby, Why?

Rayford goes deep into the woods and cuts across far behind Ida Maye's place. Today is the first time he has set foot in her yard since 1929. Thera was only thirteen years old back then. That was a bad year for everybody, with the stock market crash and all.

He stops beside a fresh water stream and squats on his haunches watching the ankle-deep water flow across the smooth-pebble bottom. It is a blistering hot day and he feels mucky and tired. He is not accustomed to losing his sleep, and the burying and digging another well were long hard work.

Rayford takes a crushed pack of Lucky Strike Greens and a worn matchbox from the bib of his overalls. He prefers a pipe and seldom smokes cigarettes. These have been in his pocket for more than a month. He flicks the white phosphorous tip of a match with his thumbnail and lights the smoke. The stale tobacco tastes harsh and dry. He throws it into the stream, takes off his boots, sticks his feet in the cool water, then falls back on the grass to seek sleep. Each time he closes his eyes, he sees Ida Maye as he remembers her from more than thirty years ago.. He sees her body in lewd positions. He sees her having sex with other men. He sees her face laughing at him the same way she laughed at Nathan when she was in his arms. No matter what he sees her doing, he feels love for her so bad it hurts.

He tries to stop the pain, to erase her image by thinking of something else. It doesn't work. She just reappears in a fresh vision more base, more crude, more vulgar. He tries to mentally change her; to make her hair another color but it remains shiny black, to make her fat but she stays voluptuous, to make her old and ugly, but she is so young and beautiful, to mar her gorgeous face - to cut it, sear it, scar it, bruise it, to burn it, to cover it, to drown it, to make it bleed like the many pigs he slaughtered, to bury it like he did his son.

But regardless of what he thinks, Ida Maye returns with a smile to mock him with a glint in her ebony eyes and strands of her glistening hair drifting rakishly across her moist, full, half-open mouth as she twists a little to the side and directs a puff of her hot breath to breeze the hair off her carmine lips. Then her mouth opens more and her tongue slithers out to run a slow circle around it as Ida Maye kneels over a grotesque oversize male body with a hideous face.

***

Elroy Knox rises to the occasion when he sees Dee's grotesquely disfigured face. It is a clear cut case of "love conquers all". She is truly the love of his life and he knows that nothing will change that. 'Who knows?' He thinks, 'This may turn out to be the best break I've ever had come my way. When Dee's face was so beautiful, every man who saw her wanted her. Now, I'm most likely the only one who will have her. Hells bells, everything a man appreciates about a woman is not just in her face. She's also smart, funny, talented, she sings just like Dolly, she's good at poker, she has a great pool stroke, plus she's a good cook and a fine housekeeper. Dee has a gorgeous body that the doctors say is gonna heal up fine. Their exact words were, "We expect a full recovery of all her body functions." Now, those body functions are what I like best about Dee. And, to top it all off she just told me last week that I'm the only man she has ever really loved. He held her uninjured left hand that had been in his lap when they slammed into the pole, and whispered softly into bandages where he thought her right ear night be.'

"Just wait until we get you out of this hospital, Dee. Me and you are going to really have some fun." He knew she was smiling at him because he could see the twinkle in her left eye.

***

Daniel scowls as 'Finicky Fred' wheels into the drive beeping his silly horn. Clyde was just telling Daniel about the details of how Roy died.

"Never mind,... RD can tell you all about it, Daniel." Clyde always enjoys Daniel's company. They are kindred spirits in many ways.

"Sure, Clyde....I hope you can find that dirty bird Sammy." Daniel trudges toward the car, gets in, rolls down the window, and with a loud hiss sends juice flying.

As Fred's car pulls onto the highway to his left, Clyde sees Thera's old Pontiac coming from the right, down the dirt drive from her house. He runs to meet her. She stops and rolls down her window and smiles.

'Miss Thera can I get a ride as far as the junk yard."

"Sure Clyde, hop in." She knows he is assuming that she is on her way to town and decides it is easier just to take him where he's going than to explain her destination.

"Are you going to see Sammy?" She rolls her window back up and shifts the air conditioner to high as she spins onto the highway.

"Yes mam...I'm going to see him alright....I'm going to beat his face in when I find him."

Thera glances at him and raises her eyebrows. "Sounds serious. What did he do?"

"He tried to kill my puppy."

"I didn't know you had a puppy."

"RD gave it to me last night."

"I didn't know RD had a puppy."

"You mean....he didn't tell you about last night?"

"I know that Roy Franklin died last night...." She shook her head. "RD tried to tell me more.... I don't guess I really gave him a chance. Why don't you tell me the whole story."

Clyde told her everything. As she drove past the Riley house, Thera noticed that it looked empty and dead.

"...Well, after I went inside, I decide to bring in the puppy and let him sleep with me.... him being so little and probably scared...you know without his mama. I had heard Sammy out on the road and when I cut out the light and peeked out the window I saw him coming toward my porch. So I went out the back door and slipped up on him trying to drown my puppy. I snatched the little pup out of the rain water just in the nick of time."

"Are you sure he did it?'

"Positive. There's just no way that tiny puppy could've got up into that washtub on his own. He's so little he can hardly move. And I wasn't inside more than two minutes. Sammy was the only one who could have done it." Clyde is visibly shaken just recounting how it happened.
"I roughed him up a little bit and he ran off without denying it or even acting like he was sorry."

"What good do you think it will do for you to beat him up?"

"Miss Thera, somebody's gotta do something. Once he seen that I wasn't going to run him down, he just started walking up the highway whistling a merry tune like nothing ever happened....What he did was awful mean."

"Horrible." The tears in her eyes said Thera agreed.

"Why would somebody do something like that?"

"Probably because somebody hurt them very much when they were little."

Chapter 21:
To Know Him Is To Love Him

Jack Fisher is a small man who leaves everyone he meets with a big impression of himself. He took over his bed-ridden father's ailing grain business when he was only eighteen, and he has been "the boss" from the day he called in the store's ten employees and told them that he was now running the show. Run it he did. And what a show it was.

Fisher's Feed and Grain has become as well known as grits throughout the state. The processing plants Jack Fisher built now provide jobs for more than eight thousand residents of the small town of Traveston, Georgia.

Jack Fisher wields power as naturally as most people get out of his way. Moving into the political arena came just as natural to him. He has served two terms in the state legislature and within six months of his first term rumors were circulating that he would make a fine governor. He has wisely let the momentum build and now the time is right to make his run for it.

Jack feels that his only serious competition will be either a racist old fool, or a rich fat cat who has bled his fortune from the sweat of the poor. He is pulling for the fat cat in their runoff. 'Hell,' he thinks. 'Once I tear into his lard ass, he'll be lucky to make it through the campaign without getting shot. But, racism is a dangerous nut to crack and beating the senile old fool could be a bloody battle.'

Katheline studies her father's serious-looking face. He is a very handsome man at forty-two. Deeply tanned with a thick crop of dark brown hair with a tinge of grey at the temples and on his short sideburns. All of his features are small; small nose, small mouth with thin even lips, small eyes that have a frightening intensity when he is angry, and his hands now held high on the steering wheel are small with short, professionally manicured finger-nails that would look feminine on a lesser man. Katheline slides across the seat and puts her own hand over one of his.

"I'm glad you let me come along, Daddy. This is turning out to be a wonderful week."

He smiles broadly without turning his head. "And I'm glad you came, Kat. What do you think of that gang who think they can make your daddy Governor?"

"As usual, I agree with you...Thera Fulton is my favorite."

He lifts her hand and kisses the back of it.

"I think you should persuade her to manage your campaign."

"Well, aren't you the clever girl? I intend to ask her today. I'm not sure some of the others will approve of a woman telling them what to do. What do you think?"

"All I know is that she will do a great job. She's about the smartest and nicest person I've met in a long time."

"Well, you seem to have unusually good judgement for a soon-to-be teenager."

"Especially when I agree with you, my dear daddy?"

"Especially! Thera's only drawback is being a woman."

"I know, daddy. If she were a man, she'd probably be the Governor."

"My, my...you are impressed with her."

They are silent for the rest of the ride. Jack contemplates who Thera will assemble at this mornings church service and those he needs to make a point of phoning while he is here in Woosterville. Katheline watches hills and hous-es pass and waves occasionally to people who stare at the long black limousine.

Katheline is a child of rare and exquisite beauty. Her soft blond hair, as light as the down on a baby's neck, falls in abundant cascades over her shoul-ders and swirls in the breeze from the partially open window to form beau-tiful shifting patterns about her lovely neck. Her face has a Renoir quality in the smooth roundness of her cheeks and her small but full lips. Her eyes are beacons of pastel blue that dance under long fluttering lashes. Her perfect-ly-sculptured nose has just a slight hint of uptilt which adds a touch of arro-gance to her expression when she is angry or upset.

But today, Katheline is full of joy. This might just be the most exciting day of her young life: staying in the finest Atlanta hotels, eating at the best restaurants, wearing her finest clothes, and meeting some of the nicest peo-ple imaginable - people who are supporting her father for governor!

She flicks the tab to fully lower her window and hangs her arm out to wave at a large party gathering in front of a church this fine morning, to greet the arrival of their favorite candidate for governor - Jack Fisher, and his lovely daughter.

They are to attend church with Thera and her teenage nephew, RD, then spend this glorious day with them, before driving home to Traveston to tell her mother all about her wonderful week with daddy.

She is confident that he will be the next Governor of Georgia. How could he lose with all these marvelous people behind him? Everybody who knows him, loves him, and he's the most well-known man in the state. And, his campaign manager is the most well-known woman.

Chapter 22:
I Saw the Light

RD sits on the church pew beside Thera , enjoying his Juicy Fruit gum almost as much as he enjoys having Katheline Fischer sitting on his right.

Katheline is waving a funeral home fan with her right hand , sending her delicious scent right into RD's face. It's the same aromatic soap that he used at Becky's, Cashmere Bouquet. But it smells better on her than it did on his hands. He tilts his head toward her to get more of her fragrant Bouquet. He has his eyes half shut and when he leans her way he finds himself staring at the top of her left breast. Her stiff pink summer suit has bent out at the top and as she fanned it revealed her budding little breast enclosed in a lacy white bra. RD could not take his eyes off of her.

Suddenly, she stands and the seat of her skirt sticks to her sweaty buttocks and he catches a brief glimpse of the back of her shapely thighs before she brushes the skirt down as Thera nudges him to stand just as the congregation bursts into a rousing rendition of **I saw the light**.

As RD stands, he becomes aware, with grave embarrassment, that he has pitched a tent in his loose grey summer slacks. He does his best to cover it with his open hymn book.

"No More In Darkness.....No More In Night..." he sings his heart out until the tent collapses. And, she is coming to his house after church! *"...PRAISE THE LORD....I SAW THE LIGHT."* Thera eyed him curiously when he sang louder.

When the church emptied, Jack Fisher and Thera stood on the porch and talked politics with a group of about twenty people, mostly men, while Katheline and RD sat on the steps bored silly.

***

Daniel sat by the card table bored silly.

"Yaa yaa.....yaa yaa...yannie. I slipped right by Dannie." His half sister, Susan, chanted from the other side. When he looked up at her, she added. "I landed on Park Place and you missed me."

Daniel drowsily studied the blue card. "That's fifteen hundred dollars with a hotel." He said half-heartedly.

"Sorreee......Mary Ann already threw the dice."

"What a nurd, you are sometimes, Susan." As he stood up both girls spoke at once.

"Where are you going?...going?"

"To the toilet....toilet."

"But, it's your turn next." Mary Ann, who was winning, protested

"Skip me."

Daniel sat down on the commode lid, thinking. 'What a miserable day! The more time I spend with these "finicky folks", the more I want to get away from them - all of them. They seem to fit in their dull little world, but, I'm definitely an outsider.'

He takes out his wallet and studies the photo of his father. 'I don't belong with these people, dad. If you were here we'd probably be flying. You'd show me how to do a loop. He waved his hand through the air. None of this boring shit!'

What a drag! RD is so lucky to be back at Thera's house. He looked again at Victor's picture. Maybe he isn't so lucky after all. Even though my daddy's dead, I've still got pictures of him. RD's got nothing...no daddy...no mama...no brothers...no sisters.

"What are you doin' in there, Dannie? Playing with yourself again?" Susan sneered from just outside his door. 'Damn. RD is so lucky!'

***

Everybody at the church is invited to "drop in" at Thera's house today. RD finally has Katheline all to himself. She was the center of attention among the group, who are now drinking lemonade in the living room and large center hall. They are all boosting the confidence of the most over-confident man in the state of Georgia.

After fighting the temptation to stare at Katheline since they left church, RD takes a good look at her sitting beside him in the swing on the porch. He has never seen anyone so pretty. Beads of sweat hold strands of corn silk hair to her brow, as a gentle breeze tugs to free them from her sweet moisture. The brow furrows, drawing him back to her inquiring eyes.

"What are your parents like, RD?"

"They were killed in a car wreck when I was born.....I don't know what they were like."

"Oh, RD...." Her voice trailed off to pensive thought.

He curved his hand behind her, curled his fingers around her temple, and slid the stuck hair loose, letting the underside of his finger pick up some of her dampness.

"I know what they looked like..." He shifts his arm off the back of the swing and nibbles at his fingers, as if thinking. She tastes even better than he expected. Her own exotic sweetness with just a faint trace of Halo shampoo. He sucks the finger so hard it squeaks, then throws his arm over the back of the swing. Her taste is gone anyway, for he reaches the flavor of his own finger, which he gnaws when he is really thinking.

"I have a photo of them that was taken at a fair...it's wrinkled all over and some parts are peeled off. One side of my father's face is missing. He has the sleeves of his white shirt rolled up and his collar loose. He has big muscles and big hands, that are lying open in his lap. My mother is standing behind him, with one hand resting on his shoulder, and she is holding something close to her side in the other. I think it is some kind of stuffed animal, that he probably won for her, by ringing a bell or knocking something over. There are tiny white lines across her face that give the illusion of a lace veil.... just wrinkles on the picture, but they look that way.... " Katheline's face is very close to his and the Halo shampoo smell is delicious. "Well, that's it....except...I think they both look happy."

Suddenly, her hands are behind his head and her lips are on his. It happens so fast that he had not brought his arms off the back of the swing before she was out of the swing, and stood smiling down at him.

"I just wanted to see what you tasted like." She nodded toward the door. "Let's get some lemonade."

Chapter 23:
Whispering Pines

"You want a drink, Rayford?"

"No. Whatdidja want to see me about?" This was the first time Rayford has set foot inside a trailer, and he is surprised how much it looks like a house.

"Bobby Riley's mother died last night. How well did you know her?"

"Can't say as I did."

"She sure knew you. She left this." TJ hands him an envelope with his name on it.

Rayford rips it open, then realizes he can't read it without his glasses. He shifts uncomfortably, then hands the open sheet of paper to TJ and asks him to read it to him.

Dear Rayford,
You have been the Ray of sunshine in my dark life. I have lots of money. I want you to have it. Try to keep my Bobby out of jail with some of it. Have fun.
Love, Ida Maye

Rayford is stone faced, apparently unmoved by the revelation.

"She's being buried this evening at six." TJ is puzzled. "I can go over the will with you anytime you like."

"I don't need money, TJ. Give it to Bobby, or just do what you can for him with it."

"I don't think you understand, Mister Franklin. She did leave you an

84

awful lot of money. I haven't totaled up all of her investments yet, but there is almost three million dollars in liquid assets."

"How did Ida Maye get that much money?"

"Seems a man named Jarvis left her some oil wells in Texas, and some mines in Alaska."

Rayford laughs hard.

"What's funny?"

"Well, Ida Maye shore loved hole diggers." Without another word, Rayford gets up, shakes TJ's hand, walks out the door, and gets in his truck.

It's a windy morning. With his windows down, Rayford hears the wind whistling through the pines around TJ's trailer. He cranks his truck and the radio plays Johnny Horton:.

"My heart is sad like a morning dove that's lost its mate in flight.
Hear the cooing of his lonely heart through the stillness of the night.
Whispering pines whispering pines tell me is it so.
Whispering pines whispering pines you're the one who knows.
My darling's gone oh she's gone and I need your sympathy.
Whispering pines send my baby back to me."

Rayford shuts off the radio, and slowly backs all the way down TJ's long driveway

***

The only reason Rayford comes near the cemetery is because he has to pass it on the way home from TJ's trailer. The only reason he stops is because he sees an old friend working there.

'Lucky' Lynn' Sledge is filling up the grave when it begins to get dark, so he has turned on his truck lights. When Rayford comes down the road, he sees him working with the lights behind him. Between him and 'Lucky Lynn' they dug most every grave in this cemetery since about 1920.

He is called 'Lucky Lynn' because he loves to gamble and his luck is so bad. 'If Lucky bet on tomorrow, the sun would never come up.' Rayford parks his truck at the entrance and continues on foot to the far side, where Lucky is shoveling steadily.

Rayford just can't understand fancy funerals.' Why do live people make such a fuss over dead ones?' He shakes his head as he passes grave markers; low blocks with last names only, tombstones with fine sayings, polished marble with sculptured vases and flowers, the dead person's head carved in stone, and even one little cement house for a tomb. Lucky says that tomb can be opened, and a man's body pulled out in a drawer, that is airtight and preserved, and the man looks just the way he did when he died. Lucky says nobody has ever come to look at him. The heavy door is locked, and you can't see much of anything through the narrow slits of windows, but it does look like there is a drawer inside. 'Crazy people.' according to Rayford. 'When they're dead, they're gone.'

Lucky is the spiffiest hole digger Rayford has ever met. He works in a short-sleeved, white shirt, and dressy, striped pants. Before he starts digging, he puts on rubber waders and gloves, pulls his fancy pants high on his chest, and tucks his pants legs into the top of his big boots. He can dig all day and not get dirt on his clothes. He is a short stocky man who says 'You have to let the shovel do the work.' His smooth use of that shovel will fool you. It looks like he is working slow, but he gets a lot more done that others who look faster.

"Yo, Lucky!" Rayford booms as he approaches.

"Lo dar, Rafe!" Lucky doesn't look up, but just keeps throwing dirt into the grave,

"Long time, no see. How ya, been?"

"Struggling'... same's always. 'Bout you?"

"Just gettin' by. Livin'... Taking a shovelful at a time....till its done."

Rayford lights a badly bent Luckie Strike Green and stands silently as Lucky fills the grave.

Lucky thinks about asking him if he is still chasing women, but he doesn't. 'Rafe never chased 'em anyway. He just took 'em 'cause they's there. If they's not there, Rafe don't worry about it.'

When he finishes with the grave, Lucky puts his tools in his truck and pulls off his rubber boots and gloves. He watches as a hearse enters the cemetery and approaches slowly along the drive lined with large oak trees. He takes a small notebook from his hip pocket and looks in it.

"The last one named in my book is number three thousand, nine hundred, and ninety-nine.... Just one more to make uh even four thousand. Whatdaya think of that, Rafe?"

"You won't have long to wait. Folks are just dying to give you business." Rayford looks out across the well kept graves. "You countin' them in Homebrew Village?"

"Uh grave is uh grave. All I need is the name to count this un."

"Well, do ya know who's in this one?"

"No idee....it's a drop-in." He says, using an old burying-trade-expression to describe a funeral attended only by the corpse. "....unless somebody puts a marker on it, I guess nobody will evah know."

"Except for me, Lucky." Rayford rubs the butt of his smoke between his thumb and fingers until the bits of ash and tobacco are sprinkled on top of the grave mound.

"You know who's in it, Rafe?"

"Yeah, but I ain't gonna tell ya."

"Guess I'll just have ta wait an' see when tha marker comes."

"You might not know then."

"One thing I do know." Lucky slaps his palm with his tally book. "I done dug a lot more graves than you dug wells, Rafe. Now, whatdaya say to that?"

"I say it don't make sense digging a hole then filling it back up again. I see a lot of markers around here, but I don't see no holes."

Lucky is undaunted. "Well, if I hadn't dug these holes, this place would stink so bad they'd have to move the town a long way down the road. But this is my last one, Rafe. That contraption up by the shed is gonna take over." He pointed to a bright yellow earth-mover at the corner of the lot.

"He starts tomorrow and Lucky's outta his job."

"We both done got too old for digging anyway, Lucky. You can write down in your little book beside number four thousand that in this grave is A WOMAN OF MEANS, and take it from me, Lucky, that's the God's honest truth. Now, how 'bout we go see Homebrew Annie and buy us a drink?...kinda celebrate you quittin'?"

"You got some money, Rafe?"

"Yeah, I got some money."

***

'Why did Ida Maye leave all that money to Rayford Franklin?' Thera sits thinking as she corrects the final entry by her mother's name in her big bible, changing the year of her death from 1923 to 1959.

TJ must be having a busy day, arranging the burial, getting Bobby out of jail, and explaining a multi-million dollars estate to an ignorant hole digger.

'Rayford Franklin will be in town!' Thera recognizes a rare opportunity. 'It's about time for me to have a talk with Irene Franklin. She's been around a long time, and perhaps that old woman can shed some light on the mystery I've been trying to solve all my life.'

Thera puts up her Bible and tells RD that she has some thinking to do and she has decided to take a long walk.

Chapter 24:
Alone and Forsaken

Irene Franklin sits by herself listening to another of her favorite Hank Williams songs.

> *"Alone and forsaken, by fate and by man,*
> *Oh, Lord, if you hear me please hold to my hand.*
> *Oh, please under-stand."*

She has cranked and played it over and over until she just doesn't have the will to wind it again.

Irene Franklin decides she will kill herself.

She is trying to figure out how to do it.

She thinks about cutting her wrists with Rayford's straight razor, but that would be too messy. She could hang herself but she doesn't know how to tie a hangman's noose, and she doesn't want to break her neck and then not die. She could burn the house down with her inside, but she hated to destroy the fine building and attract a lot of attention. Besides, there is a chance that somebody will happen by and drag her out; making her look like an old fool.

Irene wishes that she could kill Rayford instead, but she doesn't have the strength or the courage to do that. Even if she did, she would just get caught and spend the rest of her life in jail. 'I'd just hate being cooped up.'

She could eat rat poison, but that would be so painful and just thinking about being in pain really scares her to death! 'If we only had gas in this house. That would be such a peaceful way to go, just turn on the gas and go to sleep. Peaceful, like the water. That's it! I'll drown myself. I'll just go down to the old Chattahoochee; go under the water and never come up.'

Irene likes the water, always has. She doesn't know how to swim, never learned. She's too ashamed of her body and too shy to be seen in a bathing suit. She has one she bought secretly many years ago, but she never got up enough nerve to put it on. 'I'll wear my pretty bathing costume nobody's ever seen. Nobody's gonna see me anyhow.'

She digs the deep purple 'costume' out of the bottom of a trunk and puts it on. In it she looks like a dried prune. The mirror on her dresser is too short for her to see her face when she stands erect. She does have nice shoul-ders.....and her legs were once quite pretty. Now, they are marred by varicose veins which match the swimsuit. She needs shoes. It's a long walk to the river. She puts on Roy's old tennis shoes and they are much too long for her tiny feet. She puts on her oversize maroon bathrobe before going outside to make sure Rayford doesn't slip up on her and see her bathing suit.

She must hurry. Rayford could be back any minute. She walks quickly to the shed. She pushes a wheelbarrow as close as she can get it to a small bench under an overhang beside the shed. She then tries to move a large anvil off the bench but it is to heavy for her to lift.

'Mustn't panic...must stay calm.' She thinks, as she spots a coil of rope hanging on the side of the shed. She runs the rope through a large hole on the blunt end and tries to drag the anvil into the barrow. She does pull it off the bench, but it strikes the side of the barrow and turns it over, dumping the anvil to the ground.

Clyde is standing by the pigsty waiting for his pup to feed when he hears the noise and crosses the corner of the yard to the shed.

"Good evening, Mrs, Franklin."

"Whatdayawant? Whatdayawant? Whatdayawant?..." He scares the wits out of her.

"I didn't mean to startle you....I'm Clyde...the one that brought Ray home?"

"Yeah, I know." Irene is composing herself. "What're you doing here?"

Clyde tells her all about the puppy. "I thought nobody was home...else I would've asked about feeding him. I'm sorry I upset you."

"That's alright, son. You can feed your puppy on that sow anytime you want. Two of her piglets were born dead. Rayford only raises them hawgs because he enjoys killing them anyhow. We got more pork in the freezer and the smokehouse than we'll ever eat." Irene is thinking that if she can just get to that river, she has cooked her last piece of pig meat. "Will you lend me a hand and pick up this anvil for me?"

"Sure, what are you gonna do with it?"

Irene pauses for a moment. "Put it in the wheelbarrow."

Clyde lays it on its side to balance the heavy weight.

"And, could you tie that rope to it with a good strong knot."

He does. She watches carefully trying to remember enough to tie the same knot around her waist. "So, your puppy took right to that sow's teat, huh?"

"He sure did."

She lifts the handles and wheels the barrow back from under the shed. "Well, you just make yourself welcome, son. Feed him anytime you like." She smiles and pushes the barrow toward the dirt road leading into the woods.

"Do you wanta see him?" Clyde calls after her.

Irene stops the barrow and sits it down. She stands for a moment looking down the road to the river. Then she turns and walks slowly back toward Clyde. "Yes. I do want to see your puppy feeding on my sow. But I gotta hurry.....I don't have much time."

Clyde leads her to the pen. As she climbed over the fence, he caught a glimpse of her old-fashioned swimsuit. 'And those tennis shoes.....she sure looks funny. People must really dress wild when they don't expect anybody to see them. But, running around a farm in a bathing suit on a hot day ain't such a bad idea..."

"My goodness...." Irene stands in the mud smiling down at the feeding pup. "When I was a young girl, I used to work for Mister Nathan now and then. One time he brought home a baby deer and he took a cow's teat. He was a cute little fella, too. Ain't no telling what happened to him." She picked up the puppy and rubbed her face against his.

They hear a car turn into the driveway on the opposite side of the house. Irene seems to hold her breath. "OhmyGod....It's Rayford." She hands the puppy to Clyde and clumsily crosses the fence and runs toward the barrow. She lifts it and runs awkwardly down the road pushing it ahead of her.

Clyde follows her to the yard. He sees Thera round the corner of the house and stops to look at the crude headstone where the well used to be. He runs and catches Irene in a short distance.

"It's Miss Thera, Irene..... It's not Rayford. It's Miss Thera." He hands her the puppy and smiles. "Let's go see what Miss Thera wants." He turns back the wheelbarrow and pushes it along beside her. As they reach the shed, Thera comes across the yard to meet them.

Irene holds the puppy in front of her face and beams. "Would you just look at that...the little fella is trying to open his eyes. LOOK! They're open! And they're so pretty. Such pretty eyes! Almost as pretty as.....Thera's." Her own eyes are sparkling as she looks into Thera's face. She turns to Clyde who is still holding the handles of the wheelbarrow. "Son, would you please put that anvil back on the bench for me?"

He did.

"Now, can the two of you stop for awhile? I don't often get good company." She smiled gaily. "I make good coffee."

Clyde has never seen such a winning smile on such an ugly face. He nods and smiles back at her.

The three of them sip coffee and talk. Before Clyde leaves, he gives Irene the puppy and nothing could please her more. Thera watches Irene play the mother role for the small animal. She beds him, like a baby, in a blanket near the sofa.

The changes on the headstone outside have Thera puzzled:

HERE LIES ROY
~~IRENE'S ONLY CHILD~~
JULIE's BOY

Thera knows that Irene raised Julie's son, Roy. But she had changed the words ONLY CHILD to BOY? Could that possibly mean that Irene had children....girls? Thera decides to test the issue:

"You never told me about your girls, Irene?"

Irene dropped her coffee. "How'd ja know? How'd ja know? How'd ja know? Oh, dear...How'd ja know?"

Thera is retrieving cup and saucer and soaking spilled coffee into a dishrag. "Irene, your secrets are safe with me. You know you can trust Miss Thera."

"You're the only friend I've ever had."

Before Thera left, Irene told her everything she knew. The names of her two daughters are Joanie and Ida Maye.

It is midnight when a tired Thera climbs the stairs to her room and gets quickly into her bed. To end another day of worship in Woosterville, Thera lies awake reflecting upon the values of people she knows.

'Most people worship something. Jack Fisher worships power. Nathan worshiped God.

Despite his faults, he truly believed that God is love. RD loves the beautiful Katheline. Daniel loves his father, Victor. Irene loves nature.' And as hard as it is for Thera to understand, 'Ida Maye loved sex. Rayford Franklin worships nothing. He believes in nothing. Clyde believes in strength. Bobby Riley believes in violence. 'What do I believe? In one important way, I am very much like my son, TJ. We both want to think carefully about what we know are matters worthy of our closest attention. Think it through. Take all arguments to their end conclusions, as Mildred E. Clark does in her great poem "The Difference."

"Men sing of war who never knew its hell,
on harp and lute,
while those who know how rotting dead men smell
are stricken mute."

91

'I believe in life!'
   It is three in the morning when she falls asleep.

Chapter 25:
The Flow of Youth

They ride. Clyde has no particular destination. Rachel suggests none. She rests her head on the back of the seat.

"Are you hungry, Rachel?" Clyde half whispers.

"Yes. Starved." She rolls her head his way and rubs her stomach.

"We could go to the Red Oak. That's where the school crowd will be." He notices that she makes a face. "OK, I got a better idea. There's a place named Henclaws out toward my house that cooks a great steak. Have you been there before?"

"No, but I'm ready to go. Let's do it." She slides close to him, puts one arm around his shoulder and drops her other hand in his lap as she softly whispers in his ear. "I'm just so hungry, I could eat just about anything." Her hand grips him and takes his breath away as she sings along with the radio.

*"Where have all the soldiers gone? Gone to graveyards every one.
When will they ever learn? When will they ever learn?"*

Clyde shakes as if suddenly chilled as they pass the Woosterville cemetery.

"Hey, Clyde. Don't look so serious." Rachel notices his mood change as he glaces at the grave stones beside the road. "There's nothing here but dead people. I'm used to them."

"Yeah, I guess you must be, Rachel. I was just thinking about my Grandpa Addison. He left plots here for all his family in his will. One of them is for me." His mother had pointed it out to him when they were putting flowers on Grandpa's grave.

Clyde kisses her neck.

"Looking at the markers, you can see that dying can come at any time and any age. Nobody expected Roy to die so young. Makes me wonder when my time will come." He grabs her thigh.

"Well, I can tell you for sure that right now you are very much alive." Rachel laughs.

"And if you don't stop what you're doing, it may be that my time is coming soon."

" I'm glad we're going to Henclaw's. Do you think there'll be anybody we know out there this late?" She runs her fingers through the back of his hair and watches it fall as she releases it.

"Probably a few mill hands on their way home from work. Or some of the kids who live out this way." In his mind he comes up the road from the store toward town and stops at Bobby's house. He hopes Bobby won't be here. Bobby is acting mean and unpredictable since his mom died and Dee Dee got her face messed up in the car wreck. Clyde is not afraid of Bobby, he would just rather not see him for awhile. Clyde used to have fun with Bobby, but he seems different since he got out of jail.... bitter and angry all the time, like he's just looking for trouble.

It's only a couple of months since the accident, and Bobby has already tried to start two fights. The day he got out of jail he went to drag Elroy out of his house, but Irving called to warn him and Elroy was sitting on his porch with a shotgun. He started shooting like crazy long before
Bobby was in range. He didn't hurt Bobby but he did scare him away. The next day Bobby ran into Irving and beat him up so bad that he was afraid to tell anybody who did it.

As they pull into the restaurant, Clyde sees Bobby's old Chevy pickup among the four vehicles backed up on the low hill above the graveled parking lot. The local boys started parking on the slope when one of them had a car with no battery in it that could be started by rolling down the hill in gear then popping the clutch. Necessity is often the mother of innovation. Now, it is just cool to park that way. It's just the sort of cool stuff Bobby would expect Elvis to do. The others are just copying Bobby.

Clyde pulls door-to-door straight into the gap on the right, driver side, of Bobby's truck. He goes around the back oh his car to open the passenger door for Rachel, then comes back to where Bobby is leaning back over the fender across the hood of his truck on the side toward the restaurant. Bobby is shelving an almost-empty pint whiskey bottle sitting upright on his bent fingers against the palm of his right hand.

"Hey, Bobby.....Whatcha doin'?" Clyde asks.

"I'm waiting for that buu... buzz...urd ta come out cheer. He's in thur...Dee Dee, too. What's leff uh her. Juss...leave me bee...muh boy, muh boy"

Clyde knows Bobby's been drinking a lot when he slurs his words. He turns to Rachel on his left to suggest they try to get him home, but it's too late. He sees the side door leading out of the kitchen slowly open as a dark figure eases out to make his way toward them. The ground they are standing on slopes down a few feet and levels beside the building. Just as the figure reaches their corner of the building and steps into the light, Clyde sees the menacing glint of a large meat cleaver.

"Look out Bobby! Here comes Elroy, and he's got a meat ax!" Clyde turns to shield Rachel from the attacker.

Bobby rolls onto his feet and vaults toward Elroy taking giant strides down the incline and swinging a stiff arm, with the bottle still cupped in his hand, through a shoulder-high wide sweeping arc. His timing is instinctively perfect as he brings the bottle down toward Elroy's head. The combined momentum of his body moving down the hill, Elroy running toward him, and the full power of his strong arm laced with adrenaline propels the bottle into Elroy's face with such force that it explodes with a sound to match a shotgun blast. The blow sends Elroy straight back slamming his head against the cinder block wall causing him to sink to the ground like a puppet with its strings cut.

Pieces of the broken glass are hanging from his face and tiny waterfalls of blood spew over and around them. Bobby's hand is cut, too, but he doesn't seem to notice. His eyes are fixed on Dee Dee who followed Elroy to arrive as the bottle exploded.

Dee Dee stands frozen. This is the first time Bobby or Clyde has seen her since the accident. What they see makes even Clyde's strong stomach feel queezy. The entire right side of her face is a crimson scar that has nothing but a few cord-like purple wrinkles where her eye used to be. The side of her head is a massive criss-crossing of stitch marks with an odd little stub of pink meat which was all that remained of her ear. On the side of her chin is a deep sunken area where both teeth and jawbone no longer provide any support.

Bobby couldn't look. Suddenly the condition of his hand demanded all of his attention. He begins picking glass out of his palm then turns his back to Dee Dee. He stumbles back up the hill and takes a greasy rag from the truck bed and wraps it around his hand. Then he climbs into the cab, lowers his right shoulder and reaches across to start the truck with his left hand. He raises his shoulder to drive out, but his head stays down on his chest. He does not look up until he is on the highway. He never looked back.

Clyde steps forward and puts his strong arms around Dee Dee. Her body heaves in a spasm of grief. He holds her tight for long moments before speaking.

"Rachel, go inside and call an ambulance."

She does as he asks.

Elroy lives. It takes thirty-five stitches to sew his face back together and although his left eye is badly cut, he wears a bandage then a patch over it for weeks, he does regain some vision in it.

Deputy Lester convinces Elroy that he'd be smart not to tangle with Bobby and that fancy lawyer anymore. "Best just leave 'em be, muh boy, muh boy."

"Yeah, I suppose you're right, Mo." Elroy rubs the spot where one of his teeth used to be. "I reckon enough is enough. You kin just drop them charges. Besides, I got what I want."

Elroy and Dee Dee are married just a week or so after Sammy Paylo comes back to Georgia.

Chapter 26:
Away From Home

Sammy Paylo makes himself comfortable, in a boxcar on a freight train, pulling out of Dallas, Texas eastbound for Georgia. He can rest easy to the sound of "click-ity- clacks over the tracks" for a long and uneventful ride covering a distance of more than one thousand miles.

He begins singing another tune from Irene's collection of slightly warped 78s. He is pleased that he remembers every line of an old song by Jimmy Rogers, the Mississippi Blue Yodler that fits his present situation perfectly.

"All around the water tank. waiting for a train.
I'm a thousand miles away from home, sleeping in the rain.
I walked up to a brakeman, to give him a line of talk.
He said if you got money, I'll see that you don't walk.
Well, I haven't got a nickle, not a penny can I show.
Get off. Get off. You railroad bum. He slammed the boxcar door.
He put me off in Texas, a state I dearly love.
With the wide open spaces all around me. The moon and stars above.
Nobody seems to want me, or to lend me a helping hand.
I'm on my way from Frisco, heading back to Dixieland.
Though my pocketbook is empty, my heart is full of pain.
I'm a thousand miles away from home, just waiting for a train."

Sammy Paylo has put a lot of miles behind him since he got fed up with Woosterville and the old fool. Those hicks in that place don't know from nothing, is the way Sammy sees it, now. He considers himself a real man of the world - a seasoned traveler.'Man oh man, the places I've been and the sights I've seen.'

And, damn, but he has sure done some hitch-hiking! He worked the state fair in Albuquerque, swept out the stands for four dollars an hour; laid carpet in Tucson, back-breaking work but it got him some new threads and a few bucks in his pockets. Shop lifting in Sacramento was a snap. He admires the large diamond ring on his finger.. It was almost like everybody had so much they didn't mind you taking a little ring and just putting it on and walking out of the busy store. If you got in a real jam in San Francisco, you could always sell your body to the queers for a few fast bucks. Yeah, even living off queers was better than living with the old fart-sniffing fool.

'But it'll be good to be back. Rachel told me on the phone yesterday that Bobby's been let out of the clink. Nub will let me stay at the store until I get something better. And, speaking of Rachel, I still remember that she has the hottest little ass I've seen since I bought some in Vegas. Maybe it takes a man of the world, to appreciate what we got right there, in Hicksville. She's free and probably a whole lot cleaner.'

***

Finicky Fred has transferred his obsession with cleanliness to Becky. She has been driving both Daniel and herself to get the new prefab spotless before they bring in all of their belongings. They have put up sheet rock, painted and plastered, put up wall paper, washed windows, and scoured and scrubbed until Daniel is sick of the place.

Moving-in-day has been sheer hell for Daniel. He sits a heavy box of books on the edge of a shelf and begins placing the books on it. He pauses with the big red dictionary Thera gave him in his hand. Dare he look up that strange hate word Finicky Fred had flung at him yesterday?

"It's not your father you love, Daniel. It's yourself. You only love your father because he looks like you in the pictures." So said Dead Head Fred. "Narcissism - that's your problem."

Daniel leafed until he found the word:

> nar cis sism ... 1. sexual excitement through admiration of oneself. 2. self-love; erotic gratification derived from admiration of one's own physical or mental attributes; a normal condition at the infantile level of personality development.

"DANIEL FULTON!"

Daniel starts. The box of books falls with the sharp corner hitting his foot hard. His mother only uses his full name when she is angry. He slips off his shoe and sock. His big toe is badly bruised and the nail is split deep. He hobbles into the kitchen where his mother is on her knees wiping the floor.

"What do you mean tracking on this floor I just waxed?"

"I'm sorry, Mom. I didn't see it."

"DIDN'T SEE IT! DIDN'T SEE IT!" She springs to her feet and pushes the wax-soaked rag in his face. "Take a look, Daniel Fulton. That's wax. W...A...X... WAX! Have you got that straight?" She grabs him by the hair and pulls his head down. "And those are tracks....Your tracks. Daniel Fulton! Made by your feet in my wax. Do you see it now, Daniel Fulton?"

"God dam it, mom, stop it!" He pulls her hand forcibly from his hair. "Stop treating me like a child. I didn't mean to mess up the damn floor. I was carrying a heavy load and didn't look down. Get off my damn back!"

"How dare you talk to your mother that way!" Fred startles both of them as he enters from the garage.

Daniel feels his mom's hand tremble as he releases it. He looks Fred straight in the eyes. "You go straight to hell!"

Fred swings at Daniel. He dodges the blow and strikes a solid one of his own against Fred's temple, sending him reeling sideways. Fred half falls, half slips to land on his back with his head slamming into the tile. He lies stunned.

"Dannie, you hurt your foot..." his mother sees the bleeding toe for the first time. She guides him into a chair.

When Fred pulls himself off the floor, Becky is kneeling before Daniel bandaging his foot. He avoids looking at Daniel as he speaks. "I want him out of my house, Becky." He quickly goes back out the door to the garage.

The boy and his mother are quiet as she finishes nursing. As she rises, he puts his arms about her and holds her close.

"Mom, you don't have to take anything off him. You're a beautiful woman. You can do a hellova lot better than that."

She looks into his eyes and smiles. "Thanks, Dannie... You're a lot like your father."

"Thera and RD are gonna think I'm nuts. I just brought all my junk over here and now I'm gonna take it all back. I'll stay with them until I get a job and a place of my own."

"Com'on, I'll help you." As they leave the room she stomps her bare feet in the fresh wax and laughs, taking tiny little steps which leave many tracks on the kitchen floor.

Chapter 27:
Welcome To My World

The last time he saw his mama-san she dropped her grey head to her chest, cupped her hands in the sleeves of her faded sky blue kimono, and with stooped, arched back eased away from him, taking tiny little steps as was customary in Japan.

Kyoto Iwaoka (Kee-O-Toe Ee-Wah-Oh-Ka) stands rocking back and forth with a firm grip on the head-high plastic loop as bodies sway against him with each bump and rattle of the crowded train.

Thinking of his mother makes him sad. Her tired old eyes were red with restrained emotion as she held his face in her hands and tried to smile. She told him how proud she was that he had won a scholarship to study in America and that she could only imagine how hard it must be for a Japanese boy to do what he had done to earn this honor.

"Go...men..ah...sigh...yah." (Excuse me please.) "Sum...ah...sin..nay." (sorry to bother you.) The train has stopped and an especially pretty young girl rubs her soft flesh against his as she politely asks that he shift and let her pass through the close group to the door. He flushes and lowers his head to his chest.

"Doe...eee...yo." (slang for don't mention it.) Kyoto backs awkwardly causing an old man to grunt and elbow his shoulder.

The old man cranes his head over his shoulder, looks him squarely in the eye, and whistles air through his yellowed teeth to force tidbits of his last meal from between them. As the stench assails his nostrils, Kyoto turns his back to the old man. 'Bah...Kah!' (Old Fool!)

How different his life in America will be. He has seen many films. So exciting and romantic. So spacious and clean. What a contrast to this. He is suddenly more aware of the smells in the hot train car; more disturbed by the jostling; uncomfortable with the bodies bumping his.

His Grandfather is an American. His mother told him that her papa-san is named Pay-ro (Paylo - most Japanese people pronounce the English "L" sound as an "R".)

***

"You're a lucky girl, 'Lizabeth." A broad shouldered woman with a face as fresh as a polished green apple, pushed an even stack of English pound notes through the teller's window. The dear child she had nanny-ed stood before her a sophisticated young lady preparing to set off on an adventure beyond her own wildest dreams. "I don't suppose you would consider taking a sentimental old fool along with you to America, now would you?" She cocked her head and touched her ear ring with a well-kept chubby finger.

"The good people of Harrowdale should never forgive me should I whisk you away from them, Ms. Gilbey." Elizabeth removed her scarf and shook it in a billowing wave leaving a faint cloud of mist in the air, thus exposing dark black hair, drawn behind her small ears and tied at the back of her graceful neck. Her face has the delicate beauty of a fawn. Her large green eyes are alert and lively, but suggest they can be easily frightened. Her nose reminds the tight-lipped teller of the finely carved Llardro figurine Elizabeth gave her after an holiday with her parents in Spain. Her small, but full, lips appear slightly pursed when at rest giving a slight pout to her noble expression.

The lips are purple now from the cold.

"I'm sure the weather will be more to your liking in America." Ms. Gilbey is never much for idle chit-chat when there is important instruction to be given to her charge. "Right you are. Now, this is the draft the professor called in for you. And, this pamphlet explains the use of your Barclay's card." She holds the card firmly on the counter and proffers a pen. "You must place your signature here before I am permitted to issue this first draft."

"Oh, it's not at all complicated, is it?" Elizabeth signs her full name with the flowing precision she perfected during her childhood with Nanny Gilbey's hand directing her own.

Thera Elizabeth McTanis.

"I'm sure you shall find it quite simple when money is needed." Ms. Gilbey put one hand over her lips and lowered her head to hide a suppressed giggle.

As Elizabeth tucks the money and the card inside her smart leather shoulder bag, she impulsively takes the happy woman's hand in hers, draws it to her face, kisses it, then smiles into her dancing eyes. "I shall miss you dreadfully."

101

"It's I who will do the missing. You take happiness with you where ever you go." She gently but firmly squeezed Elizabeth's hand and let it fall. "Now, off with you! Your father will be furious should you make him late." Her face returned to its usual mirth with the corners of her thin lips in curls as neat as Elizabeth's pen strokes.

"Cheerio, Nanny Gilbey!"

"Cheerio, 'Lizabeth, Cheerio!"

A bell tinkles merrily as she steps out onto the narrow main street into a light chilling rain. She pauses under the sign of a chemist shop, dabs quickly at the corner of her eyes, then darts across the street to her father's Mercedes. She notices the windscreen wipers come on as she approaches the car.

Chapter 28:
Hard Drinking, Hard Gambling

A rainy night in Georgia awakens Rayford Franklin. Lucky's shack leaks. Rayford's pants are soaked from water dripping on him while he slept. His stomach growls, reminding him that he has not eaten in two days.

He drinks what is left in a pint bottle, on the coffee table, taking big swallows that make his mouth burn and his eyes water. His stomach is on fire. He holds the empty bottle on his leg under the biggest drip for a long time until it fills with water. He gulps down the water and throws the bottle across the room. He tugs on his heavy boots and ties strong knots in the halfway-up laces. 'They're all gone.' He thinks. "I guess Lucky finally won enough to get him to Vegas with a stake.'

It seems to Rayford that the last year has been one long poker game. He has lost more money than he ever dreamed he could make in a lifetime. 'Easy come, easy go.' Lucky has said a million times.

Rayford stumbles out of the shack and crosses the old graveyard into the woods. His stomach quivers and the burning deep in his chest keeps trying to rise up in his throat. He chokes back the bitter bile in his mouth and swallows hard. The strong grain alcohol is getting to his brain and his head aches.

It stops raining as he reaches the stream. He picks up a discarded bottle and tilts it into the current of the stream to fill it. He plods on through the woods rinsing his mouth and spitting as he stomps steadily along until he comes out of the woods beside the store's abandoned outhouse. It is weather-worn and rotting. The door is missing, ripped off long ago to make a rabbit trap, leaving rusted old hinges twisted and useless. The moonlight shines in on the center of a crude bench with an oval hole in the center that is worn shiny smooth from years of use.

Rayford falls to his knees before the bench as his body convulses rejecting the liquid fire in his gut. His stomach muscles tighten and relax until there is nothing left to heave, then he coughs and spits and climbs to his feet. He feels better, but that is not what he wants. He wants to black out his brain.

He trudges to Nub's back door and pounds on it with his sledge-hammer fist until he hears Nub groaning obscenities. He tries the doorknob and pushes the open door ajar to see Nub curled in a tight ball on the floor with his one arm tucked under his head and his knees on his chest.

"I want another bottle, Charlie. Ya hear me? Get off your lazy butt and get me a bottle!" Rayford puts his heavy boot on Nub's hip and shakes him.

Nub rolls one eye open and peers up at him.

"Ain't got no more....drunk it all up...." He snickers causing saliva to drool from the corner of his mouth. ".....done drunk it all up...."

Rayford can't resist giving him a solid kick before stomping out the door. He goes to the well and crawls down into it, sits on the board above the water and fishes up the net with the bottles in it. He opens one and throws back his head letting the fire-y liquid flow down his throat. Above him he sees the opening in the well and the bright moonlit sky above it.

For some reason he can't understand, a quiet peace comes over him sitting at the bottom of the well. He can hear the music from the jukebox in the store.

"Whatcha gonna do when the well runs dry? You gonna run away and hide.
I'm gonna run right by your side, For you pretty baby, I'd even die..."

Rayford sings along with Fats Domino and drinks. The drunken old holedigger thinks back on his life and the years he spent in prison and sings his favorite song, one that Woodie Guthrie wrote

"I've been hittin' some hard rock minin', I thought you knowed
I've been leanin' on a pressure drill, way down the road.
Hammer flyin', air-hole suckin', six foot of mud and I shore been a muckin'.
And I 've been hittin' some hard travelin', Lord."

***

RD is playing the pinball machine with Bobby and Sammy. He loses track of time and then realizes how late it is as he starts home. He stops at the well and is replacing the cover someone has left off when he hears Thera's car turn into the driveway of the store. He runs along the back path to beat her to the house.

Rayford has chug-a-lugged a bottle when suddenly the well goes dark as pitch.

"Yoah!...YOAH! What the hell ya doing up there?....shuttin' me up in here?" Rayford hears his own voice echo. "...in here?...in here?.." He tries to climb the ladder and falls into the water. The well is very deep and he goes completely under before kicking and struggling until he gets a strong grip on the board and pulls himself up on it. His next try is successful and he makes it to the top of the well where he viciously shoves the well cover which is merely lying across the opening and sails off and onto the ground.

Rayford climbs out of the well with fire in his eyes, raging at being made a fool of, and damn near drowning, is the way he sees it.

***

As RD reaches the back yard, he passes Daniel. Panting to catch his breath, he turns back to speak to Daniel.

"Where.....where are you...going?"

"To the store."

"Nub's drunk. Bobby and Sammy are there."

"Wanta go back with me?"

"Can't. Thera wanted me home when she got back."

"OK. See ya." Daniel walked slowly down to the store. He could hear the 'chink...chink...' of the pinball and music from the jukebox as he reached the gravel.

"Oh Cee..Cee Cee Rider... Oh See what you have done.."

As he entered the store, RD sees that Bobby is playing the pinball and that Sammy is upset. Probably mad at Bobby for playing CC Ryder. Sammy hates that song and Bobby only plays it to irritate him.

Bobby wins a game and begins flipping the toggle switch to click up all the credits the machine will register.

"Where's Nub?" Daniel asks.

"He passed out. We put him in the back room." Sammy grins and shakes his head toward the back. He pokes Bobby's arm, but Bobby is intently focused on his timing and shrugs irritably.

"I'll check on him." Daniel goes toward the back of the store with Sammy following him.

The door they go through leads into the first of three rooms that make up the living area. Daniel turns left through a narrow kitchen into the second room. He is walking toward the third room when Sammy enters the first. The lights are off in all of the back rooms. The light from the Texaco sign shines in through the front windows of the two last rooms, revealing an assortment of card board boxes that Nub has piled in them. He saves the empty boxes for the Salvation Army, but he never remembers to have them picked up.

Daniel hears Nub moaning, as he moves around a stack of the boxes, and sees him lying on the floor with a big man standing over him. Good grief! The man is kicking the tar out of him, with his big red boots.....like the ones Rayford wears! Rayford Franklin!

Daniel freezes as Sammy moves behind him and sees what is happening, then goes into a blind rage, running straight at Rayford flailing his arms madly. Rayford hits him so hard in the mouth that blood begins gushing immediately. As Sammy falls backward, Daniel runs to get Bobby.

As Bobby bounds through the center room, Sammy is on his back, struggling to get his knife out. He manages to draw the knife and flick it open but Rayford quickly kicks it out of his hand and begins kicking Sammy mercilessly. The knife sails directly to Bobby's feet. Bobby deftly picks it up and covers the distance to Rayford in two giant strides.

Daniel loses sight of them momentarily behind the boxes, then moves around the obstruction and freezes briefly in the doorway with his mouth hanging open as he sees Bobby thrust the knife deep into Rayford's gut again and again, finally twisting it and pulling up hard into the big man's chest as Rayford topples to the floor landing across the semi-conscious body of Nub.

Nub suddenly lets out a blood-curdling scream.

Thera and RD arrived at the edge of the gravel just in time to hear the commotion and rush to the open back door. Thera steps through the doorway as RD pushes in beside her and flicks on the lights,

"OH...MY GOD....MY GOD!" Thera shrieks.

Bobby stands in the center of the room with his arm soaked with blood to the elbow. He lets the knife fall and is suddenly overcome by emotion and remorse.

"I...didn't mean to....Mizz Thera.....I had to......Mizz Thera......" He stammers. "..see what he did to Nub...and Sammy...." He pushes by her in the doorway and goes outside to the well.

Thera and RD watch him draw a bucket of water and try to rinse off the blood. Bobby gives up and throws down the bucket and runs toward the woods.

When they re-enter the house, Sammy sits on the floor gently touching his badly cut lip.

RD looks down at Rayford and Nub who rolls his plastered eyes up at him.

"Git this load offva me, Bocephus.." He was pushing and straining half-heartily at the heavy dead body with his one arm.

"We had better call the sheriff." Thera said to nobody in particular. She makes her way through the house with Daniel and Sammy following her.

RD grabs the bib of Rayford's overalls and sort of rolls him off Nub's chest. As the body rolls over a ledger book sticks out of his hip pocket. RD eyes it curiously then pulls it out and puts it in his own back pocket. He helps Nub make it to a worn old sofa where he falls on his side mumbling about all the rabbits they have killed.

CC Ryder is still playing when Thera, Daniel and Sammy enter the store. Bobby must have played it six times, thought Sammy as he unplugged it. Thera dialed the operator.

"This is an Emergency. Get me the Sheriff."

***

Sheriff Dawes and "Mo" Lester arrive well ahead of the ambulance they call to pick up Rayford's dead body. Lester's mountie hat covers the scar on the back of his head. He has his thumbs hooked in his shiny cartridge belt supporting his gun and holster. His khaki shirt is stretched tight across his big belly. He walks straight to Sammy as he comes into the store.

"Hey, you were with that son of a bitch that beaned me!"

"Hold your tongue, Mo! Don't talk that way around Miss Thera." The sheriff tipped his hat politely when he addressed her. "What happened Miss Thera?"

"I don't know how it started, sheriff. But, as I mentioned on the phone, Rayford Franklin was killed. His body is in the back room." She turns and leads the way. The sheriff follows and Lester motions for Sammy to go ahead of him. Daniel and RD tag along behind the fat deputy.

When they reach the back room the sheriff surveys the scene quietly. He points to the blood-stained knife. "Is this the murder weapon, Miss Thera?"

Thera nods.

"That's this punk's knife. I saw him cleaning his nails with it the night his partner got me from behind." Lester sneered at Sammy when he spoke.

"Bobby Riley killed him. We all saw him do it in self defense." Daniel said matter-of-factly.

"Bobby Riley, huh?" Lester goes to scratch his head but stops when he touches his hat.

"Yeah, He's the same one who tried to knock some honesty into your cheating head." Sammy spat at him and tried to grin but it hurt his cut lip causing more of a scowl.

"Why you little wise ass..." Lester starts at Sammy but the sheriff stops him.

"Mo, I told you to watch your mouth around the lady. And just who do you think you are acting like that in a law officer's uniform? That boy's done nothing wrong that we know about. Now you settle down or you'll be back at the slaughter house knocking pigs in the head for a living. Go wait in the car 'til I'm done here." He turns back to Thera. "Please excuse my deputy, Miss Thera. "I just can't seem to train him properly. I know where Bobby lives. I suppose we'd better go and pick him up right away."

"I'll go with you sheriff. I know him. He's not really a bad boy. (Lester was easing slowly back toward the front of the store and patted the top of his head when he heard this.) And, I can tell you for sure that it was a mean and evil man that he killed." Thera has a look of triumph in her eyes as she glares at the body on the floor. "Daniel, you and RD go on home. I want both of you in bed asleep when I return. Is that clear?"

"Yes 'um."

"Yes 'um."

"I'll stay here with Nub and wait for the ambulance, Miss Thera." Sammy offers.

"Thank you, Sammy. Make sure you ask them to look at your cut and have them examine Nub to make sure he has no broken bones or other serious injuries."

"Yes 'um."

As Daniel and RD walk out the back door, RD notices that the well cover is off again. He replaces it and the two boys walk slowly along the path to the house. When they reach the back yard, RD turns toward the old dirt road leading down to the barn.

"I'll be right in, Daniel. I gottsa take a whiz."

The barn is run down and surrounded by weeds from years of neglect. It looks desolate and somber in the dark. Rd runs through high Johnson grass and shimmies up the rickety door that is held ajar by clumps of mud built up around the bottom of it. He darts into the loft that has been wide open since last spring when he and Daniel made rabbit traps of the doors. He walks carefully across the rotted boards making his way to the far corner where he had found pictures of girls in skimpy clothes that he had guessed Daniel tore from magazines and hid there. He took the ledger from his back pocket and slipped it under a pile of dry hay. It was soaking wet and it might dry out here, he thought, as he crept back out and climbed down the door.

"Hey, Bocephus!" He hears Daniel call him as his feet touch the ground.

"Yeah...I'm coming."

***

Bobby and the preacher's wife are sitting on the steps of the church as the sheriff's car pulls up in front of his house. Bobby has his face in his hands and Eunice is talking in tongues.

"SHANDEMA....SHANDEMA,,,,,SHANDEMA,,,,NI.."

Mrs. Hawkins has her eyes closed and is shaking her fist that clutches a handkerchief in a tight little ball.

Lester is driving the patrol car with Thera and the sheriff sitting in back. He runs around the car to open the door for Thera. The sheriff slides out behind her.

"I'll handle this, Lester. You wait in the car."

"He's a sly one, sheriff. Just call me if you need any help."

Thera walks up the path from the front of the Riley house to the church. She goes directly to Mrs. Hawkins and puts her arm on her shoulder.

"Oh, sister Thera....I'm so glad you're here. What's gonna happen to poor brother Riley next? First his mama....then his sweetheart......now this....can you help the poor, unfortunate boy, sister Thera?" Her voice is more of a squawk than talk.

"I'll do everything I can, Eunice. You know that."

"He ain't got nobody else. No money...nothing.....nothing but the good Lord's mercy. The Lord will have mercy on you Bobby. Won't he Thera?" ('Bockbock...bockbock...bockbock..' Thera thinks.)

"All I can tell you, Bobby, is that you will have the best lawyer in the state. TJ will defend you."

"Will he do that, Thera" ('BOCKBOCK...') "Oh, thank you Jesus...thank you Jesus."

"Bobby, you have to come with me now." The sheriff said softly.

Eunice embraced Bobby then turned to Thera. "Will you look in on him now and then while he's in jail? He ain't got nobody else." ('bock.')

"Mrs. Hawkins, anytime you or the Reverend want to visit Bobby just give me a call and I'll send out a car to drive you in to town." The sheriff handed her a card with his name and number on it.

She didn't thank him.

They drove Thera home and the sheriff walked her to the door.

"Miss Thera, I've been wanting to ask you.....Do you know anybody around here who might make a good deputy?"

"I'll have to think about that, Sheriff Dawes."

"I need a strong young man, but sensible. I prefer that he be at least twenty-one. If you think of anybody, let me know. Your recommendation is all he needs to get the job."

"Why, thank you, sheriff." Thera offers her hand which he grasps firmly. "I'm flattered."

"Goodnight, Miss Thera." He tips his hat.

"Goodnight, Sheriff Dawes." She stands with her hand on the door and watches him leave. As he reaches the steps she calls to him. "Oh, Sheriff....somebody has to tell Mrs. Franklin. I'll do that."

"Thanks, once more, Miss Thera. Now, if I had a deputy like you, this would be the best job in town." He smiled openly and waved goodby.

Thera stands on the porch for a minute, then enters the house in silence, careful not to disturb the boys. RD needs his rest for she has planned quite a surprise for him after church tomorrow. She puts on her old shoes and slips quietly out of the house to visit Irene.

Chapter 29:
Oh Happy Day

The busy lives of Katheline and RD have changed so much since the day she kissed him on the porch. However, the only difference in their feelings for each other is that their love has grown even stronger while they have been separated, by circumstances beyond their control, during the last couple of years.

So, shortly after church, it is a very happy RD who finds himself seated on the sofa beside the Governor's daughter with Thera giving them curt instructions.

They were not to spoil their Sunday clothes as she and the Governor would most likely bring guests with them when they returned. Chicken salad sandwiches were in the refrigerator. Only one soda each. Thera is wearing her playfully stern face as she rushes upstairs to change.

Now that they are alone for the first time, they are shy and hesitant to speak. Both are anxious for Thera to leave so that they can feel really free. They exchange nervous small talk until Thera returns.

Thera rushes through the room, pausing only to peck him on the forehead. RD follows her to the door.

"Thera, can we go to the store? We can put on some of my old clothes. I want Nub to know how bad I feel about what Rayford did to him last night. He did nothing to deserve being treated like that."

"Oh, RD, how can I refuse you when you give me your please-please-please look." His look is the same that first melted her heart when he was just a baby. Perhaps the power of it comes from the self-evident knowledge that it is always reserved for her alone. "Alright, but don't stay too long. Nub has enough to worry about right now." She opens her purse and gives him two quarters. "One for the pinball machine and one for the jukebox. Maybe the noise will cheer him up for awhile."

"Thanks, Thera. He likes that. You're the best."

"No, I'm just an old softie...and you know it." She leans his way and lets him hug her.

RD stands waving from the porch steps until she spins down the drive, then he runs back to Katheline. He stops at a chest in the hall and takes out two pair of Levis and two clean white T-shirts. As he comes into the living room, he throws one set to Katheline.

"Go upstairs and put these on...You can leave your pretty dress on Thera's bed." He winks at her and her beautiful blue eyes twinkle at him.

RD changes quickly and waits for her at the foot of the stairs. She sees him from the top step and puts one hand on her hip and holds the other out from her side with the fingers spread back and her elbow against her side. She takes exaggerated steps one at a time twisting her hips and showing off her Levis rolled up in wide folds to her knees. He catches her by the waist as she reaches him and swings her playfully in the air with her hands gripping his shoulders.

They come laughing out the back door into the bright afternoon sun. He holds her hand to lead her down the road to the old barn. She is squeamish about walking barefoot through the thick grass so he lifts and carries her to the barn door. They climb the door and sit with their feet dangling from the open loft.

RD tells her everything that happened last night.

"What's in the ledger, RD?"

"I haven't looked yet. I'll get it." He creeps back to his hiding place and brings back the still damp ledger. He cautiously separates the pages and they read it together.

My True Story - by Rayford John Franklin

This is a true story put down by me to tell how things really happened. Most folks might not believe it but this is the way it was. I am writing this at the state pen where I'm doing time for the crime that I done and I got no reason to lie. I been a hole digger for most of my life but now they got me digging lakes here at Alto State Prison. I got this ledger book from a man that works in the office. I give him three plugs of Bull Durham chewing tobacco for it so that I could write this down. I won the plugs off of Lucky Sledge who's in here for stealing. He's the only friend I got in this world. I ain't loved but one woman in my life and that is Ida Maye, Nathan Fulton's wife. All that ever done was cause a lot of trouble. Ida Maye is the prettiest woman God ever made. She is so pretty that if you ever see her, you'll go crazy if you don't see her again. Well, the first time I laid eyes on her she was already married to Nathan, had been a long time. You see, she was a good bit older than me but that didn't really matter. The trouble was that she was married to Nathan and I couldn't see her and I was going crazy. That's how I got started digging wells. Ida Maye had a sister, Joanie, who lived with Irene and her brother, CC Paylo. Joanie had a boyfriend named Charlie Hooper. Charlie was digging wells and I figured by hanging out with him I might get to see Ida Maye when she comes to visit her sister Joanie at his place. Well, it did work out that way but it took a long time. I did see her a few times at Charlie's place but the others were always around and I didn't get nowhere. I had started working with Charlie and finally we started digging a well for Ida Maye and I got to see her a lot. Well, one day Nathan was gone and Charlie had to go into town to buy a new pickax cause he broke the only one we had. Anyway, Ida Maye called me into the house and gave me some lemonade and I started telling her how much she meant to me and we got to fooling around and I made her pregnant. She had the baby in 1916 and named her Thera. Nobody ever knew that baby was mine and Ida Maye's.

"Holy cow! Rayford was Thera's father!" RD was astounded.
Katheline's big blue eyes were full of wonder.
They read on.

Well, Ida Maye asked me to come over and clean that well out a three or four months after Thera was born, but she really didn't want no well cleaned. She had worked it out so that nobody else was there and I got her pregnant again. That boy was born dead so it didn't make no difference. A few months later she set it up for me to clean the well again and she got pregnant that time too. She had a boy and named him Victor. I think that was 1920. Yeah, that's right cause that's the year I dug Joan Paylo's well. That was a real hard well. Full of rocks. Took me almost a month. Me and Joan fooled around a little and she got pregnant. Seems like every time I fool with a woman she gets pregnant. Don't it? HA HA. Well, her daughter, Julie, was born in 1920 I believe.. That same year Julie was born Ida Maye asked me to clean her well again. Her well was in soft dirt and we managed to get together a lot with her telling Nathan that the water was muddy from the dirt falling off the sides. Well, that time she had a boy she named Ned in 1921. That was a busy time and I might have some of this mixed up a little bit. In 1920 I went over cross the Alabama line to dig Ruby Newman's well.. Didn't have no luck in Alabama either cause she got pregnant too. Had a boy named Alton in 1921.

"That's my daddy!" RD presses his finger on the name.
Katheline is speechless.

I cleaned Ida Maye's well again in 1921 and she had another dead baby. She was gonna name it Rose

I remember cause I made her mad when I said something about a dead rose. That was 1922. That was the year Nathan got sick of paying to have Ida Maye's well cleaned. I'd a done it for nothing but I didn't tell him that. Anyway, Nathan bought these big concrete sleeves to put in the well to make walls so that the well wouldn't have to be cleaned so regular. That was the year I cut off Charlie's arm. When we came out to put them sleeves in the well, they were big and heavy like the ones they use to make drains under roads. Well, Charlie went to borrow a tow truck so we could lift them up and lower them into the well. As soon as Charlie left, Ida Maye came out of the house and told me that Nathan was in Atlanta and wouldn't be back until the next day. So, we went inside and was really enjoying ourselves. But, Charlie came back real quick and caught us at it. He got real mad at me and Ida Maye and said he was gonna tell Nathan and there would be no stopping him. Ida Maye was worried sick. Finally, Charlie said he had done got the truck so we better get them sleeves in the well. We had a hard time with the sleeves cause it was the first time we tried to use them. We had to dig out the sides from the top and the water was full of mud. When we tried to lower a sleeve down, it wouldn't go down far enough so we raised it back up a few feet and Charlie got down in the well to knock off some more dirt and rocks off the sides with his pickax so the sleeve would fit. We had been at it a long time and we got thirsty as could be. So Charlie asked me to go down to the store and get us cold RCs..Before I left I told Ida Maye to watch the brake on the truck so it didn't roll back and drop that sleeve on Charlie. I told her that blooming sleeve could kill somebody if it fell on them. Anyhow, when I got back with three RCs, Ida Maye was gone and the truck had rolled back all the way to the well. Charlie was screaming like crazy and when I looked down in the well I knew he was in a fix. He was caught way down in the bottom and it was all he could do to twist his head out of the muddy water to holler at me. So, I tried to pull the truck up but Charlie had the keys so I crawled down in the well with him. The sleeve had penned his arm behind it and nearly ripped it off. He was bleeding like a stuck hog and choking on the blood and muddy water. I tried to get the keys out of his pocket but he was kicking and squirming and made me drop the keys into that deep muddy water. His arm was gone anyway and I knew he would die if I didn't get him out of that well quick. He always tied his pickax to the bottom of the rope he used to climb down on, and I found it and chopped off what little was left of his arm. He was flailing around like crazy and if he hadn't passed out, I don't think I'd of ever got him outta there alive. Well, as far as I'm concerned, I saved his life but Charlie never saw it that way. He couldn't dig no more, so he started selling moonshine and drinking a lot. He acted like it was my fault that he lost that arm. Ida Maye got pregnant that time too. She had a little girl named Carol in 1923.

"Wow! That's my mother!....Rayford Franklin was my grandfather on both sides." 'Holy shit!' he thought to himself.

Katheline was thinking about the pleasant one-armed man who sold her father gas this morning. 'Whew! How ghastly!'

Nathan ran Ida Maye off just after Carol got weaned off her mama's teat. I figured she told him that baby wasn't his or something she made up but she didn't tell on me cause Nathan kept calling on me to clean out that well when ever the water got to tasting funny or had bugs or slime in it. Oh, I almost forgot to mention that I dug Cecilia Johnson's well that same year Nathan ran off Ida Maye. She had a girl named Rebecca in 1924. That was just after CC came back from overseas and Joan threw herself in front of a truck that was going like a bat out of hell down the highway in front of the junk yard. CC's been looney ever since. Guess he really loved his wife. That same year I went back to Nathan's to get a skunk out of Thera's well. Thera was a ugly little girl. So ugly it kind of made you feel sorry for her. She was so lonesome she even stayed out there with me when I got the skunk out. It smelled so bad it made me puke. Well, I worked on Thera's well about once or twice a year and she would always come out and talk with me while I worked. She was so lonely it made me want to cry. Seemed like all she ever did was study books and plant flowers. Well, I knew she would never get a man and I felt real bad about her never feeling like that, so in 1929, the year of the big crash, I put it to her and she didn't like it one bit. No sir-ee! She fought me like a tiger and when it was over, she ran right to Nathan and told him to call the law. Well, that's how I got put in the pen for these ten years. I'll be getting out next summer which is good cause the well business is always better in the summertime. Signed Rayford John Franklin on October 5, 1938

RD and Katheline just sit for a few minutes staring out over the overgrown barnyard.

Katheline fans pages in the ledger with her thumb to help them dry and spots where Rayford had picked up his narrative again. "RD, there's more." She hands him the ledger opened to the new pages.

Well, I skipped a few pages in case I remembered something I left out. I was real lucky when I got out of prison. Old CC Paylo wants me to dig him another well. Seems the one I dug for Joan has done dried up. I'm gonna start tomorrow.

Started on Julie's well today and it's gonna be a real hard one. All of Paylo's land is full of rocks. That Julie is driving me crazy after all that time in the pen. She's the prettiest woman I've seen since Ida Maye was here. Well, I ain't wrote nothing in about a week. I've been working real hard on Julie's well. I finally got her today. Took her by force. That's what I did. Just like with Thera. But it wasn't cause I felt sorry for Julie. It was because I wanted her so bad that I just couldn't stand it no more. Figured she'd be worth another ten years digging lakes. Ain't really much difference in digging wells or lakes as far as the works concerned.... except it's more cramped in a well. She had a boy she named Sammy in 1939.

Old CC talked to me today and I ain't going to prison this time. He said if I'd marry his ugly sister, Irene and take her off his hands, he's just forget about what I did to Julie. Irene's got a good piece of land the other side of Ida Maye's place. So I'm gonna do it. It's about time I got out of this well digging business anyway. I was forty last month and I'm getting tired of being a hole digger.
Signed Rayford John Franklin July 16, 1939

1949 Dug Irene a well. Irene has been bad sick. Julie has been staying with her.

1950 My boy Roy born.
1959 Roy died. Buried him in Irene's well.

Life just ain't worth living no more. I want to kill myself but I ain't got the guts. When I do die, I want my son Thomas James Franklin to manage all the money Ida May left to me. So, I got him to make up a will for me so that he can take care of it cause I know he will do right by the ones that deserve something from me.
Signed Rayford John Franklin

RD and Katheline discuss the names and dates in the ledger, until they have sorted out as many pieces of the puzzle as Rayford wrote down. RD tries to work out how he is related to all the hole digger's children, but finally throws up his hands in frustration, and puts the book back under the hay.

"I guess they are all my cousins.... Even Sammy Paylo....Uck!"
He jumps down from the loft and looks up at her.

Chapter 30:
As Time Goes By

"Come on, Katheline. Let's go to the store." He turns his back to her as she starts to climb down the door.

"RD Newman! You brought me in here, the least you can do is get me out." She hung on the door scowling . 'Damn,' He thought. 'She's even prettier when she's mad.'

"Sorry, I was lost in thought, I guess." He backs up to the door. "Get on my back. It's easier."

She hooks her legs around his waist and when he locks his arms under her knees, she lets go of the door and wraps her arms around his neck. She is choking him, but he is not about to tell her. They don't have far to go, and she feels so good that if she chokes him to death its worth it thinks RD. He carries her well beyond the grass, and is willing to take her all the way to the store on his back if that is what she wants him to do.

"I can walk now, RD." He releases her legs and she slides off his back . He turns to her while she still has her arms on his shoulders and impulsively puts his arms around her waist. He is looking directly into her big blue eyes.

He kisses her, hard. Truly 'a kiss to build a dream on' as "Satchmo" would sing. She holds him closer. They embrace until RD can feel the tent rising and knows that she feels it too. Her face turns crimson as she pulls away from him.

"I've never felt like this with anybody."

"Me neither."

"I'll race you to the store." She darts ahead of him. He runs a little stiff-legged for a few strides and she gets a good lead on him. When he settles

The Holedigger

down, he picks up his sprint and begins to close the distance between them. He overtakes her just as they reach the gravel. She stops when her tender feet hit the sharp little rocks and hops on one foot back to the grassy path, holding her stinging foot. She steps gingerly to test her hurt foot then sits down to inspect the bottom of it.

RD sits down in front of her, takes her foot in his hands and rubs it gently. "Ohhh, that feels so good."

Chapter 31:
Let the Good Times Roll

"Oh, that feels so good." CC is in the process of filling another quart jar with his excrement when he hears TJ's car pull up in front of the garage. He gets off the seat and pulls his coveralls up from around his ankles and squirms into them. He lifts a mason jar from the commode and twists a lid on it. He labels it September 9, 1959 and puts it in a large wooden bin that is almost full of similar jars. He meets TJ getting out of his car.

"Mister Paylo, I need to speak with Sammy. Is he here?" TJ was struck by the stench of CC before he came close to him.

"Little Sambo? Don't live here..no more...no more..." CC shakes his shoulders as if dancing. "Huh, huh, huh...   He's gone, gone, gone.."

TJ considers asking if CC knows where Sammy is staying, but looking into his glassy eyes, he decides to wait and inquire at the store. As he gets back into his car, CC does a walk-around viewing the lack of shiny metal on the plain Chevy with obvious scorn. When he comes to the side mirror, he presses his nose against it and smiles at himself. 'What do you say to such a narcissistic nut?' Thinks TJ. He rolls down his window and starts the engine as CC backs away from the car.

"Enjoy yourself, Mister Paylo."

"I do. Huh, huh, huh... I do, I do, I do.." CC does a little jig around the corner back toward his cage.

TJ shook his head and smiled as he pulls out of the garage drive. Old CC has been considered the harmless town joke for as long as he can remember. Nobody seems to take him seriously. Except Nathan Fulton that long ago day at the court house. TJ remembers that day vividly.

He is thirteen and rides into town with Nathan to get a tooth filled. When he comes to meet Nathan in front of the court house, with his jaw still numb with novocaine, there is a crowd gathered and Nathan is the center of attention. TJ just misses seeing him eat live bees as he pushes into the silent crowd, apparently struck dumb by the demonstration, or speechless at the stupidity of what they witnessed.

Then CC laughs. "Huh, Huh, Huh." The crowd remains silent.

"What're you laughing at you crazy old loon?" Nathan bellows.

"I may be crazy, but I'm smarter than you." CC scratches his butt and grins, drawing a few chuckles from the crowd.

"Name one thing you know that I don't." Nathan tries to intimidate him.

"I know better than to eat bees. Huh,huh,huh." The crowd roars.

Nathan's face turns red. "You ain't got the nerve, that's all."

"I got thu nerve to tell ya...The hole digger dug into Ida Maye." The crowd goes quiet again.

Nathan is still also, and lowers his head, then speaks in a whisper..."I know that."

"Do ya know that hole digger is little Thera's daddy?" CC looks at the crowd for approval.

Nathan bolts down the steps, grabs CC, and starts shaking him.

"You're lying, you worm!"

"Huh...huh...huh..." The nearby spectators pull Nathan away from him. "Huh, huh. Huh. I gotcha on that one. Gotcha, gotcha, gotcha...HUH, HUH, HUH..."

TJ never knew if CC was lying or not. But, he had played with the idea of Thera being an older sister when he learned that Rayford was his father.

'Sister Thera? No, it just doesn't sound right."

As he passes the church, he sees Thera's car among the many that fill the parking lot and spill over to the lawn of the parsonage and line the sides of the road. Woosterville has turned out in force to see their new governor. TJ drives on.

He knows now that Ida Maye and Rayford were lovers. But he is still sure that Thera is Nathan Fulton's daughter.

***

The governor's daughter sits on the bench rubbing dirt off her hands on the Levis. Her face is flushed from the sweltering heat.

"Want a co-cola?" RD thumbs a quarter through his fingers.

"Yeah. The small one."

As RD enters the store Nub is refilling the cooler. He carries the wooden case with his thumb through the handgrip and his fingers around the neck of one of the bottles. He swings it smoothly onto the cooler then lifts the opposite lid and starts adding the bottles two at a time.

"Hey, Nub! Are you feeling better today?" RD says cheerfully.

"Well, well. Hey yourself, RD. To tell the truth, I'm sore as hell. I've got bruises all over me. Don't remember much, but Sammy tells me that sorry hole digger kicked the be Jesus outta me. I hate to talk about the dead, but I hope he's burning in hell."

"Speaking of burning up..." RD changes the subject. "It sure is hot. Have you got any real cold ones in there? In the small bottles?"

"Sure do..." Nub draws two from the far corner of the cooler. "These have got a little ice in them."

RD offers his quarter.

"Well, well. I'm plumb outta change. You're gonna just have to let Nub treat you and that pretty little lady today." Nub grins and keeps putting cokes in the cooler.

"Thanks, Nub." RD goes to the Rock-ola, drops in both of his quarters, and selects twelve of Nub's favorite tunes. "Miss Thera sends you her regards and told me to try to cheer up her Uncle Charlie."

"Well, you be sure to tell Miss Thera that her thoughtfulness is always appreciated. And it's always a pleasure to see you, my boy, my boy." Nub was already among the millions who were starting to pick up on some of the cool expressions that were used by their hero - Elvis Presley

"Thank'ya, thank'ya very much." RD gives Nub a parting Elvis salute as he returns to Katheline, with the King singing "Love Me Tender" in the background.

From this moment on, Katheline will never forget that little bottle of coke with slivers of ice in it and her all-time favorite song being sung by the greatest singer in the world on the day when she knew that she had found the love of her life. She closes her eyes to thank God for this time of pure and perfect romance. RD kisses her eyelids softly and knows that he is tasting tears of joy.

They sit side by side on the bench with her head on his shoulder without saying a word and listen to the music play all of the dozen selections. RD has played two of his favorites ,just for her, and sings along with every word of the lyrics to "Earth Angel" and "My Special Angel." Katheline swoons.

Just as the last Elvis song is almost over, they are drawn from their day dreams by a metallic green fifty Chevy pulling in front of the store. RD recognizes TJ as soon as he gets out of the car. TJ wears a light summer suit and carries a rich leather briefcase.

"Hi, RD. Is Nub here?"

"Hello, Mister Franklin. Yes Sir, he's inside." RD is pleased that TJ remembers his name.

"Who's your friend, RD?" He smiles at Katheline. "I don't think we've met. I'm TJ."

"This is Katheline Fisher. Her daddy's governor."

"I am indeed honored, Miss Fisher." TJ makes a quick bow. "Jack Fisher is the only man I've ever voted for in this state."

Katheline offers her hand which he takes by the tips of her fingers and shakes lightly.

"I'm pleased to meet you, Sir. And happy to know that you support my father."

"I just passed the church and it looks as if he has all of this town turning out to show their support for him. I noticed a lot of cars belonging to people who have never set foot in that church. It goes to show that a lot of people believe in him. I think we're lucky to have him as our Governor."

He turns his attention back to RD. "RD, I would like to talk with you later about last night. I'm representing Bobby Riley."

"Yes Sir. Daniel saw all of it. If we're not here, we'll be at Thera's."

"Thank ya, Thank ya very much." TJ surprised both of them with an excellent imitation of Elvis' voice. It draws a giggle from Katheline and a broad smile from RD. "Excuse me, Miss Fisher. My first order of business is to get one of those cold co-colas."

TJ goes inside. Katheline studies RD for a moment.

"Are you going to tell him about the ledger?"

"I don't know if I should.....What do you think?"

"I think you should. He has a right to know the identity of his parents."

"Yeah, I guess I should let him see it. He's a lawyer too. He'll know what to do with it." Just as RD says this, TJ comes out of the store. He eyes RD curiously.

"Know what to do with what?" TJ takes a long drink of his coke. "Nub's no help. Says all he remembers is drinking too much and being kicked. He thinks he must have shot some rabbits, too, because with blood all over the place, it looks like somebody skinned them in the house."

RD takes the ledger out of his pocket and hands it to TJ.

"I took this out of Rayford's pocket last night." Rd looks at Katheline. "She and I are the only ones who have seen it."

TJ seats himself in the straight chair RD pulls up for him, crosses his ankles on the corner of the bench, puts on his glasses, and begins to read. Katheline sits quietly beside RD, who is anxious, restless. He picks up the three empty co-cola bottles to take them inside, and walks behind TJ to get a peek and see how far he is into the ledger. He looks over TJ's shoulder again as he returns to his spot on the bench When TJ finishes, he closes the book, stares at his patent leather shoes, and removes his glasses. "RD...Miss Fisher....I prefer that you don't tell anyone about this until after Bobby's trial."

"We won't, Mister Franklin. RD wasn't even sure that he should tell you." She stands and does an arms high stretch.

"You two can run along. You've given me much more than I expected. I may need to ask you some questions later, RD....about last night. I'll speak with Thera and arrange a time to see both you and Daniel."

TJ parks beside Thera's car in front of the parsonage. Many of the cars are gone now. Most of the hangers-on are those who stand to gain the most by association with the governor. Many of them are members of the team that got him elected.

TJ goes directly to Thera. "I must speak with you in private. It's important."

She excuses herself and they walk outside.

"This will take some time. Shall we sit in my car?"

"In this heat? Let's use mine. It's air conditioned."

They get in her car. She cranks it and when the air is cooled, they roll up the windows. They talk. She reads. They hug. She cries. She turns off the engine. He steps out of the car and stands with her door open waiting for her to get out. She sits until beads of sweat form on her forehead, then she speaks.

"Will this help Bobby?"

"It's all I've got."

"Use it. It's high time everybody knows the truth."

"The truth is that you were right about him, Thera." TJ admits. "Now, what about his burial?"

"He will burn in hell anyway. Cremate him!" Thera states bitterly.

"I couldn't agree more. After reading his own words, I'm convinced that all he did was evil."

"Not entirely. As much as he hurt me, I must admit that he did one good deed." She smiles.

"And what would that be?" TJ looks puzzled by her change of attitude.

"He gave me you." She lightly touches his cheeks with her fingertips,

"So I'm the gift of the old hole digger." He gives her a hug. "What an epitaph for my grave."

***

The sun is high over her head and her fine hair glimmers with sunlight passing through it. She leans over him and runs the tip of her finger across his lips. RD wishes he knew a way to freeze this time....stop it and keep it forever just this way. Like the photo of his parents.

'But time will not stop for us as it did not stop for them. We too will grow old and wrinkled as the picture did. One day our faces will disappear as theirs did....first in life and finally even in memory.

'Daniel keeps the memory of his father alive with photographs. I must take a mental picture of Katheline as she is now, perfect in every detail, and never forget.' RD closes his eyes as she runs her fingers through his hair.

There is a redness from the bright sun on his eyelids which fades to neutral gray. He thinks she is shielding him from the sun, but he opens his eyes to see that a large dark cloud has moved overhead making the sky gray. Then he feels a raindrop and then another as he hears a great clap of thunder and the sky opens pouring heavy rain. He does not move. Katheline springs to her feet.

"RD, we'll get soaked."

He smiles and grabs her ankle. "So?"

She tries to pull away but he holds her firm. He pulls himself into a seated position and she steps across his legs and clutches his head to her mid drift. He throws his arms around her legs and holds her against his chest. The rain is pelting them. It feels cool and fresh. The warmth of her thighs through the jeans feels so good on his sensitive cheek that he trembles and she squeezes him tighter to her warmness. His hands impulsively grip her buttocks. It is an innocent gesture; no thought of boldness from him; no suspicion of presumption from her. His hands move to hers and he slowly rises to embrace her.

Their lips do not meet in a kiss. They stare into each others eyes so close their breath co-mingles as does the rain flowing between them.. He tastes her wet neck; she his. Their T-shirts are soaked and their bodies seem to unite flesh-to-flesh. Her budding nipples are pressed firm on his chest. She pulls away and makes a dash for the porch. He watches the graceful beauty of her lithe body.

Her motion has the daintiness of petals falling and the vitality and sureness of a young squirrel darting from branch to branch in Daniel's mopping tree. RD strains to hold his feelings inside.... to make them last. As he steps onto the porch, Katheline pinches her wet T-shirt above her breasts and pulls it out from her drenched body. She moves momentarily out of his world into the exclusive realm of a feminine beauty convinced that she must look dreadful. RD can not imagine anything lovelier. Her hair hangs in wavy coils with tiny ringlets about her ears. Her face shines as her eyes flash with life. Her eyelashes are stuck together forming narrow v shapes that look like rays above dawning suns of blue.

"Come on in....I'll get you a towel."

Chapter 32:
Don't

Beads of perspiration pop out on Thera's upper lip as she hears TJ drive away. She rubs her lip and grimaces at the sour smell of the ledger on her fingers.

The repulsive odor is Rayford Franklin. Rayford Franklin pushing her into the smokehouse. Rayford Franklin pushing her down on the feed sacks. Rayford Franklin.... pushing, pushing, pushing!

"Don't...don't...don't" She screamed endlessly.

"What's the matter with you, girl?" I'm not going to hurt you."

Nathan had said the same words to her the day he died.

He came back from the courthouse raging about being made a fool of by an old fool. She enraged him even more by agreeing that it was stupid for him to eat bees. When he made a feeble attempt to explain it as an act of courage, she told him. "You don't have to prove yourself to me."

Then he had pushed her. Now she knew why. Nathan knew that she was Rayford Franklin's daughter and he hated Rayford Franklin more than anything on earth. She recoiled from the fury in his eyes. That angered him more. He shook her and mouthed Rayford Franklin's words that were imprinted in her brain like an inscription on a tombstone.

"What's the matter with you, girl? I'm not going to hurt you."

She had her pretty hat in her hand and she pushed it into his face. The pearl stickpin scratched his eye. As he held his eye the convulsions began. Thera now knew that the lethal protein poison of a Black Widow spider was attacking his nervous system. When it happened, she knew only that he fell across her bed with his muddy shoes kicking wildly making red mud streaks all over the white bedspread.

"Don't die daddy.....please daddy....don't...don't...don't..." She pleaded with him until the end.

Thera dries her eyes and blows her nose as she notices that pouring rain is cooling the day's blistering heat.

***

RD watches Katheline spring up the stairs with the towel wrapped around her hair like a turban. At the top of the stairs, with her back toward him, she peels off the wet T-shirt and turns a shoulder to toss it to him. His eyes are fixated on her bare shoulder and he misses the towel. She goes behind the bannister upstairs and in a moment sticks her head over it and tosses him the soaked jeans. With his arm high he catches them and a loose leg slaps him in the face. He hears their cars outside and goes to the front door to greet Thera and her guest.

"Hi, there......Governor Fisher..." He almost said Mister Fisher.

"Hello, RD. It seems we aren't the only ones who got soaked." Jack replies cheerfully.

"Yes Sir....We had on old clothes. Katheline's upstairs drying off.... and changing." Thera rubs his wet head affectionately.

""Why don't you get into some dry clothes?" She pecks him on the forehead.

"Hi, Daddieee..." Katheline yells from upstairs. "Be down in a minute."

Jack and Thera stepped to the foot of the stairs.

"You're beautiful. Come on down. We're late." Jack was loud but jovial." He glances at Thera and flushes slightly then smiles broadly.

Too often, Thera has seen that flash of awareness from a man after he looks at a beautiful woman or comments on her beauty, then looks directly into her own face. Just a momentary unconscious hint of embarrassment from an innate male tendency to mentally compare all women.

"Why don't you leave your daughter with us while you're in town, Jack?"

Jack looked at his watch. "I'll have a word with her. Coming up!" He bounded the stairs two at a time.

He finds her sitting on Thera's bed rubbing her hair with the towel.

"How would you like to stay here while I go to town for a couple of hours?"

"Oh, Dad. I'd love to. It's been a swell day.....RD's really neat."

"Really neat?"

"Oh, you know.....I like him a lot."

"Can I come up now?" RD shouts from below.

"If you're not afraid of witches." Katheline moves to the desk with the oval mirror above it and quickly begins brushing her hair.

RD bounds into the room wearing dry trousers and a towel around his neck and bare shoulders. "Can she stay, Sir? Can she, please?"

Jack considers the eager young man's eyes and his daughter working furiously to get her hair in order. "Maybe next time. I think its best that you come with me, Kate. I could get held up in town and we still have the drive home."

She eyes her father through the mirror. It isn't like him to make long-winded explanations. A simple no is more his style. He meets her glance. The disappointment in both her face and RD's confirms his suspicion that they may be getting too serious about each other.

"Perhaps we can visit you again soon, RD."

As Thera leads them to the door, RD and Katheline lag behind. Just before she steps out the door ahead of him, she takes his hand and presses it lightly.

"I do hope I see you again soon, RD."

"Me too..."

She drops his hand to take the white scarf Thera offers. She billows it over her shoulders and holds it high with her arms to form a shelter from the rain. As they reach the steps, she looks directly into his eyes for a moment then turns abruptly and steps briskly down the steps and rushes to the car where her dad stands holding the door for her. The light from inside the car shows her face under the scarf as she turns to give him another parting smile.

RD thinks he sees raindrops on her cheek but the rain has fallen well in front of her face. He follows the car to the end of the drive and watches the tail lights fade into a dim glow and vanish.

He knew she didn't want to leave him, because she continued looking back at him until she was out of sight. He smiled remembering an old song Thera used to sing. "Oh, I was looking back to see, if you were looking back to see, if I was looking back to see, if you were looking back at me."

Chapter 33:
Love Me Tender

"I see that you and Katheline are quite fond of each other, RD." She puts her arm on his shoulder.

"I love her, Thera....I love her."

Thera drops her hand uneasily. 'Strong words for my dear RD.' She thinks.

"Come and sit with me, RD. We need to talk about so much that has happened."

They sit quietly in the swing for a few moments, gathering their thoughts and watching the heavy rain fall blur the images of trees bordering the yard. The sudden storm has made it dark early. The lights inside the house cast window- patterned projections across the porch floor in front of them.

"TJ showed me the ledger. You made the right decision to give it to him."

"I wasn't sure....Katheline told me I should."

"Did she read it?"

"Yes. She read it with me....I had no idea what was in it."

"There were many startling revelations in it for me. Are you disappointed with me for not telling you what I did know? I was ashamed for you to know what that evil man did to me."

"No...not really.... But I don't understand why you thought it would matter. I love you, Thera. Nothing can ever change that. Once you love somebody....you always love them. Don't you?"

"Yes, RD. Yes...always."

"Thera, have you ever loved somebody the way I love Katheline?"

"Yes, I have. The man I named both you and Daniel after- Rabun Daniel McTanis. I've never talked with anyone about him." She puts both hands in her lap and laces her fingers together tightly.

"Oh, Thera. How could you hold something so important inside all this long?" He instinctively put his palm over her cupped hands. "I want to know everything. Please tell me all about it. Please, please, please."

She shifts her weight to face him and holds his hand between hers.

"I met Rabun McTanis in college...in England. I was there doing graduate work at Oxford and he was a Rhodes Scholar doing research and studying at the same school. We were brought together in 1940 as volunteers to research the growing social problems of city children being placed in rural homes to get away from the dangers of bombardment and the threat of German invasion in London.

"We met in London to plan our study in August, just two months after the British expeditionary forces were driven from Dunkirk and watched in horror as the devastation of that city became reality. We learned that some of the children were being sent overseas until a German U-boat sunk a ship with ninety children aboard. We also learned to dash for a big "S" sign when we heard the air raid sirens, and how to mark the start of another day by the sound of the "ALL CLEAR" signal at dawn. We learned that the city's own guns did little more than boost morale, and draw the bombers attention to where they were located. But, we joined in the enthusiastic cheering as they were fired."

Thera pauses to dwell on memories too horrid to share with her youthful charge. Like the morning they stepped out of the shelter onto hot pavement and saw the smouldering corpse of a young woman who had not made it inside. Nostrils accustomed to every conceivable human stench, after days of huddling in cramped shelters, shuddered when assaulted by the fumes of burning flesh and hair.

Thera's eyes are watering and she looks so sad.

"Thera, I don't want you to have to think about it anymore, if its too painful for you."

In response, she simply rubs her eyelids and continues her narrative.

"On the tenth day of September, we packed notes, address books, forms listing foster parents, lists of displaced children, and our skimpy personal goods and left London on a train for the city of Ely. From there we could reach several small villages by foot if necessary.

"The train was packed so full at Liverpool Street Station that we just managed to squeeze in at the door of a crowded compartment." Thera smiled. "We stood with our noses pressed to glass, looking out the door window, all the way to Cambridge and Rabun's only comment was 'What a lovely view of the countryside.' "

Thera pauses again, this time she is simply lost in her private thoughts of him.

"RD, in a quiet moment such as this, I have clear visions of that entire train ride."

"I understand, Thera. I've been trying so hard to make sure I don't forget anything about my time with Katheline. I already know that what is happening between us is the most wonderful experience I will ever have, and it's just too precious to lose even the smallest detail."

"You are absolutely right. I know now, that true love is the most powerful force in the world. And, I have vividly re-lived my time with Rabun countless times, over the years, since we rode that train. As we swayed and rattled out of the city, the smoke outside the window was replaced by fog. As the fog thinned, I can still close my eyes and see the coils of barbed wire bordering the tracks and the painted over station signs along the way that added to the confusion among passengers with no idea where they were going or what they would do when they got there. But, together, Rabun and I had never been more sure of ourselves and unafraid. That's the power of love." Thera rubbed her eyelids again.

" When the fog cleared, we saw open expanses of grassy fields edged with thick trees that reminded me of Brussel sprouts in s steaming bowl of pea soup. As we changed trains in Cambridge, it began to rain. It really began to pour as we pulled away from the empty platform, much the same as it is raining here now, RD.

"There was room in the club car on the train to Ely. We were seated at a booth facing each other across a small table where I had a clear view of the bar behind Rabun. I remember feeling a little nauseated by the odors of stale tobacco and beer.

"Most of the people on this train were disabled veterans on their way to the RAF Hospital in Ely. All of them looked so very tired. In contrast, a robust woman, who looked very fresh and healthy, came and seated herself beside Rabun. I slid over near the window to allow a man with a heavily-braced leg to get it under the table beside me. The four of us exchanged timid pleasantries. In answer to Rabun's questions, the woman began telling us proudly how her husband had been crippled.

"During the retreat from Dunkirk, he was shot by ground fire and lay helpless as a German plane dropped toward him from the sky. He heard the rattle of machine guns and watched the dirt fly up toward him until the bullets ripped through his body.

"While his wife talked, her husband looked at a menu card and took a single coin from his pocket under the table before ordering her a cup of tea from a passing porter.

"At the bar behind our booth the porter was drawing pints of beer for a young US Army private when a highly decorated RAF sergeant ordered a half pint. The porter placed a full pint before the RAF soldier as he brought the American youth's order to the counter. The sergeant flushed and nervously rubbed the coins in his hand as if troubled that he couldn't pay for the full pint. The young American walked away leaving more money on the counter than the RAF non-com made in a fortnight.

"The Dunkirk cripple struggled onto his crutches and fought the moving train to the edge of the bar and cancelled his order. 'Changed me mind, Guvnur..' Said he, as he slapped his only coins on the counter. ' I claim the honor of buying the sergeant a pint. Tizz'nt often you see a man still walking who's earned the Cross.'

"Then says the porter, 'Right you are, Mate.' as he takes the coin and gives the man change from the money left on the counter. 'But, he's drinkin' 'alf pints..... That's a hero's 'alf pint...Tizz wot it izz.'

"The cripple slid the change back across the counter, and said. 'I see the tea's made. Bring a cup round for me missus.' As he balanced himself on the back of the seat and swung his braced legs under the table, the sergeant toasted him.

"'All the best!'"

"He held up a finger as if correcting a child. 'Some of the best, mate....some of the best!'

"His wife beamed over her raised teacup and said to nobody in particular.

"'He may be poor, but he's a gentleman still.'

Thera stands, stretches, and walks to the front steps to put out a hand to test the rain. It is now almost a light drizzle. She turns back to RD who sits glued to his seat in the swing.

"Let me know if I'm boring you."

"Are you serious? I can hardly wait to hear more. What a story. You should write it down."

She returns to her place beside him and gives him a bear hug. He puts his arm under hers and rests on her shoulder as she picks up the story where she left it.

"The rain slowed to a drizzle as we walked out of Ely Station, me with my suitcase and a box filled with books, and Rabun with his suitcase and a sack filled with forms and notes. We saw the young American and his buddies pile into the only taxi. As the cab pulled away, a man noticed that one of them left a black instrument case on the curbstone. He picked it up and ran futilely after the taxi as it sped away. The man approached Rabun with his face a mask of disappointment and asked if he knew where the Americans were going. Rabun took the proffered case and smiled broadly and reassured the man by telling him, 'Yes, I know where they're going. I'll take care of it.'

"We walked down a grey gravel path from the station to a street we followed up a long hill. At the top of the hill, we put down our load and looked back. Far below, the street went under a trestle, beyond which was an expanse of flat open fields with the darkest soil I have ever seem. 'So, there is the fen land,' Rabun informed me.

"We turned to the right and walked into the center of the Ely market-place, where we bought fish and chips wrapped in newspaper, and ate them sitting on a long bench in the square. An old woman sat down on my left and a young lady with a small child approached on Rabun's right where he had placed the black case. He put it across his lap and the lady sat down beside him with the child standing leaning against her mom's legs. After eating his meal, Rabun started reading aloud the comics on the greasy newspaper which amused the little girl and she began to laugh. Her reaction made him laugh and his laughing was so delightful that soon all of us were laughing with him.

"Honestly, RD, I have never seen such contagious joy. For a glorious moment the horrid war had lost its grip on us and we remembered how to laugh. When the little girl put her hand on the latch of the case, he nodded to her and she opened it to reveal a beautiful new banjo.

"'Can you play it?' She asked sheepishly. He smiled at me. In the shelters of London there was often someone to provide entertainment. Once, a single accordion had led all night sing-along sessions for hundreds of people crammed into the basement of the building where they had rented flats.

"'Of course I can.' He took out the banjo and began to pick.

"The somber marketplace came alive. Within minutes, we were surrounded by a happy throng, mostly women and small children. Rabun played Bluetail Fly until his fingers bled. He confessed that it was the only song he knew how to play. His grandfather had taught it to him when he was eleven. When he finally put the banjo away, the gathering disbursed with smiling faces and bright 'Cheerios.'

"His cloth sack had fallen beside the bench and was soaked. He took soggy papers out of it and grinned as he threw sack and papers into a trash bin. 'The last thing these unfortunate people need is two dour scholars asking them questions that have no answers.' So said he to put an end to our best laid plans. I tossed my dripping box of books into the same bin.

"Just keep them smiling, Sir Laughs-a-lot. " I told him. "We'll find some answers."

"We found a bed and breakfast near the market. The next day we bought rickety old bicycles and began working from sunup to sunset, visiting people as far as twenty miles from where we boarded. Rabun slowly increased his number of banjo tunes. We often stopped at village pubs where we began to get robust greetings. "'Give us a song, Yank!'" "'A song, Yank, a song."

"I can admit to you now, RD. I have never felt more proud than when I heard their parting comments. "'A rum fella, that Yank. No flies on him.'" "'Best ever.'"

"What a wonderful man!" RD popped upright, unable to contain his enthusiasm. "I wish I could meet him. Do you know what happened to him?"

"You're jumping ahead of me, RD. "I was told when I came home that he was killed when a German U-boat sank a transport ship on his return voyage to America. I later learned that he was thought to be alive but lost somewhere in Europe during the war years. After so many years I gave up all hope of seeing him again."

"Ohhh, Thera. It breaks my heart to know you've had to live all this time without him."

"No, RD. Every moment I have ever shared with him has been a blessing."

"You've told me enough to know that he was irreplaceable in your heart. What it was like when you were missing him so much? Did you have intimate thoughts about him? Were you aroused by your memories of him?"

"RD, some feelings are just too personal and private to discuss with anybody. Especially at your age. I will say there is more to our story. Perhaps I'll tell you more details when you're older and wiser."

"OK. But, please tell me more about the time you were together in England and what you saw."

"Well, we made a pact between us that first day in Ely that we would never look sad in public, an agreement that was often hard to keep because of what we saw.

"We saw laborers with hard sinewy muscles go frail and weak as they shared their meager
nourishment with London's rosy-cheeked children.

"We saw famished eyes swell with compassion as the hunger they knew so well spread thin and gaunt across childish cheekbones, draining the very blood of life from them. And..good God!...they seemed to age before our very eyes.

"We saw America's glorious gifts come into overcrowded cottages. Wonderful, life-sustaining meat, to heat in its own little can over a peat fire.

"We saw pots, pans, wedding rings, oil, gas, and coal poured into their beloved isle's freedom fire. We knew that this, too, was nothing more than a morale booster, but we joined in praise for a local farmer who loved to tell about throwing his belt buckle into that faint flame which must out burn the hell being spread across the world by unimaginably satanic Nazi forces."'Even gave up my good 'ol brassie.'"

"But, my greatest memory of all is the evening when we rode our bikes all the way to Cambridge for an event that we had talked about for months. It turned bitterly cold, and we arrived totally exhausted and shivering, but elated to be on time. As we parked our bikes we heard a lost child crying behind a row of hedges.

"Never has there been a more gallant Knight mounting a more noble steed than when my dear love McTanis lifted the skimpily-dressed child from the cold cobblestone, wrapped it in his scarf and coat, and sat it in his big basket and pedaled his wobbling bicycle up the hill to find her house. Later that night, he told me how he found the child's home where distraught parents had spent hours looking for her."

"RD, while he was gone, I sat alone on a dank pew in an ancient cathedral to hear the timeless beauty of a boy's choir. As I left the quaint old church, icy fingers interlocked mine as Rabun excitedly told me that he had heard the end of the program, from outside the massive doors, that he would not dare enter for fear of disturbing the magical sounds." The rain has slowed to a soft patter and they are so still that they can hear it on the tin roof. Her face is aglow with a gentle, faint smile that suggests just a hint of inner peace

"Until that moment, RD, I had never dreamed that such love could enter my dull life."

Chapter 34:
If You Got The Money, Honey

Irene Paylo Franklin never dreamed that so much money could enter her dull life.

At the very moment we leave Thera and RD sitting in the swing, TJ is drinking coffee with Irene and explaining that she is the sole legal heir to the fortune Rayford recently inherited.

"Rayford has spent less than ten thousand dollars of the money, Irene. I can't imagine what he did with it. Has he made any new purchases for the farm?"

"Nothing, nothing, nothing. Not a thing that I know about." Irene is thinking hard about the money and she is worried about doing right with it. "I do know that he's been doin' some hard gambling. He's been drinking heavy and playing poker a lot lately. That's what he'd been doin'that night Bobby had to kill him to stop his mean-ness." She kept her rocker at a slow even pace. "TJ, I want to do all I can for Ida Maye's boy, Bobby. Can some of this money get him out of jail?"

"I don't believe we can buy his way out of this mess, but we do have a fine Governor with the power to release him early. He's a good friend of Miss Thera and I know she'll put in a good word for Bobby. Establishing his financial security would surely make a more convincing case for Bobby's successful prospects when he gets out."

"What about giving him this farm?"

"That could add more stability to his prospects for the future.

"Do it, TJ. I want to move into town. It's so lonesome out here by myself."

Chapter 35:
PPFFTT!

"It makes me sad to know how lonesome you must have been for so many years. Life has been so unkind to you, Thera." RD said softly.

"No, RD. Life has been very good to me. Life was unkind to your friend, Roy. He only had thirteen years of it. Life was unkind to your mother; she only had twenty-one years. Life was also unkind to my mother. She had seventy-one years, but most of them were sad and lonely. No, life has been good to me. I have been loved in the richest way, by a kind father, by a man who has always respected me for what I am, and by you."

"Everybody respects you, Thera. Everybody."

"Yes, they do. That is why I know I'll never die alone. The only person who did not respect me was....was...."

"Your father?"

"No! Rayford Franklin was not my father. He was an evil man who did nothing more than plant the seed. His mate should have been a Black Widow to kill him after the act. Nathan Fulton has been my father since I was born and, after all these years, he shall remain my father to me always." Thera spoke firmly then paused to think of Nathan. "Never forget that every day we spend in this world is a gift, RD."

RD is thinking that if Ida Maye had killed Rayford, he would not have hurt Thera.. But there would be no TJ either. And, without Rayford, there would be no Thera. Wow!....just think of the people who would not be here if there had been no Rayford.

Thera is pondering how she would look if Nathan had sown her seed. She had often wondered how such a handsome man, and a woman as beau-

135

tiful as the young Ida Maye Addison, could produce an offspring with her looks.

"Oh, I almost forgot...." RD was hesitant to change the subject.

"Forgot what?"

"Nothing important... I just wanted to tell you about the dream I had last night."

"Please tell me. What did you dream about?" Thera coaxed with eager eyes.

"Everybody was in a large group photograph...like the ones from school... except much bigger." He stood up and spread his arms wide. "Some of them were seated. Others stood behind them. And some were kneeling in front. My father sat in the center with my mother standing behind him with her hand on his shoulder. They were the same as in the fair picture, except there were no wrinkles and my father's face was complete; nothing peeled off."

"What did he look like?" Thera teases him. Of course, she knows his father's image quiet well from seeing him often while he and Carol shared her home.

"He had dark brown hair..." RD continued with what Thera saw as his self description.

"And large light brown eyes, just like yours?" Thera added with a smile. His father had looked a lot like him.

"No. His eyes were just like yours, Thera." When she didn't correct him he went on. "While I
was studying his face, my father just disappeared from the picture... then my mother.... then Grandpa Nathan... then Victor...then Ned....Roy, then Rayford Franklin..."

"I was hoping he wasn't in the picture."

"Thera, everybody I have ever seen was in it. Even people I've seen only in pictures. And they just kept disappearing one by one. At first I thought it was only the people who are dead. Then Bobby disappeared, and Sammy, and Clyde....Nub....Daniel...."

"Let me guess. I bet the last one...the only one left, was Katheline. Am I right?"

"No. She went too. She was not the last one, but I felt horrible when she did. I cried so hard I couldn't see the picture for awhile."

"RD! You were dreaming!" Thera laughed.

"But that's the way I was dreaming. It seemed so real. And everybody was just going PPFFTT and leaving a fuzzy white spot where they had been. I mean everybody.....Becky...PPFFTT...Fred... PPFFTT..."

"Did I go PPFFTT?"

"Yes, you were the last one. Then all that was left was fuzzy white paper. What do you think the dream means, Thera?"

"I don't know, RD. What do you think it means?"

"Well, I can understand the dead ones PPFFTTing but not those who are still alive and kicking. And, people I haven't seen for a long time could have PPFFTTed because they aren't around anymore. I guess they might as well be dead as far as I'm concerned..."

"No, no, no! Because they might just PPFFTT back in on you at any time." Thera was enjoying his stimulating imagination. 'Does a falling tree make noise if there is no one to hear it?' She remembers an enduring question from a college philosophy course.

RD walks to the edge of the porch and puts his hand under water dripping from the roof. Katheline had her arm out this way when she got into the car. Those were tears on her face! He turned to Thera.

"I miss Katheline so much it hurts and she just left."

"It is hard to be away from people you love."

"It must be even harder to lose the people you love. PPFFTT - just like that."

"The secret is to never give them up. I don't. I sit with them in this swing on rainy evenings such as this. I can close my eyes and see Nathan sitting right here watching me gardening in those very flowerbeds. My other Raybun was here with me when I was telling you about him. Nobody can ever take him away from me."

"Yeah, nobody can ever take Katheline away from me, or take her place, just like your Mister McTanis."

"RD, you're the first person I've heard call him Mister McTanis. He would be amused to hear that." She chuckled. "Of course, it didn't take much to amuse him."

"It's good to hear you laugh."

"He made me laugh a lot, RD. I called him Sir Laughs-A-Lot and he called me Lady Greyeyes. Can you imagine such names?"

"Yes. It's perfect for you." He dropped to one knee in an exaggerated bow. "Your court awaits you, Lady Greyeyes."

`Thera actually blushed as she smiled down at him mischievously.

"That's just the sort of thing he would do." She wipes a tear from the corner of her eye. "See? You just PPFFTTed him back to me for a moment."

"Well, I shall PPFFTT him away..." RD snaps his fingers. "He's had his share of your time tonight." He becomes suddenly serious. "I am happy that one person stayed the same after all we learned from that ledger."

She waits.

"I'm glad I've still got my Aunt Thera."

"So am I, RD..." She beams. "So am I."

"I have a confession to make. I found out that TJ was your son from the Bible foldout."

"You never fooled me for a moment." She shakes her head. "I knew precisely why you were snooping in my Bible. By the way, Daniel is the only person

I know who misquotes the Twenty-Third Psalms with 'Yea tho I walk through the shadow of death...' instead of 'the valley of the shadow of death...' She tries to look stern, but her mood is far too good for scolding. "I also have a confession to make. My mother wrote to me over the years she was away. I already knew most of what was in that ledger long before I saw it."

"I wondered about her. The ledger said Nathan ran her off in 1923 and the Bible said she died that same year. I guessed Nathan considered her dead as far as he was concerned. Where was she all these years?"

"I didn't know where she was until Nathan died. She came back here after his funeral. She was Bobby's mother."

"Holy cow!"

"She never put a return address on her letters. She told me that she would stop cars and ask them to mail them when they got were they were going."

"Did Nathan see the letters?"

"I hid them from him for years, in the attic above my closet. I should have burned them. He found them when he went into the attic to fasten those stupid lightening rods."

"Then he knew all about Rayford and Ida Maye?"

"Yes, and it hurt him really bad."

"I'm surprised he didn't kill Rayford."

"Oh, he would have killed him for what he did to me alone. But he was so afraid."

"Why was he afraid of him?"

"Oh No. That's not what I meant. He wasn't the least bit afraid of Rayford Franklin or any other mortal man. The fear Nathan had was for the wrath of God. He truly believed he would spend eternity in hell if he broke a commandment - Thou Shalt Not Kill. It was also easier for him to obey while Rayford was in prison. Nathan died only four years after Rayford Franklin came back to Woosterville."

"Nathan was a fine man, Thera, I've been thinking about how much we learned from that ledger."

"Are you trying to tell me that you finally understand the importance of recorded history?"

"Precisely."

"Then I suggest that you describe this historic day in the diary I gave you. I can think of no better way to record the day you learned of love."

"OK, I'll try it. Do you want to come inside with me?"

"No. You go ahead. The magic of a personal diary comes from expressing your most private thoughts and not sharing them with anybody. I want to sit here alone for awhile."

"To ponder your private thoughts?"

"Precisely."

"Just remember, if you're thinking of me those thoughts won't be private, because you'll PPFFTT me here with you."

"RD, you amaze me."

"Good." He left her smiling.

Chapter 36:
They Paint Dry Flowers

Becky stands on the bank in front of Thera's house waiting and watching for the dusty old station wagon to make its daily appearance around the bend near the Franklin house. She holds her breath as it comes into view and smiles eagerly as it slows and pulls off the road to put something into the mailbox marked F.B. Sanders.

She vaults down the side of the bank with her right foot plowing a trail until she pushes off with it near the bottom. She sprints to the mailbox and eagerly draws the letter from it.

It is a pamphlet extolling the accomplishments of Georgia's Governor, signed by Jack Fisher.

She crumples it and sticks it in her pocket.

She has not heard from Daniel since he left for Army basic training more than ten weeks ago. She has the sinking feeling that a Greyhound bus has taken him out of her life forever. So much has happened since Daniel got on that bus!

She is divorced. It is not easy.

Becky turns to gaze at the stark house she now hates. Nothing will grow around that house. She worked hard with trees, shrubs, grass and flowers; but everything dried up and fizzled out in the parched red clay.

The yard has not been watered since she left the house for good more than two weeks ago. The sun has baked it into a hard shell that cracks and curls occasionally, reminding her of dried lipstick peeling from chapped and swollen skin.

Becky touches her bruised lips tenderly - a slow healing reminder of her final showdown with Fred. She got her licks in. He still has claw marks on his face and the bout convinced him not to try her again. But he had raped her, and a woman can never even that score.

***

"Bobby, I want you to know that we all feel you've got a raw deal." Clyde picks up Bobby at the state prison and is driving him home a free man. "You've got a fresh start now, Bobby. As a good friend and as a Deputy Sheriff, I'm hoping that you can forget the past and get on with your life."

"Don't worry about me, Buddy. I've had a long time to think about my life, Clyde. He squeezes the patch on Clyde's starched uniform sleeve. "I've spent the last day I'll ever spend behind bars. I still can't understand how TJ managed to get me title to the Franklin farm, but it's just the break I need. I'm ready to settle down, Buddy. You'll have no trouble with me."

They rode without talking until they passed the store, where he asked Clyde to let him walk from here. "I just want to get the feel of being here."

"Sure thing, Bobby. Here's your keys. I'll stop by tomorrow to see how you're doing."

"Thanks for everything....Deputy Addison." Bobby grins and gives a firm handshake.

"You're quite welcome....Farmer Riley." Clyde watches him walk toward the farm from the store.

As Bobby walks below the red clay bank, passing Thera's house, he sees Becky kneeling in front of the prefab house and crosses the road. As he draws near her, he sees that there are tears in her eyes as she looks down at a moisture-starved mum stalk that is so limp that its two flowers and three unopened buds are drooping to the ground. "Perhaps it will still grow if replanted in good soil." He says softly.

"Bobby!" She springs to her feet and impulsively throws her arms around him. "You scared the daylights out of me. When did you get home?"

"Just now. You're the first person I've seen since Clyde picked me up at the prison." he ran a rough finger gently below her bruised lips. "You look awful, Becky. What happened to you?"

"You think I look bad, you ought 'ta see the other guy." The old life is coming back into her eyes. "I had one hell of a fight for my freedom....but I won."

"Does that mean you've divorced the bastard that did that to you?"

"That's what it means."

"Well, well...How about the two of us celebrating our freedom together?"

"Bobby, that's the best offer I've had in years." She smiles and winces when it hurts her lips.

Bobby kneels and digs up the mum stalk with his hands. "If I'm gonna be a farmer, I suppose I need to learn how to plant. I was just on my way to look at the farm."

Becky locks arms with him. "I'm afraid you've got a lot of work to do. The place has really grown up since Irene moved into town."

They cross the road and take the trail toward the back of the Franklin house. The grass in the back yard is calf-high. Bobby looks for a place to plant the mum stalk, and walks to Roy's grave marker. He sticks a broken limb from a nearby tree in the ground in front of the grave. Then he digs a hole in front of the limb, presses the rich moist soil around the dehydrated stalk, and props the flowers in its forks.

Becky goes to the new well and returns with a pint bottle full of fresh water. "Rayford drinks 'em and Irene saves the bottles." She carefully pours it around the stalk.

By morning, as pauses to admire its recovery. the mum stalk is rising straight and strong to greet the new day. This night has put new life in Becky and her lovely flower. The dawn is breaking as she walks briskly up the low end of the bank and follows the trail at the top of it to Thera's house. She steps lively to the house and bounds up the porch steps two at a time.

Chapter 37:
One Dying

Fred Sanders is being especially finicky this early morning. He wants every detail to be perfect. He set his alarm for precisely 2 am and awoke to shut it off at 1:45. He has four five gallon cans of gas in his trunk. He has a twelve gauge shell in his shotgun on the back seat of his car. He leaves an audio cassette tape in the car's player. It is set on pause. All he must do is hit play before he cuts off the engine, and it will start playing as soon as Becky turns the key, to move his car tomorrow. He puts his insurance policy in the mailbox outside her house.

He is ready. He takes the gas cans and shotgun inside the house. He parks the car a safe distance away. He enters the house and props his gun against the arm of his favorite recliner. Then he empties all five of the gas cans around the house. He pours almost a full can directly on his chair and sits down in it. Then he panics!

He suddenly realizes that he doesn't have a match! He searches frantically throughout the house and is thrilled to find a small box in a drawer under a table with a large candle on it.

He gets back in his chair, reclines it, places the gun between his knees with the barrel under his chin, takes out two matches, strikes them and lights the chair arm. Then he calmly feels for the trigger, closes his eyes, and pulls it. Right on time!

Thera reported the fire to Clyde. By the time he arrived leading two fire trucks, there is no need to put out the fire since the house is totally destroyed. Becky never hears his tape. Clyde gets in the car to move it out of the way of one of the fire trucks. As soon as he turns the key, he hears the voice of Roger

143

Miller playing on the tape.

> *"Well, I think I've found a sure fire way to forget.*
> *It's so simple. I'm surprised I haven't though of it yet.*
> *All it takes is, One dying and a burial.*
> *Some sighing, some crying, and six carrying me.*
> *I wanta be free."*

"Clyde fast-forwards the tape and Hank Williams is singing:

> *"We met in the springtime when blossoms unfold*
> *The pastures were green and the meadows were gold*
> *Our love was in flower as summer grew on*
> *Her love like the leaves now has withered and gone.*
> *The darkness is falling, the sky has turned gray*
> *A hound in the distance is starting to bay*
> *I wonder, I wonder - what she's thinking of*
> *Forsaken, forgotten - without any love."*

Clyde plays the tape for the Sheriff and they decide that the "sicko" Fred had staged it just to hurt Becky. They agreed that Becky had been hurt enough and destroyed it.

Chapter 38:
Over There

An old woman and a young man sit on the steps of the Lincoln Memorial, she to catch her breath and he to read a letter. People pass close to him as they go up and down the steps. Pigeons land to his left, very near the woman. She kicks a foot and they scatter, some taking to the air, then returning.

"Why do they keep coming back?" She complains in a loud voice as if demanding an answer from the stranger in the expensive three-piece suit. "There's nothing on these steps, but us."

"Perhaps they enjoy our company." TJ looks up and smiles.

"They annoy the hell out of me. That's what they do. Shoo!"

A single pigeon waddles back toward her as the others retreat. He shifts his tail feathers and deposits a milky splotch on the cement. The old woman ignores the dropping which, for some strange reason, reminds TJ of a map of a nasty little spot on the world map that is of no interest to most Americans.

He takes a letter from his breast pocket and removes a letter from an envelope with the seal of the President of the United States on it.

***

I completed Speciality Training last month (Combat Arms Infantry). I'm try-ing to get into the Green Berets. I have just completed three weeks of jump school at Fort Bragg and I hope to get into the 5th or 7th Special Forces Group if they accept me. Special Forces training takes about a year. I'm anxious to get started so I'm not taking leave. The next time you see me I hope to be wear-ing a Green Beret. Sincerely yours, Private Daniel Fulton, US Army

Satisfied with his letter, Daniel looks up as a company of 'boots' march past where he is sitting on the steps of the barracks.

"Get in step you CRUDDY LEGS!" He barks an imitation of his paratrooper drill sergeant, and smiles when the entire company changes step.

Daniel takes another look at his letter. 'Mom won't understand about any of this military stuff.' He crumples it. He remembers how sharp Clyde looked in his Deputy Sheriff's uniform.. 'I suppose by now he's probably married to that pretty girl who is such a good artist.'

**

Chapter 39:
Save the Last Dance

Rachel Souquet could draw before she learned to write and she was making impressive free-hand sketches from the drawings of the great masters during her pre-school years. The paintings she did as a child were as accomplished as those of many well-known artists.

Rachel's father is an expert embalmer who recognized her talent and encouraged her keen interest in his work. She assisted him at the Souquet Funeral home from the time she turned eight years old.

"Daddy, can I put on the makeup?" Her eagerness was matched by her ability.

Rachel was fascinated by the art of reconstructing facial features that are destroyed by accident or disease. She digested her father's reference books on sculpture, cosmetology, plastic surgery, and hair styling. She spent long hours in the lab experimenting with waxes, plaster, cements and cosmetics until she developed her skills until she was much better with women's faces than her father. For the last few years she has done the facial work on all the female bodies requiring major restructuring. Rachel is also an exceptional observer. She looks at the local people with an eye for details that could be useful should they end up disfigured in the mortuary

Her father has only one strict rule - she is not allowed to work on male bodies.

***

At this moment, Rachel's eyes are working over the male body seated across from her in English class. 'He seems to mold himself to his surroundings; as comfortable in that stiff desk as most people are in an easy chair. His movements are effortless as he rolls to his feet and steps smoothly across the room, his gait fast but not rushed. His build is trim and slender, strong but not muscular like Clyde.'

Rachel's eyes follow RD to where he waits in line at the pencil sharpener at the far side of the room. 'He rests knuckles on hip and shifts his weight to one leg. The fingers holding the pencil are curled; his wrist slightly bent, reminiscent of the hand of Michelangelo's David. The girl before him turns and looks too long. She is absorbed by his energy and confidence, the way his facial expression is accentuated by the movement of his loose jointed body. Embarrassed by her attention, he smiles and turns to the pencil sharpener.'

Rachel watches him return to his seat. 'He has light brown eyes and thick lashes. His hair is dark brown and he has a habit of running his hand through it when he is lost in thought, and sometimes he chews a knuckle when he is concentrating. Like now, he is hunting a word in a dictionary.'

RD is looking up the word travesty. From that root word, he amuses himself by creating a definition of the name of the Governor's hometown. 'Traveston - an exaggerated or grotesque imitation of a very large quantity of anything. Appropriate enough, since there isn't much there other than the most important person in the whole wide world - Katheline Fisher.'

RD is to attend the summer session at Traveston College. The very thought of staying in Katheline's town is delicious, to be savored. He looks up at Rachel and catches her staring at him. She does not look away, but bites her lower lip then runs her tongue slowly over it. She holds her gaze as if she is unaware that he is returning her stare.

Rachel has asked him to take her to the prom and he eagerly accepted. She wants Clyde to take her but he has to be on duty. With all the kids out celebrating it's sure to be a busy night for the Sheriff's boys. Some nasty little mind wrote 'Rachel puts out" on the wall in the boy's bathroom after she was seen with Sammy Paylo. RD has never heard Sammy talk about her, and he sure talks about all the other girls he knows that put out.

All RD is sure about Rachel is that he likes being with her. She is fun. He has never dated her, but he did sit with her at the movie one Saturday. She let him work a hand under her sweater where he found a big mound of reality. It's been a long time since anybody has joked about her large breasts being falsies. 'Perhaps the other boys are finally outgrowing their childish jokes? Perhaps they all know better from first hand experience?'

What he doesn't know is that at this very moment Rachel is trying to think of a way to get free of Sammy Paylo for good.

Chapter 40:
Let Me Go, Lover

Now that Rachel has met Clyde, she wants nothing more to do with Sammy. The immediate problem is how to get around Sammy's insane jealousy long enough for her and RD to enjoy their prom date. "'I don't want any part of that kid stuff.'" Sammy told her when she mentioned the prom to him. "'All we need is a drive-in, my Impala, and a six pack.'" As a second thought, he held up a round gold foil package. "'And one or two of these.'"

Her greatest fear is that Sammy and his vulgar talk will ruin what she has with Clyde.

**

"Careful, don't mash the flower." Thera pushed RD back a little and blushed from the energetic hug he gave her as he thanked her for letting him use her car. "Have a good time. If I'm asleep when you come in, wake me and tell me all about how the prom night goes."

**

Going in opposite directions, two cars pass in the heart of Woosterville. RD honks the horn of the Pontiac and waves to the driver of the Impala convertible. The square is well lit with spotlights shining on a cascading water fountain making it easy for RD to see Sammy driving with the top down.

RD stops for the streetlight on the next corner. In his rear view mirror, he sees Sammy make a sharp U-turn back in his direction. The light changes and RD slowly accelerates as Sammy pulls close behind him, motioning frantically for him to pull over.

RD turns left down a narrow side street that drops sharply to railroad tracks at the foot of the hill. He stops at the curb in front of a pool hall, shuts off the engine, and swings out of the car. Sammy skids to a halt just behind him and swings over the unopened door of his rag top.

"Hey, kid. Whatdaya mean foolin' with my girl?" He keeps his distance moving in an arc in front of RD with one hand in the pocket of his wind breaker. "You've got a big set of balls, RD."

"You got it all wrong, Sammy. I know you've dated Rachel, but I didn't know she was your girl. And I'm not foolin' with her. I'm taking her to the prom, that's all. Why do you think I'm in this getup? Shit, man. You know what a prom's like."

"I think you're full of shit, RD. That's what I think. But your monkey suit gives me an idea. You won't be going to the prom if I mess that suit up...will you now?" He draws the hand from his pocket, and RD hears the sharp click, then glimpses the flashes of reflections from the blinking neon pool sign.

"For Christ sake, Sammy, are you still playing with that stupid knife? Talk about kid stuff..."

"Don't get smart ass with me, RD!" Sammy steps forward with lightening speed, grabs the leg of RD's trousers, and whips a sharp clean cut about eight inches long down the front of it.

RD makes no attempt to move. His eyes look hard into Sammy's without flinching.

"Now that was really dumb. What do you think Thera's gonna say when she sees these pants? She rented them for me." RD has a hurt look on his face.

Sammy closes the knife and looks down at it. For a moment, it seems that he might drop it, but he slips it back into his pocket.

"OK, RD. I got a deal for you. You take Rachel to that silly-assed prom, but when it's over I'm gonna be waiting for her at the Red Oak, see? You're gonna bring her and then she goes with me. You dig?" Sammy's meanest expression was touched by the doubt that maybe it won't work on somebody who isn't afraid of his switchblade. "Whatdaya say, RD? Deal?"

RD surveyed the damage to his pants. "The first thing I gotta do is take care of this shit. Then I'm sure as hell going to take Rachel to the dance. After that I'll be happy to bring her out to the Red Oak, if she wants to go, we'll see you out there. It's up to her if she wants to go with you. As far as I'm concerned, your manners need some work, Sammy, and don't kid yourself into thinking that you're ever going to tell me what to do."

Sammy stands in the street and watches RD drive away. He enters the pool room and orders a beer. Then he takes his favorite cue stick from a long rack.

"Anybody in here want a money game?" He mashes the chalk so hard on the cue tip that he breaks the cube.

***

The sheriff's car turns into the semi-circular, tree-lined driveway across the road from the funeral home. As Clyde stops beside the high porch, Irene gets off the swing and walks down the wide steps to meet him.

"He's in the shed out back." She walks past him to lead the way. "I hate to give him up, Son. He's good company. The folks across the street have got a bitch dog that's been barking all night since I moved in here with him." She opens the shed and the dog runs out wagging his tail and jumping up on Clyde who pets him playfully.

"He's sure grown since the last time I saw him."

"Yeah, he's a big dog and he's gonna get a lot bigger." Irene slips a lease on the dog's collar and hands it to Clyde. "I'd appreciate it if you'd stop by now and then so I can have a look at him"

"I'll be happy to do that...." Clyde has no difficulty getting the dog into the back of his patrol car. He bounds in and sits upright on the seat as soon as the door is open, as if waiting for his master to take the wheel.

"My, my...just look at that. He seems right at home with you, Clyde."

"How do you like your new home, Irene?"

"It's fine...just fine. Good neighbors." She points across the road with a gnarled finger. The Souquets live over there."

"Yeah, their daughter, Rachel is my girl friend. RD is taking her to the prom tonight. I'm on duty and can't go."

"Well, how about that?" She smiles and claps her hands. "You can leave your dog with me when you take Rachel out on a date... or anytime you come to visit the Souquets."

***

The Souquets live in one of the best houses in Woosterville. Their estate, including the large grounds of the funeral home, is the largest privately owned plot of land inside the city limits. The entry leading up to the high-columned main entrance to the funeral parlor is almost a mirror image of the one in front of Irene's new house. Another tree-lined drive to the right leads to a bright-white colonial home with an expansive rich green lawn. All of the grounds are beautifully landscaped and impressively maintained.

As RD steps out of the car, an Irish Setter runs to him with her tongue hanging out and tail wagging briskly. He pats the friendly dog and gets her back on all fours, but her paw leaves a streak of red mud near the tear on his pants leg. He wets his handkerchief with his tongue and dabs at the stain ineffectively.

Mrs. Souquet is watching him from a large window. When she opens the door for him she is smiling and shaking her head. "I must apologize for Red. She's so affectionate that she just can't control herself." She brushes aside the hand he holds over the tear. "Oh, my. Your pants are torn. Come in and let me have a look. Rachel's not quite ready. You go in here." She ushers him into a small room. "Take them off and hand them out to me. I'm slow as Christmas with a needle and thread, but perhaps I can repair them suitably for tonight." As she closes the door, she mumbles in a half whisper. "We must take care of our appearance."

RD is amazed by her choice of words. The caretaker's wife? ...Mortician, undertaker, embalmer....What is the correct title? Which would Mister Souquet prefer? Best not to ask about his work, RD decides as he hands her his pants through the cracked door.

RD sits on a flowered sofa and eyes the contents of Rachel's study. One wall is covered with bookshelves filled with often-read books. Dog-eared, worn covers, many torn and stained, the books have nothing to boast about but their titles – <u>War & Peace, Catcher In The Rye, Pride & Prejudice, Crime & Punishment, Of Human Bondage, The Way Of All Flesh, A Farewell To Arms, The Great Gatsby, The Fountainhead, The Complete Works Of Shakespeare and many others.</u>

RD is struck by the quality of the selections. Almost all of his favorite books are among them. They seem the kind of reading that appeals mostly to male readers, especially here in Woosterville, where most women are discouraged from any interest that is not related to being a wife, mother or housekeeper. He thumbs through various selections and finds extensive notes in the margins. He recognizes the almost illegible handwriting as Rachel's from her signing his yearbook.

Stacked on a small roll top desk under a curtained window, are thick sheaves of papers covered with the same handwriting. He picks up a few of the top pages and returns to the sofa.

Above the sofa are three of Rachel's sketches in simple frames. RD recognizes them instantly; Michelangelo's study of drapery for a kneeling woman, Leonardo Di Vinci's drawings of women's heads, and Renoir's nude study for 'The Bathers.'

He is having difficulty reading the papers. Her rapid hand flows so freely that it leaves some letters by the wayside in her attempt to jot down just enough for her to recall key thoughts at a later time. He is able to piece a few of her ideas together from the pages:

"What a comfort to have friends who seek nothing, ask nothing, and are there when needed with a kind word and gentle smile at times when others are demanding from you and you have nothing to give. A fine young man has agreed to escort me to the prom, without questioning my boldness in asking him nor making me feel that I owe him in return..." RD skips further discussion of himself because he did not expect it and feels uncomfortable reading it without her permission. He leafs through a few pages then sees two more names he recognizes - Teresa Brewer and Sammy Paylo.

"You made me weep, cut me deep, I can't sleep, Lover.
I was cursed from the first day we met."

'Yeah, he wanted to cut me deep, too." RD amuses himself with the thought, and reads on.

"How can a person with the ambitions I have be torn apart by a man such as Sammy Paylo? What is it about him that brings out the worst of my animal passion? I behave like Red with him. I seem to have no self control. I find him crude and vulgar but I can't bring myself to get rid of him. I simply cannot understand my own attraction to him. Now that I have a man I love, I must prevent him from coming between Clyde and me."

RD is startled by a rap on the door. He quickly puts the papers back on the desktop and opens the door just enough to peek around it as Rachel smiles and hands him his pants.

"Your trousers, Sir." She makes a mock bow and RD's eyes caress the solid mounds straining to burst free of the V neckline of her formal evening gown. The hand that shyly covers his privates impulsively grips them. He composes himself and takes the pants. Before closing the door, he takes another delicious look at her.

"You look sensational, Rachel!" Her eyes tell him she knows he means it. Her makeup is expertly applied and her face is like a Breck girl he once saw in one of Thera's ladies magazines. Her gown is soft turquoise and flows in pleats from her small waist over layered crinolines to the floor.

RD dresses quickly and they chat with her parents for a few minutes. Then RD remembers the flower he left on the seat of the car and excuses himself to get it. Mrs. Souquet steps outside with him to call the dog.

Her parents watch with pride as he pins the orchid on the dainty lace that covers Rachel's shoulders and sweeps over her abundant breasts.

Chapter 41:
My Buckets Got A Hole In It

CC Paylo often rides his old bike up and down the highway collecting junk he finds alongside the road. Now and then he stops as he passes "Homebrew Annie's" shack and buys a quart of her brew. Tonight, his big find is a galvanized bucket that has been tossed in a ditch because it has a hole in the bottom as big as a fifty cent coin. The twisted wire basket on his bike is already full and when he manages to get the bucket tucked in among his treasures, he decides to pour the beer in it so he can urinate in the quart jar and put the cap back on it so he can add it to his collection when he gets home. While he is peeing in the jar, the beer runs out of the bucket down over his front tire and seeps into the grass. As he goes on down the road, he discovers the bucket has a hole in it, and he starts singing an old song about somebody else with the same problem as him. He was very thirsty when he got the beer and now it is gone and he is really dry.

"Dry as a bone...dry as a bone...dry as a bone..." CC keeps repeating aloud as he peddles his rusty bike up to where Nub sits on his bench about to enjoy his first pint of the evening. The old bucket is still in the loaded basket and it blocks the dim unsteady light mounted on the handlebars.

The light is powered by a small drive shaft rubbing against the front tire that is wet. Nub is laughing at CC trying to keep his top heavy bike balanced as he hits the gravel with his light going on and off haphazardly. When he sees Nub, CC just hops off the bike and lets it fall to the ground. He then speaks to Nub. "Dry as a bone...Dry as a Bone...Dry as a bone..."

"You want a drink, CC?" Nub offers him his bottle.

154

CC looks at the clear liquid and smiles. "Dry as a bone..." He turns it up, takes a long gulp, then begins to gag, cough, sputter and spit. "Sjash shaa.....sjaah...shas....sjash shaa.." He throws the bottle to the ground in bewilderment, sticks out his chin, and gives Nub his best indignent smirk.

"Damn, CC, I thought you wanted a drink. Shame to waste good stuff like that." Nub watches CC put his stuff back in the basket and wobble away to check the ditch far down the road.

***

Rachel senses an uneasy silence in the car. She bends forward and clicks on the radio.

"You're gonna need an ocean of calamine lotion. You'll be scratching like a hound, the minute you start to mess around..."

"I saw Sammy tonight, Rachel."

"Poison ivyeeeeeee...." She turns the radio down very low and shifts to face him. Her crinolines swing up and he glimpses her creamy thigh for a brief moment.

"He stopped me as I came through town. He was mad as hell about me taking you to the prom."

"I knew he would be. I do hope I haven't caused you any trouble." She bit her lower lip.

"No... I'm glad you want me to take you." RD keeps his eyes on the road as he makes a turn near a makeshift produce stand. "I told him we'd come out to the Red Oak after the dance. He wants you to go with him then. I told him that was up to you."

"Well, I can tell you right now. I'm your date tonight. That is if you want me?" She turns off the radio and waits for his reply.

"I sure do want you, Rachel...." He blurts out, then flushes. "I mean..."

She leans over and puts her hand over the wrist of the one he is using to steer. 'I know what you mean, RD." She smiles and rubs his hand. He makes her feel so good about herself.

Chapter 42:
No Call. No Win.

"I hate to admit it, but you're too good for me." Sammy grins and turns to put away his cue stick. "I've had enough."

"I'll spot you five balls."

"Five balls? You're kidding."

"Five balls."

"You're on. Lag for break."

Lucky wins the break and makes a straight run to the eight ball. He taps his stick in the pocket across the table. "Eight ball in the right side pocket." He smoothly strokes the cue sending the eight ball straight into the center of the hole.

Sammy hands him a five dollar bill. "I know when I'm licked. I can't beat that kind of shooting."

"Are you gonna quit on your break? You get the five free balls after you break and you can pick them."

"Rack 'em."

Sammy makes a good break. He carefully selects the free balls and Lucky puts them in pockets. He has two more easy shots before the eight ball and it is sitting right in front of a corner pocket. He takes his time and makes all three balls.

"You didn't call the eight ball." Lucky protests.

"It was set up right in the pocket."

"Don't matter. You didn't call it. Rules is rules. Right, Doc?"

"You gotta call the eight ball. No call. No win." Doc Jacobus is the final word on rules. He owns the place.

"But everybody in here knew where I meant to shoot it..."
"No call. No win."

***

RD holds Rachel's sweet-scented body so close that he can feel her supple breasts rise and fall against his chest. His tent is safely buried in her thick crinolines as they sway slowly, on the crowded dance floor, to the beat of every song played, regardless of tempo. When the last dance is announced, he mentally focuses on counting the crowd until his tent collapses.

As they leave the school parking lot, Rachel slides close beside him and rests her hand playfully on his leg. Her touch makes his flesh tingle under the smooth material and his tent begins to rise.

Rachel seems to know just the moment she must break contact, let him squirm uncomfortably for awhile, then drop her fingertips once more to trace the sewn line where his pants had been cut. Each time she stops he feel as if he will explode.

RD feels that he must get to a bathroom. He passes nothing as they drive across the corner of town through scattered homes and closed businesses. He pulls into the large parking lot of the public library and stops at the rear corner under a massive elm tree which shadows the car making it hardly visible in the dark.

"You'll have to excuse me, Rachel. I've just got to take a whizz." He eyes the neatly trimmed hedges lining the park directly ahead of them.

"It's not a whizz you need, RD." She drops her hand smack dab in the center of his pants and RD's entire body tightens. He trembles at the very thought of her making contact .He can't believe it!

'She is actually digging into my underwear!'

***

"There ain't no money in digging, Lucky. All hole diggers oughta have CC's name - Paylo. They all get paid low." Nub takes his bottle back from Lucky and downs another long drink and snorts. "I make more money in one good day selling hooch than I ever made in a good week when I was digging holes."

"I'd say it depends on what you're diggin'."

"Well I tried most of it. Betcha didn't know I dug a few graves, didja? Used to not pay as much as wells. Course, that was a long time ago."

"Rafe says diggin' for oil is where the money is."

"Don't believe it, Lucky. Them that does the digging don't get the money."

Lucky holds up his hand to show off the diamond ring on it. "See that, Charlie? You don't get that without money. That's what I'm talking about. Whatdaya say to that?"

"I'd say from the pool chalk on your fingers that you hustled it out of Sammy in a pool game." Nub laughs. "Sammy stole that ring in California. He's told me about it a dozen times."

"Now, come on, Nub. You know old Lucky don't hustle. I had to give him fifty dollars for this ring. Course, I got the fifty bucks from him. The young man forgot you have to call the eight ball." Lucky studies the diamond. "Now Sammy told me that it's worth about five hundred dollars." He breathed on it and rubbed it against his leg, then held it up to his eye. "Now this is what we should have learned to dig up, Nub. It's worth more money than I've ever made in a month."

"You can just stop your poor-mouth act with me, Lynn Sledge. I always knew you was making money. You never fooled me for a minute with all that talk about bad luck and losing all the time. Funny thing I noticed.....I never saw you lose. Talk's cheap, but you always won. Always saying easy come, easy go, but the only going was you going home with everybody's money in your pocket."

"Naw, I've had bad luck all my life... Course I get a streak now and then, but I always lose it all back sooner or later." He takes another drink from Nub's bottle.

"Whoowee.....that stuff sure clears your sinuses!"

***

"Do you have a handkerchief, RD?" He feels her hot breath on his wet, sensitive skin.

He arches his back, withdraws a handkerchief from his left rear pocket, and slides it sheepishly up on his leg. As he looks down at her pretty shiny hair, she cleans him and herself, then stuffs his underwear, zips his pants, lowers the automatic window, and tosses out the dirty hanky.

***

'Man, these local punks wouldn't believe there is a woman in the world who loves sex so much!' Sammy sits backed up on a low slope behind the Red Oak beside an empty wooden shed that used to house an outside jukebox when he was a teenager and this was his favorite hangout.

A part of Sammy's life had gone with that jukebox and he is lost without it. Back then, people respected his quick blade. Everybody parked on this hill would take a look when he made a spin around this place. He had been among the coolest of the cool.

He taps the visor of his Impala with a shiny chrome antenna he took from CC's cage to put on his convertible. 'Yeah, that Mia can never get enough. A real nympho, that's what she is.' Just thinking about Mia Ho Lai's

158

incredibly small, but perfectly shaped, body was sexually arousing Sammy. 'Just what the hell is keeping that Rachel?'

The first time he saw Mia she had her tiny butt on a high stool so that she could reach the flippers on a pinball machine in an all night hotdog joint on Market Street in San Francisco. She saw his reflection in the glass scoreboard and said without missing a flip.

"What choo doin'? You wanta fuck?"

Inside the three-bucks-a-night sleazy hotel with worn out carpet, she rode him like a tiger as long as she could keep any part of him inside her. He was so sore that he couldn't touch himself and he had to sit down to pee.

"Damn! Outta beer!" He throws the antenna in the back seat and starts the car. He roars down the slope spinning gravel against the shed and virtually skids to a stop at the drive-thru window. A very young girl pushes up the window and smiles at him.

"When they get here, tell 'em I'll be right back. Will ya, Patti?"

"Sure, Sammy. I'll be here 'till we close. That is, if you're interested."

For a moment, he considers her implied invitation, "Naw...Jailbait."

***

As Clyde's patrol car pulls slowly around the Red Oak, there is not a single car on the lot. Just as he drives out of sight down Airport road, RD and Rachel arrive and their car backs into the same spot where Sammy was parked earlier.

"Guess he got tired of waiting for us."

"No such luck. Sammy will never give up. I'm sure of that." Rachel rolls the stem of the beautiful orchid in her fingers, studying it carefully. "He'll be here as sure as this lovely flower will wilt and die." She balances it on the rear view mirror. "I wish I could save it....Keep it as pretty as it was when you gave it to me."

"They paint dry flowers, don't they?"

"Most people press them in a Bible, or something. But, they're not pretty....They just look like dried, mashed, dead flowers."

"Maybe, next time, Clyde will give you one."

"How well do you know Clyde, RD."

"I know he's a good person. He's been like a brother to me, and I know he's crazy about you."

"I know that.... I like him an awful lot, too."

"Do you still want to wait for Sammy?"

"I don't think we should."

"OK. But you've got to excuse me, Rachel. This time I really have to take a whizz."

"If you shake it more than three times, you're playing with it." Rachel immediately regretted saying that. Such talk was for Sammy's kind, not RD, or her for that matter.

"Hey, you want a co-cola?" RD quickly ignores her comment.

"I've got a better idea." Rachel sniffs her hand. "I'll go too. I do need to wash my hands." She swings out on his side and they skip down the slop to the back of the building. She enters the ladies' room and RD walks around to the drive-thru. Patti slides up the window.

"Sammy's been hanging around here all night. He's drinking and awful-ly mad about you taking <u>that girl</u> to the prom." Patti blushes as if speaking the unspeakable. "You know how <u>he</u> is."

"Yeah, don't worry. There's not going to be any trouble. Two large co-colas on ice, please."He hands her money and she prepares and passes him the cups. "Thanks, Patti."

Rachel rounds the corner and moves close to him, taking the drinks. Patti turns away.

"Hi, Patti." Patti pretends she did not hear Rachel.

"What a little shit!" Rachel says loud enough to make sure Patti can hear her.

RD slams the little window down so hard that he sees Patti flinch.

"Patti! Your attitude seems to reflect a little of the Paylo influence, late-ly." He is speaking very loud to make sure Patti hears him through the win-dow. "Don't you know better than that?"

He smiles with genuine pleasure as he looks deep into Rachel's eyes. He feels as if his bladder is about to burst, but, he takes the cups back. "Please, let me carry them for you."

She leads the way to the car. He opens the door for her, hands her a cup, then kisses her free hand tenderly.

"Gosh, your hand smells so fresh and clean." He puts his cup in her hand. "Now, I gotta go." He closes the door and skips down and enters the men's room.

Rachel sees the white Impala approaching from the main highway..

Sammy slides to a stop sideways in front of their car. He bounds over his closed passenger door and runs toward Rachel. She quickly puts up her win-dow and, just in time, as Sammy gropes for the outside handle, she locks her door, only to see him reach the back door and swing it open seconds before she can get to its lock. He reaches in to unlock her door and has it open before she can re-position herself in the seat. He grabs her hair, causing her to yield as he drags her awkwardly out of the car.

"I know what you been doin'." He slaps her wildly with one hand and jerks frantically at the heavy hair in his other. "You filthy whore."

RD hears the car slide up in mid-pee. He tries to hurry and drips on his pants. As he rushes outside, he sees Sammy hitting Rachel on the opposite side of the convertible that is blocking his path toward them. He vaults to step across the back seat and his foot lands on the antenna. He grabs it and jumps out directly behind Sammy swinging it madly.

The strong chrome whip whistles and strikes Sammy's back with stinging force causing him to release Rachel and stumble to his knees. RD keeps
beating him with a crescendi of rapid blows as he curls into a tight ball on
the ground, screaming like a wildcat caught in a steel trap. The strength and
intensity of the whipping is actually ripping Sammy's silk shirt from his lean
back, exposing thin strips of peeling flesh from glancing blows flicking into
his hide at lightening speed.

Rachel stays away from the singing whip with her hands covering her
face. When she sees how badly Sammy is being beaten, she speaks in a
strained, high-pitched voice.

"Stop, RD! You'll kill him!"

He stops swinging and lowers the harmonically-swishing antenna to his
side, as it winds down, along with the subsiding fury of his inner rage.

"Get out of here." RD speaks softly

Sammy scrambles on his knees to open the passenger door of his car. He
drags himself up onto the seat, pulls on the steering wheel to slide under it,
and leaning forward to keep his tender back from touching the seat, he starts
the car and drives slowly out of the parking lot.

RD escorts Rachel to the ladies' room and waits for her to freshen up.
When she comes out, her face is fresh scrubbed. All the carefully applied
makeup is gone. He admires her shiny-clean face.

"Rachel, I've never seen you looking prettier!" He kisses her on the
cheek. "Hey, I bet our colas are pure water by now."

He takes her hand and leads her to the car. They both enter from the
driver's side and as he closes the door, she reaches for their drinks. "I am
thirsty." She holds the cup up to her face and smiles, "Hey! Look at this....the
orchid fell in my drink. It looks so fresh... fresher than it did when you first
gave it to me! It's open more...it is! Look, RD, look!"

He looks, but not at the flower. He is looking at the radiant young face
with tears of joy shining on her Cashmere Bouquet cheeks.

Chapter 43:
Breaking Up is Hard To Do

Rachel watches as the car RD is driving disappears into the night. She takes a key from her handbag and walks past a Cadillac hearse to a side door of the ante bellum funeral home. Inside, she moves gracefully in the dark, making her way to the parlor.

The room is prepared for a funeral service tomorrow.

The coffin on a waist-high tier is surrounded by flowers and wreaths. Rachel likes the smell of the parlor. The remains in the casket came here in a small wooden box. The man had set fire to his house and then sat down in his easy chair and blew his brains out with a twelve-gauge shotgun. Half of his skull was blown away by the blast. All that was left of his body was some charred bones and a few hunks of fried gristle.

The casket will remain closed for the funeral, but, Rachel wants to see what her father has done with the face of the man. She lights a candle and opens the coffin. What she sees looks like a dime store mannequin. 'The color is all wrong...too pink. Not enough cheekbone.' She runs her finger over the cheek. 'Too smooth...and the eyebrows are too coarse.'

***

For a biology course, RD has written a report entitled <u>Deadly Lady of the Spiders</u>. In addition to high praise and a grade of A+, his teacher has recommended that he submit it to a leading science magazine for publication.

Thera is reviewing the report at RD's request before he sends it to the magazine's editor. He has already told her that his research confirmed that his intuitive guess, as to why the Black Widow eats its mate, was indeed correct.

"The male of the Black Widow species begins his dangerous courtship cautiously. He sends his love call to the deadly lady by tapping gently on the corner of her web in a rhythm he alone knows and she alone recognizes. When the vibrations are right, she goes into a trance and her lover comes to her."

'It is well written.' Thera observes with pride.

"The probe of the male fits into the uterus of the female with the precision of a complex lock. This precise interlocking prevents cross-breeding with other spiders, although it is unlikely that another spider would live long enough to fertilize the deadly lady.

"The probe of the male Black Widow breaks off after copulation to allow his rapid retreat as the female comes out of her trance. The male is seldom fast enough and the deadly lady usually kills and eats him to provide nourishment for her babies."

***

Rachel hears a soft tapping. She snaps her head toward the large bay windows of the parlor. Someone is out there. She holds the candle in front of her and moves cautiously forward. She sees a hand through the lace curtain with fingers tapping a tattoo on the pane. 'Ray..chul, Ray..chul, Ray,,chul.' She imagines the drumming fingers are saying. She pulls the curtain aside and see's Sammy's lips mouthing her name. She lets the curtain fall and steps back quickly causing hot candle wax to spill on her arm. She is momentarily stunned then scratches the wax off with her fingernail. She remembers the door she left open and darts for it, but as she gets there, Sammy is pushing it against her as she tries to close it

"Get out of here, Sammy!" She tries to push him back with the door.

"It's OK, Rach....I just want to talk with you." His beer breath hits her full in the face as he overpowers her and gets through the door. She backs away.

"I have nothing to say to you. Get out! Get out or I'll scream."

He closes and turns the dead bolt on the door, then follows her as she backs out of the alcove into the embalming lab.

"Nobody will hear you... except maybe that dead man you was lookin' at. Whatdaya do, Rach? Get your kicks off of dead men?" He stumbles toward her unzipping his pants.

"I got the real thing here, Rach. Better than that punk kid's, huh?"

Rachel is cornered, backing up, she bumps against her work table with a jolt that knocks out the candle flame. As the room goes pitch dark, Sammy rushes forward and grabs her arm.

163

"Just feel of this, Rach." He forces her hand around his member. "Now that kid didn't have anything like that, did he girl?"

Rachels's free hand gropes behind her until it touches cold steel. She finds the handle of the scaple and brings it down fast in front of where Sammy holds her hand.

***

Thera moves her hand slowly above her forearm and brings it down in a quick slap, killing the mosquito drawing blood from her. She flicks the insect off her arm and presses a drop of blood from the hole it made in her skin.

'She was getting a good blood meal .... to feed the babies.'

Thera once read that the female mosquito requires a blood meal to produce eggs. The male mosquito feeds on the juices of plants. Only the female mosquitoes are blood suckers.

***

If a scream could wake up the dead, the corpse in the parlor may have run through the bay windows. Sammy is on his knees with his hands between his bleeding legs. Rachel drops his still-throbbing flesh. She must stop his screaming. Her next swipe with the scalpel slices halfway through his neck and the screams stop immediately.

Chapter 44:
Watching

Thera stops reading RD's paper and goes to the window looking in the direction where the Sanders house used to stand. From this same window lookout, she had watched the fire burn it down just three nights ago. She never suspected Fred's depression over Becky divorcing him would lead to suicide. It seems he had carefully planned it all then simply followed his plan.

***

Rachel has decided what must be done. She now has Sammy's dead body on her work table; drawing out his smooth-flowing, still warm blood from the main artery sliced open in his neck; and pumping embalming fluid into a large blood vessel she has just severed in his leg. She returns to the parlor and rolls the bier with Fred Sander's remains into the lab and positions it near Sammy's body on her work table.

When Rachel finishes the first part of her plan, Sammy's embalmed body lies in the closed casket in the parlor with the mannequin-looking head on it. Fred's remains are in a body bag with Sammy's head, which has his other missing body part stuffed in the mouth. When she lifts the bag to take it out to the hearse, she is surprised how light it is. 'Well, I suppose there's not much weight in an empty head, a few ashes and a tiny little bone.'

***

'That Rayford Franklin was just bad to the bone.' Thera is trying to sort out the facts from three sources; the ledger, what Irene has told her, and the information in her Bible. She makes a list of all the people who are victims of the long chain of incest, rape and adultery. She crosses out those who are dead and is left with a list of the living who were born of incestuous stock.

The two who started it all were CC and Irene.

Next came Thera, Julie and Becky, Victor, Ned, and Alton.

Then there is the last generation - TJ, Sammy, Daniel, Susan, Mary Ann, and of course, RD. At least a dozen people cursed from birth. But perhaps even the product of a bad seed can prosper under careful cultivation. TJ just received an appointment from the President himself. Daniel is certain to do well in the Army. Susan is showing great promise, and Mary Ann might develop into a fine concert pianist with encouragement.

'And in my opinion, RD, has the ability to succeed in any field he chooses.'

'Sammy will never amount to anything, but I blame that on the fact that nobody has ever given him the guidance he needs.'

***

Rachel guides her weighted canvas bag out into the current at the end of the boat ramp, off of an isolated dirt road, at a remote bank of the Chattahoochee river. The bag floats slowly away in the muddy water. Then it begins to sink until nothing can be seen except small air bubbles popping on the surface of the water. She closes the back door of the sleek black hearse and drives it off the ramp she had backed down. She also backtracks the route she had taken to the river, and follows back streets across town until she is back at the Mortuary.

Sammy left his Impala parked on the side of the street near the foot of the driveway into the funeral home. On her ride to the river, Rachel took everything she had removed from his pockets, including his keys, and threw them on the seat of his car. She gets in it now and drives about ten blocks from her house to the same library where RD had stopped earlier tonight. She also parks in the same inconspicious spot they were in before, puts his wallet, comb, condoms and pocket change in the dash, and holds on to his keys. As she leaves the car on foot, she spots RD's handkerchief on the pavement and carefully picks it up and wraps the keys in it. She walks home, hiding behind trees or shrubs each time a car passes. Along the way, she tosses the keys and hanky into a trash receptacle at a neighborhood bus stop.

Has she covered every detail? She checks and re-checks that everything in the funeral home is clean and in its proper place. Her back is killing her by the time she climbs the long circular staircase to her bedroom. She takes off her prom dress and notices that it has blood spots on it. 'Oh, well I'll just tell mom my period started early. Besides, I won't be wearing that dress again.'

Her father usually sleeps late on Sunday mornings, except when he has a funeral to manage. Rachel climbs into her soft bed in her underclothes, just as her father's alarm goes off down the hall.

***

Thera hears RD enter the hallway and quickly folds her list and inserts it in her Bible and places it into her desk with the ledger. She pretends to be reading his report when she hears him come up the stairs to her room.

"Hi, Thera! I'm glad you're still up." He comes to lean over her and give her a hug.

"So am I, my dear." She puts down his report and turns to smile at him. "I totally agree with your teacher." She tapped the report with her finger for emphasis. " This should be published. And, how was your evening?"

"Well, to use the current vernacular...it was really wild."

"And just what do you mean by that, young man?" She rolled her eyes playfully. "I certainly hope you're not referring to your date with Rachel."

"Oh, no. Rachel's really a very nice girl. Funny, I never expected her to be so intelligent and interesting. She's actually an exceptionally bright student."

"I'm pleased to hear that you value her ability to think."

"Now, Thera, I must confess. That's not all I value about Rachel."

She slaps him on the chest with his papers. "Now that your project is complete, put this in the mail tomorrow and please dispose of the subject of your intense observations?" She hands him the mason jar with the deadly lady in it. It has small holes in the twist on lid and a twig and some insects inside for the spider to eat.

RD put in the three insects that his research told him were the Black Widow's favorite diet - a grasshopper, a June bug and a Japanese beetle. He turns the jar in front of the desk lamp. She has killed them all but he did not see her do it. When he watched her, she stayed at the bottom of the jar and her victims stayed at the top of the twig as far away from her as possible. He did see the beetle die and guessed that he just missed her attack. Now, all three are wrapped in fine silk thread.

He walks to the back yard and loosens the lid then hurls the jar deep into the field of Kudzu vines that lead to the corner of the woods. For the spider the trip was comparable to a man taking a ride in a spaceship to another world. 'Or Daniel going to Vietnam.'

Chapter 45:
Leaving On A Jet Plane

"Saigon Flight 320 now boarding..."

Daniel rises and stuffs his paperback into the pocket on his duffle bag.

"Well, Grasshopper, we're on our way." Lieutenant Rivers has two reasons for hanging that nickname on him; one is that a grasshopper squirts a brown liquid that looks just like the tobacco juice Daniel spits; reason two is that he is always ready to jump. "Where's Swamprat?"

"Most likely sleeping on the john." Daniel grins. "I'll get him, Sir."

Daniel looks around the men's room until he spots paratrooper boots under a stall. He bangs the door hard with the heel of his fist.

"Swamprat! Put a cork in your ass! We're leaving."

***

RD leaves on a Greyhound for Traveston, with Thera standing by her car waving goodbye in front of the Woosterville bus station. The trip was slow and uneventful, but he was thrilled to be on his way to summer classes, out on his own, and staying in Katheline's hometown. It is very late when he gets there, but he has a short walk from the Traveston depot to the boarding house he has booked for his stay here.

With good directions, he finds 189 Elm Street easily. It is a large Victorian-style boarding house on a corner lot, with a large porch across the front that wraps around the right side. Both sides of the porch are well-lit by the streetlight on the corner. As promised, the front door is open and he finds a note for him on a large cork board above a dim lamp on a small table

to his right as he enters. It tells him how to find his room and when breakfast will be served tomorrow.

RD rests his suitcase on a small landing halfway up a narrow staircase
that is flush with the back wall of this rather large central room on the first
floor. The landing overlooks the sitting area which makes the room an infor-
mal parlor. Directly above the landing is a very big colored glass window,
backlit by the street light, that throws a beautiful array of colored rays across
the dimly lit room and staircase. At the top of the stairs he turns left and follows an L-shaped banister-rail walkway past two large rooms on his right
then left again past a communal bath to the second small room above the
foyer where he entered the house.

The room he enters is the smallest of the four upstairs bedrooms. The
ceiling slants with the roof and the wall adjacent to the house front is only
about six feet high and mostly a window. A bed fits snugly in the corner to
his left. There is a straight chair at the foot of the bed

The only other furniture is a small dresser with a lamp to his right
between two doors; one opens to a closet and the other to a toilet with a
small sink. RD opens his suitcase on the bed and unpacks his few belongings.
He reaches the dresser sitting on the bed. He gets his clothes put away, slides
the suitcase under the bed. and looks approvingly at his new home. From
where he sits he can see the street below. Perfect, he thinks, and just three
blocks from the Traveston College Administration Building. A brick path
with low hedgerows on each side leads from the house to the street with
neatly edged grass on each side.

RD is now resting comfortably with his head at the foot of the bed. He
does a sit-up and moves the pillow from near his feet to under his head.
Much better, he can now doze off to sleep looking out the window. He gets
up, raises the window, moves the lamp to the straight chair below the bed,
plugs it in a wall outlet, and turns on the light. The cool summer breeze
brings in the scent of fresh-cut grass, and he remembers the closing lines
from "One Candle To Blow" by his favorite Poet, Mildred E. Sargent.

'He's prematurely wise: when he is tired
he yawns and shuts his eyes and goes to sleep."

RD does just that..

***

Swamprat and the others have been sleeping soundly since the plane refueled
in Japan. Daniel finishes his paperback and steps over his partner's legs into
the aisle. His real name is Kevin Bevins. They have been close friends since
the day they first met in Jump School. His is a proud Louisiana Cajun with

divorced parents. His mom and younger brother moved to somewhere in Georgia and he stayed in New Orleans with his dad until he joined the army.

The C-141 is packed with men and equipment. As Daniel makes his way forward he is met by a slim Air Force Sergeant in a flight suit who offers him coffee.

"Thanks." The plane wobbles a little and Daniel braces himself on the flight galley counter.

"Do you make this run often?"

"Oh, about twice a month."

"What's Saigon like?" He sips some coffee and is surprised how good it tastes.

"It stinks. No sanitation. Don't drink their beer." He lights a smoke and offers Daniel one.

"Don't smoke....I chew." He reveals a plug of Bull Durham in his shirt pocket.

"Most of them only have a forty year life span....Hell, I was forty last month." He stuffs out the cigarette after only a couple of quick puffs. "Their teeth are all black and rotten from chewing Beatle nuts."

Daniel rubs his plug pocket and changes the subject. "What kind of weather are they having in Saigon this time of year?"

"It's always the same. Awful humidity. Every day it rains at least an hour or so. Yeah, I sure wouldn't want your job. A couple of days a month is all I can take in that hell hole." He reads the disappointment in Daniel's eyes. "I guess it ain't all bad. Abalone is cheap here. The asparagus soup is good, too....filled with shrimp." The NO SMOKING/FASTEN SEAT BELTS light comes on with a ding and the fly boy points at it. "I gotta get back to the cockpit...we're getting ready to land."

Daniel returned to his seat, and as he steps over the sleeping cajun he feels a powerful grip on the calf of his leg. Swamprat hurls him high above his knees and throws him into his seat with hot coffee flying. Damn, but that man is strong!

"You keep that up and I'm gonna have your job." Daniel says playfully. He and Swamprat are alternates; trained to do each others jobs in case one of them gets killed. The thick neck and hard muscled shoulders tighten as Swamprat pushes the Green Beret covering his eyes back up on his smooth-shaved head. He has such remarkable upper body strength that he can do one-arm chin-ups with the other arm at his side. His black eyes are dancing.

"Jump, Grasshopper, jump." He laughs hard. "If anybody gets killed, Swamprat's gonna be doin' the killing." He pats the tattoo on his massive bicep that reads: MEANEST MUTHER IN THE VALLEY.

"Our job is to teach them how to do their own killing, remember?"

"You can teach them all you want, Grasshopper. I plan to show them how it's done."

"How many men have you killed, Swamprat?"

"Sorry, buddy, but I gotta take the fifth on that one....Speaking of fifths, I need a drink."

"The fly boy says not to drink their beer. Poor sanitation and all."

"Hell man! I was raised on homebrew with bugs floating in it. Good protein, that's all."

***

RD is awakened by the smell of fried eggs and bacon wafting up from the kitchen below.

He is still dressed in jeans and a T-shirt. He goes to his sink and throws cold water in his face and dampens his hair, runs a comb through it and brushes his teeth.

As he comes downstairs, he notices a phone on the table below the cork board and a meal schedule posted on it. Good... breakfast is still being served. The landlady is busy in the kitchen in the back corner to his left. Her master bedroom is to the right of the stairs. At the left front corner is the dining room, and it has a long table sitting before large double windows with thin pale green curtains that let in the morning light.

Illuminated by that light is the face of a beautiful young woman seated at the far head of the table. They make immediate eye contact but neither of them speaks when he enters the doorway. At that moment, Mrs. Varaugh arrives with a tray of food from the kitchen.

"Oh, there he is, Elizabeth. Our new boarder, Mister Rabun Duel Newman." She puts down her tray and waves an open palm toward the pretty girl. "And, this is Elizabeth. She's the loveliest girl, ever. None can match this one."

"You get no argument from me, Mam." RD approaches her with his hand out. "Hi, Every body calls me RD."

She rises and grips the tips of his fingers.

"Elizabeth McTanis, I am pleased to meet you, RD." She smiles at him with approval. "You must have arrived very late. We didn't hear you come in."

"It was late. I came in on the last bus."

***

A bus met their plane when it landed in Saigon and took them to a reception center where they were met by a grave army Major who briefed them on their assignment.

"Assist in training a tribe of indigenous troops in equipment operation and combat skills."

After the briefing, they declare their valuables and change their American currency. Swamprat goes straight to a bar in the airport complex while Daniel buys their commercial tickets to Song Be, a small province near the Cambodian border. There is a three hour wait for the commuter air service flight. Daniel joins Swamprat in the bar and has three American beers with him.

"I've had enough to drink, Swamprat." He declares. "I'm gonna take a look around."

"OK, Buddy. Meet cha back here. I don't believe I've ever had enough to drink. I'll save you a seat."

***

"Come, come....have a seat." Vera motions them to sit as she takes the seat to Elizabeth's right facing RD. "So, it's a nice room I have for you, RD. I give you it because of the toilet. Kee wanted the big room. He said all rooms in Japan are small. So, when Audrey moved out he took the big room. Elizabeth, did you see Kee this morning?" She looks toward the doorway as if expecting him to enter.

"No, Vera. I haven't seen Kee since yesterday."

"So, you like your room, RD?"

"Yes, Mam. It will do just fine, Mrs. Veraugh." He holds Elizabeth's chair as she sits.

"Vera, Vee rah!" Everybody calls me Vera."

"Yes, Mam....Vera." RD smiles.

"Such a nice smile. We get along fine, RD." She passes him a plate piled high with eggs and crisp bacon. "By the time you finish college you will be like family to me. Losing Audrey is like losing a daughter."

"Did Audrey finish college?" RD decides not to mention that he's only here for the summer.

"No, no. She got married."

"Gomenasaya...Excuse me, please." Kee comes in bowing as he apologizes for being late.

Vera stands shaking her head and gives him a scornful look.

"This is Kee, RD. Kee, RD is our new border."

RD stands and shakes Kee's hand. "I am pleased to make your acquaintance, Kee."

"I am pleased...pleased to meet you, RD."

Kyoto Iwaoka is the first Asian RD has met face-to-face.

***

Daniel steps out of the Saigon Airport into a madhouse. It does stink, he thought, a mixture of diesel exhaust fumes and sewage. He notices the small cars, many of them three wheelers. The street is jammed with traffic and lined with shops and peddlers.

He is light headed from the beer after sleeping less than two hours on the long flight. The humidity is oppressive. He feels sick to his stomach. He passes a fish stall that absolutely reeks!

He crosses the street, stepping quickly out of the path of a cart being pulled by a water buffalo. An undernourished stray dog sniffs at a fresh cow pie behind a parked cart full of rotting vegetables and food scraps.

Daniel stops to watch a man working a foot peddle sewing machine with amazing industry. He was much faster with the crude device than anyone Daniel has seen using a modern electrical sewing machine back home.

There seems to be naked children everywhere. They are begging him for cigarettes!

"I don't smoke!" Daniel shouts, wanting them to go away.

There is hate in their eyes. They hate him. Why?

He turns and walks back to the airport where he finds Swamprat as he left him.

Two hours later, they join about thirty people in a small two engine plane that will fly them to Song Be.

Daniel studies three old Vietnamese men seated across from him. They look frightened. He has already noticed that the older people he sees give the impression that they are content with their deplorable existence. Could it be that they have never known a better life?

"Notice how the roads below are cleverly hidden by tying branches of trees together above them." Lieutenant Rivers leans back so Daniel can see out of the window.

"Yeah, these little bastards are tricky." Swamprat looks hard at the old men.

Daniel sees a tremble run through the arm of the man directly across from him. He remembers what Clyde said to him about his puppy. 'Never cower a dog. Once a dog is cowered, you'll never be able to do anything with him."

Chapter 46:
Walk On

A dog barks somewhere in the dark, as RD steps out of the boarding house and looks up at a clear sky filled with stars and a clear crescent moon. A frog croaks as he walks along the tree-lined street with warm lights and familiar sounds ebbing from the houses he passes; a piano tinkles in one, laughter in another, a baby's soft cries subside to a lullaby drifting down from an upstairs room on the next corner.

He pauses in the shadow of a tree at the corner of a large brick house with a light in the window on the second floor where someone is playing Roy Hamilton's recording of "You'll Never Walk Alone."

> *"When you walk through a storm keep your chin up high*
> *And don't be afraid of the dark*
> *At the end of a storm is a golden sky*
> *and the sweet silver song of a lark*
> *Walk on through the wind walk on through the rain*
> *tho' your dreams be tossed and blown*
> *Walk on walk on with hope in your heart*
> *and you'll never walk alone you'll never walk alone."*

As he crosses a narrow side street he can smell bar-b-que pork grilling behind a large house on the other side of the street. He sees a small group of people moving around just beyond the hedges bordering a back yard patio. He can just make out the form of a young woman seated in a swing under a large tree beside the house. When she sees him approaching, she walks toward the chain link fence surrounding the front yard.

"Hi!" They are both so surprised when they recognize each other, that neither of them knows what to say for a moment.

"RD....I can't believe it! I thought you were.... It's really you! Come in. Come in. Nancy Harris is having a cookout.....She lives here. What are you doing here in Traveston? How's Thera?" Her eyes dance with excitement as RD opens the gate and steps inside.

He throws his arms around her and hugs her hard.

"Oh, Katheline....It's so good to see you."

She eases free of his embrace and takes his hand. He instinctively draws it to his lips and kisses it again and again.

"I wanted to surprise you. I'm attending summer classes here. I'm staying with Mrs. Varuagh. Do you know her?"

"Everybody in town knows Vera." She pulls him toward the swing. "Do you want to meet some of my friends?"

"No. Not yet. Can we just sit for awhile and hope they don't miss you?"

She squeezes his hand between hers and beams. One look at her makes every girl he has known pale in comparison. 'Wow!' He thinks. 'She does something to me that I can't understand.'

"Kat!" Someone calls her from the patio. RD puts a finger to her lips, trying to delay the interruption. No chance; a young man rounds the corner calling her again.

"That's Tony." She whispers. "Tony, come and meet a dear friend of mine. This is RD Newman from Woosterville. His aunt has the seat my father used to hold in the state senate. I haven't seen him for the longest time and just now he came walking down the street. How about that?" RD noticed that she had dropped his hand while making the introduction,

Tony half-heartedly extended his hand. 'A solid muscular young man with short curly hair that is long out of style, even in this small southern town. He is probably a real bumpkin jockstrap-er.' RD thinks.

"Pleased to meet you." RD mumbles.

"Likewise I'm sure."

RD grips Tony's hand firmly and looks him dead in his blue eyes.'Christ! What a corn ball.'

"Nancy has the ribs ready, Kat." He diverts his attention away from RD and toward her. "We'd invite you to join us, RD, but we hate to impose on Nancy. You know how it is...." He puts his hand on her shoulder to usher her away.

RD looks at Katheline. "You know where I'm at...See ya."

As he turns to walk away, she puts a hand on his arm. "I'm glad you're here, RD. Please call me."

"Well, I'm awfully busy....meeting new people. You know how it is." There was anger and sarcasm in his tone causing her to bite her lower lip and tighten her eyebrows.

"Well, don't bother if you're so BUSY!" She takes Tony's arm and wheels away from him.

He kicks the gate open and stops dead in his tracks, as he sees Elizabeth standing on the sidewalk with her arms folded loosely behind her back.

"My, my, aren't you the operator? Second night in town and you're already having a lover's quarrel with the local elite. Tsk..tsk." She is tracing an arc on the pavement with the toe of her ballerina-type slipper.

"Oh, hi Elizabeth." How much did she hear? "We're old friends, you could say." He blushed. "Excuse my silly outburst."

"Excuse my eavesdropping, but, I must admit, I do enjoy life's little dramas." She smiled. "And now our plot thickens. Nancy just called to invite me down to join her little group of players, and I asked if I could bring you along. How about it? Would you like to join the party?"

RD skips through an exaggerated about face and throws out his elbow. "Take my arm, lovely lady, we're off to the ball."

Elizabeth giggles as she takes his arm.

As they come around the corner of the patio, they see that there are six people in the group who are all eating spareribs from paper plates and look up in surprise at their arrival.

Their sauce-smeared lips and puzzled faces remind RD of kids caught stealing early bites of Sunday dinner. Nancy feels the tension, sits down her plate, and holding sticky fingers high and away from her pretty pink blouse rushes to greet them.

"Hi, Elizabeth. So glad you could come. And this must be the, quote...." She made imaginary marks in the air with her sauce-tipped fingers "....fabulous young man.... who just moved in at Vera's., ...unquote." She takes a napkin from the picnic table and wipes her lips, then still holding back her hands, leans toward him and gives him a peck on the cheek. "Hi, doll. I'm Nancy Harris."

"Hi, Nancy. I'm RD Newman."

"Easy, Nancy. This one's mine." Elizabeth gives off her warmest smile and darts her eyes at Katheline.

"We have plenty of these delicious ribs. Grab a plate and dig in."

"We'd only just finished dinner when you called, Nancy. Just thought we'd pop up for a quick chat and let you meet RD." She presses her shoulder against him, fueling the fire in Katheline's eyes.

"Well, meet my other guests." She poked her napkin animately. "Paul....he's mine. Peggy and Roy. Katheline and Tony." She retrieves her plate. "Now, excuse me, I wouldn't think of letting these ribs get cold."

Nancy, Peggy and Roy go right back to enjoying the ribs. Katheline and Tony make a determined effort to eat neatly, dabbing self-consciously at their mouths with napkins. Tony makes no effort to conceal that he is annoyed. Katheline is quiet and reserved. Paul spends a lot of time tidying up, putting trash in a can and placing empty soda bottles in a case.

Elizabeth is light and cheerful and seems to enjoy special humor in the situation. RD acts totally fascinated by her and oblivious to the others. He finds it hard not to look at Katheline, but giving his attention to Elizabeth makes it easier. Within a couple of minutes, she is apologizing for watching the others eat and almost pulling him to the swing around the corner with obvious glee over being alone with him. Katheline sits fuming and Tony is surly.

As soon as they reach the swing, Elizabeth holds his cheeks in both hands and kisses him right on the mouth. She whispers into his ear. "On, what fun!"

He is drawn to the oval pennant she wears on a gold chain around her neck. It is inlaid with jade and looks exactly like...the June bug he fed to the Black Widow....without legs.

After a few minutes of merriment and laughter, Elizabeth suggests that it is time to go. They join the others arm-in-arm. She takes a napkin from the table and makes a production of wiping her carmine lipstick from the corner of RD's mouth. With a knowing look purposefully and specifically designed for Katheline to read as her desire to be alone with RD, Elizabeth says goodnight to all, and they stroll slowly   home with his arm around her shoulder.

At the top of the stairs he touches her arm and she turns to face him. The light from the colored glass window makes a beautiful pattern on her white blouse and gives her face a soft radiance. He lifts the June bug and looks at it carefully.

"It's called a Scarab, RD." She turns it over to show him an inscription in ancient Egyptian.

"This is an exact replica of an original dating back to the fifteenth century B.C."

"Do you know what the markings mean?"

"Yes. It's a motto - May you walk through life with a friend beside you."

"It's a beautiful motto, Elizabeth....and you are a beautiful friend." He carefully re-centers the Scarab under her neck. "Thanks for what you did tonight."

"Oh, it was indeed a pleasure." She smiles mischievously. "I simply adored the look on her face when I wiped lipstick off your face. If looks could kill, Miss Fisher would surely be a murderess tonight. What fun!"

"She's very important to me, Elizabeth."

"Of course she is! I could never have given my award-winning performance without knowing that." She tosses her head high and throws kisses to an imaginary audience in the parlor downstairs. "Lady Macbeth, eat your heart out."

They are both smiling when they part company.

As they part company, Daniel watches the three jeeps carrying Swamprat, a medic they call 'ears', and the Vietnamese team leader with six of his men, leave the small group of huts to follow a narrow, rutted road until they are engulfed by the jungle. He will give them about an hour head start before boarding the helicopter that will take him to check out the drop zone.

The drop zone is about twenty miles south of the village. An encampment of Viet Cong is reported to be about ten miles south from here. Swamprat and his team will drive west to avoid engaging the VC and reach the drop zone to set flares that he will use to check wind direction and velocity prior to bringing in the men who will jump today.

Daniel studies the sky. There is a thin layer of clouds at about nine hundred feet that might cause problems. He walks to the hut Lieutenant Rivers is using as a briefing room and carries on small talk with the helicopter pilot who has flown up from MAG so that his detachment can complete their three month qualification jumps.

"Sergeant Fulton, you ain't gonna see much unless we fly under that scud layer." The slim warrant officer comments in a deep southern drawl.

"Did the Lieutenant tell you about the VC nest?"

"Yeah, he said they were reported there yesterday....but that don't mean they're there today. Them suckers keep movin' all the time."

An hour later they are flying south above the cloud layer.

"I figure we got about three more miles to the drop zone, Sergeant. I'm gonna ease on down below the clouds. We can always pop back up if we spot VC." He is descending as he makes the announcement.

Daniel walks to the open door, hooks his static line to the bar above his shoulder, and leans out. The area below them is teeming with VC. Daniel keys his mike and screams into it. "Pull up! VC are thick as ants down there. Let's get the hell outta here."

The helicopter banks hard right sending Daniel flying out of the left door.

"Them suckers are shooting.....click." Daniel loses the pilot's voice as his helmet cord snaps. He falls under the turning aircraft as his chute deploys and catches on it's front skid. The combined force of his falling body and the helicopter pulling up and away gives him such a jolt that he thinks his left shoulder may have been jerked out of its joint. The wind is burning his eyes as he holds his palm over them to look up. He is hanging from the skid and being pulled upward. The pilot is trying to drag him into the protective cover of the clouds. He closes his eyes and hangs on.

Daniel pats the reserve chute on his chest. It seems OK. If he can get free of the master chute he may be able to free fall clear then deploy the reserve. He tries to open his eyes again. The down draft from the rotor blades is stinging his face. They are descending again. They must be over the drop zone. He spots smoke on his right. Damn! It is red - NO GO SMOKE. The helicopter is turning toward the flares.

Swamprat and his men just manage to set the flares in time to evade the large group of VC who are working their way south. They are speeding away when Swamprat sees Daniel hanging from the skid. Daniel is hacking away at the suspension lines of his entangled chute.

Just as he cuts the last one, and falls free he spots the jeep below.

Swamprat is standing on the hood, waving his arms madly and screaming. "DON'T JUMP! GRASSHOPPER, PLEASE DON'T JUMP!"

The reserve chute snaps open in the stiff wind. Daniel breaths a sigh of relief. High winds must be the reason for the NO GO. He will make it. It will be a tough landing, but he will make it.

***

"Dijobi...Desho. I made it." Kee gets to the corner of the front yard before he keels over into the shrubs.

RD lies across his bed looking down on the quiet street below. Most of the houses are unlit and the soft illumination of the corner streetlight casts an eerie brightness through trees and shrubbery. A dark figure catches RD's attention as it stumbles and falls against a shrub at the far right corner of the front lawn. Pressing his face against the window pane, RD can just see a still figure lying face down on the grass. He goes quietly downstairs and out the front door.

As he approaches the body, he recognizes Kee's clothing and his 'Yankees' baseball cap.

"Kee, are you alright?" RD squats beside him. He shakes his arm. "Kee, can you hear me?"

No response. He turns him over and is surprised to see that he has vomit smeared over his face. His eyes are closed and his mouth hangs open at an odd angle that makes his lips look rubbery. The thick slime on his face has picked up slivers of the fresh cut grass.

RD puts his arms under Kee's and drags him clear of the mess. He wipes his face clean with his handkerchief and props him against the chain link fence. He sits beside him letting Kee's weight rest against him. He can feel Kee's shallow breathing. RD guesses that he has been drinking heavily from the smell of it all.

He waits. A furry caterpillar draws his body into a hump and spreads it out about a hundred times until it crosses three squares on the sidewalk before Kee stirs. At last he begins to moan and suddenly he pushes himself away from RD with a yell.

"NON DIE YO! NON DIE YO!" He looks bewildered and angry, shaking his head and blinking his eyes. A light comes on in the house next door.

RD has no idea what Kee is saying.

"It's me, RD. How do you feel, Kee."

"Sheet man....I feel....warui.....bad...bad." He topples over on his back, rubbing his eyes and temples. After a few minutes, he pulls himself up by gripping the wire fence. "How long you been taking care of me, RD?"

"How long? Not long." RD amuses himself when he realizes how non-specific his answer sounds. "I've just been sitting here with you for about a week. That's all."

"You got a smoke?"

"No. I don't." RD picks up Kee's New York Yankees baseball hat and puts it on his head.

"I'm OK now. Let's go inside." He tries to get up but falls on his butt.

RD helps him until he is steady on his feet. As they stumble onto the sidewalk, RD glances at Kee's feet and pulls him back. Too late. Kee's foot landed on top of the hairy bug.

***

The wind drives Daniel west of the drop zone. He sees nothing but thick trees ahead. By tugging hard on his right riser he changes direction slightly to the right as his body begins to scrape the treetops. His boot catches a heavy branch and his head is slammed against a tree trunk. The pain becomes so intense that his mind cannot handle the overload and out of the deepest recess of his brain comes a bittersweet childhood memory of Thera holding him in her lap on the porch swing and, thinking that he is fast asleep, singing a very sad song from her own childhood.

> *"How far is heaven, when can I go, to see my daddy, he's there I know. How far is heaven, let's go tonight. I want my daddy to hold me tight."*

Daniel cries himself to sleep. He wakes to the sound of swarming VC noisily talking and rushing through the jungle toward him. He checks his automatic rifle for a full clip, covers it with the chute, closes his eyes and waits until they step clear of the brush. They think he is dead and are caught completely off guard. He fires every round he has before their bullets begin ripping into his flesh. With his last conscious thought, Daniel wonders if his foot has been severed above the ankle.

***

When they see a shapely ankle in a ballerina slipper, RD and Kee stop in their tracks as they climb the stairs together, both looking down at the steps in the dim light. They raise their heads to follow a quilted green robe up to meet Elizabeth's green eyes dancing in the light from the colored glass window.

"It seems I'm not the only creature of the night." She smiles down on them. "Could I persuade the two of you to join me in a cup of tea? I find conversation at its peak in the wee morning hours."

"I'd love to..." RD replies without hesitation. "How about you, Kee? Are you up to it?"

"Cho toe mah tay." Kee points a finger toward the common bathroom.

"That means just a minute, RD." Elizabeth moves aside to let Kee pass. "Kee's teaching me Japanese." She starts down the steps ahead of him and speaks over her shoulder to Kee. "Meet us in the sitting room. I'll have the water boiling."

RD follows her into the kitchen and watches as she fills a kettle and sits it on the stove to boil.

"RD, I wanted to tell you earlier and it slipped my mind." She opens a cabinet and places three cups and saucers on a tray. "My father's name is Rabun."

He had just lifted the tray and the cups rattled. 'Rabun McTanis? Perhaps it's a common name in England? Could it be possible that Thera's Rabun McTanis wasn't killed during the war? Could this beautiful woman be the child of the only man Thera has ever loved? Incredible! Simply incredible!'

She places sugar and cream on the tray.

"Isn't that an amazing coincidence? Rabun being such an unusual name."

It could be much more of a coincidence that she imagines, he thought.

"Does the name Thera mean anything to you, Elizabeth?"

"Of course it does. My first name is Thera! But, how did you know that?"

The cups rattled again and RD sits the tray back on the counter.

"I didn't. I have an aunt Thera who once knew a man named Rabun Daniel McTanis."

"My, my.... This is getting more intriguing by the minute."

"Did your father attend Oxford?"

"As a matter of fact, he did."

"As a Rhodes Scholar."

"Yes!"

"Is he American?"

"Yes!"

"Do you know when he came to England?"

"Yes. But I'd rather you tell me."

"1940?"

"Yes!"

The kettle whistled.

"I'll get the tea. Then I want to hear all about your Aunt Thera."

Kee steps down the stairs as they bring the tea into the sitting room.

They seat themselves around a low table, Elizabeth with her back to the door with RD on a sofa to her left and Kee in a chair to her right.

"Kee, you and I thought it remarkable chance probability that we both had American fathers when conceived on opposite sides of the globe." She looked at RD intently while they both added sugar to their tea. "But, it is simply beyond belief what RD and I have discovered tonight."

In response to her interrogation, RD tells her all he knows about Thera's friendship with her father when she was in England during the war years. He ends the the story by telling her that, over all these years, Thera has thought Professor McTanis was on a ship that a German U-boat sank. She was told there were no survivors from that ship.

"He was on that ship. And so was I." She stirs her tea and takes a sip. "We were the only survivors. We were picked up and taken to southern France by a Portugese trawler. We lived in hiding in a small French village until the end of the war."

"What happened to your mother?"

"Both of my parents went down with that ship. I never knew her. I was just two years old when it happened. Professor McTanis saved my life. He later adopted me. He's the only father I've known."

"So he never married?"

"He explained to me that Thera Fulton is the only woman he ever truly loved." Elizabeth stands and moves to sit with RD, taking his hands in hers.

"Thera says the same about him. She named me after him." RD is touched by her coming to him. "And he, in turn, named me after her. Apparently they had such high regard for each other that they never wanted anybody else." She is glowing. "Oh, RD! How romantic!"

"Does he know she is still alive?"

"No. Since he never heard from her after she left England, he has always believed that she did not survive the war."

"Where is your father now."

"He's here with me. He has purchased a beautiful country estate a few miles from Traveston and he's living there while he has it renovated. I'll be joining him as soon as he has it completed for us."

"I guess we have proven that it is, indeed a small world, Elizabeth." RD sipped the tea he had mixed in the same manner as he had seen Elizabeth blend hers. He liked it.

***

Lieutenant Rivers personally escorted Grasshopper's body home. Thera asked him to please personally conduct the military funeral. Swamprat died trying to save Daniel. His search party found Daniel hanging from a tree limb by one foot. The wind had shifted and died down causing a silk shroud to settle over his body. Daniel killed thirty-three Viet Cong troops before he was overwhelmed by the size of the heavily-armed group. Five more good men lost their lives trying to get to Daniel's body ahead of the ruthless enemy. Four of them were indigenous, dedicated, South Vietnamese Soldiers who were willing to give their lives in search of freedom. There were nearly a hundred bullet holes in Daniel's body. It seems that every VC in the area had gone out of his way to shoot the Yankee in a tree.

***

"Kee, where is your grandfather from in America?"

"New York. He gave me my Yankee cap. His name is Payro. "

"Paylo...low low...low." Elizabeth corrects him. "Kee has trouble with L sounds. We help each other."

"Pay...low!" Kee grimaced. "I've never seen him. He sent my cap to my grandmother for me."

"I've never seen either of my parents." RD says evenly. "They were killed when I was born. I only have one photograph of them and it is in pretty bad shape."

"Kee has a photo of his grandfather. Show him, Kee."

RD takes the wallet Kee offers and leans under a lamp to study the single picture underneath a plastic cover in it. He is about to tell Kee that he knows some people named Paylo, but he thought about Sammy and CC and decided it would be better not to mention them. He wouldn't wish them on anybody, even as distant cousins.

The man in the snapshot is wearing coveralls, the same baseball cap, and is leaning on a shovel. 'Holy Cow! It is definitely a young CC!' He hands the wallet back to Kee.

"Where is your grandfather, now?"

"I don't know. Grandmother said he travels a lot. He sent her postcards from Europe. He always told her that he was coming back to Japan. She would get so excited when the postcards came. My mother told me that she would read the postcards over and over to me and show me this picture. She would tell me...."Study hard. This is your mother's father. A fine man. An American. Study hard so you can go to America. America is the best country in the world. If you go to America, you will have a good life. Maybe you will find your grandfather. If you do, he will help you. The only reason he left us is because the Government would not let him stay in Japan. That's why he never came back to us. Your grandfather is a fine man. He loves us very much." Kee sniffs and wipes his eyes. "I talk too much." He stands up.

"Gominah sighyah, Elizabeth-san. Excuse me, RD."

"Doeytashemastay."(Don't mention it.) Elizabeth looks at her watch. "Oh hi yo gozimas." (Good morning.)

"No. It's not good morning yet in Japanese. As long as it is still dark and we have been to bed, we still say goodnight - Ohyasminohsiya."

"Oh-yas-min-oh-siya, Kyoto-san." Elizabeth leans forward and takes his hand in hers. "Goodnight, my dear friend."

"Goodnight, Kee." RD searches for the right words to say. "I'm glad you came to America."

"And I'm glad you came to Traveston." Kee gently places Elizabeth's hand on her lap, bows to her and RD, then abruptly turns his back to walk away.

They sit quietly and watch him climb the stairs and proceed directly to his room.

"Kee is a very sensitive person. People like him shouldn't drink. It's his religion you know."

"His religion requires him to drink?" RD looks puzzled. He notices little comma dimples appear in her cheeks as she lowers her cup. "Of course not! He is Shinto. Which means that he believes in spending his life in search of self-perfection. He is far too critical of himself which leads to great depression. People who are prone to depression shouldn't drink. That's all."

"You seem to know an awful lot about people, Elizabeth."

"I can't help myself. I have an uncontrollable urge to know everything about everybody. For example, let me tell a truly remarkable story about Kee's Uncle... More tea?

RD tastes the tea and finds it is cold. He slides his cup in front of her on the table. "Yes, please." He is thinking that he would drink rotten eggs to keep her sitting here with him.

"His uncle's name is Leo Iwaoka. Kee says he looks just like him, but older. He was actually recruited and trained to be a Kamikaze pilot just before World War Two ended. The war was over just in time to prevent Leo from flying a fatal mission." She stops to sip her tea and frowns. "Hold that thought, I'll be right back with more good hot tea." She empties their cups into the butler and heads for the kitchen. He admires the rear of her lively little body until she is out of eyesight around the corner. She has a perfect mixture of intelligence, wit, poise, grace and physical beauty; all the ingredients that draw approval from every male who has the privilege of just being with her.

She smiles openly as she enters the kitchen. Since leaving the parlor, she has been fully aware of his attention because she watched his reflection in the dining room, where the tree beside the porch blocks the streetlight making a mirror of the windows.

When she returns with fresh tea, she prepares both cups, and they taste it, before she picks up the story of the ex-Kamikaze right where she left it.

"Next, comes the interesting part of Uncle Leo's story. After Japan surrendered, and their military was disbanded, these brave warriors, who had shown their willingness to die for their Emperor, were secretly given special identification cards that verified the commitment they had made."

"Did the occupying forces ever know about this?" RD was fascinated with the story.

"No, that's what is so amazing." She grips his knee and leans toward him. "I don't think this incredible act of secrecy has ever been discovered, nor has it's significance been recorded. When you view it in relation to the intense pride of the Japanese people, who had never been defeated throughout their long history, it becomes an important statement of defiance."

"I see what you mean. Outwardly, the entire population of Japan was cowered by their defeat, while covertly hanging on to the honoring of their heroes."

"Precisely! Kee has told me of riding on the back of his Uncle Leo's big wide-seated motorcycle and roaming the country to be welcomed as heroes in every bar, restaurant, hotel, or any other business when the ex-Kamikaze flashed his card. He was given the best they had to offer and not allowed to pay for anything by any merchant who saw that card."

"I can see what you mean about knowing everything about everybody. I'm sure you are the only non-Japanese person who has been trusted with that story."

"Isn't it wonderful!"

"Yes, it's quite a story. But it's you who is wonderful." He covers her hand with his.

"I'm more like a spy. I scheme constantly to discover people's little secrets." She refills his cup. "So, now, Mister Newman, if you have any dark little secrets you might as well tell me all from the beginning. Or else I shall spend many sleepless nights until I can solve the mystery of you."

"Why did you call me Mister Newman? It sounds funny?"

"For emphasis. I'm studying to be a writer. I wish everyone would call me Miss McTanis."

"Does that mean you don't like the name Elizabeth? After all, that's your Queen's name."

"That's probably why I got it. Actually, it sounds quiet nice with Queen in front of it."

"So, am I to call you Queen Elizabeth or Miss McTanis?"

"Precisely, Mister Newman." She pursed her lips and raised her chin in jest. They both laugh.

"I'm glad you're not sleepy tonight, Elizabeth. It's fun being with you." RD blurts out honestly.

"I don't sleep very much. I've had something burning inside me all my life. It causes me to think too much and I can't shut it off." She tops off their cups. "Writing down my thoughts helps. I have been writing since I was a small child."

"I have another friend who likes to write. Her name is Rachel Souquet."

"I'm not the least bit interested. Tell me all about your Aunt Thera, I've been waiting all night to learn more about her. She has to be a remarkable woman for my dad to be so devoted to her."

He talked. She listened and questioned. He willingly opened up to her. When he got into the hole digger's story, she put her head on his shoulder and strained not to miss a word. When he had answered all her questions, she put away the tea service and they climbed the stairs holding hands. In front of her door, he bows and kisses her hand.

"Goodnight, Your Majesty."

"Goodnight, Sweet Prince." Her green eyes sparkled and the commas popped in her cheeks.

Chapter 47:
Little Things

They sit or lean on tables in the cramped basement studio. Their first assignment in the sculpture class is to mold the blobs of clay in dumpy piles on the tables into a copy of the model their art professor is discussing.

"This model accentuates the sculptural qualities of the human head. The features of every head have similar proportions." He runs a long finger across the model. "However, no two human heads are absolutely identical. Just as every person is different in some way to every other person, so are there always some differences in sculptural structure." Jason Knight looks for questions in his students' eyes.

"That don't apply to Gooks, does it?" Tony Bevins crosses his muscular arms and glares across the room at Kyoto.

Jason snaps his head erect. "What I said is my opinion in regard to all people, even the ignorant ones who are intolerant of anybody different. What I mean is that if you don't like people who are different from you, then there's really nobody left for you to like."

"What I meant was...all orientals look the same to me....that's all." Tony props against a heavy column that supports the ceiling.

"What that tells me is that your exposure to other races must be extremely limited. There are actually significant variances in the appearance of the many cultures found in Asia. Perhaps this course will help you better see the miracle in our world that every single person is unique."

"Professor Knight, I am interested in those parts of the human form that are not easily represented in sculpture." A dark haired beauty to his left changed the subject. "How do we make clay look like hair for example."

"A good question, Rachel." She registered late, but persuaded him to let her join an already overcrowded class. "Hair is a problem for the sculptor. There are some tricks to the trade. Notice how I made the eyelid thick on this model and at an angle above the eye so that its shadow gives the illusion of an eyelash." He could see from the set of her full lips that his answer had satisfied her.

"Now, let's get to work. Your assignment is to copy this model in as much detail as you can. The best of your efforts we will use in our lessons on casting techniques."

Rachel and Kyoto face each other across their table. She kneads her clay sensuously between her fingers. He pounds his with his fist as he stares at Bevins across the room.

"Don't let that dummy upset you." She smiles. "Just look at him. Can you even imagine him not being an idiot? Maybe, he's entitled to his stupid opinions, since that's all he's got."

"Yeah, opinions are like ass holes. Everybody's got one and they all stink."

"That's as funny coming from you as the first time I heard it. I bet you didn't learn that in Japan." He tells her his grandfather is a foul-mouthed American. Her smile is infectious, and soon they are both paying no more attention to Tony.

When Rachel finishes the assignment, the only discernable difference between Jason's model and her copy is the color of the plasticine clay.

Kyoto's work resembles a green monster she once saw in a B-grade horror movie.

"What the hell, sculpture is a dead art anyway."

He pokes two holes for eyes.

Rachel laughs.

She tells him about working on dead bodies. "Most assuredly dead art."

"Why are you taking this course? You're as good as Professor Knight."

"I want to work on living persons. I plan to be a doctor, a plastic surgeon." Rachel has taken Dee Dee to plastic surgeons in Atlanta who have restored her face to a remarkable resemblance of her former beauty.

She is now determined to master their profession.

"Do you think you'll ever get good enough to make a Gook's face look American?"

"I doubt it. But, I can show you what to do with that mess you've made."

***

Irene tries to straighten her dress. Clyde brought her to visit Thera and his dog was so happy to see her that he climbed all over her.

Looking up at the lighted gable, she notices that the window is open.

"Miss Thera." She yells as she sees the movement of Thera's shadow.

"Irene?" Thera leans out the window, but it is too dark to make out her face.

"It's me. I came to visit. I haven't seen you since I moved to town."

"Well, come in...come in." Thera boomed.

Thera meets her at the door and leads her upstairs. "I'm very happy to see you, Irene. This old house gets so lonely now that all my family has moved away."

"That's why I moved into town. It's so lonesome out here." She takes the comfortable chair Thera offers her beside her desk. Spread on the desk are the large Bible, the ledger, and notes.

"Excuse my mess, Irene. I've been wracking my brain trying to put all the pieces of this puzzle together." She tapped her pen on the documents. "I wish I had more information. Old letters, anything that might tell me more about the Fulton family tree,"

"I got a letter for Ida Maye that's been in my purse for years," She takes it out and hands it to Thera. "I kept thinking that one day she'd come back here."

"Oh, my God, Irene! This letter was for me!" The letter Irene gives Thera is from Rabun McTanis. Irene had thought that Ida Maye was the Ms. "Lady" Fulton to whom it was addressed. Thera sees where Irene had made a note on the envelope and later wrote and mailed a short reply so that she did not have to open what she thought was Ida Maye's mail.

Baron Jesse Garron , RDM
C/O Pierre Pissarro
LaGrange de Langlade
24200 Proissans-Sarlat, France

~~Mrs. "Lady" Fulton~~
~~Route #2 Hillcrest Road~~

~~Woosterville, Georgia, USA~~
Ms. Fulton is dead,
Return to Sender.

Reply mailed to above address
By Irene on August 8, 1943.

Thera studies the return address and quickly recognizes that is a code name, an alias used in Nazi occupied France. **RDM - Rabun Daniel McTanis!**

Thera eagerly opens the envelope.

My dearest Lady Greyeyes,
July 24, 1943

I'm writing this letter as quickly as possible. So much has happened since the last note I sent to tell you I was on my way back to America.

The ship I was on was sunk just a couple of hours out of South Hampton. Myself and a young toddler were the only survivors. We were picked up by a Portugese trawler and taken to the South coast of German-occupied France.

Because of the war, I can't give you any details, only that I am safe and that I plan to adopt the little girl as soon as possible. I must say that southern France is a beautiful place to wait out this awful war. All that is missing in my life is you.

Unfortunately, that is what matters most of all. I live for the day we will be together again. You now have two of us to love as much as we love you. I just celebrated the second birthday of the little cast away who is fated to be our lovely daughter. I named her Thera Elizabeth, after a wild fling with some woman I met on the streets of London.

"Take good care of yourself. You belong to me."

Loving and missing you every day,
Baron Jesse Garron, RDM
"Sir Laughs A Lot"

"I see you've got Rayford's book. It's a terrible story ain't it?" Irene pulls her ear nervously.

"It certainly is." Thera puts the letter in the envelope, taps her notes with her fingertips, and turns her attention back to Irene. "It sure tells his horrible story in his own words. I've been trying to sort out all the crossbreeding and in-breeding since the Zingers came to America. I've been trying to make some sense of it all."

"It don't make sense, Miss Thera. He was just a mean man....but....but.... he never knew how much trouble he caused all them women. He was really as crazy as old CC... but, in a different kind of way. At least CC didn't bring all those helpless children into the world."

"Something I've been wondering about, Irene... When CC got Ida Maye pregnant...the first time, what happened to her baby?"

"The Addisons paid an old widder woman to raise that baby. Ida Maye was young when it happened. They were trying to take care of her; to help her make a life for herself after it happened."

"What was the baby's name?

"You mean you don't know?"

"No, I don't."

"That was Rayford."

"Rayford was Ida Maye's son?!" Thera's is incredulous. Of all the horrid truths she has learned about this bizarre family inbreeding, this is the most shocking to her.

The awful man who raped her was not only her brother, but he had conducted a long term affair with their own mother!

"Yes. But....but she didn't know it. Me and CC were the only ones who knew after the Addisons died. I told CC when he came back from overseas. I think Charlie Addison suspected it, but he never knew for sure. All he ever knew for sure was that his adopted sister went away for awhile and had a baby."

"That explains why CC didn't get the police involved when Rayford raped Julie." Thera makes a couple of notes on her pad.

"That's why he made me marry Rayford." Irene shifted in her chair. "He said we had to keep it all in the family."

"Where did the name Franklin come from?"

"Old Annie just made it up. Her last husband was named Ray John Benjamin, so when the Addisons asked her to name him at the hospital when he was born, she just decided to name him Rayford John Franklin. They put that name on his birth certificate."

"Did CC have any more children?"

"He told me he had a daughter in Japan. He really loved that woman in Japan. He said he would've stayed with her forever, but they run him out of the country. His daughter gave him a grandson in 1941. The woman he loved used to send him postcards and letters with pictures of the boy. CC sent him a New York Yankee hat and she made his picture wearing it. He sure was cute. "

"What was the boy's name?"

"I can't remember. It was a funny sort of name. He told me but I forgot it. I'm usually good at remembering names, but them foreign names are hard."

***

"Kee OH Toe...Ee Wah OH Ka...." Rachel repeats his name as they walk the few short blocks from the art building to the boarding house where he lives. She is fascinated by him. She thinks he looks like a Japanese Clark Gable with his Rhett Butler moustache and full black hair swept back over his ears in full thick strands. "Keeohtoe Ewaohka."

"You can just say Kee, Racher...It's easier."

"No. I shall call you Keeohtoe. It's a nice name. But, you can use Rach for short since you have trouble with the L sound."

"Thank you. I rike Rach. Rach sounds pretty. Rach is pretty. I rove that name-wah."

She puts her hand over her eyes and shakes her head laughing.

They enter the house. He leaves her standing at the foot of the stairs and darts into the kitchen, then returns with a bottle of wine and two glasses. As they climb the stairs together, he sees a light under Elizabeth's door and hopes she doesn't hear them.

Inside his room, he locks the door for the first time since he has lived here. Rachel places her books on the small table he uses for a desk then seats herself in the only chair he has. Kyoto pulls the end table between them and sits on the edge of his bed,

"I've been saving this wine for a special occasion. It's Akadama Plum Wine from Japan - my favorite." He pours their glasses full of the golden liquid.

Rachel takes the glass, momentarily touching his fingers as the glass passes hands. Touching her female heat momentarily catches him off guard and he instinctively recoils from it. He grimaces and quickly raises his glass in a humourous toast he learned from his Uncle Leo.

"Here's to you, as good as you are, and to me, as bad as I am.

As good as you are, and as bad as I am...

I'm as good as you are, as bad as I am."

Rachel pulls the glass away from his lips with a soft grip about his hand.

"No! I can't accept that." She lifts her glass. "Here's to Keeohtoe Ewahohka! Who, I am certain, is a far better person than I am." She clicks his glass with hers and releases his hand. He gulps down the drink and refills his glass. "What makes you so bitter, Keeohtoe?"

"Not enough sweet wine, perhaps? No sweet woman, perhaps? Or do you know that a Gook can't make out in an American whorehouse with a handful of hundred dollar bills?" He downs the second glass and pours another.

"I know you're not the smoothest talker I've met." She empties her glass and holds it out for him to fill.

"I haven't had a lot of practice. You're the first girl I've been alone with since I came to America." He filled her glass as she moved to sit on the bed with him.

"Well, tonight is your lucky night, Keeohtoe. I'm no whore, but, I do like men and I like your style. I'm one American girl who has had her fill of pushy men." She takes his glass and sits it on the table beside hers. "And tonight I want a man." She fell across the bed and pressed his hand over her breast. "I haven't had a man since I cut off my relationship with Sammy Paylo..." She said in a soft whisper almost as if talking to herself.

Kyoto is stunned. "Sammy who?" He said in disbelief.

There is a rap at the door followed by RD's voice.

"Kee, are you still up?"

Kee rises, goes to the door, and speaks through it. "So sorry, RD. I have a friend with me. I'll see you later."

192

"Sure, Kee, I thought you were alone. Sorry."

When he turns back to Rachel, she has turned back the covers and is undressing. He is dumbfounded by her eagerness. He uneasily removes his clothes and folds them neatly on the chair.

When he finishes, Rachel has slid her naked body under the sheets. She takes his hand and draws him to her. He fondles her big breasts and stares at them in wonder.

"You said you had a boyfriend named Payro?"

"Yes. Paylo. He was awful...crude and vulgar." She felt between his legs and found him small and limp.

"What was his father's name?"

"CC. Have you heard about that crazy old fool? Everybody in Woosterville knows about our village idiot, but I didn't know his reputation had reached Traveston." She was kneading his still limp flesh like she had kneaded the clay, but getting no response. "Who told you about CC? RD?"

"Do you know RD?"

"Yes. He's a good friend of mine. Please don't tell him I was here."

Yeah, he thought, don't let him know you were alone with a Gook.

She tries every trick she knows, but she can't arouse him. He grunts and groans but nothing happens. As tears fill his eyes, she squeezes his head against her breasts and speaks softly.

"Its OK, Keeohtoe. I just came on too strong." She feels his tears on her chest. "It's not your fault. Besides, it feels so good just holding you close."

"Kee?" This time it's a soft woman's voice outside the door.

Kee goes to speak through the door again. "I'm not dressed, Elizabeth. I'll see you later, OK?"

"Sure, Kee. Sorry to bother you."

"This has never happened to me, Rach." He begins putting on his clothes.

Rachel swings out of bed and also begins to dress.

"Maybe this place is all wrong, Keeohtoe. Perhaps the problem is that you feel guilty about having me here. We'll get it right next time." She pulls her bra over her large mounds and hooks it behind her back. "I better get out of here. Can you make sure the coast is clear?"

He opens the door quietly and glances around the dark hallway, then peeks down over the parlor. He leads her down the stairs and walks with her to the corner. He knows RD can see them from his window but he won't be able to recognize her in the dark. When they reach the opposite side of the street, she grabs the back of his neck and kisses him long and hard on his mouth. She grabs his crotch firmly and smiles. "There! Now that's what we were missing!"

Kee flashes a broad Rhett Butler smile.

"Well, frankly my dear Rach. I'm very pleased about that."

"Just one of those things. Another time, another place."

"I rove you, Rach..UHL."

"Goodnight, Kee."

He watches the most desirable body he has ever seen walk away. He was not man enough to take it. He slams his fist into a tree trunk and bruises his knuckles.

"Sadness hides in the shadow of the stars
Ue o muite arukoo
Sadness hides in the shadow of the moon
Namida go kobore nai yoo ni
I look up when I walk so the tears won't fall
Nakinagara aruku
for tonight I'm all alone."
Hitoribotchi no yoru.
(In loving memory of Kyu Sakamoto.)

***

"Kee, I need help." RD meets him in front of the boarding house,

"What's wrong, RD?"

"Can you take me to Woosterville?" RD had taken lifts to school on Kee's motorcycle. "I just learned today that a member of my family is dead."

"Of course I can, RD. I'm sorry about earlier. I didn't know you needed me. So sorry."

"Don't worry about it. Who's your girlfriend?"

"Ah....." Kee waves the question aside. "Just somebody in one of my classes. Let's see if my bike will start. I haven't driven it for a few days."

RD goes inside to tell Elizabeth they're leaving. In a few minutes they are en-route to Thera's.

"Who died and how?" Kee turned his helmeted head in the wind and shouted.

"My cousin, Daniel. In Vietnam." RD grips his chest hard as the bike hits a bump. "His parachute got tangled in a tree. While he was hanging helpless, a bunch of damn Viet Cong Gooks took turns shooting him." He feels Kee's chest tighten. "Sorry, Kee. I don't have anything against Asians. It's just that Daniel was like a brother to me."

"It's OK, RD." Kee screamed back. "I understand." He raised his visor and twisted the throttle full open, letting the speed of the burning wind hide the tears flowing from his stinging eyes. He can recall a famous line from Julius Caesar. 'Et tu, Brute?....You too, RD?'

***

Chapter 48:
The Inner Circle

Thera works late into the night preparing a chronological list of the long chain of incest she has discovered. The neatly printed list lies in the center of her desk under a lamp she left on when she fell exhausted across her bed. Thera did not write down the fact that the two fine young men she has been so proud of all their lives, are direct descendants of this incestuous brood. Daniel's parents had been, in truth, Victor Zinger and his half sister - Rebecca. RD's parents were the Zinger siblings - Alton and sister Carol.

THE ZINGERS (History of Incest)

MAZINE ZINGER(1833) MAZINE ZINGER

and   and

Olin Zinger (1829) -   Claude Hausenzinger (1839)

HER BROTHER   HER FATHER -

had   had

CC ZINGER (1869)   and   IRENE ZINGER (1872)

and   had

IDA MAYE ZINGER (1886)   and   JOAN ZINGER (1886)

had

RAYFORD ZINGER (1899) – This man fathered at least ten illegitimate children with the women who are named below and in the following order.

(His mother)   IDA MAYE
had....................THERA (1916)...and.....VICTOR (1920)
and.......NED (1921).......and......CAROL (1923)

195

and.......RAYFORD FRANKLIN (1899) Father was
(His aunt)   JOAN had................................JULIE (1921)
RUBY NEWMAN had.........ALTON (1921)
CECILIA JOHNSON had.......REBECCA (1924)
(His daughter) THERA had............................TO (1930)
(His daughter) JULIE had.................................SAMMY (1939)
and.......ROY (1950)

As a footnote, Thera wrote: CC ZINGER also has a daughter by an unknown woman in Japan who was born sometime in the early 1920's. She had a son in 1941.

Chapter 49:
Walking After Midnught

Rachel hears Kee's motorcycle behind her and hides in the shadow of a large tree trunk to watch them pass. The small apartment building where she lives is almost in the heart of Traveston. As she turns the corner at the main street leading from the college to downtown, a car slows to a stop beside her. The driver rolls down the window and speaks.

"Hi ya, Rachel! Can I give you a lift?"

She pauses for a moment as if remembering his name. "Oh, hi, Tony."

She walks around the car as he leans across to open the door.

"You're out late tonight, Tony."

"Been at the gym....working out." He pulls his sticky sweatshirt out from his chest. "What ya been doin'?"

"Just walking and thinking."

They are both silent. She senses his uneasiness.

"Long time, no see." He tugs at his gym shorts.

"It has been. I've noticed you don't seem to see me when your Traveston chums are around." Smug bastard, she thinks. "You didn't even speak to me in class today."

"Hey, that's only because that Gook was at your table. I just found out that my older brother has been killed by Gooks and that don't make me feel too comfortable around them."

"For Christ sake, at least be honest about it! I'm not good enough for you when your college chums are around. Admit it!"

"Come on, Rachel. You know how it is. This is a small town. People are small minded here. They think small and they talk small. It's not like New

197

Orleans. There, we can strut all over town together and nobody cares." He puts his hand on her knee. "And you are mighty good, Rachel. I gotta take you down to New Orleans with me, Girl. You'll love it."

"I'm sorry to hear about your brother." As much as she hates this silly twerp, she has to admit that the hand working its way up to her thigh is setting her body on fire.

"What was his name?"

"Kevin...But nobody ever called him that. His army buddies called him Swamprat. He became a Green Beret."

She knows that he wants nothing but her body. Is it really any different with her? She certainly wants nothing else from this creep. A fair exchange. She squeezes his hot hand.

"Can we use your place, Rachel?"

Smug bastard! She slides close to him and drops her hand under the steering wheel. He responds immediately to her touch. She knows there is something abnormal about her fascination with male bodies. As she works her hand under his jockstrap, she feels a sudden release inside her own volatile body. She knows she is weird for wanting to fondle the dead male bodies in the mortuary that her father has forbade her to touch. Tony is squirming with ecstasy. Is she a latent necrophiliac?"

Rachel laughs aloud. One thing for sure - she likes her men stiff!

***

With the motorcycle humming underneath him, Kee thinks of Rachel's nude body and a bulge grows in his pants. 'Where were you when I needed you?' he thinks. He notices the big white letters on the roof of a barn like building as they pass the field of wrecked automobiles on their right.

C.C. PAYLO - JUNK YARD
USED PARTS CHEAP

Kee is lost in his own thoughts until RD sees the light of the Texaco sign as they top the last hill toward the store.

"Pull in here! It's the house on the hill past the store." He yells in Kee's ear. As they start up the rutted drive he adds. "The lights are on. Thera's home."

RD begins calling Thera as they enter the hallway. He doesn't get an answer, and by the time he reaches the foot of her stairs, he senses something is wrong. He takes the steps in bounds and finds her across the bed.

"Thera? Are you alright?" He shakes her gently with no response. "Thera! Thera! Speak to me Thera!" He hugs her shoulders and presses his face against her neck. She is still breathing! "Kee, stay with her. I'm going downstairs to call a doctor."

198

Kee stands at the top of the stairs as RD pushes by him and races down them. The lamp on the desk draws his attention to the note. He walks to the desk and looks down at it.

"Get rid of that." He hears Thera say in faint whisper. "RD must not see that."

Kee quickly folds the note and sticks it in his hip pocket. He puts the ledger and Bible in a drawer of the desk. He walks close to her. She never opened her eyes again, but she smiled and whispered. "Thank youuu....."
Kee kisses her cheek and says. "You're wercome, sweet rady."
Thera is dead when the doctor arrives.

Chapter 50:
Why?

Rachel. the necrophiliac, is beginning to feel as if she is having sex with a corpse.

"I love youu...." Tony whispers again and again as he pounds her body clumsily.

This tryst did not go well. He had let go in her hand before they got out of the car and, after taking a shower, he was raring to go again, only to spend himself at the first contact with her anxious flesh.

She pushed him off of her. "You make me sick!"

Rachel swings out of the bed and stands looking down at him in contempt.

"Do you really think that all that huffing, and puffing, and stuffing, adds up to an expression of love? You're a smug bastard, Tony. And I'm a fool for bringing you here."

"You're sure not the one to talk about love. You'll sleep with anybody and everybody knows it. And don't think everybody didn't notice you buttering up to that damn Gook! Did he get his little prick in you, Rachel? Or, do Gooks even have one?"

"You're more than a smug bastard. You're a bigoted ball of bullshit." She spat her words. "Since you asked, I'll tell you. He's hung like a mule, and I had it nonstop from the time we left class until just before you came creeping along. And, after him, you are a sad, SAD, SAD excuse for a man!"

He suddenly becomes very aware that he is naked and exposed. He pulls the sheet up over himself and cowers.

Chapter 51:
Searching

Clyde takes a firm grip on the lease then lets his dog out of the patrol car. Lucky steps out from the other side and points down river.

"It's just below the bridge, Deputy. Down on that sandbar."

The dog begins to dribble piss he is so excited. He is so strong and high-spirited that even his muscular owner has a hard time holding him in tow.

"I was fishing in my boat when I found it. Most God awful smell in the world." The dog barks. "That dog can probably smell it from here."

They work their way along the bank to the sandbar. A canvas bag has washed up on it and now Clyde can smell it too.

Chapter 52:
Get Out

"Get out of here! I want to wash the stink of you off my body!"
Rachel slams the door behind him. Still stark naked, she walks into her bathroom where she has run a tub of water. She puts a stack of 45s on her record player, pours in a lot of oil and bubble bath, then eases into the tub as the first record drops and Kitty Kallen sings "Little Things Mean A Lot."

"Give me a hand when I've lost the way
Give me your shoulder to cry on Whether the day is bright or gray
Give me your heart to rely on Send me the warmth of a secret smile
To show me you haven't forgotFor now and forever, that's always
and ever Honey, little things mean a lot." Whether the day is
bright or gray Give me your heart to rely on Send me the warmth
of a secret smile To show me you haven't forgot For now and for-
ever, that's always and ever Honey, little things mean a lot."

Rubbing handfuls of soap bubbles over her breasts, she smiles remembering the wonder in Kee's eyes as he fondled them. No one has ever appreciated her body more than him. She closed her eyes remembering his tears on her chest. He was so thrilled he couldn't sexually respond. Drinking that wine so fast may have also had something to do with his inability to perform.

***

"I never seen anybody who loves this stuff more than you!" Nub hands Kee the fresh bottle he has just brought from the well.

"And, you, my good friend, seem to have an endless supply!"

"You sure drink a lot... for such a little fella."Nub watches him tip back the bottle and take a long swallow.

***

Rachel runs her oily fingers between her legs. She is certain that the next time she gets that little oriental Rhett Butler in bed with her, they won't sleep until the world blows up.

***

Chapter 53:
Walking The Floor

As usual, Elizabeth can't sleep. Earlier tonight RD had told her about Daniel getting killed, and explained that Kee was taking him to Thera's house. She heard them leave on Kee's motorcycle some time ago. She glances at the clock. It is just past three in the morning. She puts on her robe and walks into the hallway.

She stands in front of RD's door for a moment. This has been a hard day for him with the news of Daniel's death. He has been so close to Daniel. He has shared many stories with her from their childhood years. She feels she knows Daniel although they have never met. She was so eager to tell him about her father coming to visit her, that she didn't notice, right away, that he was crying. Oh, why did everything have to happen now? She had hoped that RD and herself could arrange a meeting between his Aunt Thera and her father. Her dad has been so lonely since she started school.

She has learned that Thera Fulton is most likely the reason he never married. She hoped to surprise him, by bringing them together, now that he plans to stay here. But, everything seems to be going all wrong. Well, dad will just have to wait a little longer for a reunion with the love of his life.

Katheline notices Kee's door is open.

She starts to close his door, then steps into his room. 'Empty wine bottle, two glasses, rumpled bed.....?' She sniffs, then lifts a pillow to her face. 'Chanel number five...good stuff..expensive. Who is Kee's perfumed lady? He said he was undressed. Could I possibly be that wrong about our gentleman from Japan?'

She has written her father all about her two nice friends at the boarding house. 'Kee could have, at least, waited until after dad's visit... before turning this place into a den of iniquity.'

But, Elizabeth is completely mystified. Kee has never been that close to any of the girls he has met here. She has never even known him to date. He attends group parties occasionally, but, she has never seen him dance with the same girl twice.

She descends the stairs and pauses for a moment in front of Vera's room. Once Vera goes behind that door at eight PM every night, nothing is heard from her until she comes out at half past four in the morning.

Elizabeth goes into the kitchen and puts on the kettle. The clock on the stove tells her it will be more than an hour before Vera starts her daily routine. 'Well, at least Vera will be here when Dad comes. I was so hoping he could meet my friends.'

The phone rings. Her first thought is that her father is arriving early. She rushes into the parlor and eagerly lifts the receiver.

"Dad?"

"Elizabeth, this is RD."

"Oh, hi, RD. I though Dad might be calling early."

"Sorry to disappoint you. I hoped you'd be awake. I thought I'd try two rings."

"Oh, you know me. I never sleep. I'm glad you called. It's so quiet with both you and Kee not here, it's almost spooky. Never mind me, how are things in Woosterville? Are you at your Aunt Thera's?"

"My Aunt Thera is dead, Elizabeth. I wanted to talk with you. Kee is on another drinking spree." His voice trails off weakly. "I don't have anybody else."

"Oh, RD, how awful." She holds her breath, trying desperately to think of the right words.

"Thera had a massive heart attack. She was all alone. She always told me she would never die alone...because so many people loved her. It was important to her...We found her too late...If somebody had been there to help her she might still be alive."

"RD! Don't even think that way! Nobody could have guessed she would have a heart attack. It's nobody's fault she was by herself. That house would have been packed, if there was even a suspicion, that Thera would suddenly become gravely ill."

"Thanks, Elizabeth. I wanted to tell you. I'm sorry I can't be there to greet your father when he comes. I very much want to talk to him."

"And you shall, RD. We'll come to Woosterville right away, as soon as Dad get here. I know it's terrible to ask you now, but necessary; do you know when the funeral will take place?"

"Thera had scheduled Daniel's funeral for Friday. I'll ask that they be buried on the same day."

"We'll be there early today. How do we find Thera's house?"

He gave her good direction then added. "If you have any problem, just ask anybody in Woosterville where Miss Thera lives. Everybody knows." RD is silent for a moment.

"I'm so glad you're coming, Elizabeth. I have to hang up now. I have a lot of calls to make."

"Goodnight my dear sweet prince....I love you and I hurt for you."

RD is so moved he can't tell her goodnight. He pushes the cutoff and weeps. There is a picture in his mind of a beautiful June bug with her voice reading its sweet message.

"May you walk through life with a friend beside you."

***

Clyde, with his good police dog beside him, rings the doorbell.

"What in the world brings you here so early in the morning, Deputy?" Mister Souquet stands in the door in his old fashioned nightshirt.

"We found a body in a bag floating in the river. It's badly decomposed. We thought perhaps you could help us identify the corpse."

"Just drive around to the funeral home, son. I'll get dressed."

***

Rachel dresses and goes to her phone. She slept well and feels rested and alive. Also, for the first time in more than a year, she feels sure about herself and what she wants. She picks up the phone and dials 411 for directory assistance.

The local operator ask her for the city and state.

"Traveston, Georgia,"

"What listing?"

"Vera's boarding house on Walnut Street...or is it Elm? Good. Thank you."

She dials the number.

"Hello, could I speak with Kee Oh Toe, please?"

"I'm sorry. Kee's not here. May I ask who's calling?"

"A friend. It's urgent. Do you know where I can reach him?"

"He took RD to Woosterville. RD has a death in the family."

"RD is also a close friend of mine. Which person in his family died?"

"Actually, two persons died very recently....his cousin, Daniel, and his Aunt Thera."

"Thera is dead! OH MY GOD!" Rachel is stunned. "And Daniel. Poor RD. They are all he has."

"I spoke with him just last night. He's taking it very hard. My father and

I will be driving to visit him Friday morning. Would you like for me to deliver a message to him....or Kee?"

"I know I sound awfully forward, but...could I ride to Woosterville with you? It's very important that I see both of them."

"Of course you can. I'm anxious to meet you, actually.....Miss..?"

"Souquet, Rachel Souquet...."

"I shall look forward to meeting you, Rachel. My name is Elizabeth McTanis. If you will tell me where you live, we'll pick you up."

"That's OK. I'm just a short walk to Vera's. I'll meet you there no later than ten o'clock. If I don't show, you'll know I found an earlier ride. Either way, I'll see you at Thera's house."

Chapter 54:
Me Without You

RD sits alone in Thera's porch swing, holding the tattered photo of his parents and a recent picture of Daniel in his green beret uniform.

Irene has turned on the radio inside, and RD feels as if George Jones is singing just for him tonight. He finds comfort in the words of the song "Me Without You."

> *"Imagine a world where no music was playing*
> *Then think of a church where nobody's praying.*
> *If you've ever looked up at a sky with no blue.*
> *Then you've seen a picture of me without you."*

If Thera were here, he knows what she would tell him.

"The secret is to never give them up. I don't. I sit with them in this swing on rainy evenings such as this. I can close my eyes and see Nathan sitting right here watching me gardening in those very flowerbeds.

> *"Have you walked in a garden where nothing was growing?*
> *Or stood by a river where nothing was flowing?*
> *If you've seen a red rose unkissed by the dew,*
> *then you've seen a picture of me without you."*

"Daniel, what am I ever going to do without you and Thera?" He says to nobody. But, he also knows what Daniel would say if he were here.

"You can only do what you must do - get over it! Get on with your life,

Bocephus. That's all you can do." Daniel was never accused of being too sentimental RD is reminded of what Thera said when Lieutenant Rivers sent
them a letter and this picture.

"They called him Grasshopper. Can you imagine such a name?'

'Thera, do you think Daniel would still be home if Becky hadn't married
'finicky' Fred?'

'RD, only God can answer such questions."

"Can you picture Heaven with no angels singing?
Or a quiet Sunday morning with no church bells ringing?
If you've watched as the heart of a child breaks into,
Then you've seen a picture of me without you."

'Oh, precious Thera, why did you have to PPFFTT?'

'The Black Widow killed my daddy.' Thera told him and Daniel.

"My daddy died in the war." Stated Daniel.

"I never had a daddy." RD said sadly.

His thoughts turn to Nub and Kee who have been sitting in front of the
store drinking all night. He sniffs and tries to smile at the only two drunks
he knows sharing their hootch. 'What makes drunks such nice people when
they're sober?'

RD closes his eyes and tries to imagine Thera in the swing beside him.

"Thera, do you think they're trying to make up for what they did while
they were drunk?"

"What would she say?"

"'RD, you amaze me! Such imagination!" Then she would let out a bub-
bly laugh he loved.   "Did he make you laugh, Thera?" He would ask.

"All the time." She would answer."He made me laugh a lot, RD. I called
him Sir Laughs-A-Lot and he called me Lady Greyeyes. Can you imagine
such names? My other Raybun was here with me when I was telling you
about him. Nobody can ever take him away from me."

"What an awful tragedy!" RD moans. "After all these years grieving
over his death, just as fate is about to re-unite them, Thera dies unexpected-
ly! Shakespeare could not have written a more tragic final act."

"It's nobody's fault......my Sweet Prince."

Now, RD sees Elizabeth with her pretty Scarab that says..

"May you walk through life with a friend beside you,"

"The Egyptians worship Scarabs, RD. They consider them sacred."

"And the Black Widow eats them." He had told her.

"I know. I read your report. You should get it published."

"Is there a Black Widow in your life, Elizabeth?"

"No, silly. Besides, I'm a woman. Or haven't you noticed?"

Of course he noticed. The dark-haired beauty with the large green eyes and trim figure is clearly focused in his mind. Those eyes seem to joke at a world that will never understand the mysterious secrets deep inside her. The commas that dimple her creamy complexion always reveal her secret mirth.

The face vanishes and in its place is the personification of feminine charm, now he sees a clear image of Katheline. Gorgeous hair rippling in golden harmony about her perfectly molded features. Large blue eyes that draw him inside to float on her dreams.

'I love her, Thera. I love her.'

Chapter 55:
Going To Seed

Irene stands in front of Thera's house admiring Becky's golden mums. Thera weeded the flowerbeds so carefully all her life. But, now, the grass is going to seed. Irene walks around the yard bending and pulling up long, seed-laden stems. She tires quickly and gives up on her hopeless effort. She walks to the edge of the high bank and throws her handful of stems down it in frustration.

The entire yard is hopeless, and they will all be here tomorrow. Even the Governor! Where are all the young men? Did they expect a ninety-one-year-old woman to prepare this place for visitors?

The happiest years of Irene's life were the ones she spent taking care of this place. Nathan Fulton was the kindest man she had ever known. She walks around the house to the far opposite corner. She had lived in a room at that corner of the house. She reflects back on an old song she heard years ago.

"Oh, if this old house could talk, what a story it would tell
It would tell about the good times and the bad times as well
Oh, if this old house could talk it would break my heart in two,
I couldn't stand to be reminded of all the things we used to do."

Everything seemed so simple and easy until that day when Rayford cut off Charlie's arm. She had been awakened by the commotion of an argument between Charlie, Ida Maye and Rayford. She heard Charlie tell them he was going to tell Nathan what they had been doing behind his back. Poor Nathan. He would simply die if he knew what Rayford has been doing with his wife. And what would happen to her daughter? Why, Nathan might even kill Ida Maye; him being so religious and all.

Irene has listened at her window as they began lowering the sleeves down into the well. When Rayford left Ida Maye watching the truck, the idea struck her. Rayford had said that sleeve could kill Charlie. Kill Charlie!

Charlie Hooper is the only man in the world that Irene ever wanted. But, he didn't want her. He wanted Joan and she wanted him, too. Irene couldn't stand seeing them together anymore. She had tried everything to get him interested in her, unspeakable things! He would take her favors, too! Then go right back after Joan! Kill Charlie! Then he can't tell Nathan and he can't marry Joan.

She had run out the back door screaming. When Ida Maye asked her what was wrong, Irene said she had seen a big spider in her room. She knew her mother was deathly afraid of spiders. Ida Maye told her to watch the truck and went inside to kill the spider for her.

Irene let the brake off the truck just before Rayford came back. She ran inside and told Ida Maye that they had killed Charlie. Through the window, they watched Rayford go down into the well after Charlie and they fell on the bed in each other's arms, scared silly.

Ida Maye was such a loving little girl, so different from Joan.

But Joan did love Charlie, for certain. When he broke off with her after losing his arm, she killed herself. She jumped right in front of a big truck. Charlie didn't even know Joan was going to have his baby, until after she died.

When Charlie called her last night to tell her that Thera had died, Irene had caught a taxi and rushed to this house. It had taken her most of the night to contact some of the people who are close to her. 'They will all be here tomorrow and this place looks awful!'

Chapter 56:
May You Always

What Irene doesn't know is that there is a small army on the way to take care of Thera's house. Bobby and Becky are the first to arrive in Rayford's old truck with everything they need to make the landscaping the pride of Woosterville. A group of her friends is on the way to clean and the ladies are planning to cook a feast fit for the Royal Family. By the end of the day there have been so many flowers delivered that there is not enough room in the house and both front and rear porches are lined with them. Letters and sympathy cards have already set a one day record at the post office.

The state legislature has decreed that tomorrow will be an official day of mourning.

Her obituary will appear in every newspaper throughout the state.

The Governor himself will deliver her eulogy.

Her legacy will be that there has never been a woman who was more loved by more people.

Chapter 57:
Playing George Jones

Nub comes out of the store singing along with George Jones.

"G-men, G-men, revenue-ers, too, searching for the place where he made his brew.
They were lookin; trying to book him, but my pappy kept on cookin;
Buuuuhuuuuhaaaahuuu, White Lightning!"

"How you feeling, Sonny?" The jukebox has finished playing the records he selected as Nub sits down on the bench with Kee.

"Warui...Bad...." Kee rubs his eyes. "Do you have more of my favorite drink?"

"Sure do, Sonny." Nub grips Kee's shoulder and pulls himself to his feet. "I've always appreciated a man who'd have a drink with me. It's hell to drink alone." He goes into the store, slaps the jukebox hard, with the flat of his hand, and punches in six more of his favorite tunes. He returns with another bottle, braces it between his knees, and twists off the cap with his one strong hand.

"In North Carolina, way back in the hills,
There lived my old pappy and he had him a still.
He brewed white lighting 'till the sun went down.
Then he'd fill him a jug and pass it around...."

"That's the best singer, we got, son. They call him 'the possum.' There's a good verse out of an old movie called "Song Of The South" that goes something like this:

"Ol' Br're Possum got a trick. How come he get so fat?
When trouble come along, he play like dead.
Now, who wants to live like that?"

Nub offers Kee the bottle. Kee holds up his hand in refusal and laughs.

"After you, Sir! I insist."

"Damn if I don't appreciate good manners, too." Sir Nub tilts the bottle to his lips.

"It's a very strong drink, Nub-san. What is it made from?"

"Corn." Nub offers him the bottle again. "We call it corn likker."

"Corn rikker?" Kee takes a long swallow'

'Close enough, pal. It's also called moonshine, and corn squeezing, and white lightening."

Bottles rattle behind him and Nub snaps his head over his shoulder as CC wheels up beside him with his bicycle basket full of old bottles he has picked up alongside the road. As Nub passes his bottle to Kee, CC drops his bike and the bottles spill noisily. He doesn't seem to notice, but runs straight to Kee trying to stop him from taking a drink.

"Don't drink it!...Don't drink it!...Don't drink it!"

Kee turns his back to him. "NONDIEYO!? (What do you mean?)...leave me alone, BAKA! (You old fool!)"

"Warui.....Bad.....Bad water." CC was making a face and shaking his head as if watching someone biting a lemon wedge. Kee was taking a long drink.

"Ni Yo. (No.) Not mesu...Good corn rikker! (Yoei)"

"You'll see, You'll see.... Huh?, Huh?, Huh..."

"Don't mind CC, Sonny. He's batty as a loon, but he don't mean no harm."

"CC?...CC Payro?" Kee spun to face him. "Same as CC Zinger?"

Nub was picking up the empty bottles CC has spilled out of his basket, but dropped the two he had in his hand and popped erect when he heard Kee say Zinger.

"No, no, no, NO!" CC shook his head vigorously. "Watashi wa...Paylo-san." (I am Paylo.)

"Anatawa Nihonjin des ka?" (Do you speak Japanese?) Kee asks.

"Hai, skoshi des." (Yes, a little.) CC replies.

Nub pats his head as if looking for his flashlight. 'Is this for real? Old crazy CC talking in tongues with this young man from Japan?'

Kee whispers his grandmother's name. "Shemora...."

"Shemora-san? Doko?" (Slang: Where is Shemora?" When Kee doesn't answer, CC pushes by Nub and grabs Kee by his shoulders. "Doko? Doko? SHEMORA-SAN DOKO?"

The smell of the old man penetrates Kee's pickled brain. He pushes CC away.

"She's dead. Shemora-san is dead."

CC seems to be looking through Kee at something far away. Tears gather in his eyes then roll down over his dirty, wrinkled flesh. Kee's simple declaration that his grandmother is dead seems to have taken his breath away and CC gasps for air.

"Suuwooooooooooo." CC gasps for air again and tries to talk over Nub's singing..."But, she's so very far away..... suuuooooo.... haven't seen her smile in oh, so many years." The effort makes him cough and wheeze. Normally, CC loves to hear Nub sing with the possum, but not now. Not now.

"Not now, Nub, I can't carry a tune in my bottomless bucket." CC comments. "Not now."

Nub stops singing. CC wants to say something but can't. He leans on the back of the straight chair and takes a deep, deep breath. "Suuuooooooo ooooo." Then whispers softly, as he slowly exhales.

"Smile for me Shemora-san..." He takes another deep gasp. "Suuooooooo....smile for, smile for me, smile for me." CC's habitual triple laugh is gone, gone, gone."Suuuooooo... Sayonara, Shemora-san,....suuwoooo....suuwooooo.... Sayonara, Sayonara, Sayonara." He stands there crying, until Nub can no longer look at him. Kee turns his back to CC and, as the old Rock-ola sends out the sweet sounds of the best country singer in the world, Kee walks toward Thera's house.

***

'I must get to Thera's house today.' Rachel decides. 'I must see RD and KeeOhToe.'

She has been on pins and needles since talking with Katheline. She has spent the last few hours pacing around the small college campus with nothing to do but wait, and she is not good at it. She doesn't want to wait another day. She feels uneasy about riding with Elizabeth and her father, and she has made up her mind to use that option only as a last resort.

Rachel is a woman of action. She must do something! She walks several blocks to Molly's Kitchen, a café adjacent to a truck stop on the main highway. She hasn't eaten since yesterday.

She enters the restaurant and takes a seat at a circular counter. She orders a grilled cheese sandwich and soup of the day.

A chubby little man with squirrel teeth is on a stool at the opposite side of the counter.

"I'll have the same as the pretty lady." He scratches his stubby beard and smiles at Rachel.

She glances at the truck she noticed outside, while walking across the lot.

216

It is parked in a direction that suggests it is going her way.

"Where you headed, Mister?"

"All the way to Florida, Pretty Lady." He bumped his teeth on his coffee cup staring at her.

"How about you?"

"I need a ride to Woosterville. It's important. A friend of mine is in trouble."

The waitress brings his soup and he leans around her to see Rachel as she speaks.

"My friend has had a death in his family." She sees disappointment in his face when she indicates her friend is male.

"Well, I'm going right through there, Pretty lady. You're more than welcome to ride with me." He turns his spoon too soon and drips soup on his little round belly.

**

Chapter 58:
I Love You

"Bobby, put your hand here!" Becky raises her gown, and he rubs her belly. "Can you feel it?"

"He's kicking like a mule."

"What if it's a girl?"

"I'll love it just like it's mine."

"Oh, you...!" She grabs his long black hair and shakes his head affectionately. He embraces her and they fall into the bed laughing. Becky is smiling with tears in her eyes and when she closes them they lie quiet and still until Bobby begind singing softly to her until she sleeps.

> *"I love you. And I'll prove it a thousand ways.*
> *You know its true. Darling, you are the only one.*
> *I'll be nice and sweet to you...and no matter what you do.*
> *I'll always love you. And I'll prove it a thousand ways."*

***

"I'm worried about our daughter, Helen." The Souquets are eating lunch alone in their large formal dining room.

"So am I, Henry." Mrs. Souquet rubs her mouth briskly with her lace napkin. "I don't think she's old enough to be out on her own yet."

He sips the clear white wine. "We have identified the body they found in the river."

"Now, Henry. Do you think that's a proper topic of discussion while we're eating?"

"His name is Sammy Paylo."

"That name means nothing to me."

"I've been told that Rachel was seen with him quite regularly before he was killed."

"Killed?"

"At the expense of spoiling your meal - Yes, brutally murdered; decapitated."

"Oh, really, Henry! Did you have to say that?" She pushed the half-eaten rare steak away.

"I could have said more." He takes a big juicy bite. "The person who did it is obviously stark raving mad and on the loose. It is possible that our daughter could be in danger should the murderer associate her with the last victim."

"In that case, I suppose it's good that she is away from Woosterville. At least until that maniac is caught."

"Exactly my feelings on the matter, Helen. I had thought of driving to bring her home this weekend, but decided against it. But, with the double funerals on Friday, I sure could have used Rachel's help preparing the bodies."

What he never tells his wife, or anyone else, is that he knows the body bag used by the killer is from his mortuary. He also knows that Rachel is the only person, other than himself, with a key to the funeral home. He does not know how, or to what extent Rachel is involved in the bizarre murder. As a precaution, he decides to dispose of the other severed organ he found in the bag with Sammy's head. He found a perfect hiding place where nobody will ever find it. It is neatly tucked away and will be buried forever in Thera's body come Friday.

Rachel will be disappointed that she wasn't here to do Thera's face. Her funeral will be the biggest he has ever done. People will be coming from everywhere to take a final look at her. He has done his best but he is sure the body would have looked far better if the job had been done by Rachel's skillful hands.

***

Squirrel-ly teeth wanted much more from her, but all he got was a hand job. He stops the truck to rest for awhile, leaving all eighteen wheels on asphalt, due to soft shoulders and a heavy load. She climbs down from the cab and walks up the low end of the bank toward Thera's house.

***

Kyoto and RD are in the swing. Kee is still sipping on Nub's bottle he walked away with from the store. "Why you no tell me about Pay-low, RD?"

"Because I'm your friend."

"And he's my grandfather!" Kee stands up abruptly and almost falls as he comes out of the moving swing. "That Baka (old fool) is the 'Great

American' I've been told about all my life."

He pulls his wallet out of his pocket and manages to remove the old photo of CC. "Since I was rittre boy, I wait to see my grandfather." He crushes the photo in his fist and tosses it at RD. "And he's the virrage idiot everybody raffs at!"

RD stoops, picks up the crushed photo and another neatly folded paper that fell out of Kee's pocket. He puts them in his pocket.

"Forget about him, Kee!" RD follows him to the steps. "He has nothing to do with you, Kee."

"Nothing to do with me?" He stumbles down the steps and crawls to his motorcycle. "Forget about him?" Kee pulls himself onto the seat. "Do you Americans know nothing of ancestral pride?"

"You're in no condition to drive!" RD jumps off the porch. "STOP!"

As Kee kicks the starter and the engine roars to life, RD sees Rachel appear from behind a large shrub near the porch. Just as the bike jumps off its kick stand, Rachel swings in behind Kee and locks her arms around his chest. When the back wheel hits the dirt, the bike rears high in front and almost throws off both of them. When the front wheel comes down, they race across Thera's flower bed and head straight for the high bank.

"TURN RIGHT! THERE'S A DROP OFF AHEAD OF YOU!" RD is chasing them, screaming. Kee does turn right, just in time to avoid going over the embankment. He hits the trail at the top of the bank, on the right corner of the front yard. By the time RD gets to the corner, they are out of sight. He hears the bike's engine and from the sound he knows they have at least made the highway. He goes inside to call Clyde for help.

***

Rachel feels Kee's body come to life in her arms. She squeezes him tightly all the way down the bumpy trail and, as they hit the highway, she moves her hands down his body. She finds him solid as the rock of Gibraltar. She whispers in his ear that she loves him.

He twists the throttle wide open, closes his eyes, and throws his head back and screams.

"KKAAA.....EEEEEE!"

"What was that?" Becky turns on a lamp.

"Sounds like a nightbird." Bobby gets out of bed and looks out the window just as the motorcycle slams into the back of the big truck's trailer."Holy Shit!"

"What happened?"

"Two kids on a motorcycle just splattered into the back of an eighteen-wheeler like bugs on a windshield!"

***

220

"It's an emergency, Dee Dee...an accident out near the Franklin farm."

Elroy is still on the phone. She taps her chest. "Sure, you can go, but we've got to hurry."

***

"Let's hurry, Dad. Just let me call RD and I can tell you all about it on the way. I'm afraid my friend is in terrible trouble."

***

Irene is terribly troubled about the mistake she made with Thera's letter. Now that she's dead it is especially troublesome. Irene has decided that she should give it to either RD or TJ. She still doesn't know what it says but she knows it must be important because of Thera's reaction to seeing it after all these years.

But, now it's gone! She can't find the letter anywhere. All the other papers, the ledger and the Bible are still in Thera's desk. But that trouble-making letter is gone, gone , gone, "Down That River Of No Return" like that song in the movie she liked so much.

RD comes up the stairs and catches her looking through the desk. He holds up the letter,

"OH, MY GOD! OH, MY GOD! OH, MY GOD!" Irene gets hysterical. "I'm so sorry, so sorry, so sorry."

"Now we know why he never came back to her." The phone rings just as RD gives the letter to Irene. Elizabeth is calling to tell him her and her father will be there at about nine in the morning.

"Rachel Souquet is coming with us."

"Rachel? Do you know her?"

"Not really. She called to speak with you or Kee. I'm to meet her tomorrow."

"Rachel is here, Elizabeth." He explained what just happened in the front yard. "I was just about to call the Sheriff's office."

"RD, we're coming over tonight."

"Drive straight through Woosterville. We're about seven miles on the opposite side of town. When you pass the junk yard, look for the first store that is open on your right. The driveway to this house is just up the hill as you pass the store."

"We'll be there within the hour."

"Elizabeth, I want to tell you now that tonight I found out about a mix up with an old letter that explains why your father thought Thera was dead all these years. I'll tell you all about it later,"

"Thank you, RD."

A kindly old hand takes the phone from him.

"I'll make the rest of the calls, RD." Says Irene,
RD puts his arms around her and gently rubs her shoulders.
"It's not your fault, Aunt Irene,"

***

"It wasn't my fault, Sheriff. I was stopped dead still in the road with my tail lights on, and they just ran right into the back of my trailer." As soon as Clyde and the Sheriff step out of the car they are approached immediately by the truck driver with Bobby and Becky also coming out to greet them.

"Why were you stopped?" Sheriff Dawes tips his hat to Becky.

Squirrel-face is silent for a moment before answering. "To adjust my seat...It slid back on me."

"Why didn't you pull off the road?" Clyde asks.

"Why? 'Cause I got a heavy load. I'm afraid of these soft shoulders, you know?"

They hear the siren and look down the road where the ambulance is fast approaching. Elroy slides to a stop beside them with tires squealing.

"No hurry, Elroy." Clyde walks to the ambulance where Elroy has jumped out in a frenzy. "They're both dead." He spots Dee Dee sitting in the seat. "Hi, Dee Dee. It is a pretty messy accident. I don't think you want to see them."

Becky had followed Clyde. "Dee Dee, you want to come inside and have a cup of coffee with me while the men are cleaning up this mess?"

"Jeeez, what are we going to do with this?" Elroy is looking at the splattered flesh in bewilderment.

"You heard the lady." Bobby began collecting parts of the bike and piling them in a neat stack. "We're gonna clean up this mess. I'll get the metal, and you get the skin and bones."

Elroy realizes who this man is, for the first time. "Bobby! What in the name of hell are you doing here?"

Clyde steps in front of Elroy. "He lives here. He's just a law-abiding citizen volunteering to help us public servants. Do you understand?"

"Sure, Clyde. I just didn't know he was outta the pen."

Sheriff Dawes pats Bobby on the shoulder. "We can take care of this now, Bobby. Why don't you go on back in your house and entertain the ladies." He winked at Clyde.

"Well, I have to admit that I'm better at entertaining the ladies than I am at picking up blood and guts. But, all of you are welcome to come in and wash up and have a cup of coffee when you're done. That offer goes for you too, Elroy."

"I appreciate it, Bobby."

222

Chapter 59:
Playing Possum

"I don't appreciate that young man just walking off with my likker that way." Nub has made at least three more slaps on the jukebox, playing nothing but the possum's songs, since he got CC seated in one of the straight chairs. That would be about an hour at three minutes a tune, but CC has not moved or spoke since. He just sits there looking far away with his eyes watering.

Nub has another bottle and he seems content just to have someone with him while he drinks. He has, however, moved to the far end of the bench to get upwind of the smelly old man.

"You sure surprised me talking in tongues with the Japan-easy boy, CC. I should've guessed you might know some of that stuff after spending all them years over there. But, what gets me is that the boy acted like you wuz making some sense. Now, why can't you do that in English? Guess he's the first Japan-easy you've talked to since you wuz overseas. Is that right, CC?" Nub burped loudly. "I see you've got a pair of them purty white pointed-toed shoes like Bobby wears, too. Clyde stopped wearing his. Said they hurt his feet. Well, you don't have to talk if you don't feel like talking. But, I swear, if I didn't know better, I'd think you wuz dead. Shoot, I reckon you might be just playing possum, so you can hear them possum records I been playing." Nub laughs at his own funny, and slaps CC's knee. "Is that it, Coo Coo?"

CC's body begins to slowly tilt forward. Finally, it just topples out of the chair, and lands in the pile of bottles that spilled from the bicycle basket. Nub is startled by the noise.

"Now, who wants to live like that?"

***

Becky has gone to quiet Mary Ann and Susan. Dee Dee is sitting in the rocker sipping coffee when Bobby enters the room. Neither speak as he takes the over-stuffed chair in front of her. He looks at her carefully and smiles.

"I can't smile back at you yet, Bobby, but I'm glad you approve of the way they fixed my face." She touches her cheek. " It takes a long time to heal and, if I smile, it hurts real bad in there."

"You look great, Dee Dee."

Becky comes back into the room. "I hope I'm not interrupting anything. I know that you two used to be awfully close."

"Yes, we were, Honey." Bobby stands and takes his wife's hand. "But, that was before I fell head over heels in love with you." He guides her to sit in the big chair and seats himself on its arm rest. "How are you and Elroy getting along, Dee Dee."

"Fine. Just fine." Her eye twitches involuntarily.

***

"Irene, Coo Coo's dead. He was just sitting in a chair down at the store, then he just killed over dead." Nub held the screen door open, but Irene made no move to come out of the house. "What should I do about him, Irene?"

"Good riddance! That's what I say. He ain't my problem. No more he ain't."

"Well, now, somebody's gotta bury him. Pay for the funeral and all."

"Well, that somebody ain't me! Get him buried there at the junk yard. That place is already stunk up with him. It's a fittin' spot to bury his smelly self!" Irene pulls the screen closed and stares through it at Nub. "Stop letting in the flies. Thera's house has got enough to worry about right now. Leave us alone, Charlie. Just get rid of him."

As nub reaches CC's body again, he notices that flies are buzzing around his filthy old head.

He goes inside and calls Lucky.

"Lucky! Old Coo Coo just killed over dead here at my store. Irene says to bury him on his land at the junk yard. Can you take care of burying him for me?"

***

Lucky's old pickup rattled into the gravel in front of the store. He backs it up to the transom and gets out. He takes a heavy tarp and spreads it on the ground beside the old man's body, sits in the straight chair and puts on his boots and gloves. Then he takes CC's white shoes off his feet and puts them in the cab, and rolls old Coo Coo up in the tarp. He drops the tailgate and speaks to Nub.

"Charlie, can you handle that end?"

Nub didn't answer. He just made a tight twist at his end of the tarp and took a firm grip with his one strong hand and lifted as Lucky picked up the other end.

"One..Two...Three...Heave!" They swung the body into the bed of the truck and closed the tailgate. Nub throws in the bicycle and all the bottles CC has collected.

Lucky says an impromptu eulogy for old CC "Paylo" Zinger.

"Whew, he stinks like carne!"

***

Elroy manages to hold on until the job is finished. When they had all of the pieces of the two bodies that they could identify in the bags and placed in the ambulance, he walks to the side of the road and vomits.

The other men have washed up and are sitting around the kitchen table drinking coffee as Elroy enters Bobby's house.

"How's Sammy doing, Clyde?" Bobby has taken a chair across from Clyde. The driver sits on Bobby's right and the Sheriff is on his left.

Clyde is slow to answer. "Sammy just disappeared some time back."

Squirrel-face put down his coffee. "Hey, I knew Sammy... He caught a ride with me one time. Helped me with the driving."

"Where did he leave you?"

"Oh..." The driver is squinting his eyes as if thinking hard. "It's been awhile..." He snaps his fingers. "It was Albuquerque, New Mexico! That's where he left me. Said he was going to California."

Clyde wonders if he can pull off his plan to cover up Sammy's awful demise. Sheriff Dawes is quiet, but his keen eyes are taking an in-depth look at each person who speaks.

"Well, I guess that explains why we haven't seen Sammy lately." Says Elroy as he pulls up a chair beside Clyde.

Bobby grins. "Yeah, once Sammy got to California, I wouldn't expect him to feel like he had much reason to come back here. I bet he's living it up out there."

The Sheriff stands and puts on his hat. Clyde does the same.

"Thank you for the coffee, Becky. I believe Bobby has finally found somebody who can keep him out of trouble." He offers Bobby his hand. "Good luck to you, son." He smiles broadly and holds up a finger. "He's a good man, Becky. But, he's got a mean streak in him. So, keep your eye on him."

"I intend too, Sheriff." Becky glances at Dee Dee.

As the Sheriff and his deputy step out of the house, Clyde says evenly.

"I lied to them, Sheriff. We identified that body we found in the river. It was Sammy Paylo."

The Sheriff put his hand on Clyde's shoulder. "I know. Sometimes it's best to keep such things to ourselves. What people don't know, can't hurt them."

***

Julie hears Lucky's truck drive into the field behind her house. She walks out to meet him. He cuts the engine, but leaves the lights shining out over the high grass.

"CC's dead. I got his body in the truck. Irene says to bury him here." He takes his boots and gloves, drops the tailgate, and sits on it to take off his new white shoes and put on the boots.

"There's no need to dig a fresh hole, Lucky." Julie points to the far corner of the back yard. "That old well over there has been dried up for years."

Lucky gets back in his truck and drives it to the well. He removes a heavy wooden cover lying over the hole and begins unloading the truck. He throws the old bicycle and rakes the bottles into it.

Julie has followed him across the field and watches him slide the tarp off the tailgate and let it fall down in the deep hole. "Before you fill in the hole, Lucky, can you bring your truck around to the back of the garage? There are some other items of his that I want you to throw into that hole for me."

Later that night, Lucky pats the soil above the filled hole with his shovel. He removes his boots and gloves and takes out his little notebook and records grave number four thousand.

'Now, that is really a drop-in.' He thinks. 'I wonder why that old fool was keeping all of them spoiled canned goods? Guess he thought we might have another war or something. Whew! That stuff smelled almost as bad as old Coo Coo!"

***

Henry Souquet is making final preparations in the parlor. He decides to position the two coffins at slight angles in front of the pews with the heads pointing toward the pulpit which has a magnificent gold-plated bible stand in front of it.

Wreaths have been coming in steadily for two days. Henry is placing the largest of them in an impressive semicircle that curves all the way from the walls of the wide room to meet in the center in front of the gilt Bible on its golden stand. The stage behind the pulpit is a solid array of gorgeous floral arrangements. As he selects the best of the best for the most prominent spot

226

in front of the pulpit, Henry reads a card on one of the most magnificent over-sized wreaths he has ever seen.

IN LOVING MEMORY OF MISS THERA FULTON
THE GREAT LADY OF THE STATE OF GEORGIA.   - JF/K

A mortician's dream come true. 'Centerpiece provided by the President himself!'

Sheriff Dawes and Clyde startle him as they walk softly and reverently into the parlor.

"Sorry, gentlemen. We are not ready to receive visitors just yet."

"We're here on business, Mister Souquet." The sheriff removes his hat. "Can we speak with you for a moment,"

"I'm quiet busy at the moment. This is the most important funeral in Woosterville history."

He gestures with pride at the amazing array of flowers. "This wreath is from the President himself."

"We won't take long. It's about that body we found in the river."

"I couldn't do much with it, Sheriff. It was badly mutilated and decomposed."

"I wanted to ask you to simply dispose of it. We know who murdered Sammy Paylo."

"Oh, I see..." Henry eyes Thera's casket uneasily.

"Your daughter was killed in a motor vehicle accident this evening, Mister Souquet." Clyde announced. "The ambulance is outside with both her remains and those of the young man she was riding with when it happened."

"OOOHHHHHOOOOOO...." Henry moans like his weak heart has just been ripped out of his chest.

"We feel that the best approach to Sammy's death is to just quietly dispose of his body. Letting this story get out is definitely not in the best interest of the living." The Sheriff explains.

"Did Rachel suffer?"

"No. Her death was instantaneous, according to eyewitnesses."

***

The first person to view Thera's body in state is TJ Franklin.

'It doesn't look like her." He observes. "She never wore makeup like that. But, what is it that just doesn't seem right?' Suddenly it hits him. He has never seen Thera with her eyes closed!

TJ calls to tell RD that Mister Souquet has everything ready for the funerals to take place tomorrow at noon. He, too, reads the card on the center wreath.

'JF/K — Jack Fisher and his daughter Katheline.'

Chapter 60:
A New Beginning

Just behind the ashes of the burned prefab house there is a long and winding road that leads up to the crest of a large plateau. Mostly the landscape is flat with only a few scattered scrub pines among knee high Johnson grass. Sir Laughs A Lot has decided that it is an ideal spot for the Thera Fulton Memorial Cemetary.

There is not enough time to complete his vision prior to Thera's funeral, but, there is time to start and to make the commitment required for it to become a reality in a few days. He has already bought the land from Becky at a price good enough for her to be delighted to sell it to him. He has already commissioned two large sculptures to be completed right away by a good friend and accomplished artist in residence at Vanderbilt University.

High on the hill across the road, in the exact spot where the "moping tree' now stands, an oversized statue of Thera Fulton will be placed on a marble pedestal to raise her eyelevel to the precise height it would be with her looking down from her window above the porch. Daniel's tree will be replanted where the ashes from the prefab house have been plowed under to enrich the soil. He has already contracted with a top notch group of golf course designers who assured him that when they finish executing his plans, this place will be as lush and beautiful as Augusta National. A statue of Daniel with a parachute drapped over his shoulder and curled around his leg covering his missing left foot will be placed under the shade of his tree with him looking up across the road at Thera's memorial. At the large gated entrance to the winding road up the hill there will be an American flag above an engraved granite message expressing the nation's graditude to the young men and women who served in Vietnam. The gravesites will be free to all veterans of all branches of the United States Military. There are still many details to work out and he has retained the services of TJ Franklin to put in place a trust fund for the long term financing and maintenace of the entire complex.

However, a most important first step begins today. Gravesites are being prepared and graves are being dug for the first two people to be buried here. They will be side by side under the shade of a magnificant solitary oak that is thought to be at least three hundred years old. It stands in the center of the plateau and when the roadwork is finished there will be a full circle roundabout orbiting it. With drives to the other sites spreading out like spokes of a wheel, or rays from the sun, across the entire plateau.

The professor was lucky to find a grave digger on such short notice. A Mister Lynn Sledge has worked late into the night and the graves are done. Dr. McTanis gave him an enormous tip by local standards and he feels lucky to have gotten the job. "Lucky" is also happy to be a part of the biggest funeral in the history of Woosterville

Chapter 61:
Earth Angel/My Special Angel

The Country Club's Cotillion Ball is the biggest social event of the year in Traveston. As the reigning Miss Traveston High, Katheline was unanimously selected by her coterie as the Harvest Queen. She is extremely popular and extremely sad. Her mom has her dressed in the most beautiful white evening gown she has ever seen in her life. Her escort for the evening is one of the nicest boys she knows and he has gone all out and rented a white stretch limousine for the occasion. This should be among the happiest nights of her life. Instead, it is, in fact, one of the most miserable days in a terrible week for her. She has been feeling awful about herself since the night RD showed up unannounced here in Traveston. She behaved terribly, and she can't blame him for turning to that lovely English girl after the way she treated him. She knows Elizabeth and RD were just trying to make her jealous, but what really happened is that she was forced to realize how much she truly loves RD Newman. She is heart broken over the fact that what could have been a great summer for them to be together has turned into this insane situation that is keeping them apart. The truth is that Katheline has never even liked Tony Bivens and the only reason she was with him at Nancy's cookout that night was because she has been deliberately keeping her distance from all suitors since meeting RD.

So, here she is dancing with Roger Jamison in this gorgeous ballroom, listening to that wonderful song that RD sang to her the last time she saw him in Woosterville, and ruining her mascara.

"Earth Angel, earth Angel will you be mine?

230

I'll love you forever, until the end of time.
I'm just a fool, a fool in love with you."

Katheline still swoons every time she gets lost in the memory of that day at the store.

"Katheline Fisher, you have a guest in the lobby." Comes a voice over the speakers.

"Excuse me, Roger."

"Are you OK?"

"I'll be fine. Thank you, Roger." She squeezes his hand before she releases it, and rushes to the lobby, where she is met by an anxious Vera.

"There you are, My dear. Your father has been trying to reach you. Thera Fulton died. Her funeral is tomorrow."

"Oh, Vera. Thank you so much for letting me know." She gives her a quick hug and rushes back to Roger.

"Can I use the Limo? I have to get to Woosterville right away."

"Of course you can." He hands her the keys. "Be careful."

"Thank you so much." She smiles and kissed his cheek. "I'm so lucky to have a friend like you."

Katheline is furious with her father for waiting until the last minute to let her know about Thera's death. This is the last chance he gets to disapprove of the two of us! RD is my choice! And that's that.

Poor RD! Losing Thera and Daniel both within a matter of days! What can he be thinking about me?

Katheline is determined to make record time from the ballroom to Nub's store.

***

"There's the store, Dad." Elizabeth leans forward and points toward the house on the hill beyond it. "And that must be Thera's house."

Professor McTanis has rented a black LTD as an appropriate vehicle for the funeral. He notices the one-armed man sleeping on the bench as they pass the store. He drives slowly up the driveway and parks between Thera's car and the one with a big star on the side labeled SHERIFF.

RD is walking with Sheriff Dawes to the patrol car when he sees Elizabeth. He runs down the steps to meet her. He opens her door and takes both of her hands and smiles.

"I'm so glad you're here. The Sheriff is just taking me to the funeral home to view the arrangements for tomorrow."

"I'm Professor McTanis. I'm happy to meet you, young man." He offers his hand. "You've made quite an impression on my daughter,"

"Thank you, Sir. The pleasure is truly mine."

"I realize you must be anxious to get to the mortuary. Can we take you there?"

"That would be great!" RD gives an enthusiastic swing with both his hand and Elizabeth's."

"The traffic is horrendous everywhere." The Sheriff tips his hat as they go to the cars. "Just follow me, Professor."

Becky bounds down the steps with something to tell them.

"Don't worry about accommodations. Irene is preparing your rooms."

***

The Governor and most of the state legislature have arrived in Woosterville for Thera's funeral. Every room in every nearby town is taken. Trailers and campers fill every vacant lot and parking place for miles around.

There are so many cars that the Georgia State Patrol has to line the drive to Thera's house and only allow a select few of them to pass. Nub sells out of gas before noon, and gives up the last pint of moonshine he plans to sell by mid-afternoon.

Evening is approaching, as the sheriff's squad car escorts a black LTD down the semicircular driveway at the mortuary. It is Elizabeth and her father bringing RD to view Thera and Daniel in state.

***

RD gets out of the car in front of the funeral parlor. The Professor drives Elizabeth down to the Souquet home. To her surprise, Clyde is there to open her door. He walks her to the door and introduces her to Helen and Henry when they answer the doorbell.

Mister Souquet goes down to let them in to view the arrangements.

***

RD goes to the bay windows and cups his hands above his eyes to peek inside. He drops to his knees to see under the thick curtains and strains to see through the thick glass. The room is dark and peaceful.

A long white limousine stops at the far side of the circular drive behind him and someone gets out of it. The LTD comes down the drive from the Souquet home on the other side.

Suddenly, it all becomes clear to him! Death is the Black Widow! Not people. Not the female.

Not women! Death! That's what they are all afraid of...DEATH!

They see RD on his knees and hear him sobbing with a muffled cry.

Seemingly, from out of nowhere, a figure dressed in flowing white, arrives over him with her palms outstretched and leans to lightly touch his shoulders and speaks softly for his ears alone.

"I came as fast as I could. I love you, RD."

He stands and turns to take her in his arms and sings softly for her ears alone.

"You are my special Angel, sent from up above
The Lord smiled down on me, and sent me an Angel to love.
You are my special Angel, through eternity,
I'll have my special Angel, here to watch over me."

"Love is life, Katheline."

Elizabeth approaches, removes the Scarab from her neck, and without a word, puts it around Katheline's neck and turns back to join Clyde and her father.

"Dad, I've decided to write a novel."

"Really, Elizabeth? What's it about?"

"It's about living and dying in the rural south of France."

"What's your theme?"

"People simply change. Death is the greatest change. And life is a gift." She touches her chest where the Scarab used to rest. 'The Gift of the hole digger.'

Professor McTanis smiles knowingly.

"No, my dear. Love is the gift."

Elizabeth says nothing, but Clyde knows she is in full agreement with her dad's words, by the way she looks, with her bright and beautiful green eyes, directly at the man who only has eyes for her.

***

The funerals are set to take place tomorrow at high noon on, Friday, the twenty-second day of November, 1963. The people who have gathered in Woosterville expect it to be the most monumental event in the history of this little southern town. However, what happens next, by comparison, will completely pale the importance of these funerals.

The President of the United States of America is shot and killed.

Chapter 62:
Secret Love

The funerals begin with full military honors for Daniel including a 21-gun-salute of 3 vollys by a seven man firing squad and taps played by a lone bugler positioned under the "moping tree." The Governor reads the inscription to be engraved on the tribute to Americans who served in Vietnam. Honoring a request from her father, Elizabeth sings a beautiful rendition of "Secret Love" as made popular by Doris Day.

> *"Once I had a secret love, who lived within the heart of me,*
> *And too soon my secret love, became impatient to be free*
> *Now I shout it from the highest hills, even told the golden daffodils*
> *Now my heart's an open door, and my secret love's no secret anymore,"*

The Governor closes the services with an inspiring eulogy for Thera and a description of the planned memorial. Her gravemarker will be a huge marble ingraving of the words to the last song she sang to Professor McTanis when she told him she was terminally ill. The song "May You Always" was made popular by the McGuire Sisters.

> *"May your heartaches be forgotten May no tears be spilled*
> *May old acquaintance be remembered May your cup of kindness filled*
> *May you always be a dreamer, may your wildest dreams come true,*
> *May you find someone to love, as much as I love you."*

When the services are over, Clyde brings RD home. As soon as he gets there,

RD goes upstairs to sit at Thera's desk. He opens the drawer where Kee put away her Bible, the ledger and her notes. He opens the gilt Bible to the center fold of the Fulton Family Tree to discover a sealed envelope with a message across it written in Thera's hand:

To be opened only by <u>Rabun Duel 'RD' Newman</u> and only in the event of my death.   Thera Fulton

RD takes an opener out of the desk and carefully opens the letter.

My dear RD,

I have lived a good life and now that it all seems near the end, I want you to know the truth, because the truth can set you free to love and live happy without me. I have lived a double life that has brought me more happiness than one person could ever dream or expect in a single lifetime.

My secret life began with my trip to North Carolina when you were only seven years old. That was when I was finally reunited with my "Sir Laughs A Lot". He learned that I was still alive when he was asked to be a Keynote speaker at the symposium with me in Chapel Hill. He planned and carried out the most wonderful reception for me when I arrived.

Simply put, we truly enjoyed only 'The Best of The Best' throughout the entire two weeks of our magical stay together in 'The Southern Part Of Heaven.'

From the time of our reunion, we have known every joy, every thrill, every excitement, and - Yes my dear RD - every pleasure God has given lovers to know. My one and only love, has been there to meet me on every single one of the many trips I have taken since we came back together after all the years apart.

We have held back nothing and we have truly made up for all the time we lost.

All of these marvelous gifts came to us just in time. I was diagnosed with severe heart problems less than six months before I knew my great love was still alive. The best physicians informed me that I could not expect to live but a few short months. I have already far exceeded their expectations. My enthusiasm and pure exhilaration with Rabun has kept my heart bubbling over with life.

My dear, dear, RD. My cup runneth over. Rabun has been here in this very room with me every day and night since you took that bus to summer school. My life is now complete in every way. My God has given me everything. I am ready to meet my maker and express my gratitude for all I have been given. Especially you.

Love Well, Thera Jean Fulton PS: Our Love is Forever until the end of time. Irene brought her old record player out here so that we could listen to our favorite song from 1942, the year we were together in England. It's on the night stand by my bed. Just crank it up and enjoy! It's a grand old song.

He winds it up, makes himself comfortable on her bed, then carefully lowers the needle to the 78 rpm record and closes his eyes to listen and picture her there.

***

Katheline has rode out with Elizabeth and her father. Clyde greets them and Elizabeth sits with him in the swing.

"I think I'll take a stroll and just look around." The Professor smiles at Katheline. "Why don't you check on RD and let him know we're here should he need us,"

"I will." She places her palm ever so softly on the side of his face. "Please know that we are also here for you should you need us."

As Katheline walks quietly to the stairs, she hears the music playing.

"You must remember this A kiss is just a kiss, a sigh is just a sigh. The fundamental things apply As time goes by.

As she reaches the top of the stairs she sees him on the bed and thinks he is asleep. She removes her heels and steps soundlessly to stand over him.

"And when two lovers woo They still say, "I love you." On that you can rely No matter what the future brings As time goes by.

She slowly rests her right knee on the bed beside his hip, shifts her left leg over his body and lays her head on his chest. RD hasn't moved but he is definitely awake.

"It's still the same old story A fight for love and glory A case of do or die. The world will always welcome lovers As time goes by. Oh yes, the world will always welcome lovers As time goes by."

***

The professor has found a great place to just think and hear the music from the house.

He is sitting in Daniel's exact spot leaning against the "mopping" tree. When the song finishes, he rises and goes to the open window of the room below the stairs. Using his best Bogey impersonation, he yells through the window.

"PLAY IT AGAIN, SAM!"

Katheline re-winds and turns up the volume as high as it will go.

When it finishes playing again, Elizabeth breaks off her kissing with Clyde just long enough to yell up from the front porch.

"HEY UP THERE! PLAY IT AGAIN SAM!"

They must have played that record a dozen times, but nobody was counting.

Eventually, all of them migrate naturally to the front porch. RD brings out extra straight chairs and they make an intimate close circle with the swing. Elizabeth's father straddles a chair facing the others with his back to the wall. He is the first to speak.

"I have decided that now is the time to share with you the Greatest Love Story ever told..

It begins when lovers meet in 1941. They are separated for eight long years each thinking the other is dead from 1943 until 1951. By a miracle they find each other again in 1951 and make up for lost time until the lady lover's untimely death in 1963. The magic of those dozen years can only be due to one reason. The lovers were the only ones who knew that they shared such bliss. It was truly a secret love

"Now that all good things have come to an end, only I am left to explain the reason for such carefully guarded privacy." He looks deep into their eyes. "And this I would be happy to do, except that I am sworn to secrecy."

"Oh, you!" says Katheline. She simply hates not knowing why they didn't tell the world.

"Oh, me!" says Clyde. He doesn't know anything, except that he is very much in love.

"Oh, man!" says RD. He hands Elizabeth Thera's letter, and motions for her to go read it..

"Oh, Dad!" says Elizabeth. She departs to read, holding a large envelope and the letter.

"Sir Laughs A Lot" says nothing.

Other friends begin to arrive. Becky, Bobby, Susan and Mary Ann walk up from the farm.

Elroy brings Dee Dee in the ambulance he has been driving since he totaled his car. Irving is here because his brother came and he has nowhere else to take his new girlfriend, Patti. Even old "Mo" Lester comes by "Just to see what's going on." after seeing the Sheriff go by bringing the Governor out here. He wanted to see Nub but the store's all locked up and Nub's not there. People are finding their own places to get comfortable, on the steps, on the floor, in the yard, standing, sitting, leaning, pacing, bringing chairs and pillows out of the house.

More are coming. Thera's friends from big "A" town. Ladies from her church. Lucky who has brought Julie in his old truck because she needed a ride. Vera has driven Roger from Traveston to pick up the white Limousine, and they stop to pay their respects. Preacher Hawkins and his wife, Eunice, have come to pray. TJ has come to stay. He's moving in with RD until he leaves for his new assignment in DC.

"Anybody seen Nub?" Shotgun asks from behind the swing. He sits on the floor, his back against the wall, with one leg hanging off the porch. His new wife sits smiling in his strong arms. He proudly introduces her to everyone as: "This is my Shirley. Shirley Shirey. Don't it just sound right?"

Irene has been sleeping in her old room at the back of the house. She comes to the door and says through the screen. "I think I've heard your record, enough! Does anybody mind if I play "Goodnight Irene?" Nobody objects and soon there is music blaring from the window up above,

"Goodnight, Irene. Goodnight, Irene.
I'll see you in my dreams."

When the music stops, RD excuses himself to cut off the record player. As he turns to go downstairs, he sees the large manila envelope on the desk. It is addressed to him. He opens it and reads.

A Brief Biography Of Ramun Daniel McTanis, PHD
Written by his daughter - Thera Elizabeth McTanis

Born in 1913 in Quebec, Canada. Raised Roman Catholic in Buffalo, NY. Undergraduate
at Fordham. Earned PHD in sociology from UNC. Rhodes scholar at Oxford (1940-1943.)

"Father is Scotch"
Father was the son in a long line of the family McTanis known throughout Scotland, and eventually the world, as makers of one of the finest scotch malt whiskeys money can buy. Many people did buy it and, over the years, the McTanis family amassed an enormous fortune. Sadly, after the war there were few male family members left to manage the vast empire and take advantage of the great wealth. Until the arrival back in England, of a not-so-famous Baron, from the south of rural France, at which time it was discovered that one male descendent of the McTanis Clan was, indeed, alive and well,

"Mother is French"

Although his mother was, indeed, a Frenchwoman, who taught him fluent use of the romance language, the Baron's French connection was the direct result of the wages of war.

"Sole Survivors"

When the ship he was on was sunk by a German U-boat off the coast of England in 1943, he and a little two-year-old girl are rescued at sea in 1943 by a Portugese trawler. They are taken to the west southern coast of German-occupied France. Aided by the French resistance, from there they are taken, under cover of darkness, to a farm about one hundred kilometers due east of Bordeaux.

They find themselves tucked away on a farm in what is known as the cradle of civilization in Langlade, a small and quiet hamlet near Proissans about one hundred kilometers east of Bordeaux.

It is here at the "LaGrange de Langlade" in the immediate vicinity of the "Dordogne'" that the Baron Jesse Garron acquires a retreat from the horrors of war, a new identity, a new life and his prestigious title.

"Baron Jesse Garron"

The french resistance operated with scant resources in virtually every category. The one exception was an abundance of auspicious, and sometimes suspicious, royal titles. It seems that when our scot scholar needed a new identity, there was found a small estate nearby that had once been owned by an obscure Count Garron. It was thought that there were no male heirs left in that family, after so many aristocratic heads rolled during the French Revolution. So, finding a surviving Baron, to carry on the name of Garron, was an occasion for great celebration and drink in the local wine country. So our professor and his little charge spend the rest of the war years in, what proves to be a superb sanctuary, as well as a warm and friendly place for a pretty English girl to grow and prosper. The best is yet to come.

"A Wealthy Man"

The end of war brought with it the freedom of travel long awaited by millions of people.

The "Baron" and his little princess return to England where even bigger surprises await them. The exchequer of the McTanis fortune informs one Mister Rabun Duel McTanis that he is the sole heir to the wealth that has flowed precisely in step with the flow of good scotch malt whiskey.

"A Man of God"

The only cork in the bottle is the fact that the Baron is now a Roman Catholic Priest. Having been raised in the French Catholic tradition by his "ma-man" and after raising his "treasured child" in that magnificent culture whose citizens are about eighty percent Roman Catholic, it is no wonder that our lone survivors are committed to their faith.

"A Priest"

Add to all this the great tragedy of the loss of his one true love, and it becomes easily understandable that the young scot scholar would turn to the church for comfort, accept the vow of celibacy, and the honorable path to becoming a Priest. It was indeed an intelligent choice at the time. Father Garron was a blessing to his faithful following. Always a kind and giving man, he gave his best to the people he came to know and love in France. However, time truly changes everything and the chance of his lifetime is on the way. Fate is about to rock the foundation of his orderly world,

"A True Scholar"

True scholars never severe their ties to the schools they learn to love. Such is the case with R.D. McTanis, PHD. When he takes his, now legally adopted, daughter to visit the Oxford campus, he discovers that many of his teachers are now gone. However, good fortune smiles on him and the professor both he and Thera were assigned while earning their degrees is still living in his same little cottage and providing counsel to aspiring young students.

"Do you remember the name McTanis?"

"No."

"Will you look it up?"

"No."

"Do you care?"

"No."

"Have you ever?"

"No,"

"Will you ever?"

"No."

"How about Thera Fulton?"

"Fulton, Thera Fulton?"

"Does that name ring a bell?"

"Yes!"

The honorable teacher digs through stacks of papers. Most of them are ungraded thesis drafts, Then he finds a copy of a small brochure and a note attached by paper clip to a manuscript..

"She sent me this and asked me if we still had a copy of this." He taps the report that Rabun recognizes on sight.

Displaced Children Of London
A study conducted from 2/11/1940 to 11/28/1942

240

by: Rabun Daniel McTanis, PHD and Thera Fulton, MA

"Oh, now I remember! That's you, right? Dan McTanis! I didn't recognize you with that beard.

"That's me."

"Well, your timing is perfect. I was about to mail it to her."

"Do you mean that SHE IS ALIVE?"

"She must have been when she wrote this letter last week." Professor Jenkins hands Rabun the letter. " You might want to look at this pamphlet too."

Rabun is stunned to discover that his Thera will be speaking at his Alma Mater next month.

"With your permission, Professor, I would like to hand deliver that copy to her in America."

"Oh, by all means, Doctor Dan." He hands it over. "Give her my best regards."

"A Happy Man"

So here we were with dad a priest and her a saint, mad with unrequited love and passion, and what could they do? They prayed to God for forgiveness and consummated their reunion with every fiber of their beings. To their surprise, they felt no guilt, felt no shame, felt no remorse, felt no regrets; they felt only the burning desire for more of the same. They also felt that the world and its affairs had interfered with the oneness that they shared for the last time. "Nobody has a need to know and what they don't know can't hurt them." was their philosophy. They did not know how much time was left for them to be together, but they made a pact to seize every moment they could in private. Theirs was truly a secret love. And it was GRAND!

And that's my story as I have learned it over the years by paying very close attention to the affairs of my father, who is the greatest man I have known thus far. I'd tell you more, but I'm sworn to secrecy.

***

As RD goes downstairs and crosses the hallway to join his guests on the porch, he hears a familiar man's voice singing softly in Irene's room.

"Goodnight Irene, Goodnight Irene,
I'll see you in my dreams."

"Goodnight, Charlie." The sound of Irene's voice stops RD in his tracks. 'If that's not Nub, then the real George Jones has come to visit Aunt Thera.'

Among the thousands who came to visit Thera one last time at her funeral today there were many who thought the real George Jones was singing "May You Always." Many of them will be trying to buy the new record by the real George Jones over the next few months. RD is fairly sure that he never recorded that song, but he should record it right away. The rendition done by his talented immitator and devoted admirer, Nub, was so emotional that it brought tears of mourning and grief from every single one of these thousands of people who covered the fields, the hills, the sides of the road, the area in front of the store, the bank in front of the Fulton house, the yard and porch of the Fulton house and the bank that ran from the store to the Franklin farm.. They cried for the loss of their beloved Thera who many revered as their "Mother of the Universe."

Chapter 63:
Sir Dan and the Tally Man

Men who lost a mother and a lover, TJ and the Professor, sit in the swing on the porch of the Fulton House while Irene packs away Thera's clothing and cleans out the upstairs room for TJ to move in with her and RD.

TJ emptied the trailer and is traveling light with all of his worldly possessions in his fifty chevy. RD has hung his clothes and stacked boxes of legal files in the single large closet upstairs while TJ loaded Thera's empty desk with his important papers.

RD is happy to have TJ with him. He has naturally and competently taken care of Thera's affairs and assisted all of the family, and their close friends, with the barrage of legal activites that have sprung up, during this time of multiple deaths, requiring the disposition of estate assets and execution of wills for those who have died. "Tallying the bananas" for them is definitely not a simple tasks due to the large amounts of money from the Riley inheritance and multiple insurance claims from property settlements and life insurance. Added to his challenging work and sense of duty and responsibility, now comes this wonderful man with his wealth asking TJ to manage large sums of money for his Thera Fulton Memorial Cemetery.

"Mister Franklin, we are all grateful to have you staying here with all the work we are piling on you." He opens a briefcase and hands TJ a folder. "Here are the preliminary drawings for the entire project. I have set aside six million dollars for your exclusive use in managing the construction and long range upkeep and maintenance of the complex. Please prepare a power of Attorney for my signature giving yourself full legal authority to make all financial decisions regarding this project. Just let me know should you need additional funding in the future. I assure you that money is not an issue as I have ample resources and I am fully dedicated to this memorial honoring your mother and the love of my life.

"Thank you for your trust in me, Professor McTanis." TJ puts the folder in his case. "I will do my best to prove worthy of your confidence. And, please call me TJ."

"You are a brilliant attorney, TJ, and your mother is proud of you. You are also a good man and that is all the assurance I will ever require. I am honored and blessed that you are here to assist me."

"And, with all your titles, how do you prefer me to address you?"

"Well. Your mother called me Sir Laughs A Lot." He flashes a mischievous smile. "But that sounds a bit ostentatious, don't you think? So why don't you just call me SIR! That's what most people call me despite my protests, so I might as well just give up on that point."

"Before you got your titles and great fortune, what did your close friends call you."

"Dan. Can you believe it? Just Dan. And I loved it. It's also what my parents called me."

"May I call you Dan?"

"By all means. I'll be delighted each time you do."

"Thank you, Dan."

"You are most welcome, TJ."

They shake hands. TJ leaves Dan in the swing alone looking out over his vision for a tribute to Lady Greyeyes.

Thomas James Franklin, Attorney at Law, now has two multi-million dollar accounts. He goes upstairs to work on more important matters that are near and dear to his heart. He sings a few lines from a popular song recorded by Harry Belefonte called "Dayo."

"Come mister tallyman, tally me bananas,
Daylight come and I wanna go home."

***

"We have a lot of work to do Mister Newman. Please have a seat." TJ gives RD a very bussinesslike handshake as they take chairs at the desk.

"You, Sir, are my first client in my new office." TJ takes a yellow legal pad from his case.

"Our first Item of business is Thera's will. It is clean and simple. Thera left everything she owns to you. This house and this property including the store, plus approximately five square miles of good timberland behind them. Her car, her bank accounts including checking, saving, short and long term Certificates Of Deposit, and stocks and bonds. These items will add up to a large sum of money. However, the most significant part of your inheritance is Thera's share of the money that Ida Maye received from her late husband, Mister Gus Riley. Irene has made me the sole executor of her estate and I have deemed your portion to be exactly one million dollars in liquid assets. I will be holding all of these assets in trust until you are of legal age, at which time they will go directly to you."

"What about Becky, TJ? What does she get?"

"Good question, RD. She also gets a million dollars in cash payable immediately upon demand. She has also just sold her land across the road to Professor McTanis for an undisclosed sum. She was recently awarded payment from the life insurance policy on Fred Sanders and the replacement cost of the house that burned down. And, as you know, Bobby was given full title to the Franklin farm and his portion of the Riley fortune will be an additional one million dollars in liquid assets. Between the two of them there will definitely be enough money to insure a bright future for Susan, Mary Ann, the child Becky is expecting and any others they may have."

"And what about Aunt Irene?"

"I will continue to manage the remainder of the vast holdings in the Riley estate and administer the funds as needed by all beneficiaries. Irene will have access to enough money to insure that she never has to concern herself with financial matters. She will be well cared for as long as she lives."

"Can I give the store to Nub?"

"No." He smiles at the disappointment on RD's face. "But I can do it for you, before we finalize all this paperwork."

"Would you? Please, please, please."

"Thera once told me that nobody could refuse three pleases from you." He put his pad back in the impressive briefcase. He did not write anything on it. "Of course I will."

RD stands and puts out his hand to shake on it. TJ grabs him and gives him a long bear hug.

"Now, Mister Newman. Would you please find your Aunt Irene and send her up here? I need to find out what she may want or need."

"Yes, Sir." Suddenly RD begins to laugh.

"What's so funny?"

"I think Irene finally has what she wants."

"Yeah, old Nub's alright, ain't he?" TJ has a good laugh, too.

THE END

Epilogue

**"May you walk
through life with
a friend beside you."**